ACORNA'S
People

ACORNA'S
People

ANNE McCAFFREY
and
ELIZABETH ANN
SCARBOROUGH

HarperPrism

A Division of HarperCollinsPublishers

HarperPrism

A Division of HarperCollins*Publishers*
10 East 53rd Street, New York, NY 10022-5299

HarperCollins®, ♨ ®, and HarperPrism®
are trademarks of HarperCollins Publishers Inc.

First HarperPrism printing: July 1999
Printed in the United States of America

Library of Congress Cataloging-in-Publication Data

McCaffrey, Anne.
    Acorna's people / Anne McCaffrey and Elizabeth Ann
Scarborough.–1st U.S. ed.
        p. cm
    ISBN 0–06–105094–6
    I. Scarborough, Elizabeth Ann.   II. Title.
PS3563.A255A646 1999
813'.54—dc21   97-51201
                                                                          CIP

Visit HarperPrism on the World Wide Web at
http://www.harperprism.com

99 00 01 02 03 ❖ 10 9 8 7 6 5 4 3 2 1

To Ryk Reaser,
science and salvage consultant

One

On the planet of Laboue, within the opulent chief residence of Hafiz Harakamian, in one of the hundreds of finely crafted, hand-joined cabinets of rare and lustrous woods in which he kept his smallest and often most precious collectibles, Acorna had once seen a display of brilliantly bejeweled and decorated eggs. Created hundreds of years ago by a man named Carl Fabergé for the collection of a Russian czar not nearly so wealthy as their present owner, the eggs had dazzled the eyes of the young girl with their richly colored enamels, their gold loops and whorls, their swags and bows of diamonds and glittering gemstones, and their tiny movable parts—the delicately wrought scenes that unfolded from within their interiors.

Now, a fathomless distance from Uncle Hafiz's home and many years later, it seemed to Acorna as if the eggs had magically grown to giant size and lofted themselves into space, where their colors shone even more brilliantly in the blackness of infinity than they had in the memories of her childhood. They formed a festive flotilla visible from the viewport of the *Balaküre*.

The flotilla had been growing in size since the *Balaküre*

exited the wormhole that deposited them just beyond the atmosphere of narhii-Vhiliinyar, the second Linyaari home world.

The imagery was further borne out by the seemingly endless number of Linyaari space-farers, the denizens of those bright ships, who paraded across the comscreen to welcome the *Balaküre* delegation home.

Melireenya introduced Acorna to each of the officers as they appeared on the screen, so that Acorna felt that she was already at one of the receptions or parties her aunt and Melireenya were threatening to give in order to introduce her to Linyaari society and, most especially, to prospective life-mates. Acorna was so excited by the sight of the egg-like ships and the spectacle of her people's home rotating almost imperceptibly beyond them that she could hardly pay attention to the images on the comscreen.

The Linyaari welcoming her to this world all looked so much like her that they could have been mistaken for her by her human friends. The figures on the comscreen were pale skinned and had golden opalescent spiraling horns growing from their foreheads, topped by manes of silvery hair which continued to grow down their spines. Like her, they had feathery tufts of fine curly white hair adorning their legs from knee to ankle, to just above their two-toed feet. Their hands, like hers, bore only three fingers, each with one joint in the middle and one where the finger met the palm.

After the life she'd led, it was a little overwhelming to be among so many others of her kind. All of the equipment and utensils she could see and touch were designed for people like her. Nothing had to be specially adapted to her anatomical peculiarities. Nothing about her appearance was unusual to the Linyaari.

However, as like her as these people were, they were all, even her mother's sister and those aboard the *Balaküre*, still strangers—strangers who took a proprietary interest in her without actually knowing her very well. Although she had ceased to be regarded as a child by the humans she had grown up among, she seemed to be regarded by her Linyaari shipmates as little more than a youngling.

This was a new sensation for her. Acorna had been jettisoned in a life pod from her parents' ship as an infant to save her from the fatal explosion that claimed the lives of her parents and the attacking Khleevi. She'd been rescued soon after and had grown up among humans. Specifically, she had been raised by her three adoptive uncles—Calum Baird, Declan "Gill" Giloglie, and Rafik Nadezda. Back when they'd found her they had been miners working in the far reaches of the human galaxies. These days they'd gone on to other things. Rafik, for example, was now the head of the House of Harakamian, the empire founded by his uncle Hafiz Harakamian, an uncommonly wily merchant and wealthy collector.

When Acorna had first met Hafiz, he'd wished to add her to his many treasures, to be displayed along with the beautiful Fabergé eggs and the incredibly rare Singing Stones of Skarrness guarding his courtyard. However, her value to Hafiz as a collectible had sharply decreased when Hafiz learned she was not a solitary oddity but merely a member of a populous alien race.

Acorna's relationship with Hafiz, and the one between Hafiz and Rafik, had improved after that to the point that Acorna now used the name Harakamian, along with that of her good and gentle mentor Mr. Li, as a surname. Dear Mr. Li had passed on a few months ago, but the more durable Uncle Hafiz had recently married his second wife and was now enjoying his retirement in her company.

Acorna, along with her uncles and Mr. Li, had succeeded in rescuing the children imprisoned in the camps on Kezdet, a planet whose economy had once depended on the exploitation of child labor. They had been ably assisted in this task by the intelligent and resourceful siblings of the Kendoro family, Pal, Judit, and Mercy, themselves former victims of the camps. Together, Acorna and her friends had been instrumental in changing the planet's laws and ridding it of the Piper, the ringleader responsible for the most heinous of the abuses. They had gone on to establish a mining and teaching facility on one of Kezdet's moons, Maganos, to nurture and educate the children they had rescued from the horrors of the labor camps.

Later, Acorna and her uncle Calum, while trying to locate her home world, had helped quell a mutiny among the Starfarers, human voyagers on a large colony ship. After being forced to watch their parents' murders during the rebellion, and the subsequent bloodshed, murder, and exploitation that the ship's new masters were intent upon, the children of the ship were able, with Acorna's help, to wrest control from the mutineers and destroy them. In the process, they rescued the famed meteorologist Dr. Ngaen Xong Hoa, and his weather control system. The people who had seized the ship had used Dr. Hoa's new system to destroy the economy and ecology of the newly colonized planet Rushima. The mutineers were spaced by the triumphant youngsters, just as the mutineers had spaced their victims, when the children regained control of the ship.

While returning with Dr. Hoa to repair the damage to Rushima, Acorna, her adoptive family, and the children fell under attack by the Khleevi, a vicious bug-like race responsible for the death of Acorna's parents. Fortunately, Acorna's aunt Neeva and the delegation from narhii-Vhiliinyar had arrived in time to warn everyone of the impending invasion. With Acorna's help, the resources of Kezdet and the Houses of Harakamian and Li had been mobilized to rout the Khleevi.

In the course of all this, Acorna had become something of a mistress of disguise, and had used her horn to purify an entire ship's poisoned air and the waters of Rushima as well as to heal the wounded in all of the hostile encounters with which she'd been involved.

This was all quite aside from her abilities to divine by seemingly magical means the mineral content of each individual asteroid her uncles wished to mine, an ability which had earned her their respect while she was still quite young. So Acorna had actually packed a great deal of activity into a relatively short life. Consequently she did not feel particularly childlike most of the time.

Nevertheless, she was a child to her mother's sister Neeva, a Linyaari Envoy Extraordinaire, or *visedhaanye ferilii*. She was considered a youngling by all the other Linyaari aboard the *Balaküre* as well: Khaari, the navigation officer or *gheraalye malivii* in the Linyaari tongue; Melireenya, the senior communications office or *gheraalye ve-khanyii*; and Thariinye, the young male whose function was still not exactly clear to Acorna, even after their travels together, but who seemed to think that without him, the mission could not have succeeded. What had been taken by Acorna's human friends for talent was apparently standard issue for her race. And many of the talents the other Linyaari possessed seemed to have been carefully developed. For instance, none of them *needed* words to communicate with each other and all of them could read the thoughts of the others on the ship—including hers, a fact which she found rather unnerving at times. She had so very much to learn. Fortunately, if her shipmates were typical examples, her people were kind and forbearing.

"Khornya, this is my counterpart in the Gamma Sector, *Visedhaanye Ferilii* Taankaril," Aunt Neeva told Acorna. Khornya was the Linyaari version of Acorna, the name given her by her human "uncles." The introduction pulled her attention once more from the spectacle of the ships outside the viewport. Acorna dipped her horn, as did the *visedhaanye ferilii*, a woman who, like Aunt Neeva, Khaari and Melireenya, was of an indistinguishable age, at least indistinguishable to Acorna.

"Khornya," Aunt Neeva said, nodding to the woman on the comscreen and relaying her thoughts to Acorna, "the *visedhaanye ferilii* is the mother of two handsome sons who have not yet found their lifemates. She regrets that she is about to embark upon a mission, but hopes you will feel free to call upon them for any assistance you need in adjusting to your new home."

Acorna smiled and nodded at the woman again. No actual words had been exchanged between her aunt and the dignitary. Even across the vastness of space, it seemed that the senior space-faring Linyaari could read thoughts. Acorna occasionally felt she was catching on to how it was done, but found the process frustrating even with people standing in front of her. Particularly when they responded to thoughts she would not have voiced, given a choice. But her grasp of the Linyaari tongue was not yet complete and the crew of the *Balakiire* found the need to communicate with her in spoken words tedious. Neeva assured her she'd get the hang of things soon enough. But Acorna still worried.

And so went her homecoming, with the space around her new home planet dancing with egg-ships full of Acorna-like beings, *all* of whom seemed curious about the formerly presumed dead daughter of the illustrious Feriila and the valiant Vaanye, *all* politely inquiring as to where she'd been all this time and what she'd been doing, *all* seemingly with unmated sons or nephews or widowed fathers and uncles, *all* shepherding the *Balakiire* into port and docking alongside her.

Acorna emerged from the *Balakiire* behind her Aunt Neeva and just ahead of Thariinye to find the docking bay crowded with Linyaari, some even holding a banner aloft. Behind the uniformed Acorna-like space travelers streaming from their ships to add to the party, a mass of multicolored creatures similar in form to the space-farers crowded onto the docking level, strumming, blowing into, pounding upon, brushing, and stamping a variety of musical instruments. The docking bay was filled with strange but wonderfully harmonious and joyous music.

Even before Aunt Neeva could explain, Acorna was overwhelmed with happiness. This was the welcoming committee. They didn't even know her, and they'd brought the brass band and the welcome mat. Aunt Neeva gave her a hug.

"We are all so glad to have you back, Khornya," she said, waving her hand to indicate the smiling Linyaari. Tears came to

Acorna's eyes as she nodded an acknowledgment to all those who'd turned out to meet her.

At last she would truly belong. At last she would no longer be an oddity. What a relief that would be. "And I am so glad to be here, Aunt Neeva," she said. "I can't tell you how glad."

Aunt Neeva looked a little puzzled, an expression that seemed common whenever she was dealing with her niece. "But you just did, child," she said. "You just did."

Two

The *Condor* lurched and shuddered and flung its captain and the human part of the crew—both parts consisting of one Jonas Becker, CEO of Becker Interplanetary Recycling and Salvage Enterprises Ltd.— against the bulkhead. As quickly as Becker fell, he was released, and rose to the ceiling like a ballet dancer in slow motion, while the rest of the crew, twenty pounds of grizzled black and gray Makahomian Temple Cat, drifted past him, the cat's extended claws grazing what remained of Becker's right ear.

"Dammit, RK, have you been pissing on the GSS panel again?" Becker groaned. RK, whose full name was Roadkill, growled back in his version of a friendly purr. His claws were flashing in and out, blissfully kneading the air, and beads of happy cat drool floated up from between his formidable fangs. His good eye was closed in an excess of feline ecstasy. Becker had never seen a cat who loved zero G the way RK did—but then he had never seen a cat anything like RK before either. The cat's stub of broken tail moved back and forth like a rudder as it floated by.

Becker gave the Gravitation Stabilization System panel a boot as he passed it. The force of his kick sent him soaring

9

upward to bang against the console of a fighter ship strapped to the ceiling above the control panel of the *Condor*. There wasn't a whole lot of room in his vessel to store cargo, and Becker utilized every cubic centimeter of extra space. This left him no soft place to land when, after a couple more shudders, the ship's gravity stabilized and Becker and RK tumbled back to the deck.

Becker massaged his hip. He'd banged it against one of the packing crates of cat food he had unloaded from RK's original home ship. The cat, always interested in those particular crates, rubbed himself between it and Becker. As usual, Becker was surprised at how soft the cat's coat was in comparison to his personality. Becker had lost the little finger of his right hand while trying to salvage Roadkill. The cat had then been nameless, of course, the spitting, hissing, clawing sole survivor left aboard a derelict Makahomian spacecraft along with the corpses of his former shipmates.

Becker didn't like to talk about the loss of his second finger, but it had to do with what he referred to as "RK's adjustment period," the time when the cat had recovered enough from his injuries to start feeling at home. When Becker went to sell a couple of choice bits from the inventory soon after he'd acquired Roadkill, he'd found them slick with yellowish liquid and stinking worse than a musk otter in heat. The cause was obvious—and so was the need for a solution.

Becker consulted the library he had rescued from a landfill on Clackamass 2. He was a sucker for information in any form: hard copy, chip, what have you. It came in handy when he wanted to identify or figure out how to operate some of the inventory.

He dug through quite a few moldy, torn books before he found the copy of *How to Care for Your Kittycat* he'd stashed in the stall of the spare head. The book advised that when a male cat began "marking his territory" by spraying it, the only way to stop the behavior was to have the cat neutered. Becker's business kept him a long way from a veterinarian, but back when he was a kid on the labor farm on Kezdet, he'd helped with the calves and goats. He'd figured a cat couldn't be that much different, so he attempted a little home surgery on RK. Turned out he'd figured wrong. The attempt ended with them both having surgeries of a sort—RK was now one nut short and Becker had another stump in place of his right ring finger next to the stump of the little finger the cat had shredded during the original rescue. You had to love an animal like that.

"That's okay, man," he told the cat, scratching it behind the right ear, which, like his own, was only partially there. The cat's purr increased in volume until it sounded like a whole pride of lions right there in the cabin. "Those gravity systems are worthless anyway."

He knew he had a replacement system someplace among his cargo, probably a better one than the one he'd installed six months ago. Only problem was he couldn't do these particular repairs in space. To the best of his recollection, the piece that he needed was buried so deep he'd have to unload the cargo hold to find it. As usual, the ship was packed too tightly to have any room inside to conveniently shift the cargo while he looked. He could maneuver around and manage it in a pinch, of course, but why bother?

"So, cat, looks like it's dirtside for us again. I was going to pass up this next trashed-out planet and head back for civilization, but it looks like we need another pit stop first. The way I figure it, with this one, we've pretty much replaced the whole ship since we last headed back to Kezdet—we'll basically have a brand new *Condor* by the time we dock there again."

This wasn't unusual. On the average, he replaced most of the *Condor* about three times a year. This was an occupational hazard, or maybe a hazard of the kind of personality that occupied Becker's occupation. He hated to pay full price for anything when there was so much good stuff, only a little used, laying around for the taking. He was an expert at improvisation, refitting, retooling, and emergency landings on remote hunks of rock in the middle of space. He could do mid-space repairs, too, but it was so much easier to land somewhere with a bit of gravity where he could suit up, toss stuff he didn't need out the hatch while uncovering what he did need, close the hatch, pressurize the ship, make his repair, then retrieve and reload his previously discarded cargo.

He ended up making some pretty rough landings occasionally, but he wasn't much worried about scratching his paint job, and the *Condor* wasn't so big that he needed a lot of level area for a landing pad. He headed for the planet he'd selected for this minor emergency. If the rock had an oxygen atmosphere, he'd even be able to empty the cat box and let RK out to do a little business.

Sometimes they found some of their best cargo on these pit stops. Lately he'd run across a whole string of planets, all pretty well stripped of resources on the one hand, but chock full of possibly profitable debris on the other hand. Becker lived for debris. His big regret was that he had not yet devised a way to strap extra cargo to the outside of the *Condor*, but so far he hadn't found a way to do so that would allow him to enter and exit atmospheres without burning up the merchandise.

The *Condor* landed on what seemed the only level bit of ground for miles around. Soil and vegetation had pretty much been stripped from the rock around this little basin in the wreckage, but here bluish grass-like plants still grew—until the *Condor*'s descent singed them, anyway. It was a rough landing. The atmosphere was tumultuous—roiling clouds of various red and yellow gases filled the sky. That was okay. According to his instruments—if they were working properly, and they seemed to be—it was still breathable out there. Even if it wasn't, he had a good protective suit if he needed it. It was the one item he bought not only firsthand but also top of the line. He never knew what the conditions would be like out here in the boonies. While he could use the robolift for most reloading, loading, and hauling jobs, some of them he needed to do by hand.

*   *   *

It took him a day and a half to repair his system. The first full day, with RK's enthusiastic participation, he devoted to rooting around among the derelict shuttles, escape pods, and command capsules in his inventory, looking for an outfit in better shape than the one he was using. As usual, much of what was on top of what he wanted landed on the ground outside the vessel until he found what he was looking for.

He eventually rounded up a replacement system and patched it in. RK "helped" again, trying to stand between him and what he was doing. Every time Becker reached past the critter, RK's low snarl warned him off. When the cat tired of that game, he sat beside Becker and periodically reached up to sink a single claw into the man's thigh. Finally, Becker opened the hatch again and the cat leaped out without a backward look. The work went amazingly swiftly after that.

Prior to reloading his cargo, Becker suited up. He was a little more cautious of his own hide than the cat was. Taking a work light, a collection sack, a tin of cat food to lure his roaming partner back aboard again, and the remote to the hatch and the robolift, he popped the hatch and disembarked. All he had to do now was throw his stuff back aboard and find Roadkill. While he was looking, he might as well take a stroll and scope out the local real estate.

The grass around the *Condor* was singed for about thirty feet from where the vessel sat, and Becker thought it was a real shame about that. All around the basin, bedrock lay tumbled as if something had reached in, pulled it up, and stirred it around. What a dump. Only this one little patch showed any real signs of life. Of course, it could be the planet was just in the process of giving birth to life, or it could be a failed terraforming job, but his guess was that this planet had at one time been alive. The little patch on which he stood was probably one of the last, if not the last, vestiges of that life. Damn shame, of course, but without ruins like this, he'd be out of business. Only problem was, the devastation here was so complete, there wasn't much left, even for him. The other planets they'd come across lately had been much the same. Each of them had a few useless remnants that gave him the creepy feeling that a perfectly good civilization had been destroyed fairly recently.

It was Roadkill who pulled him from his contemplation of mortality.

In fact, it looked as if the cat had dug up something, and was smacking it around. Space mouse? Not very likely, with no signs of plant or animal life around, excluding themselves and the puny patch of grass they occupied.

Whatever it was, RK was in love with it. Becker couldn't hear anything, but he could see that the cat's sides were pumping up and down with the force of his purring.

A few feet further on, something gleamed in the beam of the work light, and Becker bent to examine it. Like the object RK was mauling, the thing was long and thin, maybe had been pointed on the end at one time, but the tip was broken off. There were definite spiral markings on it, he saw as he brushed away the soil. It glistened in the light, refracting rich shades of blue and green and deep red from its white surface. It looked like a big, carved opal. Pretty thing. He tucked it in the sack and swung his beam around. It flashed on several other pieces like the one he had, all broken and sticking up through the soil. He took a couple of other specimens, and made a note of the precise coordinates of this location so he could land here again, in case this stuff was valuable. Then he grabbed RK and headed back to the ship.

He finished reloading his cargo. As usual, he left a few of the more expendable pieces behind to lighten his load. He had inventory scattered all over the galaxy now. Well, most of the sites where he'd stashed the stuff were uninhabited, so it would keep. He could reclaim it if he found a market later. Finally, after he got the cargo stowed aboard once more, Becker lugged RK, the new treasure firmly clamped in his fangs, back onto the ship.

First things first, he decided. He set their course back to Kezdet and lifted off. It wasn't like he wanted to go to Kezdet.

He hated the damned place, but it was—unfortunately—the *Condor*'s home port. The ship had originally been registered to Becker's foster father, Theophilus Becker, who bought Jonas from a labor farm to help with the business when the boy was twelve. The old man had died ten years later, leaving the ship, the business, and his private maps of all manner of otherwise uncharted byways and shortcuts through various star systems and galaxies for his adopted son. Becker had spent every possible minute in space in the years since.

Once the ship was out of the planet's gravity well and the course was set, Becker turned the helm of the ship over to the computer. Too exhausted to fix himself anything else to eat, he opened another can of RK's cat food and ate that before settling down for some sleep. The cat, who had of course been fed as soon as the two returned to the ship—otherwise nothing else could have been accomplished—was already sacked out on top of the specimen bag containing the strange rocks they'd salvaged from the planet.

Becker pushed the recline button on his seat at the console and slept at the helm. His bunk was full of cargo. Besides, he couldn't get to it for the stacks of feed sacks full of seeds he'd picked up several weeks before.

He woke up finally when a paw on his cheek told him he'd better do so if he didn't want another pat, this time with the claws bared. He looked up into RK's big green eyes. Something was different about that cat, but he couldn't put his finger on it. He fed both of them again, checked his course, and emptied the collection sack onto the console. Time to get a better look at what he'd acquired.

He didn't figure he needed to use gloves with these specimens, since the cat had been carrying one around in its mouth with no ill effects since they'd found them, so he dug a couple of the spiral rocks out and ran a scanner over them. No radiation, nothing to poison, burn, freeze, or sting him. He knew that, having just picked them out of the sack with his bare hands.

RK crowded in close as Becker examined the objects,

stroking them, turning them, trying to chip a piece off one with a rock hammer. The stones had a strange feeling to them—a sort of hum, as if they were alive. Maybe they were. Damn, if these were sentient life forms, he'd have to take them back. He was going to have to check this out with an expert. He dumped the rocks back into the collection bag.

There wasn't much else to do, so he slept again. When he awoke, it was to find RK standing on his chest. Becker thought the cat must have been sleeping on his arm, because his right hand tingled as if it had been numbed from the cat's weight. His right ear felt funny, too.

That was when he realized what was different about the cat. *Two* green eyes blinked back at him, the good one and the one RK had lost in the crash. The cat's right ear was also whole and perfect. At that point the cat stood up, stretched itself halfway down Becker's leg, and stuck its tail in his face. Becker was stunned to see that the tail had straightened out, lengthened to a luxuriant and elegant appendage, and now waved quite handsomely. Below the tail, well, yeah, that missing part had returned there, too.

Becker lifted his own right hand and saw that the stubs of his fingers had regrown. His hands looked just as they had before he'd come into contact with RK—maybe minus the odd scar. He touched his ear. That felt whole again as well. What in the name of the three moons of Kezdet was going on here? How could this have happened—not that he was complaining. The only thing he could think was they'd run into some kind of healing force on that derelict planet. If the planet was capable of this kind of miracle, it was no wonder somebody had wrecked the place looking for the secret. As soon as he sold some of this cargo and reprovisioned—he was getting tired of cat food—he was going right back there to see what he could find.

"Mercy, Roadkill, when we get to Kezdet we're both gonna be so damned good lookin' we'll have to watch out they don't snag us for the pleasure houses." Not that he didn't intend to go there straightaway himself. And he'd take Roadkill with him.

Hell, they didn't call those places cathouses for nothing. Must be a lady cat or two around there would appreciate the attentions of a handsome space traveler like his buddy.

The trip back was real pleasant. For one thing, the cabin and hold didn't stink. Not even a little bit. Becker had to keep looking around to make sure Roadkill was still aboard because the whole ship had stopped smelling like cat piss. It was a smell you got used to, but it was nice to get used to *not* smelling it. For another thing, they were making really good time, even though they had been traveling vast uncharted distances from their — well, Becker's — home world.

Theophilus Becker had been much more than just a junk dealer — er — salvage broker. He was a salvage broker, a recycling engineer, *and* an astrophysicist. Jonas's new master, who liked to be called Dad, was also just a tad on the reckless side. The man liked nothing better than riding the wild wormhole, finding the quirks in quarks. He'd known how to detect those places where time and space pleated up, accordion-style, to be shot through for a shortcut by a space-farer with the guts to use them. Jonas had learned a great deal from Theophilus.

So it was a matter of only a month or so before Becker, with RK trotting along beside him like a dog, showed up in front of his favorite bawdyhouse. A girl he didn't recognize came to the door. She was fully dressed in a long-sleeved coverall fastened clear to her neck, not the attire he was accustomed to in this place.

"Oh, Lord, not another one," she said.

"You don't sound glad to see me," he replied, smiling. It had never been customary to bring flowers or any other greenery here — just a few hundred credits and the courtship was complete.

"When will you men get the word that this is an honest establishment for making safety belts for flitters now? The Didis are history."

"History?" Jonas felt stupid. "I like history. What do you mean, history? Where's Didi Yasmin?"

"In jail, where she belongs. Where have you been? Outer space?"

"As a matter of fact, yeah," he said. "Why is she in jail?"

"I haven't got time enough to tell you," the girl said. "But you might try asking some of the kids on Maganos—little girls she forced into prostitution." She glared at him.

"Hey, not with me! No, don't look at me that way. I like big girls—grown up girls, women, actually. I never—aw . . ."

His hostess's attention was diverted by Roadkill, who was rubbing against her ankles. She reached down and petted him, then picked him up. "What a pretty kitty," she said.

"Lady, I wouldn't do that," Becker said. "He'll take your arm off."

But RK, the traitor, lay happily purring in her arms, butting up against her chin with the top of his head, shamelessly cadging caresses. Becker wished he could do the same thing.

"What's his name?" the girl asked.

"RK," Becker hedged.

"What does that stand for?" Now she was tickling the traitor's tummy. It was white. Becker had had no idea that the cat's belly was white. RK never wanted *him* to do any tickling. Quite the contrary.

"Refugee Kitty," Becker lied, knowing that the truth would not go down well with her. "I found him on a derelict ship—his people had been killed in a freak accident and he was in a bad way."

He hoped this would elevate him in her estimation from a simple child molester to a child molester who was at least apparently kind to animals. "And *my* name is Jonas. Jonas Becker. What's yours?"

"Khetala," she said.

"Nice to meet you," he said.

"I can't say the same to you, Mr. Becker. You'll find Kezdet has changed quite a bit since the Didis and the Piper got what was coming to them. Maybe you considered the houses harmless fun, but I was forced to work in one before the Lady Epona liberated us. I don't share your attitude."

"Hey, I understand. I was slave farm labor myself but I got adopted out. I—" She was staring at him stonily. Even he knew it wasn't the same. His voice drifted off into confusion and he reached for RK, who took a slice at him. Becker ignored the cat's reluctance to be dislodged and firmly, if painfully, extricated him from Khetala's arms. "We—uh—nice meeting you— we'll just be going now."

She turned on her heel and went back inside.

One good thing about meeting her. He wasn't in the mood any more for what he had always let pass for love. So it was time to get back to work instead. He'd always found making money a fairly acceptable substitute for most pleasurable pursuits.

Before he went to the trouble of renting a container cruiser and offloading his cargo, he made a few inquiries about the state of the market. He was gratified to find that the Lady Epona who had so thoroughly cleansed the planet of evil hadn't minded junk, presumably as long as its purveyors weren't litterbugs.

The nano-bug market was still flourishing. He took a look around before settling in for the day. It was getting harder to find a real good deal any more. The original Mars probe, still in prime condition (because it hadn't worked in the first place), had been recovered by a guy who used to work for Red Planet Reclamation—the outfit that was supposed to return planets to their pristine condition after the minerals were stripped. The guy wanted enough of it to build a whole new planet from scratch. Becker shook his head and moved on. He also found a great booth for rockhounds. He was particularly attracted to four new gemstones he hadn't seen before—bairdite, giloglite, nadezdite, and acornite. Bairdite was a multicolored opaque stone with a pebbly crystalline surface striped both ways with red and yellow—probably iron and sulfur deposits. Giloglite was the color of serpentine, only translucent and cloudy. Nadezdite was a transparent purple with gold flecks, and the acornite was a blue-green stone that cleared in the middle to the most gorgeous deep teal transparency he had ever seen in any rock, real or manufactured. The sequence of names sounded familiar to him, but he couldn't quite think why.

He and RK checked out the food booths. There was a meat chili advertised as the specialty of Ma'aowri 3. It smelled really good to him, but RK took one sniff and backed off. When Becker tried to get closer, RK gave him a look that was hard to fathom, but left him thinking that maybe the meat in the dish was a little too close to home for comfort—whether to him or RK he wasn't sure. He passed up oddly shaped fruits, cheap fructose candy and waxy chocolate, various roast beasts, some fairly bizarre vegetation, and assorted other delicacies too alien to identify. He finally settled on a good old-fashioned gyro and a cup of caf, then returned to the stall he'd rented and began to unload his container into it.

After Becker had displayed his wares as temptingly as possible, he sat in the throne-like command seat he'd taken from an otherwise totaled Percenezatorian battle wagon. RK lay on the collection bag from the last trip. It had become his bed of choice. He had been willing to part with only the smallest and most broken piece of that funny opal-looking mineral. Becker kept that piece in his pocket as a deal-sweetener. It was eye-catching enough that maybe somebody would decide that his wife couldn't live without it.

As far as sales went, the day was pretty slow going—the usual looky-loos, a couple of rich teenage boys looking for ways to jazz up their cheap transportation. Becker figured he would offload what he could here and then move along to Twi Osiam to do some major trading and restocking. About then, *she* came along, her entourage trailing behind her.

She wasn't really his type—too young, for one thing. She had a figure like a twelve-year-old boy who had been dead of starvation for a year or two. Her hair was long and curly in the back and short and spiky in the front. But she was fashionably and expensively dressed in the furs and skins of several now-extinct species. Amazing that clothes that cost so much could cover so little of what was, to his eye, fairly pointless to reveal.

Her entourage consisted of four men a little older than she was, all of whom ranged restlessly behind her. "Stay," she told them, in a tone Becker would have been a fool to try to use on RK. "Helloo," she cooed to him. Well, he had been right. He'd returned to his natural drop-dead handsomeness and now women found him so irresistible he'd get tired of it. Except, oddly enough, for Khetala. Later.

"Helloo, yourself," he said. "What can I do for you, princess?" he asked, judging correctly which endearment she would prefer. RK, on the other hand, was clearly not about to try and flatter this customer. His back was up; his tail, in its fully recovered state, would have made an excellent bottle-brush, his eyes were slits, his ears were flat, and he was hissing like a tubful of vipers. Becker stepped in front of him, to block his cat's view of this doubtlessly well-heeled customer as well as to block the customer's view of him.

"I was hoping you could advise me," she said. "I was told you know just everything there is to know about slightly used equipment."

"Not everything, but more than most," he agreed.

"I'm starting a small business and it would be a big help if I had just a teensy little fleet of ships all to myself. I can get some very good bargain spacecraft, but they all need parts here and there and I was just *wondering—hoping* actually—that you would have a few things."

"Like what?"

She snapped her fingers and one of the men appeared and recited by rote a string of instruments, equipment, systems, and parts. Becker suspected the man wasn't actually a flesh and blood type, but an android. For one thing, he didn't pause for breath during the whole fifteen minutes it took to recite the lady's shopping list. For another thing, while he was talking, RK peed on his foot and shredded his lower leg and the guy didn't seem to notice.

"Yeah, I got all that," Becker said at the end of the recitation, looking closer at the guy. Yep. Android. Its foot and lower leg were smoking slightly. Cheap model. Bad wiring job. "You want takeout or shall I deliver the stuff to the hangar of your choice? Part of it is still aboard the ship." The lady would be cleaning him out, actually, a fact that made him a little nervous. He'd have to make enough money from this sale to cover his expenses while he collected more inventory. Luckily, he was already planning to go back to all of those desolate planets and pick up the bits and pieces he'd left behind. And while he was at it, he'd check out what had done the healing job on him and RK.

"Oh," the lady said in an arch voice, "how much?"

Becker named his price. About a half dozen times more than the stuff was worth. She smiled and methodically cut it down to a pittance. He named a price more than four times what the merchandise should bring, and the bargaining began in earnest. The problem was, he was nearly selling out here. It would put him out of business until he collected more salvage. He wanted enough profit to float him and RK for a good long time, with enough left over to at least maybe take a little vacation, preferably somewhere there were still Didis or pleasure houses in operation.

"Look, I'll tell you what," he said. "I wasn't going to show you this, but you're a pretty lady and I can tell you have exquisite taste. You give me my original asking price and I'll throw this in for free." He reached into his pocket and drew forth the bit of spiral stone that RK had let him keep. "Give it to your jeweler, he can cut and shape it into a fabulous suite of jewelry for . . ."

The woman's eyes widened when she saw it, and she snatched it from his hand. She began to laugh. Not a pretty laugh either. "Where did you get this?"

"Found it," he said, with a shrug.

"Found it?" She laughed again. "On whom? I mean, where?"

"Now that would be telling," he said. "Just be glad you've got it and nobody else does. A rare find, princess." Part of him thought that if she liked it so much, he should show her the rest of the stones, but that would mean trying to get RK off the specimen bag. Frankly, he liked the cat a lot better than he liked this woman. He already deeply regretted letting her have this sample for nothing—well, nothing except making her pay a lot more than she'd wanted to for the items she needed.

"Yes, indeed," she said. "What a pity you can't get more. I have an excellent market in mind." She thrust her skinny chest toward him. "We might even go into partnership."

"Gee, just my bad luck. But you know how it is," he said with a shrug. "Sometimes you just happen onto a good thing and you may never find it again." He wouldn't part with any more of the spiral stones until he knew what she knew about them that made her so interested in the one he let her have. The things were probably worth a lot more to someone else than what she was offering him.

"Pity," she said, her eyes as hard and narrowed as RK's. For some reason she seemed to doubt his veracity. Good. That made them even.

She handed him a big wad of credits. They were issued in the name of Lady Kisla Manjari. He counted and pocketed them.

"Great. It's a deal then."

"If you'll step aside, I'll have my crew reload your container and use it to transport my merchandise," she said.

"Fair enough. Come on, RK," he said to the cat, and grabbed the specimen bag RK was sitting on. The cat spat at the woman again.

"Oh, no, you don't," she said. "I just bought *everything* here, including that mangy creature. I know a laboratory that would love to get such a specimen."

"Sorry, lady," he said. "You bought everything on the list

that your singed android friend there read. And the cat's not on that list. I can't sell him under any circumstances. Federation law prohibits it. RK here isn't a creature. He's my partner. A sentient being. The brains in the outfit really."

"I *want* it," she said and beckoned to her men. RK left bloody skid marks on Becker's arm as the cat leaped over him and raced off, to be lost among the stalls. Becker grabbed his arm and dropped the collection bag on his foot, but recovered quickly, fumbling to close the mouth of the bag before Kisla could see what he had. He didn't dare look around too much, so he didn't see that one of the artifacts had slid out of the bag and rolled under an oxygen recycling unit.

"Told you he was sentient," Becker said, grinning up at her to make sure she was meeting his gaze and not looking too closely at anything else. "Sorry about that. I'd help you load your stuff but I have to find my partner now."

He nonchalantly tucked the collection bag into his belt and tried not to clank as he walked away.

Three

*A*corna wanted a graze and a good long gallop more than she wanted anything else in this world at the moment, but before she could say so, her thought was taken up by all of the others.

"A meal? What a good idea," exclaimed a nearby dignitary, as if she had spoken her wish aloud. She had been introduced to this person onscreen but she couldn't recall who he was exactly. Someone very important.

"Yes, something to eat, and a good run. What a splendid idea!" Thariinye agreed, and others concurred with nods and other gestures of affirmation. The young male had also spoken aloud.

Neither of them had apparently read the part of her thought in which the galloping and grazing was being done by herself, alone, with the wind blowing through her hair, down in that field below. She put the thought away as antisocial, something she didn't wish to appear to be, especially now, when she really wanted to make a good impression on her native people.

So she smiled and nodded and avoided being trampled while the assembled masses poured out of the spaceport and onto the broad plain separating the port from the town. The plain was lush with lovely grasses, foreign to her but tasting deliciously of lemon and pepper, with a hint of cinnamon.

The people who had joined the *Balakiire*'s crew to celebrate their homecoming happily pulled up and munched the grasses, while wandering from one area to another chatting, laughing, and calling to each other. Acorna slid a sidelong glance at one of the nearby Linyaari. He was not white like her fellow space travelers, but a deep red color with a rich black mane. Others in the crowd were black, brown, golden with white hair, or gray with hair that was lightly dappled with a darker tint.

Neeva smiled at her, catching her thought. "You didn't know we came in colors?"

Several grazers glanced at them in a startled sort of way, then looked politely away.

"We should either speak aloud now or you must keep a tight focus upon me, my dear," Neeva told Acorna. "You send quite well, you know, and will have half the planet privy to your inner thoughts if you're not careful."

"Sorry. It's going to take some getting used to, guarding my thoughts so that everyone can't hear. I'm still not quite sure what, or even when, I'm transmitting."

"You're very strong, dear, if somewhat new to this. You tend to—well, sometimes you shout a bit. Most people won't deliberately intrude upon your thoughts, but you have to try to control your broadcasts. It's not like it is on shipboard where we're in sync with each other, thanks to long-term close association. People here on narhii-Vhiliinyar tend to use thought-speak mostly only among their own kinship groups or close friends. They tend to vocalize at events like this, both to maintain their own privacy, and to avoid intruding on the thoughts of others. Most would no more try to listen in on your private thoughts than they would try to eavesdrop upon your private audible comments."

"I'll try to be more careful," Acorna promised quietly, watching both white and multicolored Linyaari sitting cross-legged in the field or simply lying down, rolling over to get a

new nibble when they'd worn out the old spot. No one seemed
to mind about their clothing getting mussed. Acorna decided it
was time for a change of subject. "No one mentioned to me that
Linyaari came in varied colorations. I was a bit surprised, that's
all. You and the other Linyaari I've met until this moment are
white like me, so I thought we all would have the same coloring."

Neeva made a wry face. "The color of our coat, or lack of it,
among those of us who travel in space has until recently been a
matter of pride to us. It shows our people who we are, and
where we have been. The white coloration is known as becoming star-clad, wearing the white and silver of the distant stars.
A space traveler proudly sheds his or her color the way a child
sheds his or her toys. We're not sure why, but a Linyaari's natural coat color bleaches to white during his or her first space
voyage."

"It's not genetic then, as coloring is among humans?"
Acorna asked.

"Not the white coloring, no." She said, "Since the evacuation, when many people who would have preferred to retain
their original pigmentation lost it, being star-clad has come to
be considered, at least among some circles, as an abnormality
that should be addressed. Our researchers are being asked to
study it as a 'condition.' The last I heard, they had postulated
that the change is caused by a combination of factors: the deprivation of natural light during a typical space voyage, which
results in the destruction of certain photosensitive pigment-
producing elements in our skin; and the lack of certain nutrients in our diet which are only found in plants native to
Vhiliinyar, and which will not grow successfully in hydroponics gardens. We can store the plants in seed form for transport
to suitable new environments, of course, but during the space
voyage, we simply have to do without them, with the resulting
effects on pigmentation. Between the two processes, Linyaari
space-farers lose all coloration in their skin during the course of
a typical space voyage."

Acorna looked down at her own arms and hands, trying to imagine them red or black or any of the other colors she saw around her. "Will I change colors now that I'll be in the sun and eating the right nutrients, then?"

Acorna imagined, in rapid succession, herself in each of the colors she saw on people around her, then herself with bright purple skin and a violet mane. Everyone nearby was clearly listening in, in spite of what Neeva said was polite. There was a scattering of laughter around her, and a few frowns. She deliberately broadcast an image of herself rainbow-colored. Conversations all over the meadow stopped and the laughter turned to embarrassed coughing. Even the frowns looked puzzled, and more people stared at her with politely quizzical expressions. Hmm.

Neeva laughed. "You can see, Khornya, that you'll need to learn to refine your range when you send thought-images. Some of our people have no sense of humor, and they will now think that you are not one of us at all, but some strange second-cousin to the Linyaari who started life as a—what is the little lizard from those vids? The one who changed colors?"

"A chameleon," Acorna said, blushing. "Can I send an apology?"

"Perhaps it would be better to leave well enough alone for now," Neeva replied, still amused. "Otherwise, they will see your blush and think you are trying to tell them you were originally pink. But in answer to your question, sister-daughter, once star-clad, always star-clad. The varicolored Linyaari you see here are younger than you are, born on narhii-Vhiliinyar since the evacuation." She sighed and stood up. "You know, I haven't spent a great deal of time on-planet since shortly after your parents disappeared, so perhaps the experts who see being star-clad as a disease are now close to finding a 'solution.' Perhaps I could return to being gray with spots if I wished. As it happens, I most emphatically do not wish to. I like what I am."

Acorna chewed thoughtfully on one last mouthful of the cinnamon-flavored grass. She caught several frankly annoyed stares and thought less strenuously. She was getting the distinct impression that it was rude to chew and broadcast at the same time. Oh dear, she hadn't been here long at all and already she was afraid she'd get a reputation for unfortunate behavior. It was hard fitting in when she didn't know the rules. . . .

She lowered her voice and moved closer to her aunt, and tried not to think too loudly. She was beginning to feel rather overwhelmed. For one thing, while no one was deliberately sending to her, under the vocalized chatter and laughter she was aware of a constant buzz of random thoughts. For another thing, even though her aunt had told her that the evacuation had happened after her parents and she, as an infant, had left Vhiliinyar for their pleasure cruise, somehow she'd thought narhii-Vhiliinyar would more closely resemble the place she saw in her dreams—that wonderful land with rolling fields leading to snow-capped mountains, with crystal clear rivers and streams cascading into waterfalls and pooling into emerald lakes and ponds when they weren't winding through green fields and wildflower-filled meadows. Nice, cuddly, furry animals drank from the waterways and birds darted everywhere.

Here the hills rolled slightly, the mountains were conspicuously absent, and the plains stretched off to the far horizon. She saw only the Linyaari people; no other large life forms at all. It was a pretty enough place, but lacked the gorgeous scenery and amazing biodiversity of her dreams. Of course, she hadn't seen the entire planet yet. It was unlikely the whole place was like this. Possibly there were many more interesting places on it.

An older white Linyaari male joined Acorna and Neeva.

"*Visedhaanye* Neeva," he said, inclining his head.

"*Aagroni* Iirtye, what an honor it is to see you again, sir."

"The honor is mine, *Visedhaanye*."

"Allow me to present my sister's daughter, Khornya. Khornya, *Aagroni* Iirtye is one of the founders of narhii-Vhiliinyar. His team located this world. He headed the terraforming committee, determining what would be needed by our people to sustain life here, and he customized and implemented the programs and processes necessary to create a new habitat for us."

"An awesome responsibility, sir," Acorna said.

"I'm glad you realize that, young lady," Iirtye said. "I could not help but overhear how disappointed you were at the lack of certain topographical and biological amenities we enjoyed on the old home world."

"Oh, dear. I am trying very hard to learn not to think so loudly, sir, but I can't seem to find the volume control on my mind." She smiled self-deprecatingly, hoping he would have a sense of humor.

It appeared that he didn't. "I see no reason that you should be less than honest," he said with a frown. "But you must understand how little time there was to prepare. Some of the features of the old home world were not only unnecessary, but were at times dangerous. A flat and fairly uniform planetary surface was most efficient for terraforming under the circumstances. This planet had such a surface. As for the other fauna, while we introduced all the essential species—single-celled life forms, invertebrates, and some of the smaller vertebrates like birds and reptiles—during the course of the terraforming process, we were still in the process of gathering breeding populations of the larger vertebrates to transplant when we were notified that the evacuation of our people was to take place immediately. The Khleevi invasion had overtaken Caabye—"

"That was the third planet from our sun back on Vhiliinyar, Khornya," Neeva interjected.

"We had no time to waste. Getting our people off the planet and on the way to safety took priority. We had to mobilize our entire fleet—those ships that were not already away from the planet, that is."

Acorna did not need to invade his thoughts to realize that he was making a posthumous reprimand aimed at her parents because they had taken a spacecraft—and the director of weapons development, which was her father's title and position—away from Vhiliinyar at such a critical time. Though how her parents could have predicted the moment was at hand so quickly when the speed of the final Khleevi invasion took everybody by surprise, Acorna couldn't imagine. Nor could she imagine that her parents would have left the planet if they'd had even an inkling of the fate that awaited them. But she wasn't about to point either of those observations out—if she could help it—to this man.

"In anticipation of the Khleevi invasion, we had furnished this new world with sufficient dwellings, equipment, and provisions to sustain us for the first year. We crowded our people into the colony ships in a mad rush to escape the invaders. We loaded whatever animals we could as well, but the populations were small, and have not flourished here, probably due to a lack of genetic diversity. We have teams searching other worlds now to find similar life forms to supplement and replace the native creatures we lost to the Khleevi."

"I meant no criticism, sir," Acorna replied softly. "You were responsible for saving our people and making this new world. No one, least of all me, could possibly find fault with that. I was only thinking of the world I saw in my dreams."

"Yes, I saw," he said, and turned on his heel and walked away.

Neeva and Acorna exchanged looks.

(I thought being psychic meant that everyone would understand everyone else,) Acorna *whispered* to her aunt.

Neeva patted her shoulder and whispered—vocally—in response, "Some people can hear nothing but their own inner voices shouting at them so loudly that they come to believe the shouting is coming from others. The *aagroni* was a zoologist before he was assigned to the terraforming project. The loss of so many of the native animals was shattering for him."

Acorna gazed after the man who had disappeared into the throng.

"Never mind him, Khornya," said Neeva. "The man is a relentless perfectionist. Despite his efforts, like all worlds, this world is less than perfect. Of course, Vhiliinyar was less than perfect, too, but no one remembers that now. So the *aagroni* does not count the lives he saved or lives of all the children born on this new world when he measures his accomplishments. He is acutely aware, however, of every single complaint about the weather, the lack of animals, the monotonous scenery, the bugs, and natural upheavals that are all too common on a recently terraformed planet."

Just as Neeva finished speaking a breathless young person skidded up to them, almost falling in her haste to reach them.

"Your pardon, *Visedhaanye* Neeva," the young person said. Her skin was a soft mocha brown and her hair a darker brown adorned with large white splotches. She was almost stammering in her haste to convey her message. "The *Viizaar* Liriili wishes to see you immediately on a matter of some urgency."

"The *Viizaar* Liriili?" Neeva asked. "When did Liriili become *viizaar*?"

"A *ghaanye* ago, *Visedhaanye* Neeva," the girl said. "When *Viizaar* Tiilye stepped down to pursue *Haarha Liirni.*"

Acorna consulted the vocabulary she'd learned from the LAANYE, a translation device usually used by Linyaari emissaries to sleep-learn the languages of other species. In her case, a LAANYE had been recalibrated so that she could more rapidly learn Linyaari. A *viizaar* was some kind of high political office. The other term the girl used seemed to mean "higher learning." And Acorna knew a *ghaanye* was roughly a year and a half in Galactic Standard time.

"We were just coming to report in," Neeva said with extra warmth in her voice to reassure the girl, warmth that was quite at odds with the dismay Acorna felt emanating emotionally from her aunt. "I know Liriili will be so pleased to meet Khornya."

The messenger girl looked Acorna up and down quickly, even a bit skittishly. "So you're the one who was captured by the Khleevi," she said. "How did you get away before getting tortured and killed?"

"Captured by the Khleevi? But I wasn't captured by the Khleevi," Acorna said, confused. The two of them fell in behind

Neeva and Melireenya as they made their way to the road to the city. Khaari had found old friends among the greeting committee and was, judging from the exchange of lively facial expressions, deep in animated conversation with them. Thariinye, flanked by two younger female Linyaari, followed Acorna and the messenger.

Acorna became aware of a mental exchange between her aunt and Thariinye.

(Thariinye, where do you suppose this child would get the idea that Khornya was captured by Khleevi?) Neeva asked.

(Not from me. I only said that the beings who intercepted Khornya's pod after her parents' death were barbaric and in some ways Khleevi-like. I never said she was captured,) the young male replied.

Acorna and the messenger girl looked at each other. Acorna was all too aware of the psychic communication that took place between the mature adults. But according to what Acorna had learned, psychic ability only began manifesting itself in the Linyaari youngsters at puberty. This girl was definitely prepubescent.

"I wasn't kidnapped by the Khleevi," Acorna told the young Linyaari. "I was brought up among an alien species called humans. My adopted uncles were very kind, as were many other humans I encountered. I'm sure you would have found Mr. Li in particular most . . . Linyaari-like. Am I using that correctly? There were other humans who were pretty barbaric, it's true, but my contact with the harsher aspects of humanity has been limited."

The girl looked extremely disappointed, and for a moment Acorna thought it might be the sort of bloodthirstiness she knew from the children on Kezdet.

"I'm sorry to have got it wrong," the girl said. "I didn't mean to upset you. I was hoping that you *had* been captured. I mean, not that I wish you ill, but especially when I saw that you looked so unharmed, I was hoping you had been through the torture and survived it because. . . . Oh well, it's not important right now. You didn't endure it, and I'm glad you're all right. My name is Maati, by the way. I know that you're Khornya."

"In your—our language—yes. At home I was called Acorna," Acorna said, allowing the subject to change since the girl was evidently too flustered by her mistake to make a great deal of sense. Acorna did not find the child easy to read and wondered if this was because Linyaari children lacked psychic ability. It was clear from this youngling that the lack meant that the children not only lacked the ability to receive thoughts but also to transmit them nonverbally, consciously or unconsciously.

"Acorna? That's an odd name," Maati said. "So is Khornya, for that matter. I mean, the word means 'one horn.' All of us have one horn and nobody has more than one, so what's the big deal?"

"No one else where I was living had a horn," Acorna told her.

"They didn't? How did they heal things when they got hurt or sick? And what if the water was muddy in the stream where they were, or there was a fire and the air was smoky? How did they fix it?"

"Sometimes they didn't. If they were hurt or sick, and I wasn't handy, they went to medics who fixed them with all sorts of tools and tonics and pills. As best they could, anyway. And if the water was muddy, they drank muddy water or went thirsty. If the air was smoky, they breathed it or moved to where there was cleaner air. Again, unless I was handy."

"I'm surprised they let you come home if they're that backward and you were that useful to them," Maati said stoutly.

Acorna sighed and refrained from trying to explain any more about human society.

They were walking across the edge of the field now. The sky was a clear cloudless turquoise. Acorna saw the road from the city to the spaceport just ahead of them. Standing on the road were several men in elaborately decorated uniforms, each uniform a different color. Standing beside them, decked out in

beribboned and bejeweled blankets that matched their attendants' uniforms, were animals that looked something like
horses—except that they had horns, just like the Linyaari.

"Madam," one of the men said, though he said it in Linyaari,
of course, "our Ancestors will now convey you to the home of
the *viizaar*."

"Ride? The *Ancestors*?" Neeva sounded shocked. "When did
we start using the Ancestors as transportation?"

"Ancestors?" Acorna asked, intrigued. She reached out her
hand and touched the velvet nose of one of the gorgeously blanketed creatures. Up close, though they mostly looked like
Uncle Hafiz's horses, they also looked a tiny bit like goats, with
little beards on their chins. They were somewhat more slightly
built than the horses she'd seen in Hafiz's stables. But they
were entirely identifiable as something else she'd been associated with by her human companions all her life. "These are Mr.
Li's *ki-lin*!" she said. She looked at Neeva. "You didn't tell me
about them."

"Well, no," Neeva said. "One doesn't speak of the Ancestors
off the home world, not even among one's closest companions.
They do not care for offworlders, no matter how *Linyaari*,
knowing about them. In the past, they have had great reason to
be frightened of other species. Not of Linyaari, of course. The
Linyaari have, since the Ancestor's great tragedy and rescue by
the Ancestral Hosts, evolved from them, but their kind are
long-lived and adaptable. These are descendents from the original species. Most are far older than any of us. Their species, all
of the Ancestors, remain as they always were, unchanged since
those long-distant days before our kind had yet to be born."

To the man in the fuchsia uniform standing beside the fuch-
sia-blanketed unicorn Neeva now repeated her question. "*Ride?
The Ancestors?*"

Acorna's normally serene aunt was clearly so taken aback
she'd shouted without meaning to.

The fuchsia-clad man rubbed his temples and grimaced in
pain. Very slowly, as if he was unaccustomed to speaking aloud,

the man said, "Yes, *Visedhaanye* Neeva. It is the wish of the Ancestors that you and your crew ride upon the backs of these Ancestors to Kubiilikhan. It is traditional."

"Traditional? Since when? I am not aware that we ever rode upon their backs since—well, since the Linyaari race began."

The man rubbed the area around his horn, as if continuing to block pain, and said, "It has become traditional over the past *ghaanye* and a half, *Visedhaanye*. Since the Ancestors noticed that in the continued absence of flitters, our space-farers have been walking into Kubiilikhan from the spaceport. The Ancestors feel that this lacks dignity. They feel that a lot of two-legged creatures simply walking down the road to the capital provides no sense of circumstance or occasion befitting the importance of our space-farers."

"Now *that* is odd," Melireenya said. "Back on the home world, the Ancestors never quite approved of space-farers. Such dreadful things had happened to them in space, you know."

"During the evacuation, madam, the Ancestors became aware of the important functions those who brave the perils of space fulfill these days on behalf of our people."

"I don't understand," Acorna said, feeling a little like the girl who had fallen down a rabbit hole in a rather odd old story she had once read while aboard her uncles' mining ship. "The *ki-lin* here are our Ancestors, and they want us to ride them because there are no flitters? Why aren't there any flitters? Isn't it awfully hard to get around on the planet just walking or maybe riding on—on the Ancestors?"

Aagroni Iirtye, who was in the group of people rounded up by messengers to go to the *viizaar*'s house, spoke up. He demanded of her as if she were stupid, "How much room do you think a space fleet has when it has one chance only to evacuate an entire planet full of people and the essentials for helping them survive? Flitters are large. They take up vital room that is better used by other cargo. They are easily replaceable. Organic creatures are not."

Acorna couldn't help herself. She had to reply to that. "Of course the living must come first, sir. But wasn't it difficult to settle the planet without some sort of small scale ground transport?"

"We had steps, ramps, and ladders . . . and we had feet, young lady!" the scientist said. "And each transport ship had a shuttle fleet which was perfectly adequate for transporting people and supplies to various locations around the planet as necessary. Our current dwellings and devices are quite sensibly easily portable, and as a people we've always kept the complex machinery we require in our home environment to a minimum. Flitters were, during the chaos of the evacuation, simply a convenience that took up room we needed to transport the Ancestors to our new home. The Ancestors, after all, are sentient beings. They could hardly be left to the nonexistent mercies of the Khleevi."

He shook his head at the general stupidity of his fellow beings and allowed an attendant to lead him to his designated Ancestor.

"And afterwards," someone said in a small voice, "even though the council did get around to ordering flitters eventually, they've been on back-order for almost an entire *ghaanye*."

"I don't quite understand," Acorna said. "You mean it's been three years and you haven't even started replacing them?"

"It's all right, dear," Neeva told her. "You need not understand everything right away. There will be plenty of time to explain later."

"I'm just surprised that . . . never mind. Since the Ancestors wish to make such a sacrifice, please tell them I am deeply appreciative," Acorna said, dipping her own horn toward the unicorn. She turned back to Neeva and whispered to her in a quiet aside, "It was just a surprise that the Linyaari have no more mundane form of ground transport when they have such a glorious space fleet." She indicated the ships neatly docked nearby, so many fanciful eggs in a crate.

"The ships were necessarily brought along during the evacuation. We used everything flyable in our haste to leave our old home before the Khleevi came. The flitters were expendable, though, as were many of the technological devices we'd commonly used back on the old planet. We concentrated on saving the biological wealth of the home world. As is always the case in any forced migration, there were things we lost along the way," Neeva said.

"We have all we need to sustain us," the attendant replied, overhearing the quiet conversation. "The Ancestors in their wisdom indicate the path of truth, as usual. By their example, they show us how to use what is important to substitute for that which is less so."

"It takes time and credits to resupply a transplanted world," Melireenya said, as, after a deep bow to the unicorn blanketed in blue, she was helped by the creature's attendant to mount. "Fortunately, our space fleet was equal to the demands that we made of it, both during the evacuation and now. Good engineering and buying quality paid off when we were in dire circumstances."

"The ships weren't manufactured on your old home world?" Acorna asked, surprised.

"Only partially. They were assembled off-planet by manufacturers who cater to our trade and then brought to us to be customized to our specific needs and tastes by Linyaari techno-artisans."

"I see. But why off-planet? I thought, with the LAANYE and the other devices I've seen, that you—we—were a highly advanced technological society with the infrastructure to support a great deal of industry."

"Having the capability isn't the point, child," said another of the Linyaari greeting committee.

The attendant of Acorna's Ancestor cleared his throat and said, "The Grandmother says that in the day of her own grandmother, the Ancestral Hosts did a great deal of manufacturing. It was very messy. It took up valuable grazing area and required either living workers who would much rather be elsewhere or else mechanical workers who themselves had to be manufactured."

Another attendant chimed in, as if reciting a litany. "It was a pernicious system, which devoured increasingly more grazing area as time passed. Fortunately, the Ancestral Hosts took advantage of space travel and relocated much of our manufacturing to other worlds where the beings didn't mind living without adequate grazing area. These days, even though we have a large community of techno-artisans who are superb designers and engineers, the vast majority of our manufacturing is done under Linyaari supervision on other worlds."

"Which is a very good thing," Melireenya said, "because we're always in need of grazing land."

A Linyaari woman wearing a long multicolored robe said, "The example of the Ancestral Hosts has served us throughout our history. Most of our people feel that living a life centered in plants and creatures is much more Linyaari than dealing with metals and tools."

"But our people don't mind if others spend *their* lives working with metals and tools," Neeva said wryly. "And some of the Linyaari find their calling in doing just that. Just as some of us live our lives in space or on other planets. Our people trade with other worlds for the items, materials, parts, or processes we need to have manufactured."

"What do we trade if we manufacture nothing ourselves?" Acorna wanted to know.

"Think about it, Khornya," Thariinye said. "What problems do industrial societies have that we can cure?" He didn't wait for her to answer. "Pollution, of course! Their manufacturing processes create toxins we can neutralize."

"But mindful of the example of the Ancestors," the attendant intoned, "our envoys, emissaries, and tradesmen do not disclose the true source of our power."

"Of course not," said another of the white-skinned Linyaari greeting committee. "Our trading partners do not realize the purification power lies in our horns. They think it is a mechanical process—centered in these little devices we take with us which they believe effectively dispel pollution and contamination on their worlds. Though they've also figured out the devices only work in the hands of Linyaari technicians."

"Thus, profiting from the examples of the Ancestors and the Ancestral Hosts, the vast majority of our people can live a pastoral lifestyle uncontaminated by the processes which would compromise those things we value," a golden-colored Linyaari concluded.

Neeva interjected, with a mixture of amusement and annoyance, "Fortunately for those who embrace only the agrarian lifestyle, our people are not of a hive mentality. While we sometimes communicate telepathically, that by no means indicates that we all agree, or think alike. There *are* many of us who find endless pastoralism stultifyingly boring and tedious. Some Linyaari prefer to study science and physics, to enjoy the challenge and adventure of space travel and other more technological pursuits. We have many among our kind who are inventors, who design the devices, techniques, and programs we need, and adapt alien technologies to our purposes. We space-farers serve our people as envoys and traders to supply new markets for Linyaari skills and goods, and to bring back those things our people prefer not to manufacture for ourselves."

"And we are content that you do so, *Visedhaanye*, and even grateful for the many conveniences, improvements, and innovations you bring us, so long as you do not undertake to do your work *here*, or make us join you out there," said another white-skinned Linyaari with a slight shudder. "One journey in the blackness of space will serve most of us for a lifetime. And how you can live out most of your life inside a large machine, however beautifully decorated, is beyond me."

"I must admit," Khaari said, "after *ghaanyi* in a space ship, I do love coming home—to the agrarian life where one grazes, not from a hydroponics tank, but in a real garden or field with bugs and birds and unexpected treats among the wildflowers and weeds."

"There are not many birds here, honored lady," the peridot-green-uniformed attendant of the peridot-blanketed Ancestor Khaari rode said sadly. "Great grandfather here sadly misses their singing."

"As do I," said the *aagroni* sadly. "As do I."

Four

Kisla Manjari's pout at losing the junk man and his wild cat as victims rapidly disappeared when her sandaled foot encountered a hard object on the ground. "Ouch!" she said, and bent down to pick up what she had thought was an offending rock, in order to fling it after Becker. Then she saw what it was.

"*Two* unicorn horns? That girl only had one, Daddy," she said to her father, a figure she alone could see. She saw him as she always saw him now, dressed in his finest ceremonial clothes with the blood just beginning to flow from the wound in his neck, the way it had flowed the day he died. "Where did the other one come from? The junk man said he gave me the only one. He said he had no more. He was lying, the low-born space scum."

"You must never let people get away with lying to us, Kisla. You should punish him," her father told her.

"Oh, yes. I will, Daddy, of course I will. I'll make him tell. But if these horns are real, which one is hers, do you think?"

"Kisla, I think this is a grave matter upon which you should consult your Uncle Edacki. He will be able to advise and help you."

"Yes, Daddy, I'll do just that," she said. She turned to her staff. The androids were quite accustomed to Kisla's seemingly solo conversations and paid no attention to them. "I want you to finish loading the container and then stop at the registration office and find out the junk man's name and where his ship is docked. We'll be wanting to pay him a call later. Right now I am going to visit my guardian. In the meantime, take these things to my personal hangar and have the workmen begin integrating the useful parts into my vessels. Await my instructions there."

"As you wish, Lady Kisla," said the latest model among them. Since most of Uncle Edacki's human servants were too slow and stupid to suit her, he had instead given her four of his androids for her staff. They were obedient, and were not always crying or bleeding like the human servants.

Count Edacki Ganoosh gave his ward a slow, appreciative smile as he handled the unicorn horns she had brought him. Kisla Manjari was psychotic, of course, but she was not as stupid as many people assumed. And perhaps the craziness would lessen, over time. After all, it was bound to be a shock to a young girl to see her father kill her mother and then himself after being denounced as an arch-criminal in front of the most respected citizens of Kezdet. He'd been there that night, and it had certainly shocked him. Since Kisla was a very self-centered girl, one might have assumed that discovering that she was adopted, and had been born the illegitimate daughter of a prostitute, would have been the main shock of that night to her, but once it turned out that her parents had died before the state could officially confiscate all their holdings, and that she, Kisla, was their only heir, that part of the horror seemed to have slipped her mind. The government had still confiscated most of the Manjari empire, but Count Edacki, as the girl's appointed guardian, had pleaded that the girl was not a criminal and should be left with certain holdings among the Baron's legitimate enterprises, enough to constitute a solid trust fund for her upkeep, education, and a hefty income for the remainder of her life. Count Edacki secretly suspected the girl also knew of certain secret holdings the government had not yet located. Large holdings, he believed. It was such a difficult job to gain the trust of an orphaned child. The count was thus pleased for more reasons than one that she had decided to show him the unicorn horns.

"Excellent, my dear Kisla. You've done well," he said, stroking the horns and wondering if it was true what the legends said of such horns having aphrodisiac properties.

"I don't need you to tell me that, Uncle," Kisla seethed. "I need you to help me find out why there are two and which one belongs to that girl who is responsible for the deaths of my parents and the theft of my property."

"You are impetuous, little one," he said, laying the horns aside in order to rise from the soothing bath of rose-colored gelatinous mud from the fragrant swamps of the Haidian rain forests. Having dismissed his valet at Kisla's insistence, the count was forced to wrap himself in his massage robe of the deepest purple plush. He then made himself comfortable on the bed-like couch that bracketed the gel pool. "While it is certainly possible that one of these may belong to Acorna, I believe word of her death would have reached us, and it has not. However, these horns might well belong to one of the others of her kind."

"*What* others?" Kisla demanded.

"Why, the other unicorn people who came to fetch the girl a few months ago."

"I knew nothing of this," Kisla said.

"My dear, you were still distracted with grief. That and the legal affairs your late lamented father left concerning your legacy. I did not feel it was a proper time to trouble you with the news then. Oh, yes. Four others, I believe. It seems Acorna was not a goddess, as the little child laborers believed, but simply an alien creature who, being as highly evolved as they are all generally supposed to be, took it upon herself to correct what she considered our less fortunate social behaviors and economic practices."

"These horns could belong to them then, to those other uni-corn aliens who came to get her?" Kisla asked. She could see a plan dawning in Uncle Edacki's eyes.

"Oh, yes. Or any others of her race, though they were unknown to our species before your little friend arrived."

"She's no friend of mine." Kisla spat.

"No, of course not. I was being facetious. The junk man will have to be questioned, of course. If there are two of these, there may be more, and he must tell us where he obtained them."

"I'll take care of him," Kisla said.

"Yes, my dear. But be careful. We don't want him to die before we've learned all that we need to. In the meantime, I think we really must sacrifice one of these to determine its properties and composition. I have heard miraculous things about Acorna. That her horn could heal and purify and even — no, now I'm confusing rumor with ancient legend."

Kisla had seated herself on the edge of the couch beside his head and now she leaned over him and spoke into his ear. "Don't misunderstand us, Uncle. If there is a profit to be made from these, we want it, Daddy and me. But most of all we want that girl, and all of her family, and all of her friends dead, the same way she killed my family and chased away all of my friends."

The count smiled up at his ward. The truth was, Kisla had never had any friends at all, but it would do no good to mention that. Nor to point out that she had, in the same breath, referred to the late Baron Manjari, her adopted father, as if he was still alive, and yet also admitted that her whole family was dead.

Count Edacki patted Kisla's hand. "Have no fear, child. I think that if these horns prove as useful as they are said to be, Acorna and her kind will soon become hunted throughout the galaxy as any other creature with a built-in treasure would be hunted. There are already those who seek them. But with these" — he tapped one of the horns — "and the use of a bit of research and a few contacts used wisely, I believe we may con-trive to be the first to find them."

*   *   *

Once the skinny girl disappeared, and her henchmen had loaded Becker's container with the goods she'd bought and left, RK crept out from under the table where he'd hidden, jumped up on its surface, and scattered the stones there as he made himself comfortable among them.

And that was where Becker found the cat later, entertaining the strokes and pats of the children of the stone vendor and idly batting one of the smaller and more precious stones back and forth between his paws. The rock glinted blue, green, aqua, then back to blue again as the cat rolled it from paw to paw.

"Nice cat, mister," a boy of about five said. "What'll ya take for him?"

Becker cocked an eyebrow at him. "That's the second offer I've had today."

"Don't be dumb, Deeter," a girl of about seven with the same red hair and freckles said. "You don't buy and sell cats like this. Can't you see he's a Makahomian Temple Cat? They're sacred, you know. Probably part of this man's religion. I bet he's a priest or something."

"Pope at least," Becker agreed. "Him, I mean. I just work for him."

The vendor himself was rooting around in a box and when he stood up this time, Becker finally remembered his name. "Reamer! You're Rocky Reamer!" he said.

"You got it, buddy," the man said. It was clear he was the daddy of these kids. He had the same red hair and freckles. "And say, I thought I recognized you, too, but if you're the guy I'm thinking of, you look a little different. It's Joe Becker, isn't it?"

"Joe, Jonas, whatever," he said. "Yeah, that's me, Becker. You know what? I just remembered why those stones I was looking at earlier sounded so familiar. What were the names again? Giloglite, bairdite, and nadezdite?"

"That's it," Reamer said. "They're from new deposits the kids on Maganos found and named for the Lady's uncles. See, that one with the red and yellow in it that has a kinda plaid look to it? That's for Calum Baird, who's a Caledonian Celt like me. We had a geology class together once. The serpentine looking one is for that Iroid partner of his, Declan Giloglie, and the flashy one for his *nouveau richeness* himself, the heir and current manager of the House of Harakamian, Rafik Nadezda."

Becker grinned. "That's what I thought. So Rafik's uncle made him heir, huh? I never could tell if he hated the old man or admired him."

"A little of both, I guess. You know those guys, then?"

"Yeah, we been chasing each other around the same big rocks for years. They were looking for the unoccupied ones and I was looking for the occupied or formerly occupied ones, so we didn't get in each other's way much."

RK had knocked the stone he was playing with off the table and was allowing himself to be distracted by a string dangled by Deeter.

Becker picked the stone up from the ground. "And what did you call this one?"

"That's acornite."

"Where's it from? A planet where all the plant life is also mineral? You maybe grow already petrified oak trees from it?"

Reamer's face was blank for a second, and then he grinned and chuckled.

"No, silly," the little girl said. "Don't you know anything? It's named for the Lady, of course!"

"I thought her name was Epona . . ." Becker said. "If it's the same one, I mean. I was told that was who was on Maganos, anyway, and you said that's where Gil and Calum and Rafik are these days."

The little girl looked unsure of her information at this point and turned to her dad, who said, "Nah, that's one of what you might call her titles. See, she and old man Li—he died this year, did you know?"

"Delszaki Li died? Shards, I thought he was immortal in spite of the wheelchair."

"Nope, he finally died. Turned out he was head of the

Liberation Movement that saved Kezdet. Li had already done some of the groundwork for the revolution, but nothing really got moving until Gil and his buddies brought the Lady down here. She didn't know much about politics, but she knew for sure she didn't like to see kids being sold into slavery. Took her about a year to bring down the houses and the Piper and start up the education and mining center on Maganos. Of course, it helped that she also forged an alliance between the houses of Harakamian and Li so she had almost unlimited money behind her. Anyway, the kids got real superstitious about her and some of them thought she was some kind of goddess, depending on the religions they'd had where they'd come from. So they call her Epona, Lady Lucia, or the Lady of the Light, but her name's really Lady Acorna Harakamian-Li."

"Maybe I'll go look up my old buddies then," Becker said. "I'd like to meet this lady. I was a slave when I was a kid. If it hadn't been for my adopted dad, I'd probably be dead now."

Reamer rubbed the red heads of his offspring. "I'll tell you what, buddy, it sure makes me feel better knowing those places have been shut down. In case anything happens to me, I don't have to worry about my kids getting sent to the mines or some godawful thing."

Becker thought for a minute, then pulled out the collection bag, carefully extracted one of the opalescent objects, and kept it concealed in the palm of his hand except to open the hand a little to let Reamer have a look. "While I'm at it, I think I just made a big mistake letting some of this go to a customer. It didn't come from Maganos, but I've never seen anything like it anywhere. Do you know what it might be?"

"Ho-oh-oly hematite!" Reamer said, touching the thing as if afraid it would burn him. "Where *did* you get that, Becker?" His voice was not very friendly this time, and his blue eyes had gone ice cold. "Kids, I want you to leave the cat alone and go get yourselves some candy," he said, dropping a credit in each hand.

"But, Dad . . ."

"Scat!"

They ran off and RK emitted a mournful and, for him, curiously resigned mew, watching his new friends disappear into the crowd.

"That's why you look different. You were missing an ear the last time I saw you!" Rocky said. It was an accusation.

"What about it?"

"People say the Lady's horn can heal. Then you turn up with one like it and your ear fixed, so what am I supposed to think?"

"Keep it down, will you? Jeez! I found it, I tell you. Does this lady of yours control everything? Wipes out child labor, closes the pleasure houses, and now you're about to kill me because she has a horn like mine? So what? Maybe she found hers the same place I did."

"I don't think so," Reamer said coldly.

"No? Why not? She might have."

"No way. Hers is growing from the middle of her forehead. At least it was, the last time anybody I know saw her."

Five

The crew of the *Balakiire* and the dignitaries among the greeting committee rode the Ancestors into Kubiilikhan with as much pomp and circumstance as the Ancestors could give them. Acorna feared that if dignity was what the Ancestors wished to impart by having others ride them, in her case it was rather a lost cause. Her long legs dangled below the belly of the Ancestor she rode, so that her feet were almost as low as the unicorn's cloven hooves.

Riding the Ancestors certainly didn't make the trip quicker, either. It took almost an hour to ride the two or three miles between the spaceport and the town, which at first seemed to be a tent city of massive gem-hued, gold-trimmed, tasseled pavilions the size of the circus tents Acorna had seen pictured on vids and in the books at Uncle Hafiz's. Walking would have been much quicker. The *ki-lin* of legend were supposed to be fleet of foot. If so, you couldn't tell it by the Ancestors, who kept their pace to a slow, deliberate strut.

Maybe it is because they are so ancient, Acorna thought, and immediately felt an impression of reprimand at the notion.

(We're as spry as we ever were, impudent youngling, and

can beat you in a race any time, any place, just try us.)

Oops. She was sure the thought hadn't been loud or deliberately sent, and no one else seemed to have picked up on it, but
the Ancestor she was riding rolled a rather challenging eye
back in her direction, and snorted.

The Ancestor's attendant noticed the eye rolling. He
stepped away from his charge for a pace, stroked the Ancestor's
nose, and cast a reproachful glance at Acorna.

By that time their party arrived at the first structures in the
Linyaari settlement. She supposed, since the spaceport was
nearby and they were being taken to see the *viizaar*, this place
must be the main city on the planet, but it was not of any great
size.

The circus-tent-like buildings of the city were clustered
around an even larger central circus tent, where each section
sprouted another tent-like tower from its center. Actually, these
dwellings were not so much like tents as like the pavilions she
had seen depicted in films of ancient Earth medieval encamp-
ments. Each was, like the attendants' and Ancestors' costumes,
decorated in a different gaudy hue, and liberally trimmed with
loops, swirls, swags, fringe, and tassels of contrasting metal or
fabric or rope.

These pavilions had no windows of the sort Acorna was
used to, but each section of each tent had a large arched doorway open to the outdoors and several had whole wall sections
removed.

"Behold Kubiilikhan, our principal city, honored lady," the
attendant said.

"It's—*very* colorful," Acorna said politely. And tried to think
the same thing, though the attendant frowned a bit so some of
her concerns were clearly leaking through her guard. "But you
must suffer greatly from the dampness during the rains."

Maati, who had fallen back from her trot at the head of the
procession, laughed. " No, wait till you dismount. Excuse me,
Great-grandmother, but she's got to see this!" the girl said with
an affectionate but not particularly reverent pat on the nose to

the unicorn. The Ancestor snorted, but rather fondly, Acorna thought, very much in the same way a tolerant grandparent might act toward a well-loved but rambunctious child.

Acorna dismounted with a horn dip to the unicorn, who ignored her. She followed Maati, who was now stroking the silken-appearing wall of the large purple pavilion. "Feel!" Maati commanded.

Acorna reached out and touched the fabric. Surprisingly, she found it hard and unyielding. Rapping on it with the backs of her fingers, she heard a metallic ting. "It's solid?" she asked.

"Yes, and you can open the pores so the air comes through nicely—but not the wet."

"And you don't get chilly during the cold season—you do *have* a cold season?"

"Oh, sure, outdoors when we're grazing. But then we can just go inside, close the flaps, and adjust the pores so that they heat the air as it comes inside. *Very* scientific," she said, as if she hoped that it being scientific would please Acorna.

"It certainly is," Acorna agreed.

Neeva beckoned her into the tent. "Come along, Khornya. Liriili is not a particularly patient person."

Acorna followed her, with Melireenya and Khaari close behind. Maati scrambled to get ahead of Neeva and while Acorna's eyes were still adjusting to the dimmer light inside, she heard Maati say, "Grand *Vüzaar* Liriili, presenting *Visedhaanye Ferilii* Neeva, the crew of the spacecraft *Balaküire*, and Khornya, sister-child to *Visedhaanye* Neeva and daughter to the late Vaanye and Feriila of honored memory."

Vüzaar Liriili was, Acorna saw, seated at a desk. Like the other space-farers, she was pale skinned and silver maned, and her eyes, when they met Acorna's, were deep pewter-gray. Her golden horn was twined with glittering silver thread and she wore a gown cut to compliment her rather sturdy figure in a fabric that matched the thread. Her mane was cropped short around her face and neck and her face was a bit longer than that of any of the other Linyaari. In fact, she rather resembled the Ancestors.

Thariinye's unguarded thought came to Acorna, (What a beauty!)

The *Vüzaar*'s eyes twinkled as they rested upon the handsome young male for a moment, and then she turned her attention to business. "*Visedhaanye* Neeva, dear Melireenya, Khaari, my child, Thariinye, we are all so delighted at your return especially in view of the terrible dangers you faced to warn others. And most of all, Khornya, we are thrilled that you have finally rejoined us."

"I am thrilled to be here," Acorna assured her.

"You will of course be joining us at the reception this evening, *Vüzaar* Liriili?" Neeva inquired.

Liriili smiled. "*I* will be there, certainly, *Visedhaanye* Neeva. You will be happy to know your instructions were all implemented and everything is in readiness. Unfortunately, neither you nor your core crew members with the exception of Thariinye will be there, I'm afraid. As you were disembarking, I received an urgent message from one of our trading missions. I must discuss this with you privately and then you must leave again, as soon as you have had time to refuel."

"But my lifemate is expecting me!" Khaari cried.

"He is on that trading mission, Khaari," Liriili told her. "That is one reason I wish the *Balaküre* to undertake this particular task."

"But what about Khornya?" Neeva asked.

"Why, she will stay here, of course, and learn to know her people and attend the fete as you have planned. While she will sorely miss your guidance, we will try in your absence to make sure that she is not lonely and learns what is needful for her to know."

"Excuse me, *Vüzaar* Liriili—" Acorna interrupted as politely as possible. She did not much care for being discussed as if she was not there.

"Yes, Khornya?"

"It's just that—well, even though I was very much looking forward to doing these social events with my aunt and friends,

I really would rather not attend them by myself. Is it possible to postpone the reception so that I could accompany them on their mission?"

Liriili laughed. "My dear Khornya, you will hardly be by yourself! I shall be there, and Thariinye, and most of the cream of Kubiilikhan society including many young males most eager to make your acquaintance!"

"Yes, ma'am, but I'd rather be with my aunt. Perhaps I can be useful on the mission."

"You're very young and have a great deal to learn," Liriili said as if that settled the matter.

"Khornya is a very capable young lady, Liriili," Neeva told the *viizaar*, and projected images of some of Acorna's adventures.

"I'm sure she is, *Visedhaanye* Neeva," Liriili said, then turning to Acorna, repeated, "I'm sure you are, my dear, but you are not yet versed in our ways sufficiently to undertake a mission of the delicacy this one requires. And there will probably not be enough room for you on the return trip. Or for Thariinye, which is why we are not sending him. So you young ones may as well remain here and enjoy yourselves. The reception can hardly be postponed. Everyone has been working ever so hard preparing it and many, many people will be most disappointed if you are not there. Run along with Maati now. There's a good girl."

"Excuse my persistence, *Viizaar*, but what *is* this mission?" Acorna pressed her case. "Maybe I could help. I have good friends in many high places."

The *viizaar* gave her an exaggeratedly patient look. "That may be so, Khornya. But whoever you know and whatever you have done before is irrelevant to this mission, which I cannot discuss with you because you are not fully conversant with thought transference, and I am reliably informed that during unguarded moments your every fleeting notion is broadcast to the whole of the planet; information could be disclosed that I have no wish to disseminate at this time. In your aunt's absence,

Thariinye can continue your tutoring in our communication forms and customs. Now *do* please go with Maati and freshen up. There is not much time before your shipmates must leave, and I must brief them. In private."

"Yes, ma'am," Acorna said, feeling more like a schoolgirl than she ever had done when she was of the age to have been one.

"Excuse me, Liriili," Neeva said, dropping the title in her annoyance. "I would like to take leave of my niece before we are sent back into space, if you can wait a few more moments before briefing us. I had to wait three and a half *ghaanyi* to find her and who knows how long it will be before I see her again?"

"Very well, but be brief, please. We have much to discuss," Liriili said, and turned her attention to the others.

Leading Acorna outside the pavilion, Neeva touched horns with her and Acorna, impulsively, hugged her aunt as if she never wished to let her go, which indeed she did not.

Neeva's eyes were full of tears when they stood at arm's length again. "Oh, that insufferable woman!" she said. "This had better be a truly urgent mission or I am going to have her before the Council!"

"You think she'd send you out again without a good reason?" Acorna asked. "When you've been away so long?" She frowned. "I thought if everyone could read each other's thoughts and feelings, they would be kinder."

"We are, but there are still jealousies and insecurities and all of the other baggage that goes with being sentient. And Liriili has more than her share of those emotions. She isn't really a bad person, and she can only do just so much without the say-so of the Council, but she has no love for our family. While I doubt she'd try to actively harm you, don't count on her for help either. Just stay out of her way until we return, if you can."

"I'll do my best, Neeva. But return soon, please?"

Neeva ran her fingers down her niece's face and smiled. "We'll do our best, youngling. You know we will. Now, you go with Maati to my pavilion and get ready for the party tonight. I've ordered some things sent over for you to try on. I wish I could be there to see the faces of the young males when they set eyes on you!"

"Farewell, mother's-sister, safe journey and quick return."

"Farewell, sister-child, till we meet again."

"Let's go through the courtyard," Maati said, taking Acorna's hand and pulling her away from the pavilion. "I always go that way when I can."

"Why—oh, I see," Acorna said, as the child stepped onto the path paved with several sets of the Singing Stones of Skarrness, similar to the ones Uncle Hafiz had at his compound on Laboue.

"Yeah, look," Maati commanded her, and proceeded to play hopscotch—and a little tune—across the courtyard.

Acorna smiled, applauded, and followed suit with one of the tunes she used to hopscotch on Uncle Hafiz's stones. She found it as hard now as she had then to stay unhappy when the stones sang.

Maati led the way to a pavilion at the far side of the town. "This is the *visedhaanye's* home. Oooooh, look at the dresses!"

Walking into the pavilion was like walking into a particularly well stocked closet. Gowns of every color, cut, and description lay and hung on every possible surface and protuberance. Also in abundance were gleaming gemstones and little pointy objects, like hats, the size and shape of her horn. These were decorated variously with gems, with flowers, with pom-poms, with ribbons, and gilt threads.

"*Pom-poms?*" Acorna asked.

Maati giggled. "They're all the rage at the moment especially among the girls of color who are entering society." She stuck one on her own slightly smaller horn. The effect, with her dark skin and mottled hair, of the yellow and pink pom-poms, was certainly festive and not quite as clown-like as Acorna had supposed.

"Why do people decorate their horns?"

"Well, it's not just decoration. The covers also mute tele-pathy to some extent," Maati said. "It's for flirting, too. I mean, this way if a girl likes a boy, she doesn't have to show it right away and neither does he. Before anybody can read anybody else's mind, they can kind of see how the person they like is act-ing first, or if there's anybody else interesting."

"I see," Acorna said. "When is the party?"

Maati shrugged. "It starts at moonrise, in about three hours."

"I'd better get busy then," Acorna said. All of the gowns were far too elaborately decorated for her taste, with layers and layers of different colored skirts, and frills, lace, ruffles, bows, and flowers completely covering whole bodices or skirts. Fortunately, life in a society where women were normally much shorter than she, and the occasional necessity of disguising her horn with an elaborate costume, had taught Acorna to be an excellent seamstress herself. She narrowed her eyes to blur the bewildering details of the gowns so that she could get some idea of their background color. Turning slowly, she spotted a lovely soft mauve-rose brocade fabric and reached for it. It was the undergown of a dress with a rainbow assortment of skirts that stuck out like tutus from the hipline to the ankle.

Without the tutus the rosy underdress was slightly too sheer so she looked around again until she saw that one of the flowing veil-like overskirts of another gown was a beautiful lilac color that complemented both her own complexion and the color of the undergown. That would do.

When she had bathed and dried her hair, she slipped into the rose-mauve dress and pulled the length of lilac fabric under one arm and joined it at the opposite shoulder, pinning it, after some deliberation, with a stunning brooch of pale amethysts and rhodolite garnets set in silver. The brooch had earrings that matched.

She was able to locate lilac slippers in the mass of shoes that was spread everywhere dresses and jewels were not.

"Horn?" Maati reminded her.

"Oh, yes," Acorna said, picking up the lilac horn cover that matched the outer skirt. "This means no one else can read my thoughts, then?"

"Well, not clearly anyway. You know, so if you think something—well, about reproduction, you know, the other person can't—"

Acorna giggled at the younger girl's attempt to sound adult while discussing the mating rituals of which she was not yet a part. "I think I get the idea. I will try not to broadcast so loudly I overpower the muting effect of the horn cover." She looked at the cover again. "But this spiral of wisteria has to go."

"Maybe just a few at the base of your horn?" Maati suggested, looking dismayed to see the pom-poms and wads of the purple *lii* flower Acorna called wisteria falling to the floor.

"Yes, that's nice. Thanks."

"The decorations are so pretty," she said, sadly, picking up the culled flowers.

Acorna was firm. "Less is more," she said.

Maati looked baffled by the idea.

No sooner had Acorna dressed than a great herd of seamstresses, jewelers, and cobblers descended upon the pavilion to carry the excess merchandise away.

"We'll deliver daytime ensembles for your approval tomorrow morning, Khornya."

"Oh, please don't bother," she said. "If Maati will show me where your workplaces are, I would love to see where you make these pretty things."

She had the horn cover firmly in place then and could afford a diplomatic fib. The creators of the two dresses she had altered to make her gown tried to hide their frowns but a couple of the others were eyeing her with a speculative expression.

As the last of the clothiers departed with their wares, uncovering Neeva's furnishings and returning the pavilion to some semblance of a dwelling, Thariinye arrived.

"I'm sorry, Khornya," he apologized—with some effort—

aloud. "I thought you would be dressed by now."

"Oh, but I *am* dressed!" she said, twirling. "Like it?"

He didn't say anything for a moment, then realized, with an expression of relief, that she was wearing her horn-hat, as she thought of the ornamental shields. He gave her a huge false grin and nodded so hard she thought he'd shake his own horn off. He was a *budding* diplomat, after all. In the mainstream of Linyaari culture there would be little opportunity to lie and he was unaccustomed to the practice. She supposed she should give him credit for knowing when a fib was called for.

He quickly donned a horn-hat that coordinated with his own ensemble. It had a three-dimensional stylized red fabric bird perched on the tip to match the birds quilted, stuffed and embroidered on his flowing waistcoat, the cummerbund at his waist, and perched on each shoulder like epaulets, and delicately poised upon an oversize codpiece.

Acorna politely broke into a fit of coughing to disguise the portion of her reaction not softened by the horn-hat. Linyaari fashion was going to take some getting used to. Strange that in her travels around the galaxy she had never for a moment entertained an ethnocentric attitude, had never even considered that the clothing or customs of others might be ridiculous. She supposed she felt more strongly about the Linyaari customs because they were, after all, *her* customs and she was supposed to adhere to them. One of her disguises as a Didi would have fit right in but her own natural style definitely did not.

"I saw the crew off on the new mission," Thariinye said. Acorna was glad his tone was grave. It helped her keep a straight face. She heard just a hint of censure in his tone, as if she should have been there to say good-bye, too. But surely he had heard her being ordered by the *viizaar* to ready herself for this occasion?

They did not speak as they crossed the Singing Stones again, enjoying the music instead, as it blended harmoniously with the Linyaari music emanating from a pavilion even larger than the one the *viizaar* occupied. This one had bundles of flow-

ers decorating it on the outside, and streamers of ribbon added
to the gold tassels. People were flocking into it—or perhaps a
better expression was that bouquets of people were gathering
themselves into the pavilion and onto the dance floor spreading
all around it like a carousel containing only unicorn people.

Ridiculous as the dresses and men's clothing looked indi-
vidually, collectively they were rather breathtaking, like a field
of multihued blossoms, studded with brilliant stones and even
ribbon that looked amazingly like flowing water.

Several of the men wore bird costumes such as Thariinye's,
while others wore designs depicting other animals, or elements
such as fire and water. One or two had embroidery resembling
the fleet of starships. A few had celestial themes to their clothing. The total effect was far more attractive than Acorna would
have imagined.

To her surprise, the huge tent was used not for dancing, but
for the reception line and dining. Her graze of the afternoon had
worn off, and terraces and tiers of all sorts of vegetation growing
right from the soil inside the pavilion looked delectable. The
pavilion had a large central panel which opened to capture sun-
light. It was now raised, to admit the fresh breezes and an excellent view of the heavens that so recently had been Acorna's
home.

"Ah, Khornya, Thariinye," the *viizaar* said. "Please stand
next to me to greet your guests. My aide will introduce you to
each."

Thariinye saved them both by saying, "Certainly, *Viizaar*
Liriili, but if we may have a moment to dine beforehand? I
haven't—that is, neither Khornya nor I have eaten since landing and the journey was quite long."

The *viizaar* beamed up at him again. "Of course, dear boy.
But I'm afraid the line to meet Khornya is already quite long.
Why don't you harvest some of the most succulent foods and
bring them to her to sample?"

Thariinye demurred charmingly. "I'd be happy to, ma'am,
except that Khornya's peculiar upbringing makes it impossible

for me to guess what her tastes might be."

The *viizaar* glanced pointedly at Acorna's gown. "I do see what you mean. Very well then, but return to us quickly. The line is getting longer."

Following the *viizaar*'s hand, which waved at a line that stretched out beyond the pavilion and across the dance floor, Acorna saw that the *viizaar* was not overstating her case.

"Just a little snack then," Acorna said placatingly. But the *viizaar* didn't acknowledge her remark.

The pavilion was arranged more beautifully than one of Hafiz's gardens, she saw as she followed Thariinye through the crowd, which was partaking only lightly of the gorgeous flowers and leafy greenery sprouting and blooming from floor to ceiling on cleverly designed terraced platforms, with little walkways between levels like paths up a hillside. A fountain in the center of the structure splashed and sparkled and watered some particularly succulent-looking reeds and grasses. Thariinye need not have worried about Acorna's tastes. She loved everything. Her native food at least was very much to her liking.

After sampling a few of the plants on the lower level, however, and gathering a few to munch on while greeting the long line, she said to Thariinye, "I suppose we'd better return now, then."

"No hurry," he said casually. "It's just a formality anyway. The *viizaar* realizes that you and I are meant to be lifemates and the others are only here to make the process appear to be fair."

Acorna looked up at him, blinked several times, and said the first thing that came to mind, the sort of thing Delszaki Li used to say when faced with something preposterous. "Really? How very interesting." Suddenly, returning to the line seemed very attractive indeed.

"The other guests . . . ?" she said, with a lifted eyebrow, and a wave back to the reception line. "We wouldn't want them to think us inconsiderate."

"Yes, of course—oh, wait! Is that *rampion?* I wonder where

they got that! I don't think it was native to the old planet. Want to try something really wonderful?"

"Perhaps later," she said, moving toward the line.

"Suit yourself," he said. "You go on ahead. Everyone knows me already. It's you they want to meet."

Acorna was amused and annoyed at the same time. How quickly the young male's priorities could change! She slipped back into the receiving line, between the *viizaar*, who was reluctantly deep in conversation with the oldest Linyaari Acorna had seen so far. The woman's face was actually lined and her neck and jowls sagged slightly. Acorna found that sign of mortality oddly comforting among so many smooth and flawless faces. The aide—a white and silver veteran of space like herself, the *viizaar*, and Grandam—acknowledged her return her with relief.

"Grandam Naadiina has been holding up the line while you were gone. The rest of the people are starving," the aide whispered. The male before her was as young or younger than she was, she could see, as his skin was golden and his hair a pale cream. "Now then, Khornya, this is the scion of Clan Rortuffle," he said, from memory, not from reading a list. "Hiirye, meet Khornya."

Acorna tried her best to be gracious to Hiirye and gave him a big smile. He stepped back, flustered, and did not accept her hand. Instead, he pulled the aide aside and whispered urgently to him, then retreated. Several other males dropped from the line as well, following him.

Acorna wished again she could read minds better. "What was the matter with him?" she asked the aide, but the aide had turned to the *viizaar* and begun a frantic whispered consultation with her. Meanwhile, the Grandam Naadiina turned back to fill the place in line vacated by young Hiirye. Acorna saw the youth, rather than continuing on to eat, had been going down the line, talking excitedly to other people. Each person he spoke to abruptly left the party.

"Really, child," Grandam said. "These affairs Liriili insists upon foisting on us are tiresome, but did you really need to become so hostile?"

"Hostile?" Acorna asked.

"You bared your teeth at that boy in an extremely aggressive fashion. I'm sure he mistook you for one of those . . ." Grandam looked around to make sure no one else was eavesdropping, then put her lips close to Acorna's ear and said, "Khleevi. You scared the living daylights out of the lad."

"Oh, dear!" Acorna remembered now the thought patterns she had heard from her aunt and shipmates about the peculiar custom humans had of baring their teeth. *They* understood, because of their contact with her people, that an open smile was a gesture of good will. But this was not yet known to the rest of the Linyaari. If only Thariinye's appetite had not gotten the best of him, he could have explained. His smile and social lie earlier about her dress showed, or so she had thought at the time, his willingness to try to adapt customs familiar to her in order to put her at ease. Now she wondered. Perhaps he had been actually baring his teeth in the Linyaari sense of the gesture after all?

Whatever could she do to correct the appalling impression she seemed to be making?

"Calm yourself, girl, you look as if you're about to fly apart," the grandam advised.

"But what will they think of me?"

Grandam snorted. "No less than you should think of them, particularly Liriili, dragging you out to this thing before you've had time to rest from your journey and have a bite to eat. And before you've been properly introduced to your new home and had a chance to meet people in the normal way. It was unforgivable, her sending Neeva and the others away and leaving you alone among strangers except for that uppity young stud, Thariinye." She snorted. "These young ones are making such a fuss over culture, but culture begins with kindness. I was just saying so to Liriili when you bared your teeth at that young ass.

Not his fault, of course, but I daresay in your position I would have done the same."

"Oh, but you see, I wasn't trying to bare my teeth at all—I mean, I did bare my teeth, but where I come from, among the people I grew up with, one shows one's teeth to be friendly, happy—it's an expression of greeting and cordiality, not at all one of hostility. I have been told, actually, that it isn't viewed the same way among your—our—people, but I got a bit flustered and . . ."

"There, there, child. You needn't explain to *me*."

She firmly took Acorna by the elbow and led her to the highest of the tiers where the delicious foods grew. In a long and rather shrill Linyaari utterance that sounded eerily like "Hiiire me!" Grandam Naadiina stopped the music, the dancers, the talking, and drew all stares to herself and Acorna.

Acorna noticed, meanwhile, that both *viizaar* and her aide had left the pavilion hurriedly, looking worried. She suddenly had the feeling that the crowd's reaction had more to do with Liriili's exit than her social grace.

"My children, you have all gathered here to meet our long lost kinswoman, Khornya, daughter of the late lamented Feriila and Vaanye. She only just this afternoon, as many of you know because you were there, arrived on the planet from a journey of many months. Her closest relative and only acquaintances among us had to ship out immediately on another mission, leaving the child here among us. Yes, her accent is strange and her dress is a bit of the old fashion instead of the new, and because she was not properly instructed, she greeted a prospective lifemate with an expression interpreted differently by the culture from which she comes than it is in our own, but she is a good girl, I can tell, a nice girl, and she'll be glad to meet any of you later on when she's had a proper chance to rest, collect her thoughts, find her way around, and get a decent meal or two under her belt."

As Grandam spoke those words, many people stopped dancing. Rather than paying attention to their elder, they were looking toward the flap of the pavilion where Liriili had exited, as if they were waiting for something to happen. Something far more important to them than Grandam's slap on their collective wrists. They were waiting, Acorna thought, for Liriili to return and explain what business had compelled her to leave.

Six

K isla, precious, you look fatigued," Uncle Edacki said.

"I confess that horrible junk man and his nasty beast upset me, Uncle. He cheated me—told me he was selling everything but kept the cat *and* more of the horns he lied about having. You just can't trust anyone these days."

"No, indeed, pet. It's a hard cruel world and it distresses me that you've had to learn that so young in life. But fortunately, I am here to protect you and see to it that you don't wear yourself out. Now then, if you want the junk man, it's a simple matter of sending your droids over to collect him and the cat and checking his computer banks for information about how he acquired the horns. No need for you to go yourself."

"I *can* be there when he's questioned though, can't I, Uncle? And have the nasty cat to play with?"

"Whatever you wish, dearest. But you'll want to be at your best so run along now and let Uncle Edacki handle it."

"I'm sure you know best."

"I'll need the horns, dear one."

She got that sly, calculating look that reminded him so of her late, unlamented father. "I can let you have one, I suppose. I'll keep the other." She handed him the more broken of the two. "Here, you take this one. I think this one I have is probably hers."

He sighed and smiled as if it didn't matter that he indulged her this time. "One will do nicely, thank you, Kisla. Now off you go. Leave it to me."

When she had gone he sprang into action, after his own fashion. The first thing he did was call her droids away from the hangar where they had been unloading her cargo.

"KEN637, your mistress tells me you were instructed to check on the whereabouts of a craft belonging to a certain dealer in salvaged goods?"

"It is docked at outer bay four niner eight, sir," the droid replied.

"Very well. I would like for you and your friends to call upon the gentleman at his ship and invite him to my warehouse, the one on Todo Street, number nineteen?"

"I know the one, sir."

"Yes, and the animal, too. But first, have him show you around his computer banks. And if he is not there when you arrive, access them yourself. Your mistress wishes to know where he obtained the horn he gave her."

"Certainly, sir. Suggested force level, sir?" Unlike the androids in early science fiction epics, those employed by Edacki Ganoosh's various corporate enterprises had no programming prohibiting them from harming human beings.

"Maximum without damaging any of the components."

"Yes, sir."

With the tip of his finger, Ganoosh then accessed the considerable data banks on the unicorn girl and her associates. Many of these files had been compiled by Kisla's late father, the baron.

He found a number of useful connections. The first name he noticed was that of General Ikwaskwan, the leader of the Kilumbemba mercenaries, a group he himself had employed from time to time. The reason that name particularly caught his attention was that he had been intending to contact the general for some time on another matter.

It would be late in the day in the Kilumbemba Empire, but the general was a man of business and if he was presently unemployed, the man would no doubt be thrilled to hear from Ganoosh. The comscreen showed nothing but static for a few moments and then, in a very distracted tone, from off screen, Ganoosh heard Ikwaskwan's voice saying, "Nadhari, by the Gods, woman, this is business. Untie me before you accept incoming calls."

"Certainly, Ikky," a woman's deep and sultry voice purred. "And if I do, I assume I have your promise?"

"Yes, mistress. Never again shall I sleep when you have rubbed my back with oils before I do likewise unto you."

"Very good then." There was the sound of a kiss. "I know it's difficult, Ikky, after all these years of rape and pillage, for you to remember that we women have our needs, too, and in an alliance such as ours, it is imperative that you meet them graciously. There, now, I return your dignity."

"Yes, my ferocious flower." The sound of another, more prolonged kiss. Very prolonged. Ganoosh cleared his throat.

"Ah! Nadhari, it is Count Edacki Ganoosh. Count, you have met my second in command, Colonel Nadhari Kando?"

"I have," Ganoosh said. "Though we were not formally introduced." The woman had been glowering menacingly by the side of Delszaki Li when they had met, looking as if she would cheerfully bite off the head of anyone who so much as frowned pensively in the direction of her employer. Now, she stood naked, obviously female but extremely well muscled, behind Ikwaskwan. Ganoosh was as unmoved sexually by the sight of her as he would have been looking at any other dangerous predator. She regarded him with a long stare that made him feel as if he were the one who was undressed, or perhaps dressed in the hunting or culinary sense, then slowly she shrugged her lithe muscles into a dressing gown patterned with glittering fireworks.

"Hmm," she said, in his direction, then muttered to Ikwaskwan, "The officers will be waiting for their briefing," and turned and left.

Ikwaskwan gave Ganoosh a rather silly grin and winked and shrugged as if to say, "Women."

Ganoosh chuckled far more indulgently than he felt. Even hardened mercenary killers weren't of the same caliber these days.

"General, I'll come right to the point. As you know, our government here on Maganos has undergone a great purge of corruption and through the good works of Delszaki Li and his ward, we are finally free of the tragedy of child slavery."

"I've been meaning to send my congratulations for some time, Count," the general said dryly, "but I haven't found just the right card to express my joy."

"Now, now, no need to be bitter just because your people are now deprived of the income they received for delivering war orphans to our facilities from time to time. You surely must realize that while this dreadful injustice has cleansed us of moral turpitude, it has also created a great hole in the labor force of the planet's economy."

"I had understood you were going to mechanize?"

"Hideously expensive, as you know. It occurred to some of us—me, for instance—that rather than giving machines skilled jobs that can be done less expensively by human beings, we should perhaps find another labor pool. Now, you have occasion from time to time to fight in wars where one side or the other is totally devastated."

"When my troops are involved, that is inevitably the case," the general said.

"Rather than execute the wounded or allow the survivors, if any, to either be butchered or starved, why not bring them to us? We could reeducate them into useful professions. We'd be saving lives, really, and making the universe a better place. No one could object to that."

"Humph," the general said, stroking his whiskers with the

backs of his knuckles. "The only problem with that is it would require a certain amount of restraint and gentleness on behalf of my troops. Usually by the time we finish with the losing side, they are not in any shape to work for themselves or anyone else."

"This brings me to another issue. A question really. I have heard rumors—perhaps myths—of the healing power demonstrated by the unicorn girl who was the ward of the late Mr. Li."

"She was also the ward, remember, of Hafiz Harakamian," the general said. "The Lady Acorna is not a being to be trifled with, as I know from recent experience."

"*Really?* Tell me about it, do."

"She is not just any girl, for one thing. She's a member of a race of unicorn people. A very sophisticated people no one in this side of the universe had heard of before, but who apparently have been making contact with other worlds for some time. My troops formed an alliance with Li and Harakamian against an old enemy of these Linyaari, as they were called, and liberated a planet called Rushima. Afterward—I could hardly believe it myself—Lady Acorna and the others of her species healed all of the wounds as if they had never occurred. I heard that a time or two she has revived the dead, though I didn't personally witness those events. Not only that, but some young renegades aboard a Starfarer's ship were heard to say that she had purified poisoned air aboard their ship, and the people of Rushima claim she gave them a magical device to purify tainted water that had covered their world. Purified the whole world's water supply. I hear it's the horn that does it."

Ganoosh was fairly purring to himself. "How wonderful! How marvelous! Why, just think, if you had a Linyaari medic among you, or someone who possessed the power of their horns, you could instantly heal your wounded and send the same people back into battle after battle. Your troops would be practically immortal."

"Hmmmm, yes . . ."

"And so would these poor souls you would bring to me for

reeducation. Frankly, some of the jobs that used to employ children will be a bit riskier for adults. There could be increased on-the-job injuries. How wonderful again, if we were to have such healing power to keep our workers whole and productive."

"As far as I know, Lady Acorna's people don't hire out for such things though, Count. I think you're barking up the wrong tree there."

"Perhaps no one has made them the right offer?"

"They're," the general spat, "pacifists. Wouldn't even fight to save their own planet from these big bug things we destroyed to liberate Rushima. They're plenty scared of them though."

"Hmmm—do these bug creatures have any allies, I wonder?"

"I'm told the only use they have for allies is at meal times."

"And perhaps it wouldn't be necessary to have an actual member of this alien race to which the girl belongs to work the wonders. If the power is all in the horn, all one would need is the horn."

"Yeah, but where would you get one of those?"

Ganoosh smiled. "I'm a resourceful man. And I do appreciate our little chat, General. Think about what I've said. See if you can come up with a proposal, a bid, for a solution to these little problems. And I will continue to research this matter."

"I'll do that, Count. But—uh—please, if you don't mind, utilize the code we set up for the last job I did for you after this. Nadhari is rather softhearted and sentimental about her former alliances. I wouldn't want to upset her—"

"I understand perfectly, General. Good day, and er, victory and glory to your armies."

"The same to you, Count."

Hafiz Harakamian, eh? There was an interesting footnote or two on his dealings in Manjari's files. For instance, there was the first wife, whose death Manjari had helped fake when the lady, unfulfilled by her marriage to her inattentive and unappreciative spouse, had wished to return to the spotlight she had only begun to occupy in the recreational sex industry that was one of the pillars of Manjari's empire. That wife, as her beauty waned, had retired into a profitable position as Didi of a house of pleasure. She was a particular favorite of Manjari as she had also divulged a great deal of information about her former spouse and his enterprises, associates, and most helpfully, the layout and security system of his compound on Laboue.

The poor girl had been languishing in prison with the other Didis at the behest of her former husband's ward. Ganoosh clicked his tongue. How sad. How very sad. Fortunately, he, Count Edacki Ganoosh, would be able to effect a happy ending.

He lay back on his couch, his hands steepled over his abdomen and his face wearing a smile of satisfaction. Family reunions were so touching. He must arrange for one between this poor, ill-rewarded servant and her bereaved husband, who, unfortunately for the lady, had recently remarried.

The information she had provided Manjari over the years would prove useful in effecting the reunion as the proper surprise that made such occasions so memorable.

And of course, she should have a wedding present. Ganoosh picked up the piece of horn and fondled it, imagining he could feel its much-vaunted healing and purifying energy coursing through his being. Couldn't have that now, could he? Being purified was the last thing he wanted. Picking up a heavy crystal ornament, he smashed the horn to powder. There now. That was a start. He kept a bit for himself—the aphrodisiac powers might work as well powdered as whole, and were far easier to slip into some victim's beverage that way. He himself, of course, needed no such stimulant. Bringing out the baser emotional and physical responses in others served him very well in that regard.

With a bit of a chemical additive from one of his other business ventures and a bit of a lure of the sort Harakamian was well known to covet, this was the perfect bait. If anyone knew where the unicorn girl and her kin were going, or how to find the planet where all of those magical horns on the hoof lived, it would be Harakamian.

With the right messenger, the right bait, and—ah, the properly dramatically delivered tale surrounding the gift—not too much, of course, just enough to lead the rival in the right direction—Harakamian was quite likely to be concerned enough for the welfare of his ward to wish to personally check on her welfare. And where Harakamian could go, so could Ganoosh. Or Kisla. Dear little Kisla, who *soooo* needed to be healed from the death of her beloved parents and who would not hesitate to murder each and every unicorn person while they slept.

Nadhari Kando showered and dressed in fatigues prior to reviewing her troops. As the sonic waves cleansed her skin of sweat and sex she felt the need to be cleansed of something else as well. Edacki Ganoosh, hmm? Now, what would he be calling Ikky for?

Ganoosh was not in the same league with the Piper—at least, not while Manjari had been alive—and the investigation into the child labor and sex industry businesses hadn't turned up anything conclusive linking Ganoosh's businesses to Manjari's. But he was the appointed guardian of Manjari's adopted daughter, twisted little piece that she was. He also controlled the few legitimate enterprises the council had allowed Kisla Manjari to retain for her maintenance, as they had been very meticulous about not punishing the child for the sins of her adopted parents.

And now he was calling Ikky on private business. This didn't sound good for the hopes she had had for the general. She shook her head at her own foolishness. He was a good-looking man, fit and steely like herself and well able for the games she enjoyed. Bedding down with him, to use the term loosely, was a bit like a good day in battle, kept the body honed and the wits sharp. But she had felt, as she twisted his arm to join the forces of Li and Harakamian in battling the Khleevi, that he had taken some pleasure in helping the comparatively defenseless settlers of Rushima. Of being a good guy for a change, or at least of working for the good guys—who were for once the highest bidders. It was that, more than the blackmail or his attractiveness, which had made their fling turn into more of an alliance.

She'd known he was getting restless, though, and from the men she had heard some things she didn't particularly like. She had been, in fact, thinking for the last couple of days of bailing out.

She bloused her trousers in her boots and took the back way down to the quadrangle where her men would be waiting. The com suite was on the way. She thought it might be wise to leave a message with the kids on Maganos and maybe Harakamian's security forces as well, asking them to check for new activity on Ganoosh's part.

But as she drew level with the door to the communications suite, she heard Ikky's voice. One thing about being a CO. Your voice did tend to carry after all those years of barking orders.

"What I want you to do," Ikky was saying, "is go back into our banks. Find the signals we received from that Linyaari ship when we were all on Rushima, up against the bugs. Isolate their signal, analyze it, and send word to our allies to do the same thing, and so forth, until they find it again."

"And once they find it, sir?"

"Jam it from going any further then track it to its source. Keep me posted and when we have contact, I'll issue further orders."

"Very good, sir."

Nadhari managed to be well down the long corridor before Ikky entered the hallway himself, but she felt his eyes between her shoulder blades and she knew he would know that she had heard. Normal people, maybe, wouldn't jump to such conclusions. But she and Ikky were trained by the same people and they thought very much alike. He knew. She had to make an effort not to stiffen, waiting for him to call after her, or even shoot her, perhaps, though that was less likely. But what he did was reenter the com shed.

When she finished reviewing her troops and returned to "write her letter home," Sergeant Erikson told her the computers were down, even though she could see very clearly that they were up and running. He kept his hand near his side arm as he said it and she knew that this was the sergeant's rather respectful way of telling her Ikky had made the com suite off limits to her.

Seven

The androids, KEN model numbers 637–640, stood at docking bay 498 staring at the *Condor*. It did not compute.

"I have tried the proper codes," said KEN637, "and the hatch will not open."

"I have attempted a manual override of all known computer codes for opening hatches with the result that we now have access to every other ship, flitter, chopper, and pizza delivery fly-by on the planet, and still the hatch will not open," said KEN638.

"I have tried hammering on the hull with all of my nonorganic attachments," said KEN639, "and still the hatch will not open."

"Perhaps a can opener would be of benefit," suggested KEN640, the one with the wet and smoking shredded pant leg. Fortunately for the other KEN models, they did not have olfactory sensors as part of the standard equipment.

"What is a can opener?" asked KEN637.

"An antique device for accessing the hatch of food containers and opening them," KEN640 said.

"Where may we obtain one?" asked KEN639.

KEN640 opened a panel in his forearm and his own array of nonorganic tools swung into view: a hacksaw, chisel, fingernail file, scissors, screw driver, two different knife blades, and a rotary tool with several different burrs attached. And—a corkscrew. And finally, a flat piece of metal with a knobby bit and a cut-out crescent shape. "Here!" KEN640 announced.

"Oh, is that what that is?" KEN637 said, opening his own arm. "I was wondering. I had noticed it in your assembly before and wondered what it was and why we earlier model numbers didn't have one."

"I believe I was designed as a special commission. My original employer had some rather old-fashioned tastes."

KEN637 said, "Perhaps you should try it on the hatch then. From my observations, I would say that Jonas Becker, CEO of Becker Salvage and Recycling Enterprises, Limited, also has antiquated tastes."

KEN640 obligingly mounted the movable scaffolding that the androids had brought from the central facility of the loading docks. Modern vessels all had a fairly standard hatch location but the older ones were often made by a variety of manufacturers with a variety of specifications.

KEN640 was still replacing his auxiliary components into his forearm while he mounted the scaffolding. Suddenly, his foot, which had developed a short and, consequently, and involuntary twitch from the attentions of RK, slipped off the top rung. He threw himself against the scaffolding to catch his fall and escape damage. The scaffolding banged hard against the hatch, which flew open, showering several tons of spare computer components, ancient nose cones, small flitters, and one long stretch of metal grating down onto the other KEN models, who had been standing directly beneath him, looking up to see what the ruckus was about.

KEN640 lost his grip and made one last leap to try to regain purchase on something to stop his fall—and found it. His fingers closed on the edge of the hatch. He tightened his grip and swung himself aloft and into the hatch. As he slid away from the opening, the hatch closed behind him. He banged on it. Nothing. He pushed with all his might. It remained sealed shut.

"Assistance!" He projected his vocalization so that it would carry to the units below. "Assistance is required. My sensors do not detect any accessible openings into the ship from here, and no means to operate the opening to the outside. Please assist me at once."

When time passed and he received no assistance, nor could further searches discover a mechanism to either allow him inside the ship or out of it entirely, he shut himself off to conserve power. Kisla Manjari did not appreciate it when her units wasted power.

Just before his visual sensors shut down, however, they replayed a fleeting image he'd seen—of the debris from the hatch superimposed on the prone forms of the other KEN units, who presented during this flash an uncharacteristically two-dimensional appearance, as if they were mere splashes of plastiskin, machined parts, and various lubricants smashed onto the pavement beneath rather than their usual selves.

Back at the nano-bug market, Becker was recounting his life story to Reamer and his family in an attempt to persuade Reamer that he was not the kind of guy to go bumping off idealistic young unicorn ladies to get at their horns. After all, he hadn't even known what they were till he showed them to Reamer, had he?

The redheaded rock hound was just starting to relax his suspicions again when the remote alarm went off. Since it sounded like the Klaxon horn on an old bicycle playing the first bar of "Dixie," everyone heard it. RK growled.

"That would be the skinny little princess and her heavy metal boys trying to board the *Condor*," he told Reamer. "I hate it when people do that. Maybe I forgot to leave off the NO TRESPASSING sign. Or maybe she came before I got back to pick up the rest of her purchases."

"Kisla Manjari is nobody to mess with," Reamer advised. "I'd stay away if I were you until she has what she wants, then go back and pick up the pieces of your vessel."

"Good advice, huh, RK?" Becker said, thinking it over. Then he said, "Naaah, a man's vessel is his castle. Besides, she won't be able to get in without this." He tapped the remote, which was also the source of the alarm. "C'mon, RK." The cat hopped up on Becker's shoulder and the man began jogging back toward the flitcycle he had brought along for personal ground transport.

"Wait a minute," Reamer told him. "Manjari and her droids could trace your movements through the market to us. I don't want to wake up in the middle of the night to find *that* particular woman anywhere near my bed or my kids insisting I answer a lot of questions about you when I don't know anything to tell her."

"So better you should come along and find out all my secrets so you'll have some juicy stuff to save your collective asses with, right?" Becker said. "Come on, then."

Reamer called to the woman in the Ogonquonian Ornamentation booth, "Watch the kids for me, okay, LaVoya?" and sprinted after Becker.

Becker had purposely docked as far out in the boonies as the docking bay went because he didn't like a bunch of officious inspectors messing with his vessel. The problem was, security wasn't very good out here either. A lot of semiderelicts were warehoused in this part of the bay until they could be refurbished or junked, and it was very tricky trying to tell if the *Condor* was one of them or not. However, if anyone had been passing by, they'd have noted that the *Condor* was evidently crewed by untidy personnel, as a large pile of miscellaneous technogarbage was heaped on the pavement to one side of the ship.

"Looks like the princess came by, okay," Becker said, scratching his chin. "Guess she went back for more help. Whatever she wanted seems to have been too heavy for these guys."

"Are you kidding?" Reamer asked, most sincerely, because it was hard to tell with Becker sometimes. "She sent her goons to break into your ship! I bet she was after the horns—"

"Shhh, not so loud," Becker said with a finger to his lips. "Now that I know what they are, I wish I hadn't mentioned it. In fact, I need to pull a disappearing act real quick now, before her highness returns with more goons. Look, tell you what—hang onto this." He gave him a piece of the horn. "I swear to you I didn't get it off of anybody alive and didn't even see any bodies. RK and I found these things lying around on a trashed out planet. You decide what to do with it. I'm outta here."

He thumbed the remote, which played another tune Reamer didn't recognize, and what appeared to be an exhaust chute for a Mytherian toxic waste transport extruded a broad platform that Becker and RK stepped onto.

"Don't you get beamed up?" Reamer asked, as Becker and RK ascended into the chute.

"Nah, that stuff makes the cat nervous," Becker said. "Say bye to the kids for us."

"You got it," Reamer called back, waving. Becker had forgotten the flitcycle so Reamer climbed back on it and proceeded to put as much distance as possible between himself and the pile of junk with the squashed androids at the bottom.

Reamer was thinking hard as he bombed through the back streets, trying not to make a clear path to the nano-market and his kids. Despite his customarily mellow attitude, education from the school of hard knocks had taught him a healthy amount of street-smart paranoia. Damn the red hair anyway. Between that and his height, he sort of stood out, and anyone who had seen him riding with Becker was likely to identify him to Kisla Manjari. Neither he nor his kids would be safe now. Even if nobody had spotted him on the way to Becker's ship, the nano-market was a hive of gossip and it wouldn't lighten Kisla Manjari's purse by much to find out that Becker had spent quite a bit of time at Reamer's booth. The nice, anonymous life he had built for himself and the kids, not attracting attention, not violating laws but at the same time not possessing anything anyone else would want enough to hassle them for it, was now totally blown. Well, these things happened. It was time, maybe. The important thing was to get the kids to safety and also to let Baird, Giloglie, and Nadezda know about the horns.

Reamer's heart settled back down in his chest when he saw his children working the crowd as usual, sizing up prospects for the Ogonquonian Ornaments with the same expertise they used to determine who could be tempted by the rocks and minerals in their own booth.

"Come on, Deeter, Turi, we have to pack up and get out."

"But, Daddy, we've paid in advance for our space for the season," Turi, his little business manager, objected.

"Baby, haven't I told you there's things more important in life than money? Now hop to it!"

He was thinking fast about where they would go from here. The authorities were only nominally clean, even in these reform days. Kisla Manjari's guardian, the count, was a man of vast influence and many of the security patrolmen were in his pocket. They were far more apt to frame Reamer on some charge and detain him at Kisla's convenience than they were to be helpful. It was all fine when the Lady and her uncles and Delszaki Li had lived here but without their physical presence . . .

Reamer suddenly remembered the little story Becker had told of going to the pleasure house and running into Khetala. Reamer had had a similar encounter with her himself, for similar reasons. But she was one of the Lady's people, one of the children Acorna had saved from the mines. Khetala would know what to do about the horn. She could help him and the kids escape Kezdet, too. She *would* help them. She had to.

Eight

The eyes of every person in the pavilion were focused on the opening. The flap spread wide. Dancing stopped although the band played on.

Then, abruptly, the band stopped, too, and Liriili, horn uncovered, strode through the crowd gathered outside, then the crowd inside, and stepped up onto the bandstand, where she appropriated the tiny amplifier. "I am calling an emergency council session in the *viizaar's* pavilion immediately. Meanwhile, all prep crews of all space vessels are to report to their ships and prepare for takeoff, and all other crew members are on standby. Commanders of the ships and all emissaries, envoys, and ambassadors will please attend the council meeting now."

Then she strode off, a great number of the white-skinned Linyaari following her, or leaving the party behind her.

Grandam, apparently undeterred by affairs of state from reminding people of their social graces, led Acorna down from the heights of the grazing platforms and she herself went to the bandstand and picked up the amplifier. "My children, those of you whose presence is not required elsewhere, please remain and dance with your loved ones as long as you may. There is still

much good food on the platforms and many of you have not yet
met Khornya."

Acorna protested. "This seems to be an emergency.
Whether people meet me or not is hardly important right now.

But from several directions she could hear low mutterings
to the effect of, "She seems to have brought trouble with her."

"Good manners are always important, " Grandam told her
crisply. "Besides, you'll give people something to take their
minds off of more worrisome matters. I must attend the council
meeting, child," Grandam told her. "Young Maati can show you
the way to my quarters when you're ready."

"I want to come, too," Acorna said. "If something has happened to the *Balaküre*, to Neeva and the others, I want to
know."

"I doubt you'll be permitted to attend, child. But if the
emergency concerns the *Balaküre*, be sure that I will let you
know when I return, and also, I will see to it that you are given
a berth on one of the outgoing ships. If you'll excuse me?"

Acorna had no choice but to agree.

The revels had been most effectively stopped by Liriili's
announcement but still everyone stood around waiting for further developments. At last Liriili and the council members,
including Grandam, returned to the reception and the *vüzaar*
addressed the grim-faced, ridiculously dressed crowd.

"My people, I'm sorry if I have caused you undue alarm.
The council, however, agrees that although there is no major
emergency that we are aware of, nothing really to become
overly concerned about, prompt action may forestall future
emergencies. The *Balaküre*—"

Acorna held her breath.

"The *Balaküre*, which was just dispatched to investigate a
disturbing report from one of our trade missions, sent us a message that they were unable to receive transmissions from either
the trade mission in question or any of our other ships or missions abroad in space or on other worlds. It is the belief of the
communications officer that some sort of universal equipment

failure is responsible for this silence. For that reason, in order to reestablish communication as soon as possible as well as to ensure the safety of our people in space and on other worlds and, if they are in any danger, to evacuate them as soon as possible, we are deploying the remainder of our fleet to simultaneously travel to all of the known destinations of our other ships. They will in all likelihood simply assist with the repairs of our transmitters, but if their assistance is needed in other ways, they will be there to provide it. For this reason, for all of our space fleet personnel, shore leave is cancelled and you should report to your duty stations by mid-sun tomorrow."

Acorna and Thariinye both rushed forward to volunteer to go back into space but the *viizaar* only smiled at Thariinye and said, "You're needed here." Then, ignoring Acorna, Liriili turned to go. Acorna, with two quick steps, placed herself in front of the *viizaar*. "If my aunt is in danger, I want to help. I need to be on one of those ships."

Liriili regarded her very coolly. Acorna saw that the *viizaar* once more had her horn-hat firmly in place and besides, the *viizaar* seemed to be even more adept than most at concealing her thoughts. "If it becomes necessary for our ships to evacuate our people from space or other planets, excess personnel may cost lives. I cannot possibly take the responsibility for that risk simply to allow you to indulge your curiosity, Khornya. I hope as you spend more time among us, that you'll become less self-centered and willful. Perhaps among the barbarians, your Linyaari intelligence made you best qualified to make decisions and lead expeditions, but here you are a mere child among those older and wiser than yourself. Your aunt left you among us to learn our ways, so I suggest you apply yourself to that goal and leave the crisis to those of us trained to deal with it."

Fortunately, at that moment Grandam rejoined Acorna, hearing only Liriili's last stinging words.

"Come along, Khornya. I tried to convince the council that you should be sent out on one of the ships being dispatched, but I was overruled. Certain know-it-all youngsters agreed with

Liriili that you hadn't had a chance to evolve enough to be useful on a mission yet. Humph. Well, we older ones are considered by some of our so-called respectful descendants to be relics of a less-evolved time, you know." Her expression was wry. "That's why I thought perhaps as long as you are stuck here, you might be more comfortable staying with me. We less-evolved types should stick together, don't you think?"

Acorna gratefully agreed.

"At least we know, since word of the malfunction—or whatever it is that is occurring that's keeping our people from being able to contact us—came from the *Balakiire*, that Neeva and the crew are safe. As a precaution, the ships going up now are having their com units equipped with special filters and boosters as well as the repair equipment for existing transmitters. New communications programs are being installed tonight as well by the prep crews, with extras being sent along for the ships already abroad and of course, the main receivers, transmitters, and computers are being checked for some sort of fault in their space relay systems as well."

"What do you suppose could be causing the problem?" Acorna asked.

"I don't know. Perhaps a meteor storm between us and the closest transmitters in the relay system? Maybe some kind of mechanical difficulty in the transmitters themselves—or even a programming flaw? A sun going nova? Liriili is right about one thing—I'm sure the problem, whatever it is, is one our crews are well equipped to sort out by themselves."

"You don't sound as if anyone believes there really would be a need to evacuate our people elsewhere, more as if the silence is a technical problem. In which case, why not just send out crews to the most likely areas of interference? If there is a larger problem, all of your—our—ships could be cut off from communication with the planet, maybe even each other, and we would have no idea what was occurring. Wouldn't it be wiser to risk fewer personnel?"

The animation left Grandam's face and her mouth settled

into a grim line. "We are *hoping* that this is a technical problem. If so, the council's reasoning is that the more ships we deploy to the most places, the sooner the problem will be mended. The communications channels are a lifeline to our ships, and through them to our allies, as well as a lifeline for us. It would be impossible to devote *too* many resources to their preservation. And in case there is a more ominous threat"—Acorna heard with her mind rather than her ears that the council was most deeply afraid of a new, heretofore unheralded attack by the Khleevi—"we need to cover all options as quickly as possible so we can learn of the danger, assist if possible those affected by the threat, evacuate those it does not yet affect, and have our ships return home." She paused and said, "We would not need them for evacuation from narhii-Vhiliinyar. We do not, at this time, have an alternative home ready so evacuating this planet is not an option."

"But—if nothing else, people could go to Kezdet, Maganos moon, Rushima. All of the human worlds are compatible with our species."

Grandam took a deep breath, let it out, and said, "Of course. There are other worlds as well. But until we know there is a threat and if so, where it comes from, we would hardly know where to run, would we? The personnel in space could well be safer than those of us here on narhii-Vhiliinyar. One option seems about as good as another. If this place is not safe, Khornya, is any place?"

She shuddered and Acorna realized that the elder was not only deeply worried but also deeply frightened. Since there seemed to be little either of them could do about the situation, Acorna deliberately changed her focus.

This was not hard to do once they arrived at the Grandam's pavilion. It shimmered with a ribbon of silver streaming around teal green under the light of the two moons, one blue and one golden, and although there was nothing about it that seemed familiarly cozy it nonetheless exuded a charming warmth and hominess.

Grandam Naadiina waved her hand and soft light emerged from beautifully patterned glass pillars that upheld the center and corners of her pavilion. The flaps farthest from them were open so that once more the moons were visible, and all the stars. Naadiina beckoned Acorna to follow her toward the flap, where three soft beds were arranged. On one of these lay Maati, sound asleep.

"I like to sleep with my face to the stars, and my memories of my lifemate on the old world," Grandam said, peeling off her gown and sliding beneath the top blanket of the bed. Acorna did the same, grateful to be rid of the makeshift finery.

"Maati lives here, too?" Acorna asked.

"Yes," Grandam said. "I think her parents felt that I could use the assistance and would be grateful for a strong young person to run my errands. Since it has become clear that they were not coming back, and Maati was orphaned, she has remained with me. She hardly remembers them and is useful as a page for Liriili and other government officials."

"I'm so sorry," Acorna said. "What became of her parents?"

"They could not adjust to the loss of their two sons, Aari and Laarye. They tried to—they were here almost two *ghaanyi* and had time to conceive and give birth to Maati. But her mother went into a deep sadness and at last the two of them announced that the only way to solve this sadness was for them to return to the old home and try to learn what had become of their sons. They have not been heard of since. This may be a good thing. The Khleevi have not sought to entertain us with films of either them or their sons being tortured to death, so perhaps they met with a diversion along the way or perhaps their boys were rescued in some other way and they are pursuing them still."

"But—I thought everyone escaped when you left the old world. Neeva gave me that impression anyway. You mean you left children behind?"

"What could we do? The need to evacuate happened quite suddenly. And they were young men, not children. We had learned of the Khleevi before, of course, and we had already located this planet as our refuge and had our plan in readiness. But not everyone could be gathered in time for the evacuation. A few—very few, I'm happy to say—were left behind to save the majority. Maati's parents could not accept that their sons could not be found. They would have stayed behind to search but we could not allow that, much as we hated to leave anything behind for those monsters. It was agony to leave at all. I myself could scarcely bear to leave the grave of my lifemate on the same planet with the Khleevi."

"Will you tell me about your lifemate, and what it was like on the old world?" Acorna asked.

"Oh, yes. But aren't you tired after your journey and the so-called reception?" Acorna did not have to be very psychic to feel the scorn in the old lady's tone.

"Not really," she replied. "But I *was* overwhelmed. I don't think *viizaar* likes me."

"The *viizaar* was already prejudiced against you long before you arrived, my dear," she replied. "Your mother was chosen by the lifemate Liriili had already decided was her own. Unfortunately, Vaanye didn't agree."

"Oh, that must be it then. Neeva mentioned some bad feeling toward my family. But it doesn't seem sensible to take it out on me."

"Prejudice and jealousy are seldom sensible. Liriili's is not a flexible or forgiving nature."

"I thought that people who could read minds would be incapable of that kind of pettiness."

The old lady grunted. "Except when they are healing, and really concentrating on extending empathy, or dealing with some crisis among their nearest and dearest, most people have psychic communication down to a very superficial art. One's thoughts and feelings have many layers, contradictory layers at that. And even in thought, some people are more reserved than others—or repressed, perhaps. Liriili is used to filling her mind with the details of administration and can use those to mask her feelings even from herself, as no doubt she is doing in your case."

"Oh. Speaking of feelings, is it true that it's already decided that Thariinye and I will be lifemates?"

Grandam hooted and in the dark her eyes twinkled like the stars as she rolled on her side and grinned at Acorna, only baring her teeth just a little. "Who told you that? Thariinye? I can see that he did! Of course no one has decided such a thing! Except maybe him! You've nothing to worry about there."

"I'm glad," Acorna said. "I want it to feel—right."

"You're a very clever girl. Are you very sleepy?"

"No, not really. I feel rather restless, to tell you the truth."

"That makes two of us. Would you indulge an old lady and tell me of your life? Neeva indicated in her reports that you had had some adventures. I should very much like to hear of them. Since coming here, our people have been a rather dull lot, and I do like a good story."

"Very well," Acorna said, and began with her earliest memories of her uncles and the mining ship.

She had not quite finished when both of them fell asleep.

The next morning, Acorna awoke to the sound of birds singing and a stream burbling very nearby. She sat up.

The stream was running right behind her head, as a matter of fact, down one glass column, across the floor of the pavilion, where it was joined by the waterfall flowing down the glass column on the opposite side of the floor. Acorna cupped her hand to dip out a drink, and found that the water was actually covered by glass. So were the singing birds that flew from another column, across the top of the pavilion, to disappear into the column opposite the one where the flight had begun. Within the bird's path, clouds drifted with seeming air currents and, at the base of the pillars, the branches of bushes seemed to bob in a breeze.

Acorna yawned and stretched. The pallet beside hers was empty. Then she noticed that beyond the bird column, the flap was closed and voices were coming from the other side.

She rose and pulled on the undergown from the previous night, wishing she still had her flight suit instead.

The front flap opened, and Grandam Naadiina entered the pavilion. Her arms were full of various items, bouquets of wild flowers, notes, and sheaves of edible grasses and big leafed vegetables.

"Here, let me help you," Acorna said, rushing forward to relieve her hostess of some of the burden.

"You may as well take them all. Young males haven't left such tributes to me in a long time."

"You mean these are for me? But—why?"

"Your welcome home reception was interrupted and your guests did not get properly introduced. I suppose these are by way of being an apology, if not an invitation, on behalf of some of your guests. Perhaps some of them were fellows who are going off planet now and will have no chance to meet you until they return." She paused. "Besides, the Ancestors seem to approve of you, whether or not Liriili does. The opinions of the Ancestors carry a great deal of weight with our people."

Acorna shook her head, disbelieving, as she deposited some of the edibles—the wildflowers were edible, too—on one of the low tables near the eastern wall of the pavilion. There was no kitchen facility, or rest room either. Like Acorna, the Linyaari of course tended to graze, eating only fresh vegetables and grasses, so a food preparation area was unnecessary. They buried their waste in the ground, too—or in an area of the hydroponics gardens, as Acorna and her shipmates had done aboard ship. There was no taboo about this. Linyaari recycled food with a clean efficiency that made the waste excellent fertilizer, Neeva had told her. Acorna's human upbringing made her wonder at the lack of squeamishness about this function, but then, humans often used recycled urine for water while on long voyages, too, and the connection was at least one step more remote in this case.

"I'm glad they approve," Acorna said. "It was rather difficult to tell."

"It always is, for anyone other than an attendant. Your brow is wrinkled. Why is that? What's bothering you?"

"Just that I made a fool of myself last night, and then there was the emergency and here I am being given gifts, when everyone is so very worried. I don't want people to give me things because they feel guilty or intimidated. I want to make friends, to learn to know and understand our people."

"You are a very sensitive girl and your attitude does you proud. However, many of the people last night, including our leader, were most ungracious to you and the gifts show that they realize that. The emergency no doubt kept some of them from making complete asses out of themselves. These gifts are actually quite a healthy sign—that in spite of the crisis, some of them cared enough about your feelings to apologize. Once this would not have been at all unusual but our people have changed, since the evacuation." Her voice drifted off, sadly. When she spoke again, it was to change the subject. "Now then. Tell me more about your adventures."

Acorna was surprised. She was not used to talking as much as she had talked the night before. It was easy to talk to Grandam though. The funny thing was, sometimes Acorna knew that Grandam didn't merely hear her words—that she saw Acorna's own memories as well, felt what Acorna was feeling as she remembered, felt as she had felt while experiencing the events the memories recorded. But with Grandam Naadiina, Acorna didn't worry about what was thought-talk and what was verbal. She knew without needing to question that Grandam understood what she was trying to communicate, however she communicated it. And that, Grandam's willingness and ability to really know her, was what had drawn her out. It had been that way somewhat with Neeva and the others, but there had always been their own thoughts, their considerations of what was and was not Linyaari, that got in the way.

Grandam smiled at Acorna in the brief pause the girl took before speaking and nodded. "I see that you have shared enough with me already. It has been my pleasure hearing your tales. They are so different from anything else one hears on this planet, among our people. Never fear, granddaughter, that you are unworthy. Our people don't yet know you or understand you but they will."

Acorna took a deep breath and straightened her spine. "Not if I don't make the attempt to get to know them, Grandam. Apparently I cannot help out with the crisis in space, but perhaps I can at least offer comfort to those left behind here on the planet. The gifts have given me an opening. First, I must try to learn who sent each bundle and thank them, and visit with them, and not bare my teeth." Her mouth curled in a smile but she determinedly kept her lips closed. "I must also speak with the people who designed the dresses they so kindly sent—and pay for the two I altered to suit myself."

"That is not necessary, you know. It's all been put on Neeva's account at her instruction."

"Nevertheless, I fear I insulted them and after I saw how everyone was dressed last night, I better understood the intent of the designers. I would like to tell them so."

"That would be most gracious, my dear. They *are* very silly though, these fashions."

Acorna could not truthfully debate that point, but continued. "Be that as it may, I was told that there was a possibility that some day I would return to Kezdet and Maganos and my human friends as an ambassador of the Linyaari. I don't seem to be making a good start of it yet. So perhaps, since I don't yet know exactly what it is to be a Linyaari, I should begin to explore that and in the process, practice ambassadorship by trying to represent the culture from which I've come in a more positive manner than I seem to have done so far."

"Bravo!" said Grandam Naadiina. "You have a splendid attitude with which to begin your work, I must say. And perhaps with your broad experience of other worlds, you will be able to ease some of the fears people have for their loved ones in space."

Acorna's mind was already so busy planning her day she

simply nodded to acknowledge Grandam's approval. "And also, I would like to meet some of these techno-artisans Maati was telling me about, the ones who design, alter, and adapt the technological trade items to Linyaari tastes."

"They have their own community, actually, but it's not too far from here to walk, though the path is a bit overgrazed. And you must realize that many of them spend considerable time on other host planets, learning the basics and keeping up with the new developments. A few of them will be on the crews shipping out but by no means all."

"So they spend a lot of time in space?" Acorna asked. "That's very interesting. No one in any place I have ever been has ever seen a being like me before the *Balaküre* came looking for me."

"Is that so? In some parts of the universe we're quite a routine sight, you know. But those are peaceful parts, and if they cease to be peaceful, we cease to be seen there." Her tone had a wry twist to it that made Acorna realize—with some surprise— that the words had been thought and not spoken, for she saw an image of Linyaari techno-artisans in training hastily vacating a planet where hostilities were erupting.

"Is this all right to wear to go calling?" Acorna asked, indicating the gown she had worn the night before.

"My dear, it wouldn't bother a soul if you went out unclothed altogether. We aren't fussy about those things around here, not for modesty's sake, anyway. But the weather does turn suddenly. Allow me to loan you something. You'll be pleased to know extreme fashion is only utilized in formal clothing. For daytime wear we are rather more practical."

Grandam raised the lid of one of the low tables, and inside were folded a variety of garments. From among these, she selected a simple knee-length tunic with long full sleeves and a neckline cut low in back to accommodate the hair that grew down Acorna's spine and that of every other Linyaari. Acorna slipped it over her head.

"Very comfortable," she said.

"Yes, but it does need a touch. It's a bit too floppy on you. Here, this will do nicely." Grandam handed her the most gorgeous belt Acorna had ever seen. The edges were intricately braided and interwoven of some strong but supple material, while the body of the belt was patterned with faceted gemstone beads woven into the design of birds and water, flowers and distant mountains with a stream flowing the length of the belt. Acorna had to stroke and admire it a moment before buckling it around her waist. The buckle continued the pattern of the belt in a slightly wider motif of a very tall mountain with one sun setting and another rising on the other side of it.

Grandam smiled. "It suits you. Niciirye made it for me to wear for our ceremony of union when we were still courting. Unfortunately, it lacks a few *düch'se'* of meeting around my waist these days. The scenes, as you may have guessed, are from our original home world. It was the only home Niciirye knew."

"What became of him?" Acorna asked. "If it isn't too painful for you to tell me?"

"Not at all. He was even older than I and died peacefully in his sleep. He was well enough, and an excellent healer, but his parts were simply worn out. I begin to understand that problem myself. I do miss him though—his foolishness as much as his guidance. Ah well. I hope you can find someone you care for and who cares for you as much."

Acorna sighed. "Right now I'll settle for not making an outcast of myself."

"I'm sure when people get to know you, they'll be sincerely glad you've come. I think you will have much better luck talking to one or two people at a time. You are not a shallow person, and small talk is essentially a shallow form of communication. It will not be necessary when you are alone with other individuals. Just be yourself and be willing to take each person as you find him or her and you'll do well."

"I'm sure you're right," Acorna said. "Now, how do I find these places?"

"I'll send for Maati." Grandam poked her head out of the tent, ready to call.

"Oh, no, surely with the crisis, the *viizaar* will need her more than ever today. Really, if you'll just tell me, I'll find my own way. I don't want Liriili to have another excuse to resent me."

It was Grandam Naadiina's turn to sigh. She moved back into the tent. "I suppose you're right. Very well then, I'll draw you a map. When you're ready to visit the techno-artisans, come back here and I'll take you myself. I've left a heating unit with Kaakiri for repair and it should be ready by now."

Nine

Hafiz Harakamian regarded his second wife, his most lusciously beautiful bride, with alarm bordering on panic. "Karina, my little pomegranate, you grow thin and pale!"

Indeed, half of her second chin had disappeared, and the lovely little roll of belly below her amethyst-encrusted lavender bra and bolero and above the amethyst-studded band of the diaphanous lilac harem pants she wore was eclipsed from its usual full moon to little more than a quarter.

"Tell me, oh my garden of delights, why do you wither away to nothing? Is there some wish I have not fulfilled? Some food you crave I have not had fetched from the corners of the universe to delight your delicate palate? Some garment you would desire to swathe your so lovely figure"—and he almost drooled as he said it, for his new bride was all that he had hoped she would be—"that I have not had made for you from the finest materials by the most talented and skillful seamstresses available? Some redecorating, maybe, you'd like to do to our homes?" he asked in desperation, as the first two questions were meeting with no response but a slight trembling of her lower lip and flutter of her eyelashes.

"Oh, Haffy, my darling figgy pudding hubby," Karina said, for she was not to be outdone in hyperbolic compliments to her wealthy husband who, if he was not exactly handsome, still had a wonderfully compelling personality, tremendous vitality, enormous charisma, quite startling capabilities in the bedroom, and marvelous taste in women—not to mention oodles and oodles of lovely money, "you have done everything to satisfy my body but my spirit remains unfulfilled."

"Why is that, o beloved whose face is like unto a blossoming white rose, whose eyes are brighter than the twinkling stars, whose . . ."

She cut off the flow by burying her face in her heavily be-ringed hands. "I fear I allowed myself to be distracted from my own spiritual journey by the suddenness of our passion. So overcome was I with the newness of our love that I grew complacent about what I knew was my true calling, my greatest spiritual quest—to aid Acorna and her people and teach them to channel their energies and use their gifts in a proper"—and profitable, for Karina thought wealth was very proper—"manner."

"But, my little oasis of carnal conviviality, Acorna went with her people to learn their ways and will soon return to us. Surely you need not pine?"

She sighed deeply. They were sitting beside the fountain in the courtyard, where they had just partaken of a fabulous meal. She had only picked at the third course and had barely touched her sherbet. She popped another of those little chocolate egg truffles into her mouth though. Hafiz was right. She had to keep her strength up. "Oh, Hafiz, my wise and wily warrior in the world of wealth, you are such a debonair fellow, so learned in the ways of commerce and the battle of the marketplace, that in your munificence of spirit you no doubt saw the beautiful Linyaari beings as like yourself, as sophisticated as they were soignée.

"But I, who communed with them on both a deeper level and a higher plane than any among our own kind, recall their childlike innocence, their need to be nurtured and tutored along the great spiritual pathway that it has been my privilege to travel lo these many years. Their incredible healing and puri-fying powers which really need sharp management so they don't go exhausting themselves by giving all that valuable stuff away.

"I was to have been Acorna's mentor in just such a way, but now our lovely Lady of the Light has gone with them to this secluded home world of theirs, a place where no one can find them, a place where our beloved Acorna and all of her potential are lost—not to mention the potential of a whole planetful just like her!—to me and all who love her."

Hafiz scratched his bearded chin, pondering the words of his wife, words which he had come to learn had many levels of wisdom.

Then he shrugged as if it were all a small matter. "Acorna said she would return, and her people were of the opinion that she would be given honors and rank among them and sent to us as an envoy. I'm sure she and they will be with us again soon, O my heart of butter. And this home where they live is only in space, beloved, not in that land where our esteemed friend and colleague Li now resides. And if these people can locate it in space, so can the finest engineers and navigators in my employ—that is to say, the finest engineers and navigators available. And this planet, if need be, could be visited. Especially by a friend."

"Friend? Why, you are practically the only family she has! Apart from your nephew and his friends, she had only Mr. Li. And while I am in constant contact with him, his guidance is lost to her. In fact," she added shrewdly, "it is his guidance in this matter, his insistence that Acorna and her people should still have access to our advice and assistance, that has caused me to dwell on this matter while neglecting my diet."

Hafiz was momentarily incensed. "You have been having clandestine visits with Delszaki Li, my old rival, and neglecting to feed the body upon which I have lavished so much love?"

"He *is* dead, Haffy," she said reasonably.

"But you entertain his counsel!"

"My darling, it is my calling to succor such spirits, to keep open the channels of communication between the planes. I cannot reject the spirits any more than you can reject a profit!"

"But Li himself organized her departure, outfitted her ship . . ."

"Yes, but he says he always intended that one or more of her guardians should go with her. Had she not left prematurely, I would have intercepted her and been aboard the vessel that carried her away the first time. Of course, it didn't occur to her aunt to invite me along. What with us being newlyweds and all." She blushed, a flush that cast a roseate dawn upon the exposed globes above her overflowing bodice.

Hafiz, never one to be outdone at the bargaining table, even of love, reached for her. "Perhaps I am at this moment too distracted with concern for your health to consider these matters, my little couscous. Come, I cannot speak of this further until I have once more personally inspected the possible damage your dietary deprivation has wreaked upon your beauteous body."

Karina, who was not yet over the novelty of having a man so besotted with her that, while he insisted she wear her flowing robes in public, it was only so that she could wear, if anything, skimpy little outfits like this one for him and him alone to drool over in private. His hands were very skillful and the look in his eyes made her feel, as always, quite faint with desire.

Besides, he was always more reasonable afterward.

As for Hafiz, he was even more aroused than usual, recalling the words of his voluptuous vixen, the ones where she pointed out that there was a profit to be made in the talents of Acorna and her kind. His Karina was not only lusciously lovely but also had a head for business—a true helpmeet at last!

Before he had time to explore this side of her along with the others, a discreet cough from behind him made him turn toward the lacey latticework of the door leading into the garden. "Your pardon, Lord and Master and gracious lady, but a matter of great urgency has arisen that requires your presence,

Master, something you and you alone must attend to."

"And so I will when it pleases me," Hafiz said with a glower at the servant, who had been in his employ since boyhood and certainly knew better than to interrupt him when he was engaged in the pursuit of marital bliss. "It should be obvious to you that it does not please me *now*."

"Yes, Great Lord. But I swear to you upon the Three Books and by the Three Prophets that though you reward my impertinence with a thousand lashes for this interruption, you would redouble that punishment if I neglected my duty in informing you of this matter."

"This is so?" Hafiz asked. He had not risen to his present position by ignoring urgent business when it was brought to his attention, even when it was so wretchedly inconvenient as it was now.

"Even so, Great Lord and Master," the servant said with a bow.

"Ah, very well then." He kissed Karina tenderly on the cheek for he dared not kiss her lips or he would never leave, gave her belly a longing stroke, shoved the gold enameled dish wrought with nightingales and piled with chocolate truffle eggs into her hands and said, "Eat, my dainty doe of deliciousness. You will need all of your strength when I return."

"As will you, my love," she said in a sultry voice that all but drove him mad.

Didi Yasmin, currently unemployed since the combined forces of Delszaki Li and the peculiar horned girl had put all of the pleasure houses of Kezdet out of business, was still in mourning. This fact distressed her, as black was not one of her better colors. But a son was a son and hers was dead and her husband and supposed widower no doubt had something to do with it. Therefore, he should pay. Would pay.

He would never miss it, she thought, looking around at the thick red-patterned carpets, the crimson and emerald silk-covered cushions of the divan, the endless cabinets of lustrous and exotic woods filled with equally lustrous and exotic treasures, the masses of fresh blooms plucked from his gardens, which were cooled by no fewer than a thousand flowing fountains.

And he owed her. She had given him the son and heir he demanded of a wife and he had wasted the boy and given away his empire to that asteroid-hopping nephew of his. But the worst of all was that he had had the gall to remarry without even bothering to make absolutely certain she, his real wife, was dead.

True, she had gone to elaborate lengths to fake her death so that she might return to her own profitable career in the sex industry, but it had always galled her how easily and with what apparent relief he accepted the exaggerated reports of her demise. He had been glad, back then, to have the boy to himself. She had been glad to leave her son as well, then. She had found motherhood extremely taxing, despite a whole platoon of nannies, and even then had hated to have anyone thinking she was old enough to be someone's mother!

But it had suited her purposes and those of her employers that she keep track of both her husband and her son. Her son had frequented the houses of her colleagues and even, on a couple of occasions, had graced her own establishment, though of course he didn't recognize her.

A fine boy, a strapping boy. Too bad he had caused such damage to the women he had used that they had to be replaced, at great expense, of course. After that, she reluctantly banned him. As for her dear husband, she was kept well informed of his movements and interests through those enemies she had happily supplied with detailed maps of his compound, an inventory of his most treasured possessions, the names of all of his personal guards she could recall, and other readily marketed information.

It was these people who finally secured her release from prison and these people, also, who engineered her arrival at this same compound where once she had been mistress, who got her past the guards, and who supplied her with one other little thing.

Hafiz delighted her by gaping at her as if she were indeed the ghost he supposed her to be.

"Yasmin!" he gasped, as his well-fed and gorgeously robed form appeared from among the glittering beads of the curtained doorway.

"Greetings, husband," she said sweetly. "I was told you have recently remarried. I am assuming from this that you have recently embraced at least Reform Neo-Hadathian customs and have become polygamous, since we two are still legally twined in wedded bliss." His face was turning the exact shade of scarlet she had hoped to see. She smiled sweetly. "No, no, my darling husband, do not imagine that I object. A senior wife can always use a young one to relieve her of some of her more distasteful duties. But I am surprised she is not here to greet me as well. Is this new girl perhaps indisposed? I had so hoped to meet her and see if she can live up to my standards—and of course, to instruct her in her duties to me, as your first wife and *khadine.*"

Hafiz stared at Yasmin, with whom he had once briefly been so infatuated and whom he had long believed to be dead. He had never mourned her properly, it was true, for despite her beauty as a young woman, and her apparent ardor, she had not been a very good wife. She was vicious, vain, and somewhat stupid, so much so in fact that like many petty criminals her own emotional shortcomings even got in the way of fulfilling her greed at times. And Yasmin had been a very greedy woman.

Unfortunately, it seemed she was also alive, because she did appear to be breathing even though she very much looked the part of a ghost. Her once-charming face had been resculpted, had had its wrinkles repeatedly removed by poison and knife blade so often that her skin looked as if it had been stretched over her skull bones like the skin of a goat on a drum. It was shiny, not from youthful moistness and freshness, but rather, it appeared, from some sort of pickling process that made it look thick and coarse. Little veins had broken in her cheeks.

Her mouth was puffy with the injections she used to keep it from falling back into its former thinness—but back then, though thin, that mouth had been ready for bawdy laughter, and that was part of what had attracted him to her. Now it looked as if it pained her to speak. Her eyes had had the lids lifted and brows tattooed above them.

Thick eyelashes had been implanted to augment her own. But none of this disguised the dull, stony glare of her eyes. Beneath black veils trimmed in a tasteless manner in black spangles, her hair was stiff with gilt metallic dye.

"Yasmin, you are dead by law if not in fact, and even if you remain my wife, it is only in name, and that will not be for much longer, now that I know it is a problem. Had I realized that you still lived, I would not have divorced you before, for the sake of our son, but now that he is gone—"

"Murdered," Yasmin whispered, her eyes narrowed to slits. "Foully murdered and yet I understand that you, his father, did nothing to avenge him! Have in fact, it is said, with unseemly haste replaced him with that asteroid-hopping nephew of yours as your heir."

"Tapha had it coming. He was our son, it is true, but it is also true that he was a vicious and ignorant pig."

"He didn't get that from my side of the family."

Hafiz waved his hand in dismissal. "No matter. There is no longer any 'your' side of the family. Your side of the family, apparently through your own contrivance, is extinct. And you have not been a member of my family in many years. It grieves me to tell you, oh dear departed mother of our late unlamented son, that I would have disinherited Tapha even if he lived. The boy managed, despite his legitimate birth during our marriage, to be a bastard of the worst kind."

"You have no sense of family! It is a good thing that I have returned, as your *khadine*, to instruct my junior wife."

Hafiz looked as if he were about to explode, and said in a

slow, dangerous voice, "You will not speak to her, you will not so much as lay eyes upon her. You are not *khadine*. You are no longer even my wife."

He took a deep breath and began chanting the expeditious ancient Hadathian method of ridding oneself of unwanted marital attachments, "I divorce you, I divorce you, I—"

Before he could say it the third and decisive time, she interrupted in a shrill, high whine that would not allow him to ignore it.

"You think you can cast me out, just like that, kill my son, marry another, and dismiss me as if I were someone of no consequence?"

"I am certainly about to," Hafiz told her.

"There's no need to get so unpleasant. As you recall, it was I who left you. I was only testing you," she said with a poisonously sweet smile. She pulled a beautifully jeweled box from her robes and offered it to him. "I confess, I was afraid you might react this way, that the shock of my resurrection would prove too much for you and that the years we have spent apart would have put too great a strain on your affection. Still, although I do not care for the way you've treated me, I am a broad-minded woman. And to show there are no hard feelings, I have brought you a wedding present. One I know will be of great interest to you."

"I have no wish for your gifts—but, ahhh—is that a rare Terran early nineteenth century inlaid vermilion and jade snuffbox similar to the one from the court of the French emperor Napoleon Bonaparte?" He must at least inspect such a treasure. His fingers itched to do so, as they did with any fine and rare collectible object. Perhaps he was only imagining the sneer that crossed Yasmin's red swollen mouth?

"The very one. The emperor himself gorged his very nostrils from this same box, oh avaricious husband. And now it holds a new rarity, a treasure of particular meaning for you. Go ahead, take it."

He started to accept it from her hand and then thought better of it. "No, you open it. Show me. It would be like you to have had it fitted with some poisoned clasp . . ."

"You wrong me, beloved," she said, and wondered how the man who sold her this box had known that Hafiz would say this. She touched the catch and the lid popped open. "You see? Nothing in it but fine sparkling powder, like ground moon-stones or opals."

"I do not traffic in drugs, Yasmin," Hafiz said huffily. He didn't either. Not any more. Not for many years. Well, not on a regular basis. It wasn't really profitable any more.

"Ah, but, husband, this is no drug of the sort to which you refer. This is a very special powder indeed. It will heal any wound, neutralize poisons, and will act as an amazing aphro-disiac to any man or woman who takes only a few grains in a drink or food."

"This is so?" Hafiz asked. "That is a wondrous thing indeed, mother of my deservedly-deceased son. And something I will happily accept if only you will tell me, why is it that you, who have never, so far as I could discern, borne love for any part of me but my wealth, bestow this upon me? As a gift," he reminded her hastily. A gift was, after all, a gift, though for a remedy with such powers as this powder was said to have, he might well have paid a great deal.

"Because, dear husband, it is said to come from the horn of a humanoid being who has but a single horn in the center of her forehead. Since you once showed favor to such a being . . ." She laughed, and taking a deep breath, blew the powder from the open box into his face, and into his eyes, blinding him with a starry swirl that also, somehow, silenced him and made him swoon so that when he regained his senses, he was lying upon the central pattern of the Garden of Paradise carpet, and the living ghost of his late wife had vanished.

*   *   *

He was one with his home world, gray-brown and broken, and to an onlooker would have been almost indistinguishable from the rubble. He no longer knew which was rock and soil and which part of his own body, except for the pain. He had had no fear, when the ship landed, that either the small furry animal or the cumbersome monster who kept flinging things in and out of the vessel would notice him.

But he watched when they landed once more with far greater trepidation, and with relief that he had already removed from its resting place the sacred trust that undoubtedly drew the outsiders.

Ten

The House of Harakamian chemists reported that the powder was a mixture of the ground pollens of the rare Wahanamoian Blossom of Sleep and another substance difficult to analyze, but appearing to be calcified tissue of the horn variety, about which they could say nothing further except that one of the men who had cut himself accidentally a little earlier spontaneously healed upon coming in contact with the powder.

Hafiz mentioned nothing of this to Karina. Until he could finalize his divorce to a supposedly dead woman, he did not wish to jeopardize his marriage by mentioning the inconvenient vitality of his late spouse to his present one.

But he was very troubled indeed. Surely, Yasmin had obtained the powder through her underworld contacts, which he was certain she had, as who else would have financed her all these years while she plied the trade that she seemed to feel made her a star? But if these people had somehow contrived to murder Acorna and the delegation from her home planet, Hafiz felt sure they would have said so more directly—he himself would have done that, though he was often the most indirect of men. Therefore, this powder was a warning. And yet—where could the horn material have come from?

A sickening thought occurred to him. Before he had met the Linyaari, they had broadcast as a warning vids of the Khleevi torturing Linyaari prisoners. Was there some faction of the sort of worm with whom Yasmin consorted so low as to actually have contacts among the Khleevi who would sell them Linyaari horn?

If so, this was a very grave matter. Acorna and her people should know of it at once. Hafiz wished to contact his nephew and heir about the matter but decided on balance it was best to do so in person rather than trusting the com units. Hafiz was far too practical to be overly brave, and Yasmin's ability to come and go without his knowledge had shaken him profoundly.

He forbade his house staff to say anything of the surprise visit to Karina until he could decide how to tell her himself and ordered the entire compound searched for the presence of his late wife. As he suspected, she had disappeared utterly and completely while he lay drugged on the floor of his own home.

At last, only three hours' time from when he had last been at Karina's side, Hafiz appeared in the marital bedchamber, where his bride lounged upon their connubial couch. She had been sleeping, he thought, but had awakened at his step.

"Karina," he said, "You have convinced me. Our ship is being prepared and we shall soon depart for the Linyaari home world to visit Acorna and the others."

Karina would have known at once that something was amiss even if she had not already encountered a deeply troubled and no doubt deluded woman claiming to be Hafiz's true wife. She naturally assumed that the woman was a ghost, since Hafiz's first wife was dead. Of course, she could have been one of the holograms Hafiz was always constructing to surprise a person in odd nooks and crannies, but why would he make an ugly hologram that claimed to be his wife? Had to be a ghost. Karina attempted to soothe and comfort her, to tell her to go back into the light, but the specter had merely looked annoyed. Presumably she had then gone on to haunt Hafiz, or had just come from haunting him, as the very next time Karina saw him he was behaving in a very peculiar fashion, as those who had received visitations from the other side sometimes did.

For one thing, Hafiz addressed Karina by name instead of calling her by one of his lengthy endearments. For another thing, he gave up without even a token tussle, totally unlike him, and let her have her way about seeking out Acorna's people. And for a third thing, he hardly ever did anything in haste, but always with slow and deliberate preparation.

His sudden acquiescence so alarmed Karina that she backtracked slightly.

"My darling, perhaps we should wait a little after all," she said, easing him down beside her with a light tug on his hand. "You look unwell. You perspire and your color is not at all good. I think you need a course of some of my special herbal teas and perhaps we should burn a cinnamon candle tonight to ease your—"

"Pack it, beloved!" he said. "Pack all of the tea and candles you wish. Pack your gowns and jewels, pack your cards and stones and your crystal ball. But we cannot deprive Acorna and her people of our guidance for another day."

Nor could they wait a moment longer, he thought privately, for Yasmin to return and spoil the honeymoon any more than she had already done. Hafiz worried his first wife's troublemaking would be even more distressing next time—and more obvious to Karina. He wouldn't allow that. Women were extremely difficult to understand, even for a man of his considerable amatory experience. But what worried him more than Yasmin's tricks was that the security of his stronghold had been breached. If he was to go, it had best be in all haste, before Yasmin's unsavory associates followed her here.

In the meantime he had ordered a complete restructuring of his security strategies, changes in locks, codes, and passwords, and that the compound be totally remodeled and its defenses reinforced. In his early days of affection—very well, lust—for Yasmin, he had shown her everything—*everything.*

He deeply regretted that now, for even though he had added and altered several systems since the time of his first wife, still she knew too much. He and Karina would not truly be safe here, in his own home, until the presence of Yasmin was purged.

His personal vessel was kept in readiness at all times and well equipped for his comfort on journeys around most of his customary haunts. He commanded that it be readied for an extended cruise and had retrieved the data plotted by Calum Baird and Acorna for their originally planned journey to the Linyaari home world.

They would travel with the bare minimum crew—pilot, navigator, physician, and communications officer, plus one trusted personal attendant for each of them, including the ship's officers, who must be relaxed and at peace to do their jobs well.

Hafiz himself was a competent pilot but for such a long journey, and one that had not actually been previously successfully completed by anyone of his acquaintance, he preferred to employ a specialist.

He would have preferred to take along his personal chef, the hairdresser and dressmaker, manicurist, massage therapist, valet, lady's maid, and other servants they were accustomed to, but most of these functions could either be performed by the personal attendants or were well within the ship's ability to provide electronically. For entertainment, they would have his holograms to amuse them and add a bit of spice and variety to the atmosphere. He had been constructing and collecting holograms most of his adult life, first as a business and now as one of his little hobbies. They were lightweight, took up no actual room, and could be surprisingly useful.

In the interests of maintaining security—both his own and that of the Linyaari, he decided that perhaps they had best rough it on this journey. His skeleton crew was handpicked and had been raised and educated within the House of Harakamian. They were loyal and trustworthy.

Then there was the additional problem that, in the interests of establishing rapport with Acorna's people, he felt he could not carry the usual arsenal on board, or any obvious security guards. Although the crew and attendants were well trained in security functions, that was not their primary job. Perhaps braving the unknown without sufficient weaponry or an army at his back was foolish, but there were always the ship's built-in defenses that could be deployed if necessary. He doubted even the Linyaari would suspect they were there. Given his mission, it was either go this way, or not at all.

In the unlikely event that Acorna's people did spot his ship's defenses, the Linyaari would simply have to understand. He was sincerely attempting to come in peace—very possibly at the expense of his people's safety, as well as his own. He could only hope their departure would be rapid enough that Yasmin and whoever it was she worked for would be unable to launch a pursuit.

Karina was rather distracted on the journey from Laboue to Maganos.

"What troubles you, my love?"

"My spirit guides keep looking over their ectoplasmic shoulders, darling. I'm just sure they're trying to tell me I've left something important behind or perhaps we forgot to turn off some major appliance—"

"You are having a flashback to your days of penury and poverty, flower of my soul. You have servants to see to those things now, remember?"

She gave him a wan little smile. "So we do, O beloved. Still, I wish the communication was clearer. It's very disorienting to spirit guides moving from planet to planet, you know. They get very attached to the places from whence they entered the other side."

"Indeed? You are a fountain of information, best beloved among women. I had no idea."

"Oh, yes!"

"Tell me, love of my life, is Delszaki Li still among your otherworldly friends?"

"Oh, my, yes."

"Then tell him your husband said that he's to explain himself at once and stop worrying you, precious pearl of psychic perception."

Karina giggled. "Oh, Hafiz, you are so cute when you're indignant. I couldn't say *that* to Mr. Li. But I will mention that you are concerned, too, and see if he can offer enlightenment. I must meditate in solitude to concentrate my energies. Now, where *is* that twenty-carat amethyst crystal you gave me?"

"I believe you loaned it to the physician to try to communicate with his bacterial specimens, my love."

"So I did. Well, I'll simply have to borrow it back. I must have the proper tools of my profession, after all. *Can* you manage without me for a while, beloved?"

"Each moment will be as a dagger in my heart, sweet and succulent spouse, but I will valiantly endure."

They kissed and she departed.

To the communications officer, Hafiz said, "Please alert Maganos Base to have my nephew standing by when we arrive."

A moment later the Maganos communications officer said in the high and low cracking voice of a boy going through puberty, which he no doubt was since the moon was now a training facility for youngsters and the trainees provided the personnel for almost every phase of the operation, "*Shahrazad*, this is Maganos Base. We weren't expecting Mr. Harakamian!"

"We're aware of that, Maganos Base. That's why Mr. Harakamian wishes to speak to his nephew. Can you contact him please and put him on screen?"

"I'll try, *Shahrazad*. Just a tic."

But the face that appeared on the comscreen was not Rafik's but Calum Baird's. Hafiz placed himself in front of the communications officer so that his own face and voice would appear on Baird's screen.

"Ah, senior and ugliest wife of my nephew, how goes it?" Hafiz asked, delighting to see the color rise above Baird's red beard at the mention of their first meeting, when Baird, as well as Acorna, had worn veils and a long gown to promote the idea that Rafik had become one of the fundamentalist polygamist Neo-Hadathians.

"Not so bad, oh robber baron who makes Ali Baba's forty thieves look like rank amateurs," Baird responded. "But I regret to tell you that Rafik had to go to Rushima. Dr. Hoa had a spot of trouble he had to discuss with him."

"In that case, don't wait up for us, my friend. We will go to Rushima instead for I must speak with my nephew personally. Ah—Baird?"

"Yes?"

"How is my nephew's junior wife? Has anyone heard from her or the other members of the harem?"

At first Baird looked puzzled and then he said, carefully, "We last heard from them as they were leaving this quadrant, about twenty days ago. They were all well and uh—looking forward to being united with their families."

"I see. And Baird?"

"Yes?"

"Your last cruise with the junior wife—would your plans have brought you to the destination you wished? Did the other harem members give you a clue?"

"Why, yes, as a matter of fact, they did. We would have come within—uh—the anteroom of the seraglio, so to speak. Why?"

"Oh, no reason. Just curious. A small wager I had with my own navigator. Nothing of any importance."

"Right," Baird said, in a tone that clearly meant "pull the other one."

"*Shahrazad* out," Hafiz said cheerfully.

"Have a nice voyage," Baird replied sweetly and with an exaggeratedly effeminate wiggle of his fingers. His bushy eyebrows were twisted with concern, however, and Hafiz knew that the Caledonian understood something of the nature of the business the *Shahrazad* had with Rafik.

The *Condor* contained certain modifications that were not purely born of mechanical necessity. A bank of multifrequency scanners was arrayed directly in front on the control console. Next to the cargo, these scanners were the most important item contained on the ship, aside from the captain and first mate.

Becker was constantly keeping a weather eye and ear open for distress signals, blips where there shouldn't be blips, homing beacons, any sort of indication that some vessel, station, planetoid, or whatever might now be or have been in trouble in the recent past. Of course, Becker had a first aid kit and was perfectly willing to assist survivors if necessary, but his interest was not solely humanitarian — or alienatarian, as the case might be. He simply wanted to know where trouble had been, where vessels or settlements might be abandoned, leaving behind equipment and other good stuff for an enterprising scavenger. His scanning devices were aided by other sensors that detected the physical presence of largish items in the *Condor*'s vicinity and, just as usefully, detected the absence of the usual detritus, an indication that one of the useful holes or folds in space might be at hand. While some of these things could be plotted, others sometimes occurred where they never had before. "Space moths," Becker Senior had postulated. "Damn space moths been chewin' in this sector again. Shall we see where this one goes, boy?"

It wasn't that it hadn't ever occurred to Theophilus Becker that he might guide the *Condor* into one of these little byways in space that made life jolly for astrophysicists and never find his way out. It was that neither he nor Jonas usually had an actual schedule or anything so he felt free to poke around. While it was certainly possible they could become lost in infinity, as the old vids were always postulating, the senior Becker held the opinion that there was a pattern and a predictability to these wrinkles in the space/time continuum within a given area. It was an opinion he hadn't shared with much of anyone but Jonas, who figured what was good enough for Dad was good enough for him and took the same cavalier attitude toward wormholes and such, new or used.

Normally he didn't go out of his way to pay these instruments undue attention as long as they were working. If he didn't notice, RK often did and would sit staring pointedly at one screen or another until Becker did likewise.

But he was a little nervous about being followed by Kisla Manjari and company and also was on the lookout to restock the inventory as soon as possible.

As soon as he had cleared Kezdet and her moons, he turned his attention to the scanners. He hadn't expected to be sought real soon, actually, but one of the short-range scanners was keeping up a continuous, pulsing bleep. It had to be close, but he couldn't see its source on any of the screens.

"Well, doggone it anyway," he said. "Where are you, little bleep?"

It bleeped again. Still nothing on the screen though he looked fast, as if he was expecting the visual manifestation of the sound to be playing peekaboo with him.

By the time the *Condor* had cleared Kezdet's solar system and warped through a couple of wormholes, Becker was getting pretty tired of the beep. He also noticed that RK wasn't hanging out on deck much any more. When they were back to cruising through what was usually calm empty space, Becker went below decks with a can of fish he'd picked up on Kezdet before hitting the pleasure house, intending that RK should be able to take it as an offering to his temporary mate. There was quite a bit of time before the *Condor* hit the next "black water," as Theophilus Becker liked to refer to the pleated, holey portions of space where he found his best shortcuts.

"RK? Hey, cat! Where the hell are you?"

He finally found the cat by the smell and the noise. Since acquiring the sack of horns, Becker hadn't smelled RK's particular perfume but right now C-deck reeked of it. Which reminded him that RK was once more a fully functional male cat with the begetting capabilities and prerogatives thereof, supposing there had been a lady cat who was interested.

Which fortunately there wasn't. Becker didn't even want to think of a ship with a whole bunch of little Roadkill clones playing hide and seek through the cargo.

Meanwhile, if the cat was going to stink stuff up, Becker would just have to wear nose plugs or carry a hanky with something pleasanter to counter the stench—garlic maybe. If it worked with vampires, maybe it would work with cats.

It better, because Roadkill was damn sure going to *stay* fully equipped. No way was Becker going to go through *that* again. It made his two formerly missing and now mostly restored fingers ache just thinking about it.

Finally, the stink led him to the cat, claws scrabbling at the side of the cargo hold that opened to the outside. This hold had been the airlock of the hatch of an ancient model of Antirean space craft, and it fit well into a hole Becker had to fill during one of his impromptu redesigning sessions of the *Condor*.

"Mrrrrow!" RK said, looking up at Becker as if to say, "It's about time you got here, you damn fool. Help me out with this, huh?"

Becker had rigged a bin-style entry door to the hold that opened outward. The door was totally slimed with RK's personal signature testosterone blend.

"Okay, cat, why didn't you say so before?" Becker asked, but realized he had been busy at the controls when he wasn't sleeping. Besides which, RK was used to keeping his own counsel. He knew how to get Becker's attention when he wanted it. He had obviously just preferred to work on his own so far. Becker had to admit that *he* couldn't have improved on the job RK had done on the cargo hold door. It was well and truly slimed—a piece of feline artwork in its own way. Becker had to find a piece of cloth to wipe off the mess before he could punch the button that opened the hold.

The hold door fell open, rather than sliding. And lying on the inside of it was what looked like a dead man.

A familiar-looking dead man—and not just familiar *looking*. Becker knew who the fellow was from the torn and stinky pant leg.

"No wonder you were carrying on," Becker said aloud to Roadkill. "It's your old scratching post, hitching an unauthorized ride."

He put his hands under the android's armpits and started hauling him out of the cargo hold. There was a pulse. Funny. These older models didn't have a true circulatory system. There was something strangely familiar about that pulse though, and as soon as Becker hauled the guy back to the command deck and heard the little steady bleep again, he knew what it was.

"Well, RK, here's our little homing pigeon, giving away our position with every beat of his heavy metal heart. Shee-it. I wonder if you can hear this thing through wormholes?"

Kisla Manjari pitched a fit when she saw what had become of her mechanoid henchmen. "He killed them!" she told her uncle. "Smashed them with his junk then took off with one of them— stole it. Stole *my* KEN unit! He can't get away with that—oh, no."

"Certainly not, my dear," Uncle Edacki said smoothly. He could see the scene in question on her portable comscreen. "Most unwise of him indeed."

"I wonder why KEN640 doesn't answer when I try to reach him," Kisla said. "He is still operational, according to his sonid button. He should answer and obey my command to kill the junk man and bring his ship back here."

"Hmmm, perhaps," Uncle Edacki said. "But, Kisla darling, are you sure that would be the best use of this fortuitous situation?"

"What do you mean fortuitous? They were *my* units! Now who will help me assemble my fleet?"

"I'll get you some others. But for the time being, you say you are still receiving the signal from 640's sonid, and 640 is presumed to be with Becker in his craft going — where? To their next destination. Which will be — where do you suppose?"

"Back to where he found the horns?" she asked, the light dawning finally.

"And the sonid signal, with its tiny trail of electrons — "

"Will let me track him and everything!" Kisla said, very excited. "Oh, Uncle, *may* I?"

"Yes, sweetie. You are doing so well today — first finding the horns, then cleverly arranging for your unit to be captured so we can track Becker by the signal. Just for that you may hand-pick a crew and take command of the *Midas* in order to follow Becker's trail."

"Oh, Uncle, you are the best!"

"Nonsense, my dear, you've earned the privilege."

Edacki Ganoosh signed off with a feeling of satisfaction at a job well done. He would have his horns one way or the other now, both with Kisla tracking her android to find Becker's source, and then there was the little matter of sending the *Pandora* to follow a similar sonid implanted in certain key employees — such as Yasmin, who was even now emitting her signal from her hiding place aboard the *Shahrazad*.

Honestly, the things a girl had to do to get out of jail. Confronting her almost-ex-husband wasn't so bad — there had always been a better-than-average chance he might try to buy her off, if she had been able to act sad enough about poor dead Tapha. Well, she hadn't. Tapha was no great loss to anyone. And really, she would have almost paid for the opportunity to see Hafiz's face when he realized what the powdered horn was. That made up for all the cracks about her acting and dancing ability when they were married.

Actually, what with being supplied all the security codes she didn't already know, it had been no trouble to smuggle herself aboard the *Shahrazad*, like her bosses told her. It wasn't that Yasmin wasn't perfectly comfortable either, even though she felt that as Hafiz's senior wife she should have been occupying the master suite instead of the quarters generally assigned to the pedicurist. She chose those herself because, as the pedicurist was one of the lesser servants, her quarters were farthest away from those of the family and other crew members. Here Yasmin could be as inconspicuous as a little mousie while all the time the transmitters she would sprinkle about the *Shahrazad* could send signals back to her bosses so they could monitor its movement.

But what got to Yasmin was that it was just too, too cruel of the bosses to make her go along on a "honeymoon trip" with Hafiz and that big cow he had married, thinking to replace *her*.

Never mind. She'd fix the wedded bliss stuff. It had never been all that blissful for her. All those cracks Hafiz had made about which end she thought with, all that worry about trying to keep her looks so her rich husband wouldn't get ideas. Keep her looks, hah! To think of all the dieting she had done to keep her shape and here he was with that—that—rhino-whale in purple robes!

So even though she was supposed to keep a low profile and let the *Shahrazad* lead her bosses to the unicorn people planet, where the bosses would then put *her* in charge of punishing Hafiz and his new playmate, Yasmin couldn't resist playing a few little tricks. Well, if a girl couldn't turn a few tricks, the least she could do was play some, huh?

She had, of course, bugged the boudoir. She really couldn't imagine failing to do so. It was a standard security measure in the brothels. Kept the girls from cheating by keeping tips for themselves, or the customers from becoming enamored with a particular girl and trying to run off with her.

She was delighted, on hearing the pillow talk between her husband and his new "wife," that neither of them had told the other about their encounters with her. These little deceptions on their part opened many exciting possibilities for trouble-making on hers.

Her familiarity with Hafiz's tastes and habits helped, as well as Karina's penchant for "meditation" and believing her super-stitious nonsense about dreams and communication from the dead, that sort of thing.

Yasmin might not be a brain but she was a very practical woman, in her own way, with no sentiment in her makeup. She believed in the physical, and in what she could buy and sell. If anybody thought she was *jealous* of Hafiz's new bride, or even of the lap of luxury Karina had fallen into, they should just think again. After all, she, Yasmin, had abandoned all of that to follow her personal star.

But she thought it was really insulting that Hafiz had been able to forget her, to replace her with someone he actually claimed to like better! She, Yasmin, was the unforgettable beauty, the suc-cubus who haunted men's dreams. How dare another woman think she could fill Yasmin's place in Hafiz's bed!

Of course, despite her considerable premarital experience, Yasmin had been little more than a gifted amateur when she married Hafiz compared to what she knew now, but she couldn't imagine how, after tasting her own charms, Hafiz could so much as bear to look at that fat, ugly, insipid cow who was not fit to fill Yasmin's douche bag!

When Karina returned to her "meditation chamber" to con-sult her spirit guides, as she had done before, Yasmin hovered on the floor above, listening through the replicator that was connected in the same spot on the wall through both levels. She'd discovered how easy it was to hear Karina's spiritual rantings quite by accident while planting one of the transmit-ters in the replicator shortly after the journey began.

Karina tended to "meditate" out loud when nobody was around.

"Yoo hoo, Mr. Li! It is I, Karina, your dear friend and faith-ful follower. I ask you to manifest answers for me. Hafiz—

that's my husband, you know him, Hafiz Harakamian, you did business together in life? He wishes to know what you would have us do. You see, Mr. Li, I keep getting this image of you looking back over your shoulder. Are you disturbed, gentle spirit? Are you disoriented by this departure from your home planet? Or—" The fat woman paused and her voice quavered as she asked, "Are you trying to *warn* us somehow?"

Yasmin couldn't think of any reply to that so she waited. And waited.

So did Karina until she said finally, "Mr. Li, you know you can tell me. Come on, what is it that's troubling you? Funny, but I can't even get an image. It's as if there is some sort of interference in the ether. Oh well, perhaps you're not feeling very sociable today. Hmm. Are there any other spirit guides who wish to make contact? I am here to help you."

Yasmin's lips curled back in a snarl that would have earned her a severe scolding from her cosmetic surgeon for making unsightly creases in his work. While it was true that while in a vertical position, Yasmin was not an imaginative woman, she was after all an entertainer of sorts and as such had a highly developed flair for the dramatic. She wasn't about to pass up an opening like this one.

Wishing she had the gauzy veils she had danced with and discarded in one of her old numbers, the better to haunt Karina with, she settled for letting her low voice rumble through the replicator. "Beeeewaarrre . . ." she said, trying to sound all dead and ghostly.

"Well, yes," Karina said. "I do realize that I should beware of a great many things. I'm afraid you'll have to be a more specific—er—entity. Can you tell me who you are? I've never encountered a haunted replicator before."

Yasmin was far too clever to give her own name, of course, especially since she had, very much in the flesh, confronted Karina, who nevertheless had failed thus far to mention the visitation to Hafiz. From that omission, Yasmin gathered that she must have been mistaken for one of Karina's less corporeal acquaintances. The fat idiot thought she was a ghost.

Yasmin quickly stripped her right ring finger of the four rings she had piled on top of the dinky gold wedding band in the shape of a snake Hafiz had bought for her and sent the wedding band down the replicator chute. On the inside of the ring was her name entwined with Hafiz's, and their wedding date. Yasmin hated to let go of even that insignificant amount of gold, but it would almost be worth Karina's weight in gold to see the stupid sow's complacency shaken up.

Yasmin saw Karina's plump fingers with the medium amethyst ring surrounded by moonstones scrabble in the replicator bale and remove the ring. "Uh, thanks," she said. "A serpent—how, uh, emblematic of mother goddess, in a creepy crawly sort of way. But I am puzzled, oh spirit. I don't see what it has to do with anything."

Yasmin was trying to form a suitably cryptic clue, something to imply that Hafiz had murdered her and maybe a whole harem of other girls and kept their bodies locked in a subcellar someplace. Something like that to really put a scare into the smug little wifey. But before she could let out with so much as another ghostly moan, somebody knocked at the door. "Madame Harakamian, please join the master on the bridge and secure yourself for landing."

"Hearing and obeying," Karina declared.

Yasmin made haste to secure herself for landing as well. It would be very helpful if the lot of them left the ship so that she could have an opportunity to plant additional monitors throughout. She was having a certain amount of remorse about the ring now—gold was gold after all—but the stupid slut would probably lay it down somewhere soon and Yasmin would be able to retrieve it.

The Rushiman administrator, who was deep in negotiations with Rafik Harakamian, insisted on throwing a banquet for Rafik's uncle and his new bride. Hafiz had been instrumental in gathering the forces which helped Rushima repel the invasion of the Khleevi and it had been his ward, Rafik's "niece," who had purified the putrid waters of the planet and ultimately arranged for Dr. Ngaen Xong Hoa, the meteorologist turned weather manipulation wizard, to help heal the planet's climate.

That same climate had been damaged by Dr. Hoa's techniques, while the man was being coerced by another group foiled by Harakamian's niece. So it was for his connections, as well as his wealth and power, that Hafiz was made welcome on Rushima, and Hafiz, with his typical perspicacity, understood this distinction. He was uncharacteristically grateful, particularly in view of the possible threat to his ward, of whom he was as fond as he was capable of being.

His business with Rafik was of the first priority, however, and since he did not wish to discuss it in front of Karina, he had, with the complicity of the captain and his Rushiman relatives, made certain arrangements to keep his beloved busy while he was otherwise engaged.

Therefore, when they disembarked, Hafiz gave the captain a wink and the captain addressed Karina. "Wise and enlightened mistress, during your meditations I was in contact with my sister, who has settled here on this isolated world. The people here are in much need of spiritual guidance and insight. My sister, on behalf of a delegation of the particularly troubled, hoped perhaps that you would be so beneficent as to share your gifts with those most in need."

"Certainly, Captain, I would be happy to," Karina replied with a gracious nod of her head and a queenly wave at the ragtag populace assembled to greet them. "And since this is the request of a family member of yours, I will happily provide my services at a very great discount."

"Barter is the usual method of exchange here, madam," the captain said.

"Hmmm," Karina said. In the old days, when she traveled to fairs and festivals throughout her home world, she had acquired many small bits of jewelry and stained glass doodads, hand-carved salad forks and once, a Mytherian fang-cleaning device, in exchange for readings. Now that she was a person of considerable means, these things would be more of a liability than an asset to her well-ordered home.

"Very well, then, Captain, I'll tell you what. Suppose you arrange the means of payment. What I cannot use, because we are traveling and our space is somewhat limited at the moment, perhaps we can take credit for on future exchanges with these people. I have been given to understand that due to the turmoil caused by the recent wars, the crops have not been particularly plentiful. I would not wish to take food from someone's children at this time." And of course, at a later time, the pickings would no doubt be better.

"My lady is gracious, as always," the captain said. "I shall be happy to perform this task for my lady and for my sister's adopted people."

First, however, Rafik, quick and graceful as ever, sprang forward to plant a kiss on each of Karina's cheeks and each of his uncle's. Mercy Kendoro was beside him and she greeted Hafiz and Karina a bit more sedately. She was not as yet one of the family but Hafiz thought she would make a fine addition. Broad hips, good for making children. And rather lovely, in an otherwise delicate sort of way, and very clever, too. Rafik was choosing his wife far more intelligently than Hafiz himself had—the first time, at least. Hafiz noted this with relief as it was another sign of the boy's suitability for the responsibility of leading the House of Harakamian.

Karina and the captain separated from the group to greet the captain's sister, who had been briefed ahead of time, and her fellow seekers of enlightenment. The remainder of the crew was invited to the community hall at Rushima's chief settlement and Hafiz gestured that they should accept. After all, this trip was from all indications to be a fairly long one and who knew when another opportunity for shore leave might arise? They were to return in time for refueling and taking aboard a few more provisions to top off the ample quantities loaded aboard at Laboue.

When he could be sure they were alone, Hafiz filled Rafik in on the visit from Yasmin.

He did not, of course, come straight to the point, but told the story in proper narrative fashion, building suspense so that when he spread his hands in alarm to show his reaction to the powder Yasmin had blown in his face and how he had lost consciousness, Rafik, used to drama as he was, widened his eyes with alarm.

"I presume there is some point to this, Uncle, to drive you from your home and honeymoon and into space—other than a visit by your former wife who wished you to sleep?" Rafik asked.

"Nephew, has the responsibility I have laid upon your shoulders caused you to become impatient and rude? I am coming to it, I am coming to it, and all shall be made clear. You see, I had the powder analyzed. In addition to the sleeping powder there was powdered horn—and the powder, as it touched an injury on one of the technicians analyzing it, healed that injury." Hafiz let the sentence hang in the air, where it would soak into his nephew's brain like rain into thirsty soil.

"Linyaari horn? But how did they get it?"

"Alas, Yasmin was not disposed to disclose such information, though had she not disappeared by the time I awakened, I assure you I could have persuaded her otherwise."

Rafik went quite pale for someone whose usual skin color was the same golden tan as Hafiz's. "Acorna?"

Hafiz shook his head, a small, careful gesture. He could see the horror and fury building in his nephew's eyes. "We do not know that, Rafik. The universe is wide—it could have come from anyplace. But just in case, Karina and I are making a social call upon Acorna's newfound kinsmen. We will use the charts prepared by Calum Baird and Acorna for their journey. Once we are sure all is well, we shall return."

"And if all is not well?" Rafik asked. "I should go with you."

Hafiz shook his head and waved both hands in negation. "No, no, no, no, my nephew who is like a son to me, you are my heir, the new head of my household. Think of the many enterprises that would fail, the people who would lose their employment, the joy of our enemies, if both of us should perish. You are needed here. If there is a need, we will signal you."

"How? No one here has ever received a transmission from Acorna's home world. It is quite probable that our transmitters and other devices cannot penetrate the depths of space within which the Linyaari planet is located."

Hafiz shrugged. "True, it is possible. But trust me, I will think of something. I was sailing among the stars long before your birth, puppy. I am a resourceful man."

"Also true," Rafik said. "But—"

"My son, is it not written in the Three Books that however small and randomly picked the pebble, if the aim is true and the intention firm, it may yet strike its mark?"

"Still, Uncle, I would feel better if you took an army of other pebbles with you."

"And if all is well with Acorna and the Linyaari? Do you think these people who so prize their privacy would welcome an army? Perhaps one old man and his nubile bride, perhaps even the crew of their ship, but an army? Do I remember incorrectly that these are people so peaceful they would not even fight the horrible Khleevi?"

Rafik smiled and laid his hand on his uncle's shoulder. "Maybe I am wrong when I remember that an elder relative of mine was so frightened by clips of these same Khleevi that he would not leave his compound, much less go face them without an army behind him. Are you mellowing as you age, Uncle Hafiz?"

Hafiz shrugged and scratched his chin. "Perhaps. Or it could be that I do not think these Khleevi, horrors that they are, would have given Yasmin the horn powder without taking parts of Yasmin in return. Therefore I do not feel it is Khleevi with whom we are dealing.

"And I am also of the opinion that anyone less savage than the Khleevi can be bought off. And as my dear Karina does not seem to sense the possible harm to Acorna, I see this journey as both a way to reassure myself and her other adopted relatives of our girl's safety and as a splendid opportunity for commerce. One which I would not have sullied by the presence of an army, for who knows to whom each individual soldier owes loyalty? No, my son, this pebble must fly alone—in a manner of speaking. But my aim is as true as the charts drawn up by Acorna and your ugly senior wife, and my intentions, though more diversified than those of which the Three Books speak, are nonetheless pure. I remain convinced this is the best course of action. Karina and I and our handpicked staff will go alone. We will go cloaked and shielded, of course, and if we find danger, we will return for assistance."

Rafik continued to frown and Hafiz saw with amazement that it was not only Acorna he worried about but his wily Uncle Hafiz, who had chosen his nephew over his son not only because the son had stupidly gotten himself killed but because the nephew was the only family member who could outsmart him.

It brought a brief sentimental tear to Hafiz's eye, which he quickly blinked away as an unproductive waste of moisture. Perhaps he was mellowing. Ah well, that was what a new marriage and retirement were for. But now was not the time to relax his vigilance or dull his wit. He clapped Rafik on the back. "Come, my son, let us see how your new aunt fares at reading the fortunes of these farmers."

Karina had done readings on credit for four mangy chickens, a basket of half-spoiled assorted fruit, a primitive handmade wooden musical instrument whose tone much resembled that of a squealing pig, the squealing pig that resembled the musical instrument, and a set of tea towels embroidered with the patches of the various branches of the Federation service that formed the career path of the embroiderer, who was a burly bearded six-foot-two tractor mechanic with hair the color of butter and eyes like razors.

"Please," Karina said wearily to the captain. "I grow fatigued with the power of my visions. No more, please, no more."

"Just one, Madame Harakamian, oh please, just one," begged a young boy leading what appeared to be a very elderly and crippled individual who looked as if what was left of her hair had never made the acquaintance of shampoo. "My granny sorely needs to see you, ma'am. She's been waitin' on you for weeks and weeks. I'm sorry if we're late, but she has a mighty hard time gettin' around."

"Oh, come now!" Karina said, snapping just a teensy bit. She had been enjoying getting used to leisure and luxury, and these locals had put her through a very grueling day for a few pounds of garbage she would have had to have been very hungry to eat even at her poorest. "How could she have been expecting me for weeks and weeks? My husband and I decided on our journey quite suddenly, made first contact with anyone outside of our own staff only a few days ago, and have not actually been traveling for weeks and weeks."

"Nonetheless, ma'am, she was expectin' you. Granny has her ways, she has. Now then, Granny, sit a spell and visit with the purty lady."

Karina paused. He did seem a very *bright* boy, after all, and with excellent taste and eyesight, so she gestured to the chair vacated by the last seeker of enlightenment and the boy helped the crone be seated.

"Now then, Madame," Karina began, shrewdly guessing that the old lady probably didn't want to know when she was going to find her true love, "can I put you in touch with some departed soul of whose happiness you wish to be assured?"

The old woman fixed her with one clouded eye and one quite bright green one and said in an insultingly mocking voice, "No, Missus, you cain't put me in touch with some dead person. I can do that for my own self if I've a mind to."

Where *did* these people come up with their atrocious accents? Most of them had been required to have quite good educations before being allowed to settle here not so very long ago. And how did this woman get so *old*? Surely the original settlers would have had better genetic material than that!

The old woman, as if reading her mind, cackled at her. "No genes gonna keep me from lookin' old when I'm a hunnert and three years old, Missus. Kept me from bein' fat earlier on though. Looks good on you though, if I do say so, and pleases that husband of yourn. Oh, good, here he is now. He can hear what I have to say to you, too."

Karina was glad for Hafiz's presence as he came to stand behind her, taking one of her hands in his.

"If you don't wish me to contact the departed for you, then what is it you wish?" Karina asked very sweetly, considering.

"I wish you'd quit jawin' and let me tell you what I come to say. I want to put you in touch with the living, girly-girl. I reckon as how you and your man are off to help that horny-headed gal come to save us from them buggers awhile back. It's your man been in touch with his dead, only she weren't dead, and she's been in touch with you, too."

"Why? What do you mean?"

"You got yourself a new golden ring in the shape of a *pie'son'us* serpent, ain't you?"

Karina dug in her pocket and pulled out the ring.

"Look inside of it, you darn fool."

Hafiz groaned and tried to snatch the ring away but, failing, covered the lower half of his face with one hand.

"Hafiz and Yasmin Forever Entwined," was inscribed on the inside of the band.

"A *wedding* ring?" Karina asked.

Hafiz groaned again. "Yes, beloved. I can explain, my heart."

Karina turned back to the place where the old woman and her grandson had been. The chair was empty, the table vacant. She looked at Hafiz, then, truly baffled.

"But—how did you—where did she go?" Karina asked Hafz and the captain.

"Where did who go, madam?" the captain asked.

"The golden-aged woman who was just here? She and her grandson?"

"I saw no one like that, Madame Harakamian," the captain said.

His sister replied, "Machinist Johansson was your last reading, Madame. There's been no one here until Mr. Harakamian arrived."

Karina looked from one of them to the other. "You're wrong. There was a young boy and a very old woman just here. She said she was one hundred and three years old."

The sister exchanged looks with a couple of the other people who had already had readings. "It couldn't be."

"Couldn't be who?" Karina demanded. "Who was she? How did she know about the ring? Where did she go?"

It didn't occur to her that, as the psychic reader in the room, perhaps she should not have had to ask.

The captain's sister looked abashed. "I—I can't say for sure, Madame, but the only person ever did live here by that description was old Alison Ward as used to run the herb farm."

"Well, yes, Naima, but her grandson died in that avalanche years and years before old Alison passed on."

"Passed on?" Karina asked. "I'm sorry, but she was right here, sitting in this chair."

"Oh, old Alison will do that from time to time if she reckons there's something you need to know. Don't let it upset you none, ma'am," a rawboned farmer said gently. "It's just her way."

While the locals were all saying things like "you can't keep a good woman down," and "Alison always did have to get her two cents' worth in," they all nevertheless continued steadfastly to deny having seen the crone or her grandson. Karina, who found she was far more disturbed than she expected to be at having once more encountered what was apparently a quite genuine apparition, turned to Hafiz.

"But you saw her, didn't you, darling?"

Hafiz shook his head slowly, and pointed to the ring. "I do, however, behold that band, the very one I gave to my first wife, who up until recently I fondly believed to be dead. Tell me, Karina, where did you get it, and when, and why did you not mention it to me?"

There ensued a heated discussion—their first argument!—as to why neither of them had told the other about Yasmin. Fortunately, Hafiz was not so distraught by his current wife's omission to mention encountering his first wife that he neglected to order the ship searched from stem to stern.

Yasmin, hardly the sort to trouble herself to escape through any possible handy ventilation systems, emerged, roughly escorted by three crew members and four or five enthusiastic locals. She smoothed her skirts against her thighs and glared at them defiantly.

"Get your hands off my husband, you fat bitch," she said to Karina.

Hafiz thundered, "All bear witness! Yasmin, I divorce you, I divorce you, I divorce you! There! Now, what were you doing aboard the *Shahrazad* and where did you get that powder you blew into my face?"

"Yeah, honey, what's the matter?" Karina asked in a voice she hadn't used since middle school. "Didn't you have the price of a flitter ticket? Is that why you stowed away?"

"I regret only that we did not discover your presence aboard before we landed," Hafiz said. "The customary punishment for stowaways is spacing. I would have greatly enjoyed pushing you through the lock with my own two hands."

"Bully!" Yasmin said. "You'll get yours when my friends catch up with you."

"Where did you get the powdered horn you blew in my face, daughter of evil but idiotic ifrits?"

"That's for me to know and you to find out," Yasmin said.

Hafiz turned politely to the planet's administrator and asked, "Have you a very dull axe, like the one you use to butcher wood for your fires, perhaps?"

"Sure thing, Mr. Harakamian."

While the administrator was sending for the required

implement, Hafiz whispered to Rafik, "Already I regret the necessity for us to arrive unarmed among Acorna's people, to demonstrate respect for their customs and possibly their religious beliefs, you understand."

"Under these circumstances, I can understand that regret, Uncle," Rafik said.

"Alas, I was unaware of Yasmin's presence and her onboard activities. There are other ways to defend oneself than conventional weapons, of course. As you'll see when they bring me that axe. Nonetheless, I shall have to reevaluate our internal defenses in light of this breach of security."

When the axe arrived, it was handed to Hafiz, who bowed graciously to acknowledge the generosity of the person or persons who lent it to him. To the administrator he said, in a voice loud enough for all to hear, "I hope you have no quaint native customs forbidding the execution of criminals? I assure you, my former wife has been convicted on many counts of many heinous crimes."

"No, sir. Out this far from civilization, we don't have the luxury of bein' overly forgiving. You just go right ahead, sir."

Karina saw her husband accept the axe. He nodded to the captain and Johansson, who grabbed Yasmin's arms and maneuvered her into position, her neck exposed and pressed against a handy tree trunk.

Karina held her breath. She could not believe he would do this without recourse to judge and jury.

The crew and the settlers looked extremely calm about the matter, however.

Hafiz took in a deep breath and swung the axe back over his head.

Yasmin, who had known him in his younger and more impetuous years, did not take the situation at all calmly. "Wait! Stop! You can't do this!"

Hafiz lowered the axe and smiled. "Rest assured, seed of a syphilitic she-camel, that I can, and I shall unless you answer my questions."

"I don't know where the powder came from," she lied. "The lawyer who had me released from prison gave it to me. He told me to give it to you and then follow you."

"Follow me?"

"Well, hide myself on your ship." She reached into her décolletage and pulled forth what looked like a tiny jewel. "I've been wearing this, you see. So they could follow you."

"Follow me why?"

"I don't know—robbery, I guess." Hafiz raised the axe again and Yasmin squealed. "Aiyee! I—I don't think they know where the horn powder came from either. They wanted you to lead the way to the unicorn girl."

"Aha!" This made sense to him. They were business rivals, these patrons of his former wife, and wanted to make contact with the Linyaari for nefarious reasons. They hoped Hafiz would lead them to Acorna's people. That made very good sense.

"Administrator, perhaps you need a spare field hand," he said. "If you keep this one in chains, she may be useful to you. But keep her among women only. If she is left alone with men she will be on her back in the twinkling of an eye."

Yasmin spat at him but was led off to the detention cell, to be fitted for chain jewelry. Karina called after her, "Just think of how much karmic clearing you'll be doing, dear! It will stand you in such good stead in your next incarnation!"

"May it come quickly," Hafiz growled. He ordered the ship swept for further transmitters and four more were discovered.

Then the Harakamians and their crew turned their attention to the celebration being held in their honor. Karina wore something even more floaty and lavender and silver than usual and Hafiz thought he had never seen her looking more radiant. "You are a precious pearl among women, my love," he told her. "Lesser females would have upbraided me for concealing a not-quite-former marriage."

She dimpled at him. "Hafiz, you are so *cute* sometimes. Obviously you meant to divorce her—and you did, once you knew she wasn't dead. I *am* attuned to the secrets of the universe, you know," she said. Besides, the servants gossiped, comparing the current Mrs. Harakamian to the last one—favorably, she was happy to hear. "I *did* know you'd been married before. I am only a little regretful for your sake that you chose someone with quite as many Pluto problems as that woman undoubtedly has. But then, we all have our lessons to learn, don't we?"

"Yes, my beloved."

Karina sighed and looked deeply into his eyes. "However, oh mountain of manhood, while you are not now a widower, or a bigamist, but instead have become a properly divorced man, you have nonetheless had your wicked way with me under the guise of a false marriage. I was never a legal wife and so now am only your concubine, your plaything, your—"

He looked back into her eyes, but his hands itched to make the contact more than visual. "A grave matter indeed, my sumptuous slave of scintillating salaciousness. One we should discuss immediately, perhaps, in our bower aboard the *Shahrazad*?"

"And shame me further before all of these good people?" she breathed, but took a step backward. "Oh, master, you are too cruel."

He snapped his fingers and the planet's administrator, Rafik, and the ship's captain all came running. "I wish to remarry my wife at once. Captain? Administrator? You will say the words."

"We're not on board at the moment, sir," the captain said.

The administrator quickly stepped forward and said, "There is a ring?"

Karina slipped off her amythest wedding ring and gave it to the man, who said, "By the power vested in me, I pronounce you man and wife."

"So it has been said, so it will be written, so let it be done," Hafiz said. "You are satisfied, my flower of feminine virtue?"

"Not yet," she breathed and gave him a wink worthy of

Yasmin during their heated youth. "But I expect I will be when we return to the ship."

Hafiz responded by kissing her hand repeatedly, his kisses going higher and higher, up her sleeve and onto her shoulders, portaging the wisp of fabric that covered the shoulder until he ended at her neck, at which time they were called to dinner.

The community hall was not quite large enough for all of the settlers who came from miles around to enjoy the party, so tables were set up outdoors. The weather was ideal for such alfresco dining, thanks to the manipulations of Dr. Ngaen Xong Hoa.

"Useful, this weather wizardry," Hafiz said, scratching his beard.

After a bit of preliminary table hopping, Hafiz, Karina, Mercy, and Rafik took one table, and were soon joined by Dr. Hoa and the planet's administrator. However, some matter or other required the administrator's attention and he was called away.

Dr. Hoa leaned in and spoke confidentially to the three members of the House of Harakamian. "I wish to go with you, Mr. and Mrs. Harakamian. My work is done here and indeed, I have repaired all of the damage I was forced to do while I was a prisoner aboard the *Haven*. My only wish now is to retire to a place where I will not be asked to exploit my discovery any further."

Before Hafiz could speak, Rafik raised his hand, palm out, to stop him, and said, "Uncle, I have known for some time of Dr. Hoa's wish to leave here for a place where he and his discovery will be safe. He wishes to go—where you are going, and regretted that he was not able to accompany our mutual friend there when the first opportunity arose." Rafik, of course, was deliberately employing vagueness and circumlocution in the event that the conversation was overheard. "Therefore, I took it upon myself to inform him of your destination."

"So long as he is the only one, nephew," Hafiz said with a nod to Dr. Hoa. A long journey with the man might provide

Hafiz with the opportunity of convincing the doctor to allow the House of Harakamian to market some small portion of his enviable discovery. "Dr. Hoa is of course always welcome in my home, whether it be on land or in the cosmos."

"You are too kind, sir."

"In fact, I have been pondering a certain dilemma that has occurred due to the tender sensitivities of my wife and me for the beliefs of our dear little Acorna and her people. Perhaps you will be able to advise me."

Dr. Hoa nodded, though he looked a little wary. Hafiz, however, felt certain that the simple homely solutions he was beginning to envision to his security problem would not be offensive to Dr. Hoa's beliefs, any more than they would be to those of Acorna's people.

As soon as the banquet was finished, they made their apologies and took off again, Dr. Hoa smuggling himself aboard with the crew to avoid embarrassing confrontations—or good-byes.

None of them were aware that the detectors used to find homing transmitters were unable to separate the signals given from the transmitter from those emitted by another similar device—such as a replicator.

Eleven

Rocky Reamer and his children, shepherded by Khetala, arrived on Manganos moon base. Khetala had been concerned when she saw the children that they were leaving their home—she was very big on children having a home, since she hadn't had one.

But Turi and Deeter fielded her careful questions about what they were leaving behind with questions about what lay ahead. They were tired of the nano-bug market, and had knocked around the planet with Rocky since they were babies, living in a motley collection of used recreational vehicles tastefully outfitted as combination bedrooms and merchandise warehouses for the jewelry and rocks. They each brought with them their few changes of clothes, a couple of their favorite stones, and, for Rocky, his tool kit, and left the rest for the other traders to scavenge.

Rocky didn't care. Possessions came and went. His family was with him and they were going to be safe, and that was what mattered. Not only that, but he had been able to help Becker and was helping the Lady Acorna and her extended family, and he was sure that was the right thing. To be able to be safe *and* do the right thing was a terrific combination, as far as he was concerned. He breathed a lot easier once Kheti's little craft left the planet, and he and the kids got a big kick out of taking the trip off-planet, the first they could remember, together.

Jana, Chiura, and the other children Kheti had protected while in the mines had heard from the communications officer of the day that their friend was returning to the base. They rushed forward to meet her. Reamer's kids jumped up and down in excitement to see so many other children jumping up and down, even though they weren't quite sure what all the fuss was about.

Close on the heels of the former child slaves were Acorna's "uncles," Calum Baird and Declan Giloglie, accompanied by Judit Kendoro.

Giloglie and Reamer exchanged cautious nods, acknowledging their long-ago acquaintance in a geology class, and Khetala made introductions and explained the situation, then asked Reamer to produce the horn.

Reamer hesitated for a moment. "Do you really think—in front of all these kids—I mean, it's pretty serious and from what I've heard they look at Lady Acorna as some sort of goddess."

Kheti's hard brown face turned up at him and she said, "These kids, as you call them, have already lost most of their illusions. If Acorna is truly in danger, they will want to know and they will want to help in any way they can. If this horn belongs to her or any of the other Linyaari, someone is going to find that we're plenty adult enough to make them pay dearly for harming our friends."

So Reamer showed the horn and everyone looked. Some wanted to touch it and some put their hands behind their backs and looked frightened. One girl, Jana, began to cry softly.

"I remember when I'd been beaten in the mines so badly I could hardly move and Acorna touched my wounds with her horn and healed me—it was the first comfort I had had in years and years. This just *can't* be hers, Kheti. It just can't."

Calum Baird regarded Reamer suspiciously. "Did you

bring this straight to Khetala for her to bring it here?"

"Yes, sir, I did. Becker was having trouble with a lady who seemed to want to rob him or kill him, so he and the cat took off."

"I guess that would explain why he didn't come to us himself. That and the fact that if he thought the horns were valuable he'd want to secure his source," Baird said. "Who was the lady? Did your friend say anything about going to see Hafiz Harakamian by any chance?"

"No, sir. The lady, and I use the term loosely—I'm sorry to be so judgmental but it's true—is about three nuggets shy of a payload. Her name is Kisla Manjari. Her father used to be a big shot."

"We know all about her and her father," Baird said shortly.

"Oh." Reamer blinked. "Oh, of course you do. You guys and Lady Acorna helped bring him down, didn't you? Well, anyway, Becker and the cat figured they should make themselves scarce but he didn't say anything about visiting Mr. Harakamian. He said he knew you guys, though, so maybe he met him through your partner, Rafik."

"It's possible," Baird said thoughtfully. "Laxmi, can you secure a channel for us to talk to Rafik? Uncle Hafiz was headed for Rushima. Let's see if he got there."

They were told that the *Shahrazad* had just left, but that a spy had been discovered onboard. When Rafik told them who it was, Gill let out a low whistle. About the time his cousin Tapha had been killed, Rafik had regaled his partners with a few stories about Tapha's dear departed mother, Uncle Hafiz's first wife.

"So she's still alive, huh? That whole family is amazingly hard to kill," Gill asked. "Well, Yasmin's interference probably explains the unexpected journey Hafiz and Karina are taking in the middle of their honeymoon."

"Oh yes," Rafik said. "My honored aunt blew some powder in Uncle's face that turned out to have ground Linyaari horn as part of its chemical composition. You can well imagine where he's going now."

"Yes, but do you think it's wise for the *Shahrazad* to go alone?" Calum asked.

Rafik repeated the conversation he had had with Hafiz, adding that Dr. Hoa had gone with the Harakamians.

When the transmission ended, Judit was shaking her head. "I don't like it. I just don't like it at all. Maybe an army isn't a good idea, but Hafiz and Dr. Hoa going together—it just sweetens the pot for unscrupulous people like the Piper's daughter." She gave Kisla Manjari's father the nickname the enslaved children had called him when he was still an unknown evil controlling their destinies on Kezdet.

A moment later, the communication with Rushima was reestablished and Mercy Kendoro's face appeared on the screen. "Judit? I think it's about time we got in touch with our brother and the Starfarers, don't you think? If the Piper's daughter and some of his old network are able to penetrate even House Harakamian's defenses, we need to be thinking about security. Has anybody heard from Nadhari Kando?"

They continued talking about a lot of people, most of whom Reamer had only heard of, if that, in grave tones that suggested danger. It was way too heavy for Reamer. He'd done his job and brought the trouble to the attention of the people who should be able to fix it, and had managed to take himself and his kids out of harm's way. He didn't want to hear any more. He didn't want to *know* any more. He was a peaceful sort of guy who mostly minded his own business and let other people mind theirs.

All he wanted was a place to make his living and raise his kids without somebody trying to kill or imprison them. Security arrangements were best left to people who enjoyed being on red alert all the time. He personally was not one of them.

He drifted to the back of the throng of adults and children crowded around the comscreen. A boy too small to see over the heads of the others admired Reamer's belt buckle, which he was at eye level with.

"That's beautiful, mister. What's the stone?"

"Turquoise. Pretty rare now."

"I like the frame you put it in. Is that metal silver?"

"Yeah. I made it myself."

"Wow! I wish I could do that."

Reamer shrugged. "It's not that hard. I brought my tools and a few supplies with me. Want me to teach you how?"

"Boy, do I! I'd love to make something like that with an acornite in the middle. It would make me feel somehow—you know, closer to her."

And so Reamer and his kids stayed on Manganos moon. Reamer began teaching the other kids more about looking for gemstones and how to set them in precious metals. Baird and Giloglie looked in once in a while and expressed the wish that they had time to learn.

Khetala stayed, too, at the insistence of the Kendoro sisters, who felt the younger woman would be in danger from Kisla Manjari's contacts if she returned to Kezdet right away.

And then one day, while Reamer was teaching laser torch work to the little boy who had first expressed an urge to learn metalwork, a new ship called for landing clearance on Manganos. The duty officer, Jana that day, called out to the rest of the people in the com center, community hall, school, and administration building rolled into one, that it was the *Haven* and someone had better fetch Mercy—Rafik and Mercy had returned from Rushima by that time—and Judit. Their brother was aboard.

Reamer went over to the com station to see what all the fuss was about as the *Haven* docked, the hatch opened, and out poured dozens of children of all ages, plus one guy a little younger than he was and another guy a whole lot older, and very familiar.

"Johnny Greene!" Reamer cried when he saw his old friend.

"Well, I'll be, if it isn't Rocky Reamer!" Greene responded, pumping his hand and clapping him on the back. "Who set off enough blasting powder to get you into space after all these years? I thought your feet were rooted dirtside."

Reamer explained.

He had first met Greene through some rock hound friends, years ago, and Greene had had him make a piece for some lady he was interested in back then. They'd hit it off and since then had run into each other off and on over the years when Greene was dirtside, where he liked to cruise the nano-bug markets, or needed another piece of jewelry, or had found some interesting mineral specimens he wanted to unload. Though up until now Reamer had been a wayfarer and Greene had been a space-farer, their paths crossed often enough for them to know they liked each other. When you had similar interests and some of the same friends, it could be a pretty small universe.

"I didn't know you had any kids," Johnny said, when intro-duced to Turi and Deeter. "When did you get married?"

"Right after you were on Kezdet last," Reamer said, pre-tending to look only at the tops of his children's heads to hide the fast blinking he had to do when he talked about Almah. "We had a good life for a while there." He tried a grin and man-aged it. "Now Turi has to look after us."

"They're a handful, too," Turi said in a dry way that made Johnny laugh.

"But look who's talking," Reamer said, indicating the scores of young people and children that now swarmed into the build-ing. "These all yours?"

"Not by a long shot," he said. "The *Haven* is a Starfarers ship. These kids are the survivors of the original crew. The ship took aboard some banditos pretending to be refugees, and they overpowered the adults in charge of the ship and spaced them. Fortunately, Calum there"—Johnny lifted his arm to wave at Baird who was crossing to meet him—"and Acorna were able to help my buddy Markel liberate Dr. Hoa, who was being held by the bandits, and provide sufficient diversion that the kids of the original Starfarers' Council were able to regain control of the ship and do unto the bandits as they had done unto the

Council. I was already aboard as tech crew and the bandits didn't bother me, so I was able to help Markel and the others when the opportunity came. Pal Kendoro also came aboard later to help out. He got a hail from his sisters and the whole ship felt like it was time for shore leave. So here we are."

Reamer shook his head, laughing. "Never a dull moment, eh, Johnny?"

"Not if I can help it. Though there were times when I wished life was a little less exciting, to tell you the truth," Greene admitted.

Later, in the dining hall, when the moon base community was taking its evening meal, the Starfarers joined them. Adreziana, Pal Kendoro, Johnny Greene, his friend Markel, and other members of the Starfarers' Council sat at a table with Baird, Giloglie, Nadezda, and the Kendoro sisters. Normally the adult administrators spread themselves throughout the dining hall, making themselves available to hear any problems or complaints from the student/residents. But the kids were all aware by now of the Linyaari horns that had been found and everyone was anxious to make sure Acorna and her people were well and that no harm had come to them.

Reamer joined the table at Baird and Gill's invitation. Khetala was there, too. He smiled at her as he sat down, but Kheti never seemed to smile. He thought that what had happened to her in the slave labor camps—and after—when she had been taken by the Didis—must have been pretty horrible for her to be so grim.

The other kids from her camp had told him how she had protected them and taken beatings herself to save the younger, weaker ones. And then when she grew too big to work the mines, she'd been sold to the Didis. After Acorna freed her, she had gone right back to the house where she had been brutalized and raped, to help the other girls there learn skills that would let them earn their livings without having to sell their bodies.

Reamer felt ashamed that he had never actually considered that the girls he had occasionally enjoyed in the past might not be enjoying themselves at all, or what might have been done to them to make them flexible and willing parties to any whim he happened to have. His face flushed to match his hair every time he saw Kheti now, or found her looking at him.

Turi and Deeter were at another table that had been joined by some of the younger Starfarers. His kids were listening wide-eyed to the adventures the travelers were telling about their most recent journeys. Poor kids. He had never had the wherewithal to take them off Kezdet. He had been so terrified, after Almah's death, of ending up unable to support them and having them taken from him and sent to the camps.

"Rocky, would you tell 'Ziana and Pal what you told us about the horn?" Judit Kendoro asked. The horn Reamer had brought with him was making the rounds of the table.

He repeated his story. The frowns of the Starfarer captain, her advisors, and the council members deepened as they listened.

"You say your uncle has gone to find Acorna alone?" 'Ziana asked Rafik. She was a bright young lady and not hard to look at, Reamer thought. He could see Pal Kendoro shared his opinion.

Rafik nodded. "It's a big ship but he took no extra weaponry with him, for fear of alienating the Linyaari. Of course, his people are all well trained at hand-to-hand combat, and the ship is equipped with certain long range weapons that would be almost impossible to disable. Still, for threats like the one posed by Yasmin or her employers, he doesn't have much protection. I could see that it worried him, but he told me he would deal with it." Rafik shrugged. "If anyone can take care of himself in a wide variety of circumstances, it's Hafiz."

"Still," 'Ziana said, "they should have some backup. Not to invade narhii-Vhiliinyar, of course, but just to make sure they don't come under attack."

"I wish Mr. Li's forces were still available to us," Pal said.

"House of Harakamian has that kind of resource," Rafik

said. "But I don't think Uncle would appreciate it if I under-
mined his decision by sending an armed escort after the
Shahrazad."

"No," Mercy said. "It would be hard for Acorna's people to
understand that an unarmed Harakamian arriving on their
world followed by an armed House of Harakamian escort is not
the same thing as an armed Harakamian. Besides which, the
course mapped out by Calum and Acorna to narhii-Vhiliinyar
is not common knowledge. It shouldn't be."

"We could go," 'Ziana said. "We're known to Acorna and
the people who were with her. Even though we're armed, we've
a shipload of children. We won't be suspected of trying to incite
a war or coerce anyone, but we could still guard Rafik's uncle."

"We owe Acorna and all of you big time," Markel said. "Not
only for helping us free ourselves from our parents' murderers,
but for healing our wounded and helping us restore the good
name of the Starfarers by taking Dr. Hoa to repair the damage
his weather-control device had done while we were controlled
by Nueva Fallona and her Palomellese gang."

Pal interjected, "That's true enough, Markel, but even
though the current crew of the *Haven* has won a couple of bat-
tles and has some weapons, you're not an army or a police
force. And as you yourself said, you are, when all is said and
done, a ship whose crew is mostly comprised of children."

"That's to our advantage though," 'Ziana pointed out. "We're
Starfarers. We go everywhere and everyone knows it. No one
will suspect we're deliberately guarding the *Shahrazad*. They'll
believe us if we say it was a chance encounter."

"I see that," Pal said, "But we're still not soldiers or police.
Many of our number are still under twelve."

"Some of the fiercest fighters in history have been kids,"
Markel said.

Kheti had been very silent, but now she said, "It's good to
know how to fight to protect yourself and others but Pal is
right. We are none of us professional fighters and if Kisla

Manjari and her uncle are using some of the same network her father once employed, they are very professional indeed."

"Training is all we need," 'Ziana said. "That and maybe a little advice. And the coordinates where you believe the Linyaari home world to be, Mr. Baird. We won't need your course." She glanced at Johnny Greene. "We Starfarers have our own methods of navigating."

The Council members were all nodding. Reamer could see Pal and the others were outnumbered. Pal sighed and said, "Okay, but if *this* adviser could give one more piece of advice—the one member of Mr. Li's staff who is still available, as far as I know, is Nadhari Kando. If you have to have one trainer and adviser, she's the one."

"The last I heard, she was staying in General Ikwaskwan's compound, helping train his troops," Mercy said.

"Now, that's handy," Pal said. "If we need extra fire power it's right there. We could apprise the general of the situation, too. With your authorization, Rafik, we could retain the Red Bracelets on a standby basis in case your uncle runs into further problems."

"That's a good idea, Pal," Rafik said. "Meanwhile, I can speak with Federation officials about possible sentient rights violations. Trafficking in the horns of non-Federation peoples known to be sentient surely must break some kind of law."

"And I can get the authorities on Kezdet off their duffs and launch an investigation into Ganoosh's illegal activities," Gill said.

"I think someone could just try using the secure channels on the com lines instead of everyone going rushing off into space," Judit suggested.

Calum shook his head. "I wondered why Hafiz didn't do that instead of seeking out Rafik in person. Even when he spoke to me, he used a kind of personal code. I realized that he suspected his own security had been breached. As a precaution, I took a look at *our* equipment and programs. They're all manufactured by Kezdet-Kom, which is a wholly-owned subsidiary of Interlay Enterprises, which is owned by a company owned by Ganoosh. Our security programs are manufactured by another of his puppets."

"Just can't get good help these days," Gill growled.

"We'll go find her," 'Ziana rejoined

Kheti said, "I'm going with you. Pal has been out of the camps too long. I can identify quite a few of Manjari's perverts for Nadhari and the general if they need me to. If the Piper's cronies are causing trouble again, I want to personally make sure they're stopped. None of us will be safe until that whole machine is destroyed, once and for all."

"I think that's a little beyond the scope of our mission, Khetala, but you're very welcome," Markel said. The other council members nodded assent.

"Daddy, we should go, too," Turi said. Reamer had been so engrossed in watching the proceedings that he hadn't noticed his kids had wandered over to stand behind him, where they had apparently been taking in every word. "The horn is ours. Mr. Becker gave it to us to help the Lady and her people. We should be the ones to take it to them."

Reamer didn't much like conflict of any kind and the idea of kids doing battle with people like Edacki Ganoosh scared the living daylights out of him. But so did the idea of his kids being plucked up like ripe fruit for Kisla Manjari and her uncle to use as they wished.

If there were going to be lessons for youngsters on how to take care of themselves from a former captain of the notorious Red Bracelets like Nadhari Kando, Turi and Deeter should be in on them. Him, too. Not that he'd be much good at combat. But maybe he could repair weapons or something. Bound to be able to make himself useful one way or the other. And it sounded like a wild adventure.

Johnny Greene clinched it by growling into his ear, "If the manure hits the ventilator in Kezdet, you and the kids will be well out of harm's way coming with us to see Nadhari and the general. You don't think the Kendoros and Acorna's uncles would agree to the Starfarers taking on the recruiting mission unless they thought that was the best way of keeping the Starfarers our of harm's way, do you?"

"Yeah," Reamer said, hoping he wouldn't be sorry. "Count us in, too."

Twelve

The entire city—or village, as it seemed more to Acorna—was filled with the sound of people bidding farewell, the sight of people touching horns, and a long line trudging up to the spaceport, duly accompanied by the Ancestors at their deliberate pace which would make any space traveler itch for warp speed. In a matter of an hour or two, the Fabergé egg crate spaceport was emptied of ships.

Grandam Naadiina, who had been so reassuring the night before, looked suddenly much older as she gazed skyward watching the eggs bounce into the air and disappear beyond the clouds. Then she became very busy about her quarters for quite a while. Maati's lower lip trembled. "What if they don't come back?" she asked aloud.

"The whole fleet? Not come back? Don't talk foolishness, child," Grandam said briskly, but Acorna knew the old lady was as upset as the child.

Thariinye appeared at the open flap. "Just thought I'd check up on you ladies. Liriili felt it was important that at least one responsible, well-traveled male remain dirtside to look after the women and children and show a bit of leadership for the other males."

Grandam's mouth quirked with annoyance.

Thariinye continued. "Of course, I could have had my pick of berths, but I wished to honor Liriili's wishes. The poor lady is overwhelmed right now with so much happening."

"She's hardly the only one," Grandam said sharply. "Khornya was going to go visiting this morning but I hardly think people will be in the mood for guests. Perhaps this would be a better time for her to see the compound of the techno-artisans. Thariinye, perhaps you could demonstrate a bit of that sterling leadership capability of yours by showing Khornya the way?"

"Certainly, Grandam," he said with an eagerness that indicated spending time with Khornya was exactly what he wished to do.

The walk was not long but it was very dull. Thariinye went on at great length about his importance in different organizations and families. Acorna saw some long blue grasses she would have liked to ask about, but he was in the middle of a story of how he came to be elected the *gürange* of the Order of the Irriinje, which he did bother to explain was the name for a noble bird which, on the home world, had lent its name to the similarly noble members of the organization. His babble was annoying, but she knew him well enough to realize it was partly because while the emergency had galvanized him to action, there was no action required of him. His nervous energy had nowhere to go. Had she not had so much else to worry about herself, she might have reacted the same way.

Once they reached the techno-artisans' compound, however, the trip became very interesting indeed. The pavilions were as large as landing bays and had a great deal of shiny machinery and many comscreens, plus huge bins of various metals, rocks, and gemstones. Acorna was enthralled by the central area of the huge main pavilion, where a large egg-shaped spacecraft in the process of having its outer decoration applied brooded over the bustling techno-artisans. It rather looked as if the egg was presiding over the chicken yard, instead of the other way around.

"The hull was shaped two pavilions over," the artisan in charge told her. He was a fraternity brother of Thaarinye's and had been introduced to her as Naarye.

Beyond the ship under construction, in the background, sat two gigantic hulls, their hatches gaping and cavernous. Hulking as they were, they had escaped her notice at first, as other work proceeded in front of them and regardless of them, as if they weren't there. Unlike the ship in the middle, which looked like a flitter by comparison, the leviathans had plain dark paint jobs with no decorations.

"I've never seen such large ships used by the Linyaari," Acorna said. "What are those for? Are they here for repair? Is that why they aren't up at the port?"

Naarye shook his head. "Now those are a piece of Linyaari history, Lady. It just happens that right now they're a piece nobody wants to look at. They're the two big evacuation transports that brought the people of our fair city from Vhiliinyar to Kubiilikhan. The port was built after we arrived, and they're too big to fit up there; besides, nobody much wants to look at them. It takes a crew of at least twenty people fully trained and checked out on that particular model to fly them and far more fuel than we could scrape together at a moment's notice."

Acorna could only imagine that the monster ships would need to escape the planet's gravity well.

"We could have them operational again if we absolutely had to, but it would take time and plenty of muscle to tune up the drives, fuel the vessels, and get them out of here, especially if we hope to leave both them and the pavilion intact. We keep them here because it gives our people a little sense of security knowing they're available, but at the same time, the people don't want to be reminded they might need them again."

Naarye was being more than polite to her but he, too, was clearly affected by giving the transport ships too much attention, so Acorna returned his courtesy by changing the subject.

"I'm fascinated by the decorations on the ship you're working on and the others I've seen. The *Balakiire*'s pattern, for instance, was quite different. Do you determine the designs personally?" she asked. The craft in front of them was being adorned with multicolored panels forming a sort of flame pattern, outlined in what appeared to be gilt.

Naarye beamed and waved his hand in a lordly way toward the spacecraft. "Handsome, isn't it? It is the pennant pattern of Clan Haarilnyah, the oldest clan extant among us. In answer to your question, we"—and here he said a word in Linyaari which was unpronounceable to Acorna, even though she was becoming more facile with Linyaari every day. She understood it to mean outer hull embellishment specialists—"adapt the designs for the hulls from the pennants of a clan or an individual distinguished enough to have a personal banner. We are doing it in rotation according to both their geographical and astrological position on Vhiliinyar in relation to the moons and also according to historical date, in inverse order. We keep very strict records. No one must be offended."

"Of course not," she said. "I'm afraid I don't yet have enough of a grasp on how your—our—society works to understand the importance of the order you mention, but I'm sure it's very fair."

"Actually," Naarye said with a twinkle, "it's entirely arbitrary and meant to sound as complicated as possible so that if anyone takes offense because their pennant has not yet been represented, we can make a baffling enough excuse that they will get off our backs, grateful not to have to hear the explanation of how a geographical and astrological position can be plotted according to moons we can no longer observe and translated to some sort of time order sequence. This lets us do whichever design strikes us as prettiest and most appropriate for the ship at hand."

She chuckled.

Naarye, pleased at the reaction to his wit, gave Acorna a frankly curious glance. "So you are still learning our ways, then, aren't you?"

"Yes," she said.

"I saw you at the reception last night but didn't get a chance to say hello," he told her. "Before the evacuation I worked with your father on the development of some defensive weapons against the Khleevi. Unfortunately, your family disappeared and the invasion struck before we could test them. He and your mother were fine people, though."

"Thank you," Acorna said.

"Did you know that your great-grandmother was responsible for the design of our ships?"

"She was?" Acorna asked, and found she was eager for more information about her family. "What was her name? Did she travel off-planet to study, too? Did she have many children? And what would her pennant have been like?"

The artisan smiled. Like her, and the majority of people in this pavilion, he was white-skinned and silver-maned. His features were not quite so regular as Thaarinye's, however, and the skin of his face had a rather rough, dry appearance, with ridges where his goggles lay against his cheeks and brow, just beneath the horn. His hands were blackened, too, and his clothing speckled with pigment—purple and fuschia on the top layer, along with bits of glittery stuff.

He answered, "Her name was Niikaavri of Clan Geeyiinah. She didn't find a lifemate till late in life, I understand, after she had been traveling in space, learning of alien technology and studying for many *ghaanyi*. She designed the first egg ship with the outer hull in the pennant of her lifemate, as a bonding gift. Her own pennant—ta da!—you see before you."

"Odd that it wouldn't have been one of the first," Acorna said.

He wagged a finger at her. "Don't you start on me, too. The truth is, she never knew what it looked like. Distinguished historical persons are often awarded a special pennant posthumously. This one is a fairly recent design actually not conceived until we left Vhiliinyar and came to this world. You do understand, don't you, that besides beautification, outer hull embellishment has a very serious function as heat and friction shielding material?"

"No, I didn't know that."

That information and other new ideas she gathered as she talked to the techno-artisans intrigued Acorna throughout her tour of the fascinating if baffling processes and techniques performed by the artisans. The most entertaining artisans were those who stamped the large casings and decorative moldings—they performed this function with both hands, equipped with a special glove that joined the fingers in a single block on the end, and feet, and their work resembled a kind of wild stomp dance that they did with great concentration and precision, but also with a touch of amusement at their own antics. Acorna clapped appreciatively and they bowed toward her before returning to their work.

In the next building, the artisans were busy designing flitters. "Oh, so you are going to get them?" she asked.

"Oh, yes," the designer told her. "We have the prototype nearly complete. It's non-polluting, and very beautiful to behold. Once it's finished and we have customized the model, we will return it to Kaalin where it will be manufactured, then shipped back to us fully assembled."

Acorna admired the design, which made a Linyaari riding in one of the airborne vehicles look as if he were a winged creature, the wings spreading out just behind the rider's shoulders, at the joining of the clear overhead canopy with the body of the flitter. The wings were purely decorative of course, but decoration was no small part of technology to the Linyaari, Acorna was learning. Everything the Linyaari artisans made was stunningly beautiful.

Speaking of beauty, Thariinye was quite a favorite with the younger females who worked in the compound. Acorna almost feared she and Thariinye would be asked to leave because of the disruption he caused among them. But the techno-artisans seemed glad of the distraction. She spoke with many of them about their relatives or friends who were studying or trading on other planets, and their worries were almost palpable.

When at last she returned to Grandam's, leaving Thariinye to stroll away with a pretty techno-artisan on each arm, it was dark already.

Grandam was not inside and Maati was already asleep. It took Acorna a long time to settle into sleep, and during that time Grandam returned and touched horns with her, acknowledging Acorna's concern. "I was called out to another general council meeting, pet," she said wearily. "We're still receiving signals from the ships dispatched this morning, but so far none have identified the reason why we are not receiving the more distant signals."

The following morning Acorna tried to visit the homes of the people who had left their gifts at Grandam's door the previous day.

She carefully gathered the nicest grasses she could find as a peace offering, then set out for the home of the young male she had grinned at. At the flap of his pavilion, she inquired if she might come to visit.

After a few moments the flap was opened by an older female, who announced that her son had gone off visiting his former schoolmate. She projected a picture of a lovely black haired, black skinned Linyaari with a white blaze from her horn down the center of her mane/hair to the middle of her back. Also in the thought was that the girl's full coloring, her long face, very down-turned, slightly flared nose, and curveless arms and legs were far more beautiful than Acorna's pallid coloring and somewhat shorter jaw line and nose.

"I'm happy to hear that, ma'am," Acorna replied. "I simply wanted to apologize for my social error at the reception. Where I was raised, baring one's teeth is often a sign of friendliness and welcome rather than hostility, as it is here."

"You must have been raised by rather strange people," the woman said with a lift of her brow.

"Very good people, actually but, well, I'm glad your son is enjoying time with his friend and not—"

"Not in space?" she asked dryly. "He serves a vital plantside function as a communications officer. Our people do not *do* space given a choice. It is good of you to apologize, but quite unnecessary. We were all very fond of your parents, of course, and Neeva is a fine lady, so when we heard you were returning, we were anxious that our son meet a girl from such distinguished stock. We hoped he would find in you some of those qualities that make the rest of your family so admirable. But with your, shall we say, unusual, background, I fear you just aren't really suitable for our son. So you needn't bother to call again. Now, if you'll excuse me, I have much to do. Good day."

Acorna was glad tent flaps could not be slammed.

Other than that, no one was actually rude to her but, as the pavilions all had both a front and back flap, and the people Acorna was going to visit could undoutedly hear her coming long before she arrived, it simply appeared that everyone she wanted to see was extremely busy that day, each going about his or her typical Linyaari day, whatever that was like. From what Acorna could tell, it seemed to consist of grazing. Far away. She sighed and nibbled on the handful of grasses she had. Making friends was going to take a while.

Somehow, she decided, as irrational as it was, because her arrival coincided with the crisis, she was being held responsible for it.

Grandam Naadiina was busy with the council and often came home late. She briefed Acorna on what developments there were, but actually, there weren't that many. The main thing that took time was the Linyaari desire to reach consensus in decisions, which required a great many discussions and much trying out (at least hypothetically) of different tacks until one they all agreed on worked. Of course, in this case, without more input from the persons off planet, not much could be decided. Grandam Naadiina was a bit disgusted. "It's a wonder we ever got off planet before the Khleevi arrived," she said. "I'll bet it took them less time to invade our world and turn it to rubble than it did for the council to decide what we would call this world."

Maati was exhausted when she came home at night, after running errands and carrying messages all day long.

Acorna spent much of her time visiting with the techno-artisans, who didn't seem to mind if she watched them work or asked questions. Daytimes not spent with them were difficult for Acorna, who nevertheless tried very hard to learn all she could of the rest of her people.

Linyaari always seemed to be walking in pairs or larger social groups, and when she approached, they were always heavily engaged in intense conversations about matters she had too little knowledge of to even ask an intelligent question. On the rare, desperate occasions when she tried to interrupt, people would politely but pointedly excuse themselves and turn their backs to continue their conversations. Even the business establishments seemed to be closing just as she approached.

"Is there no school I could attend, no class to take, no tutor on Linyaari culture to teach me what I need to know?" Acorna asked Grandam Naadiina.

The old lady looked rueful. "We learn our own culture from our parents, from growing up in it. There has never before been an outsider—so there has never been any need to teach how to be Linyaari to one of our own. And truthfully, you seem fine to me. Except for that smile at the reception, I cannot tell you any particular thing you are doing wrong. If you had grown up among us, no one would criticize or complain of any of your words or actions. But you did not grow up here, you see, so even though you are Linyaari the others still see you, if not as a barbarian, at least as someone *not* Linyaari. And neither I nor the Ancestors can tell them differently. Ours are a very *stubborn* people about some things."

"I see," Acorna said. She did, too, and she didn't like it. As different as she had been among the people who raised her, still, many had been willing to give her a chance, to at least find out who she was. They had not just fed and clothed and educated her, they had loved her, even when they must have found her appearance and her behavior extremely strange. They had simply worked around her differences and helped her adapt to their world. Here, where she looked so much the same, she felt different as she had never before felt in her life. Remembering Gill, Calum, Rafik, kind Mr. Li, the clever Kendoros, and wily Uncle Hafiz, she could have wept with longing for them.

She shook her head slowly. She would never have imagined that her own people, the people Neeva and the others had said could read feelings and heal wounds, as she could, would be so hard for her to reach. "It is almost as if they are afraid of me," she told Grandam.

"Perhaps they are," Grandam Naadiina said. "Your arrival has shown me that our people have become very skittish since our exodus from Vhiliinyar. I don't really know what to tell you, dear, except to be patient with them."

Acorna nodded and did her best.

When she returned for the fifth time to try to pay the dress-makers, they were closed, as they had been every time she approached. She noticed that the pavilion beside theirs was quite busy, however. Two lines of Linyaari went in and out.

One line consisted of pale-skinned, silver-maned Linyaari such as herself. They were going in.

The other line was comprised of the more colorful, and pre-sumably younger Linyaari, spotted, brown, black, red, gray, golden, so many different colors of hair and skin colors.

Acorna decided that since she had nothing better to do and these people did not appear to be engaged in private conversation, she would, very quietly and trying hard not to think any alien thoughts, join the line.

She told herself simply to be receptive, to learn what the line was about. What she heard were remarks such as, (Brilliant! I don't know why no one has thought of this before!) (It's the very latest. Everyone is doing it. Except those who— you know—go *out there* all the time.) (And to think, remember when we were children, and everyone *wanted* to look like that? All colorless and bleached out? This look is so much healthier!) (I think it's only because it is so much younger looking—perhaps because we've become conditioned to think of Linyaari of color as the young ones who did not endure the journey and who do not remember the home world.)

When she reached the pavilion, she began to notice that some of the multicolored Linyaari emerging were wearing the same clothing as the strictly white Linyaari who went in. So. Acorna couldn't help smiling. Gill might say they were now horned horse people of a different color. When her turn came, she was offered a smock by an attendant wearing a horn-hat. This was interesting. Acorna had thought the horn-hats were only for formal wear but perhaps those working with the public sometimes wore them to partially shield themselves from the multitude of thoughts, feelings, and attitudes coming at them from several directions at once.

"Please enter the minipavilion, remove your clothing, don the smock if you wish, and ring for your personal colorist," the attendant told her. Acorna was moving away as she heard the attendant repeat herself four different times. That would be a good job for a robot instead of a sentient being! Or a shelf full of smocks and a recording!

But Acorna went inside, took off the dress and the beautiful belt, put on the smock, and rang for her "personal colorist."

The colorist was of a reddish brown color, with her mane golden streaked with white. "What do you recall as being the skin of your birthright?" the colorist asked.

From the friendly way she spoke, the colorist no doubt had failed to recognize Acorna as the pariah of the planet. Acorna said, "I was born in space and so I have always been this color."

"A shipborn and you want to try color?"

"Yes. Is—is that forbidden or somehow against custom?" she asked, fearing she was making another social faux pas.

"Oh, no, my dear. Simply very daring. The star-clad and the space-going caste have always been, shall we say—vain—of their lack of coloring up until the great transference. Now, with most of us having been bleached out by the journey—" The colorist's golden eyes were rueful as she spread her arms and shrugged.

"You, too—you used to be the same color as me?"

"Still am, darling, under the cosmetics and dye. Tomorrow I could be black if I liked, or roan. But today, this is the real me. Now then, what, do you suppose, is the real you?"

"I hardly know. Are there—rules about color?"

"Not really. Of course, your paints tend to breed paints and that sort of thing, but we Linyaari have been very open about that for generations. You can be anything you like at all. I myself am not exactly au naturel." She tossed her head so that the fringe above her golden horn flipped in a saucy way. "I call this look aural sorrel. None of us were ever born this way but so what? It is my art to improve upon nature. So, sweetie, how about you? What'll it be?"

Acorna was tired of trying to blend. "Stripes," she said. "Zebra stripes."

"Zebra?"

Acorna projected a mind picture of the beast she had viewed vids of while still a child aboard the mining ship. The colorist giggled and began working on her.

"You'll stand out for sure in these," she said. "I must say, it's rather an attractive look."

"I seem to stand out whether or not I wish to," Acorna said.

She had made herself conspicuous, to some extent out of rebellion against being isolated from her fellows, but her unusual appearance had the opposite effect, at least on some of the younger Linyaari. They commented favorably on the stripes and asked about them, then invited her to a ring-toss tournament.

Watching the boys and girls catching circlets of flowers on their horns and tossing them back and forth, keeping them away from the opposite teams, made her feel unusually young and giddy again, a feeling that continued until a loud crack of thunder heralded sheets and spears of red and green lightning splitting the sky as an earthquake might split the ground, and torrents of rain poured down on everyone, washing all of the colorful paint jobs down into the grass, beating the flowers into the mud and making footing so slippery that many people stumbled and fell running for shelter.

A great wind came up, so forceful that Acorna fully expected to see the pavilions tumbling along the ground like wheels, but of course, the structures only gave the appearance of being fabric and poles. They were actually quite sturdy. In fact, the storm gave her an opportunity to observe another feature of the buildings. As the ground flooded, the floors of the pavilions rose, extruding ramps leading up from the ground to the raised floor. The central poles pulled in, too, so as not to attract the lightning. In fact, other poles suddenly appeared on the outskirts of the compound, specifically raised to attract the lightning.

"Power collectors," a very wet Grandam Naadiina told her. She came in shortly after Acorna and laughed to see the running black dye on her skin and hair. Grandam herself was thoroughly drenched but after a brisk toweling for all three of them—Maati had been closest to the pavilion when the storm broke—and hot herbal teas all around, Acorna was back to her original color of hair and skin and all of them were a great deal drier.

It was a very noisy night, but the miraculous pores of the pavilion fabric kept out the damp and most of the wind, leaving only a heady feeling due to the ions charging the air.

"Tell us a story, Grandam," Maati begged. "Tell the one about how the Ancestors left their old home to come to Vhiliinyar."

"Very well," Grandam said. "Long ago, very long ago, before the first Linyaari was born, the Ancestors lived among other species on a distant planet. As they do even now, and as they have passed down to the Linyaari as their legacy to us, the Ancestors possessed horns with the power to heal and to purify air and water.

"They were, as we are, peaceful creatures, who desired nothing more than harmony among themselves and with all the other animals. They were shy and fled at the first sign of trouble, and would stand and fight only to defend themselves or one another, or occasionally some weaker animal preyed upon by a stronger one. They lived high on the mountains and deep within the forests and their powers were valued by all so that they had no natural enemies.

"And then one day to the forests and the mountains came a new species that walked on hind legs, as we do, and carried tools and weapons with its forelegs. These creatures were not overly bright, they were not kind, and they were very, very arrogant. They cut down forests and diverted streams and rivers. They dug up plants and laid bare the ground to plant crops of their own choice. Some of these crops the other creatures, including our Ancestors, found quite tasty, but the newcomers were selfish and did not wish to share and slew any animal they could find who wished to sup upon their crops.

"The Ancestors thought that some misunderstanding was occurring. They believed all creatures to be reasonable, as they were, and except for food and mating needs, to be peaceful, as they were. But it was quite evident these new creatures—men, as they were called—were not understanding their place in the scheme of things.

"The Ancestors decided to attempt to communicate with them but they feared the males, and so they would attempt to find one of the younger females when she was alone and converse with her, show her how the air and water could be pure, show her how wounds could be healed. This was a grievous mistake, for the most part.

"The young females told the males, who felt that the horn's power was inconveniently attached to large, swift, shy creatures who knew where and when they wished to deploy the power. The men began systematically to hunt our Ancestors until many many of them were dead or captured.

"Of the captured Ancestors, some were slain but some also escaped, after observing the ways of the men in their dwellings. They felt that some of the things the men could do were very great powers as well.

"But overall, it was a tragic situation for our Ancestors, and they used the power they had always had to communicate with other species and each other to cry for help. As they were hunted and harried, the cry became louder and more desperate until at last it was heard.

"Off-world spacecraft arrived and offered refuge to the Ancestors, taking them aboard but at the same time, causing an atmospheric disturbance that produced a great flood that covered all of that planet. The Ancestors grieved to see many of their fellow creatures destroyed, but they found it hard to grieve for men.

"The beings who had found them were the Ancestral Hosts. They, too, communicated by thought, but unlike the Ancestors, they stood on their hind legs like men. They took the Ancestors to Vhiliinyar. Over the years, the Ancestral Hosts, because of the love between the two species, began to genetically blend with them. Eventually, a race arose made of the best of both the Ancestral Hosts and the Ancestors—the Linyaari. Gradually the space-faring race blended with our own, and then left, or perhaps just died away, for they were shorter-lived than the Ancestors.

"But the Linyaari remained, and many of our Ancestors remained, and we all remembered, to remind us of the dangers the Ancestors had once faced on that other world, and to teach us that while we must sometimes share our gifts with others, we must also beware and keep our home hidden from them, lest our enemies find us once more."

"We *are* the *ki-lin*!" Acorna said excitedly. "Or rather, the Ancestors are! My guardian, Delszaki Li, told me of the Ancestors from mankind's viewpoint. He came from a very old people whose memory predated the great flood of which you speak. They revered the Ancestors almost as much as the Linyaari."

Grandam yawned. The herbal tea was taking effect. "I'm glad our story pleases you, Khornya. I haven't seen you look so animated since you arrived."

"I think I'm finally starting to adjust," Acorna admitted, sleepily.

But the next morning, as she was leaving for the techno-artisan compound, Acorna was intercepted by a breathless Maati, whose eyes were round, wide, and wet. "Khornya, Khornya, I came right away to tell you. We're not getting the routine signals from the *Balakiire* anymore."

"Since when?" Acorna asked.

"Earlier this morning, about three *kii* ago." A *kii* was roughly fifty-seven minutes of Galactic Standard Time, Acorna had learned. "Everyone else is finding out now but I wanted to come to tell you myself," Maati said. "Khornya, I'm sorry." The young girl began to cry, which helped Acorna to control her own fears enough to put her arms around the child, hug her, and rock her.

"There, there, Maati. They've probably just been affected by that same problem that's blocked communications from the other missions—the one all the ships went to try to fix. Grandam says most likely it's some sort of equipment failure and as soon as one of the crews identifies it, it will be fixed and we'll be hearing from everyone again."

"Do you think?" Maati asked.

Acorna was glad that Linyaari children weren't psychic, so that Maati couldn't tell how frightened for Neeva and the others she really was. "No doubt. If the *Balakiire* has lost contact, that means they're also closer to the source of the problem. The others won't be far behind on their way to their own destinations, so probably one of them will have an answer for us soon."

But the answer, as the days progressed, was that with one ship after another, contact was lost. Relatives and friends were informed of each successive failure to receive a ship's signal. In the interests of security, signals would not be sent from the planet to a ship which could no longer be heard from. Everyone knew that the Khleevi could be listening, and find narhii-Vhiliinyar by tracing the signals. That was not a thing that could be risked. All over Kubiilkhan, all over narhii-Vhiliinyar, eyes turned heavenward as the planetbound searched skies which were silent except for the sound of thunder and the clatter of rain and hail.

It seemed as if the storms brought with them such an unescapable wash of anxiety, regret, fear, and grief that Acorna paced with restlessness.

"Grandam, I feel so useless. I need to be active, to be of service. You and Maati come home exhausted every night. Can I not relieve some of your burdens somehow? If not yours, then perhaps Maati's? Surely if a child can do her job, I could, too."

"Hmmm," Grandam sighed wearily, sinking onto her pallet, which was still dry thanks to the raised floor. The inside of the pavilion was dark now and confining rather than cozy with the flaps closed against the rain. "A very good suggestion, Khornya. Our people need more than ever to stay in touch with what's happening, with the crisis, with what the government is doing about it, and with each other. I, for one, would welcome your help."

While heading toward Nirii, the crew of the *Balakiire* distracted themselves from worrying about what might await them by imagining the parties they were missing.

(I just hope we'll make it back in time for Acorna's bonding ceremony,) Khaari joked.

(I think you're being a little premature,) Neeva responded. (I'm afraid if the new *viizaar* has her way, my niece will be put to work picking seeds from the grass and replanting them by hand or some such chore. Liriili is unbonded herself.)

(I get the feeling she prefers it that way,) Khaari said. (I think you are being too hard on her.)

(Not intentionally,) Neeva said. (But Liriili is a very complex person. I fear all of her thoughts and motivations are not known even to herself—possibly that is what makes her such a good administrator. She would convince herself that whatever she was doing or not doing was for Khornya's good or the good of the planet.)

(If you mean sending us to Nirii, at least we've learned we have lots of company. Other ships were dispatched not long after we left,) Melireenya put in.

(I wonder that they didn't leave more of the fleet on narhii-Vhiliinyar,) Neeva said. (What if the Khleevi should attack while we're gone?)

They all shuddered and tried to suppress images of all the people planetside biting down on suicide capsules.

(That's not going to happen,) Neeva said firmly. (The Khleevi got a taste of their own medicine at Rushima and will not think we're such easy targets again.)

(At least not any time soon,) Melireenya said. (But after this current crisis is dealt with, our government needs to put a bit more thought into defensive strategies and weapons again.)

(And we must find another world to evacuate to. It's not enough to keep ships and personnel on hand at all times should evacuation be necessary. We need a place to go,) Khaari said.

(No,) Neeva countered. (Wishful thinking is no substitute for the kind of defense we saw at Rushima. We simply cannot just keep running from world to world and letting the Khleevi destroy everything we leave behind. When we return home, I believe we should approach the Council about getting our trade allies to join something like the Federation Khornya's people belong to. I believe the time has come to take a stand.)

As they approached Nirii, it was decided among them that Neeva, as the ambassador, would take the shuttle to the surface, landing in the Linyaari-occupied district of Nirii's principal continent's principal city. The rest of the crew would remain aboard the *Balakiire* in orbit around Nirii.

Because the crew of the *Balakiire* did not know what to expect, the ship had not made her usual contact with the com base in this sector of the planet. When someone of Neeva's stature paid a visit, it was customary to do so. But under these circumstances, the notice was waived as an unnecessary risk.

Neeva stepped out of the shuttle and onto the empty docking bay. Normally between five and ten shuttles stood here at any given time. As she gazed around the cavernous space, Neeva knew that something very wrong had occurred here.

She had made her landing cloaked and under cover of darkness, a moonless night with a light snow falling from a dark pewter sky emptied of light. The rest of the city was full of lights, all white, all small, and seemingly strung along orderly grids. This time of night the streets and skies were empty. Though there was no curfew and little superstition on Nirii, the people were nonetheless extremely conservative and self-contained. They conducted their business during the day and their home life at night, period. Like the Linyaari, they were inclined to use thought-talk, but they did so only privately, among friends and family, after heavy mental shielding was released. There had been no crime here for a number of years, nor had there been any war, making the people of this planet ideal trading partners for the Linyaari, particularly since they were a highly scientific and technologically inclined people.

The Linyaari district was not required to follow Niriian customs but usually did, in Neeva's experience. But she saw no signs of life, no footprints of people or animals or any other species as she walked down the street between two of the four large dwellings that faced each other across a square. Centering the square was a park where athletic events, lectures, entertainments, and meetings were held. The building appeared, at least from the outside, to be totally deserted. She entered the door to the building on her left. It was unlocked, and irised open at her touch. This wasn't too surprising. The residents of Nirii did not lock their doors as a rule.

The building felt sterile, devoid of life or any evidence of it. The doors to the cubicles had been removed, and gaped at her as she walked past them, peering into empty apartments containing no furnishings, mementos, or equipment. Each building had contained eight apartments, and all of these were empty, in each and every building. Neeva could catch not a whisper of thought, not a spark of raw emotion.

She returned to the outside, her skin crawling with the unnatural silence and emptiness of the places where some of the best and brightest of her people had lived while learning, teaching, trading.

As she stepped out onto the park, her feet disturbed the layer of snow on the ground. She noticed that the native grasses her people had planted here were untended, dead. Nor had there been anything remaining to eat in the indoor gardens that each apartment customarily boasted. There had, in fact, been no way to tell which room served which function, so completely empty had the former dwelling places been.

But beneath her feet the soil, snow-covered as it was, was beginning to tell her something at last. Anger and fear, confusion, interrupted sleep, interrupted mating, longing for loved ones who were not there, the cries of frightened children and some, not much, but enough to scare any resisters, actual pain.

She was so busy absorbing these impressions that she failed to hear the snow-muffled footsteps of the party approaching her until it was too late to run back to her shuttle.

Leading the party was the large, double-horned, heavily built form of her old friend and primary negotiating contact, Runae Thirgaare, along with some other Niriians unknown to her. And behind them, four uniformed people who looked very like those who had sheltered Khornya.

"*Visedhaanye ferilii* Neeva," the Runae said to her with less warmth than usual in her greeting. "I am afraid we can no longer welcome you and your kind among us."

"Why not?" Neeva asked. "Where are the others?"

One of the uniformed strangers stepped out from behind the Runae. "We will take you to them, *Visedhaanye ferilii* Neeva," a hornless woman almost as large as the Runae said. "We are Federation forces and have detained your people to assist us with our inquiries into certain criminal irregularities we are investigating at this time."

(Runae, please, speak to me yourself. What is happening here? You know I have only just come from my own world. What crimes could my people have committed? You know us as well as your own!)

(Not quite as well, *Visedhaanye*. Your people *are* inclined to some wildness and peculiar practices. They are unpredictable. Ours is a well-regulated world. We have no idea what trespasses you may have committed elsewhere. It's to be expected, of course, of those who are deprived of the stabilizing influence of a second horn. I'm sure there is nothing to worry about. These people are from the regulatory body for a large federation of allied worlds far beyond us. We are, at their behest, considering membership at this time. So you see that of course we must respect their request for extradition.)

"For what criminal irregularities are we being charged?" Neeva demanded of the hornless beings.

"We'll explain it all along the way," the woman said.

She looked very familiar to Neeva. Her uniform particularly looked familiar. Wasn't it very much the same one as was worn on Rushima by the troops that had assisted in the repulsion of the Khleevi attack?

Neeva pondered this as she was hustled past her own shuttle, which was being transported to the same place she was, a larger vessel with some official-looking markings on it. It wasn't until the uniformed woman began to push her into the hatch, pushing down her head so that her horn did not catch on its upper flange, that Neeva recalled that the troops who had assisted on Rushima were not allied with any Federation. They were a private army of mercenaries under the command of one General Ikwaskwan.

Thirteen

Grandam was as good as her word. Acorna joined Maati and several other couriers in carrying messages back and forth from the governmental compound to the citizens at large. Despite grave concerns about the situation in space, Acorna felt better than she had done since her arrival now that she was able to be useful and somewhat a part of things. Being a government messenger also gave her a much better idea of the communities in the area and the scope of settlement on narhii-Vhiliinyar than trying to make contact on her own had done.

Besides the central compound, mostly composed of government officials and workers and their families, many of which included one or more members who were now on active duty as emissaries in space, and the large techno-artisan compound, there were many other petals to the flower that formed the populated area of narhii-Vhiliinyar.

Naturally, Acorna had realized there had to be more people than she had met thus far. From the air she had seen what looked like a large flower garden spreading out over the continent upon which the *Balakiire* landed.

Now she realized that this flower garden was but a single

bloom—the center was the government compound, and extending from it, connected by road and common grazing fields and plains, were the technoartisan compound, an educational compound (mostly for those who wished to study off-planet cultures—it was assumed that Linyaari would need no studies in how to be Linyaari, unfortunately for Acorna), an agricultural experimental farm where new food stuffs were developed and tried, and other functions.

One compound was mainly devoted to very senior elders who did nothing but contemplate higher philosophies and mathematics. The remainder of their compound was staffed by junior people who studied with the elders and supplied their practical needs. Grandam Naadiina said she had gone through that phase fifty *ghannye* ago and found it far more entertaining to be with the younger folk in the central compound. They were much more amusing, and laughing, she said, helped her stay youthful.

Narhii-Vhiliinyar had no mining and very little manufacturing, despite the bins of raw materials in the techno-artisan compound. Those were all imported.

Surrounding these compounds were the communities whose labor and expertise staffed the various enterprises, while beyond them, in semicircular clusters, were smaller units of the same sort, independently producing other products and supplying other services to their communities. Beyond the plains were low mountains and there, she was told, was where the Ancestors dwelled when not performing the ceremonial functions they had taken it upon themselves to offer.

Acorna could well understand why Maati was so tired at the end of every day. She could also understand why the young girl did not need to be in school. Walking and even running to the various homes, businesses, agencies, and other message stations within the central compounds was quite educational in and of itself.

Thariinye complained that Acorna had so little time to walk out with him and accept his "tutelage" and indeed, when she was not on duty, she was far too glad to be off her feet to wish to walk anywhere with anyone. So she was quite surprised when carrying a message to the agro-farm one day to sense great hostility from a young woman, with ruddy skin and black hair who was sorting seeds into packets for distribution throughout the planet.

"Have I done something to offend you?" Acorna finally asked, though she couldn't imagine what it might be, aside from the usual prejudice she had felt when she first arrived.

That had diminished somewhat now that she was frequently seen to be serving an important function among her people. She supposed it was also that she was harder to avoid and too busy to notice, most of the time, any lack of friendliness.

The woman's anger and dislike were evident not just in unvoiced thoughts, however, but in the stiff way she held herself, the angry way she wrestled the seeds into their packets and sealed the packets as if imprisoning the guilty seeds for life. It was evident in the flashing of her big green eyes as she darted glances at Acorna while she was delivering her verbal message from Liriili, and in the snappishness of her voice when she finally attempted to dismiss Acorna.

"Isn't it obvious? First you bring trouble to us so that my father is sent off-planet to solve it—"

"Wait, wait. What trouble? Who is your father?"

"*Aagroni* Iirtye. He criticized you and you used your influence to have him sent away."

"My *influence?*" Acorna said. "Feel free to read my thoughts. I have no influence here. If anything, I have the opposite of influence. And I have nothing to do with the problems that sent your father off-planet."

If the woman took her up on her offer, she did it very quickly, and she looked away for a moment, confused, and then back up. "And then—and then there's Thariinye. Why won't you release him?" the woman demanded.

"Release him?" Acorna asked, quite baffled.

"You don't care for him, you don't even like him, I can see that, so why are you taking him as a lifemate? He means nothing to you and he m-means *everything* to m-m-m-me!"

"You're telling the wrong person this!" Acorna said. "You should tell him if you feel that way! I have no claim on him whatsoever. He was the first Linyaari male I met and is an old shipmate with whom I've shared certain adventures, but it's his idea entirely that we should be lifemates, not mine!"

The girl looked puzzled, and wiped at the tears of anger and frustration that flowed down her cheeks. "I can tell you're speaking truly, but I thought . . ."

"What *I* think," Acorna said with sudden insight, "is that Thariinye is no more interested in me than you seem to think he is in you. I believe he likes all of the attention from all of the eligible females and doesn't wish to settle yet with one—by seeming to choose me, when he must know I don't feel that way about him—I suppose he feels free to take his time making another, more suitable choice. He's not unkind and I doubt it occurs to him that he is causing you pain."

"It's true he—he doesn't know how I feel. I knew he was promised to you and so I concealed my thoughts, thought pointedly of plowing furrows and planting when he was around and"—she blushed—"I suppose he took my metaphor literally." She sighed. "He is such a *lusty* fellow, it was very hard, I mean difficult, I mean . . ."

Now Acorna was amused. "I definitely think Thariinye is the one you should talk to. Good luck."

Her amusement faded as she went about her other errands. It was true that Thariinye was not her choice for a lifemate, but on a whole planet of beings similar to herself, with many eligible males, she had not thus far met anyone who was.

In fact, Pal Kendoro, who was not even the same species as she was, inspired more warm feelings in her than almost anyone she had met here so far except Grandam and Maati.

So if finding her a mate was part of the reason for her being here, it wasn't working out. And she would much rather be taking her chances with her aunt and the rest of the *Balaküre's* crew, or any crew, than stuck down here with no real purpose and no ability to influence events or people.

What if the Khleevi had returned, what if the radio silence was because the ships, the crews, the other planets even, had all been destroyed, invaded?

Acorna firmly shook her head and put that out of her mind. It did no good to worry about such things. For the first time in her short life, it did no good to do much of anything but wait and watch and hope for the best. She did not think she was going to be very good at it.

"What do you mean 'detained,'" Melireenya asked the official on the comscreen. She had a hard time believing she was having this conversation. The Niirians were the last people she would have expected to behave even rudely to the Linyaari ambassadors or tradespeople. Niirians were courteous and ethical, like the Linyaari themselves, punctilious and moral almost to a fault.

"We do apologize, madam, but the circumstances were totally beyond our control, as we explained to *Visedhaanye* Neeva. Probably your ship will only be impounded for the time it takes to retrieve your original representatives and return them to you, but in the meantime, our orders are very clear."

"Not to me," Melireenya said. "And I'm good at reading minds. So please enlighten me. What is it that your orders say?"

"All Linyaari coming within our spheres of influence are to be detained for diplomatic reasons. I'm afraid I'm not privy to the reasoning behind this. I am so sorry to be the bearer of such distressing tidings, madam. You have been a good friend for many years."

Melireenya softened. The young official's voice held genuine consternation and his horns seemed to droop with shame. "As you have been to me, Snoraa. I suppose there is no alternative but to trust our old friends one more time?"

"None, I fear. But I will take it as a personal matter of honor that no harm befalls you or your crew."

"I appreciate that assurance, Snoraa. Did you issue the same courtesy to my lifemate?"

From his silence, Melireenya guessed that Snoraa had — or at least had concerned himself with the fate of Hrronye and his students.

"May I speak with the *visedhaanye*, please?" she asked politely. Neeva had taken the shuttle to the planet's surface, feeling it a wise precaution until she knew what had become of the missing Linyaari and why they had sent a distress signal home.

"The *visedhaanye* has been detained as well and is presently incommunicado, madam. Please dock your ship in bay one one four and present yourself and your crew to the guardians who will greet you there. I will do what I can to assist but my job, you understand, is to insist upon your compliance with my orders at this time."

Melireenya had attempted to send another message back to Vhiliinyar. Like her previous attempts since coming within the planet's orbit, her transmission met with no response.

Unable to contact base for further orders and worried about what was happening to Neeva, she saw no viable alternative but to comply. From the transmissions they had been receiving from the other Linyaari spacecraft, she and Khaari had determined that most of the fleet, if not all of it, was now deployed. Unlike the *Balaküre*, the rest of the ships were not investigating a distress call, but rather a widespread radio silence on behalf of the diplomatic, trade, and educational missions stationed on various planets. She opened all channels in an attempt to reach the other ships, to apprise them of Nirii's odd behavior, but was met with the same silence that greeted her calls to home base. Something was very wrong.

She sent out a general Mayday, with no response whatever. Her only consolation was that none of this seemed even remotely like a Khleevi attack or invasion.

But as she prepared to land, she felt a deep sense of panic

like none she had ever experienced. She thought that the elders must have felt this way in the old stories when, attempting to make contact with a hostile species by communicating with its least dangerous members, the young females, they found themselves instead surrounded by armed males and were taken into captivity, the purpose of which they did not truly understand to this day.

Her fears were well founded. No sooner had she landed than a team of uniformed people, not Niirians but very much like the people among whom Khornya had been dwelling when the *Balakiire* located her, boarded the ship. Two of them forcibly removed her from the command seat while two others removed Khaari from hers and still others swiftly took over the controls at both of their stations and demanded the access code to the ship's computer.

"Who are you?" she demanded. "What gives you the right to tamper with a sovereign Linyaari vessel? I demand to see Runae Thiirgaare at once."

"Take it easy," a burly young man who seemed to have no hair at all told her. "You are under arrest by the Federation Forces and your ship is being impounded."

(Don't worry, Melireenya,) Khaari's thought came to her. (They will have difficulty impounding us unless we cooperate.)

(Then why do I feel us lifting up again?) Melireenya returned.

(Oh, dear. This must be one of those tractor beams we've been hearing about that allows us to be towed by another ship. I didn't see one, though, did you?)

(No. But they may have been cloaked.)

Over the com system, Snoraa's voice could be heard demanding that the vessel ask for clearance but the uniformed people paid him no heed.

"What are the charges?" Melireenya asked. "And for that matter, what are the mysterious crimes that our people are supposed to have committed?"

She was picking up a welter of feelings and confused

thoughts, most of them violent, angry, or lustful toward her or her fellow crewmen, or disrespectful of the bovine-like Niirians. They were lying, that much she knew. All of them were lying. But they were following orders, which was how they earned their living.

"Well, let's see, ma'am, what were those charges again? Resisting arrest, fleeing custody, failure to render assistance in a medical crisis, nondisclosure of residence, crimes of omission against the various environments under Federation protection. That's for a start. When we think of others, we'll let you know."

"That's nonsense!" she said. "Narhii-Vhiliinyar is not part of your Federation!"

(And to think, we were just discussing whether or not it *should* be,) came Khaari's thought.

"Oh, yeah, that's the other charges," said the uniformed ruffian. "Criminal trespass, entering Federation galaxies without a license, abduction of a Federation citizen."

"Abduction? The only person who accompanied us was the niece of *Visedhaanye ferilii* Neeva and she came willingly and eagerly to her home world."

"We'd just like a chance to check that out, ma'am," he said. "Suppose you set this egg back on course for your home world and we'll ask the citizen in question ourselves."

"We can't do that," Khaari said.

She had been watching the woman who took her seat trying to access the navigation system.

(Create a diversion, Melireenya,) Khaari said.

Melireenya screamed and lunged forward, pointing and screeching out the words to a Linyaari poem she remembered from her youth.

Khaari took advantage of the distraction to slip in closer to the woman sitting in her seat, who had swiveled around to see what the commotion was. Khaari was able to make two swift keystrokes before the woman turned back.

(There!) she said. (Thanks.)

(Were you able to delete the course information?)

(Naturally. Had we been able to complete our sequence before they boarded us, it would have done so of its own accord. It's a good thing we Linyaari have good memories for navigation.)

The woman in the navigator's chair swore something ugly and violent.

"What's the matter, Brill?" the man with no hair asked.

"It's gone!" she said. "I had almost accessed the route when—you erased it!" she said to Khaari.

"It's self-deleting," Khaari said, which was true enough. "After all, we know where we've been already."

"Yeah, but how do you know how to get back there?" the man asked.

"That is a matter of planetary security," Melireenya said. (If they can talk like petty bureaucrats, so can we.) "Now then, speaking of abductions, if you are the people who have abducted our ambassador and other members of our diplomatic community, we must insist you release them and us immediately."

"Yeah, well, tell us who is going to make us and how we can get to talk to them and maybe we will," the man said.

Khaari was staring at them. (Those aren't the uniforms of Federation Forces, Melireenya.)

(I noticed that. These are the same uniforms worn by the troops on Rushima. Mercenaries. Now, what do you suppose they are up to?)

(I have the unhappy feeling we're about to find out.)

Fourteen

There was no doubt in Becker's mind whatsoever that he should space the android. The damned things had homing beacons that left indelible electron trails for the owners to follow in case of loss, theft, or, on very rare occasions, defection. Furthermore, there was no way to remove the damned beacons that Becker had ever heard of. Even if he inactivated or destroyed the android completely, the beacon would take the lickin' and keep on tickin.'

Of course, if he spaced the android, the homing device would go into space, too, and kinky Kisla could follow it into infinity for all he cared.

The thing was, Becker just could not quite bring himself to throw out something so useful, so potentially salvageable. So ultimately valuable. He hadn't actually *tried* to deactivate the homing beacon on an android before. People abandoned androids very rarely and if an android happened to be the sole survivor of an unfortunate space accident, it was unlikely there'd be anybody left to follow the beacon, even if whoever found the droid could not legally claim salvage rights. Surely if he tried, he could do it. But Kisla wasn't a problem to be sneezed at.

RK jumped on the droid's chest and kneaded big rents in its tunic. This was accompanied by a lot of drooling and the cat rubbing the top of his head under the android's chin, then rubbing the sides of his mouth against the droid, cat lip curled upward as if smelling something nasty.

"You don't think you marked this thing enough already, huh?" Becker asked. "Come on, cat, we have to space this dude."

But when Becker started to lift the android a second time to haul him to an airlock, RK took a swing at him that would have ripped his hand open if it had connected. The cat's back was up and his tail bristled.

"Hey, look, I know he followed us home but you can't keep him, dammit, and neither can I. He's bugged."

For a cat in the business RK was in, the feline member of the crew did not seem to take technical difficulties as sufficient reason for infringing on his territory. He snarled menacingly, ears flat, eyes narrowed, back feet clawing on the android's chest much in the way bulls were known to paw the ground before charging.

Becker swore and sat back on his haunches, hearing the cat on the one hand and the steady bleep on the other. "I've got half a mind to leave you both off on some rock and let *him* take care of you if you're so crazy about him," Becker said. The cat remained unimpressed. They both knew that Becker would not do this, however unreasonable RK was, as the android would sooner or later attract Kisla Manjari and he would not wish her attentions on his worst enemy, much less his usually more or less convivial shipmate.

"Okay, okay. Will you let me haul him up to the bridge then so I can watch where we're going and probably, who's coming with us, while I try to disable the beacon?"

The cat marked the android again, then lightly jumped to Becker's shoulder and wound purring around his neck, claws close to his jugular, just in case he tried something funny. Becker hauled his and everyone else's asses up to the bridge just in time to spot one of those rare wormholes, uncharted by anyone but Theophilus Becker.

"You're beautiful, baby!" he said, blowing a kiss as the *Condor* dove into the hole.

He wasn't sure how effective those electron trails were through wormholes but with any luck at all, maybe he could buy a little time this way.

The hole spit them out in the same chewed up galaxy where he had discovered the trashed planet with the horned cat toys.

Becker returned his attention to the android. Now he really had to get that transmitter disabled. He dug in to the task at hand. The cat looked on as anxiously as an expectant father.

Becker kept hoping that if he fooled around long enough, the cat would do what he usually did and get bored and wander off someplace to sleep, but of course, that was what *Becker* wanted so no way was RK going to do that.

Becker was concentrating so hard he was sweating, and meanwhile that annoyingly regular little bleep continued. After a while, RK's possessiveness subsided enough for the cat to start noticing the bleep, too, and taking an interest in it. An intense interest. The cat stalked up and down the recumbent length of the robot, across the open control panel, waving his newly fluffy tail under Becker's nose as he walked between Becker and what he was trying to work on.

"Look, cat. A little cooperation would be appreciated."

RK, much to Becker's surprise, backed off a little, looking offended, sat down and began washing his right front paw. Both ears, now that he had two again, were cocked forward at an extreme angle. Becker stopped working for a moment to watch the control panel again.

When he glanced back at RK, he saw that the cat's ears twitched very slightly with each bleep, and the critter was hunkered low, into stalking posture, his hind end wiggling with suppressed excitement as if he was about to spring.

"Don't look now, cat, but unless the digital navigation system is on the blink again, we're homing in on the planet where we found the horns. What do you think? Should we give it a fly-by? I think we've probably got enough time to disable the transmitter. We've been weaving through wormholes like a demented spider. It's gonna take Kisla and company awhile to get here. I vote we land and get this over with, then split."

RK did not vote out loud, but instead sprang for the android's neck, where the cat began biting and digging at the plastiskin with his claws.

"Oh, is *that* where the homing beacon is coming from?" Becker asked. "Okay, if you'll move your furry carcass I'll see if I can disable it and reprogram this dude."

With a little physical persuasion, and the inducement that the man was actually doing what the cat wanted him to anyway, RK eventually subsided and Becker was able to concentrate totally on the android—so totally, in fact, that he lost track of time and place. He felt peckish and grabbed a handful of cat food but, after having to fish some of the food pellets out of the android's inner workings, he gave up on snacking.

He had set the *Condor* on voice control for most functions. The voice control had the voice of Buck Rogers. For a while, Becker had used the usual ploy of having the computer sound like a husky-voiced woman, but he'd found he wasn't getting much work done. He was always heading back to port to find a pleasure house. Now he used the voice of a heroic space voyager. He figured that would help him be proud and happy to be voyaging among the stars.

So, with Buck's backup, and having committed himself to the task of debugging and rehabilitating the android, Becker gave it his full attention. Locating the main axis of the homing beacon wasn't the only problem. The damned thing was thoroughly integrated with both the central nervous system and the circulatory system of the android. The wiring had to be removed completely and redone with minimal harm to the KEN unit.

Becker was very good at this kind of thing, when he wanted to be. It was one of his talents, prolonged intense focus on a single complex problem. Unfortunately, although the ship was still under his command, the part of his brain not devoted to work-ing on the android was occupied fully with the problem at hand. The ship told him about wormholes and black water, space pleats and folds, and he took physical control long enough to negotiate through or around these, but all the best part of his brain function was devoted to the problem lying on his ship's deck. He really didn't register how long his work was taking until the *Condor* came within the orbit of the planet where they'd found the horns.

As he was just then managing to extract the last of the hom-ing beacon, the *Condor*'s computer had to clue him in. "Captain Becker, do you wish to land? Or would you prefer to crash in a dramatic, explosive ball onto the surface when at last we have orbited until we run out of fuel?"

Becker looked up from his task. The extraction of the hom-ing beacon had been successful. The bleep was gone, though it was almost as if he could hear the echo of it in his head, he'd been listening to it for so long. RK had finally gone to sleep and had opened one eye when the computer spoke.

"What? Oh, guess we should crash. No, just kidding, Buck."

"Not funny, Becker. You programmed me with a sense of humor, but I did not find that amusing. I was already imple-menting the orbit by the time you said no."

"Of course I programmed you with a sense of humor—oth-erwise I'd have taken a crowbar to you years ago. The cat isn't much for laughing at my jokes."

"I'm waiting, Captain Becker. This planet, however, is not. It continues to exert its gravitational force upon me."

"Oh, yeah, okay. Let's set down in that green patch where we found the horns the last time—you have the coordinates, right?"

"Accessing . . . can't seem to find them, Captain Becker. Will that open volcano crater do just as nicely?"

"What? Huh? Are you crazy? Of course not!"

"Just kidding. I accessed those files nanoseconds and nanoseconds ago!"

"Now I know why usually I run the ship myself and talk to the cat!" Becker grumbled.

He figured he would have plenty of time to put the android back together after they landed. He'd have to wait to dispose of the deactivated beacon in space again. He certainly didn't want it to lead Kisla Manjari to this planet. He finally returned his attention to the landing procedure.

"How's it going, Buck?" he asked the computer.

"A-okay, captain. There is just one little thing I thought you might wish to be aware of, however."

"What's that?"

"The tail of a space liner seems to be extruding from the outer atmosphere. It looks as if it means to set down beside us."

"I don't suppose we could take evasive action?"

"You're kidding again, right? Where would we take it? Between the last few centimeters of atmosphere left—well, not any more—between ourselves and the ground? Sorry, Captain, we've landed. The other craft must have been cloaked."

"I don't suppose we have that capability, do we?"

"Afraid not. Besides, they know where we are," the ship said.

"Well, just a minute then." He spoke to the comscreen. "Hey, you, with your tail hanging out, identify yourself! This is Captain Jonas Becker of the *Condor*, flagship of Becker Interplanetary Recycling and Salvage Enterprises, Limited. My company has already got dibs—staked salvage rights, I mean, on this planet. Uh . . . ," he continued, as there was no answer, ". . . I don't suppose you're a derelict in distress looking for a tow, are you?"

Kisla Manjari's face appeared, grinning, on the comscreen.

"Nope, I didn't think so," Becker said, disgusted. "What's the matter, princess? Forget your receipt?"

"Oh, no, Captain Becker. It's just that you go such interesting places and find such interesting things, I wanted to come along. I sent my droids to find out where you were going next, but you killed them. Well—all but the one whose track we've been following."

"There now, RK, what'd I tell you?" Becker said to the cat. "Another fine mess you've gotten us into!"

"Oh, is the nice kitty there? I still really really want to play with it," Kisla said. "I've heard so very often that there's more than one way to skin a cat and I really want to find out."

By now, Becker had a visual on the *Midas*, totally uncloaked and a largish dot in the multihued twilit sky.

"You're a sick cookie, you know that, don't you?" Becker asked.

"Why, thank you."

Meanwhile, he opened the emergency cat flap in the hatch. Normally, from the hatch's opening to the ground on a given planet was a bit of a leap for RK, and the cat used the robolift for an elevator in the same way that Becker did. But Becker had rigged the flap up for just such occasions as this—not that there'd been many occasions such as this, but Becker had a healthy imagination and a goodly amount of paranoia. He turned off the comscreen, grabbed RK before the cat had a chance to protest, and shoved him down the chute that led to the cat flap. He then opened the cat flap with the remote. He got a visual of RK sitting among the grass on the ground, licking himself vigorously, and then, as the other ship landed, bolting for the rough ruin of the landscape beyond the grass. RK would have sense enough to steer clear of Manjari, as long as he was free to do so, Becker knew. Becker was pretty sure he himself could outmaneuver her, but RK shouldn't be trapped in the ship. In fact, if he left the ship himself, he might succeed in escaping her and it might not occur to her to attack the *Condor*. After all, the only thing he could think of that she wanted from him was the horns and this was where they'd come from. She had what she wanted. If she couldn't find him, she'd more than likely take her booty and run off to do whatever it was she meant to do with it. Finance a fleet made from a higher caliber of cast-off parts, maybe.

He didn't suit up this time. It would just slow him down and he already knew he didn't need to for this atmosphere. He did slip on antigrav boots, however, the ones he wore on planets with gravity far heavier than that of Kezdet. He didn't want to take the time to lower the robolift. Instead, he opened the hatch and jumped out. The boots bounced him back up a couple of meters, and he sprang for the hinterlands, as if he was Jack wearing the seven league boots from one of the old fairy tales Dad had encouraged him to read in between physics texts in an attempt to give him back a little of the childhood that had been stolen from him on the labor farm.

He should be able to get away before Kisla emerged from her ship, he thought, feeling very cocky as he left the grass for the rocks. It wasn't until the bolt from a stun gun mounted in the ship's side sliced through him that it occurred to him, in one last flash of thought, that Kisla probably had no need to leave the ship to bring him down.

None of the people who invaded the holy place were able to see him, so well did he blend with his surroundings. But he saw them. Saw the first spacecraft land and the small furry animal, the same one who had come before, first fall from the craft's belly, only to twist in midair and land on all four paws. It momentarily licked itself, then came running—straight toward him. None of the people had seen him, but the small furry creature headed his way immediately, past the sacred place and into the rocks where he lay concealed.

The other ship descended and as it did, a man bounced out of the same ship as the one that had carried the animal. The second ship landed, and a bolt of light shot from it. The man was on his third bounce, almost safe behind one of the hillocks of rubble created by the Khleevi when they destroyed this world. The man was the same one who had come before with the animal. He had the same smooth face and forehead. He did not look like a Khleevi and he did not act like a

Khleevi. The Khleevi did not run in fear. They caused others to fear.

The animal had reached the hidden one, had greeted him with soft twinings and loud rumblings, seeking sanctuary. It had watched, wide-eyed, as the man fell. It had changed its body so that it grew to twice its size and the pointed ears lay flat on the head. The rumbling had given way to the sound air makes when escaping the lungs of someone punched in the stomach.

The second craft landed. Four people came out of it. There was a small one with a loud voice, and three larger ones. The small one moved with certainty, the others had less.

The small one walked right to the man, pointed to him, and indicated that the others should carry him. They did so, carrying him back to the grass between the two ships. The small one began to kick the body all over.

That was when the little animal burst from the rocky cover and leaped across the grass, into the midst of these intruders who, although they looked like the first man, appeared from their actions, from their—energy—to be Khleevi after all.

The hidden one shook and felt sick. He could not bear the Khleevi again, he was sure he could not. They had hurt him beyond repair before. He could not face them again, not even to save their new victim, for he knew he could not save him.

The little animal had less experience, though. It dove straight into the middle of them in a howling, angry whirlwind of fury, blood, snarling, and screaming. The blood appeared to be mostly from the small biped in the center. The noise seemed to be coming from all of them.

And then, all at once, another light bolt and the furry creature fell to the ground. A silence fell upon the group.

The people still standing looked much different now. Their clothing was torn, one of them covered an eye with his hand, and their faces were a network of scratches. The small biped had her—for the voice sounded female to the hidden one—hand to her throat and red blood streamed from between her fingers.

She sent a vicious kick into the body of the little beast and it flew to the edge of the grass.

Then she began once more to beat the unconscious man, until one of the other men stopped her.

The hidden one rocked and cried and grieved and wondered if perhaps—perhaps the little animal could be saved without the Khleevi noticing. There was enough power nearby to heal it, if the wounds were not already fatal.

On his belly, the hidden one slithered toward the edge of the grass where the small body lay.

Fifteen

ecker had definitely had better days. The pain in his leg was intense. Kisla's kicking reminded him of the time he had dropped one of those Myrathenian morning stars on himself while trying to store the damned thing. Lots of little sharp pains. Speaking of which, it looked like Kisla and her gang had lots of little sharp pains themselves. RK had apparently come back; their faces definitely bore his signature. But where was the little demon anyway? Becker raised his head to look around. The eye that wasn't busy swelling shut saw the small furry body by the edge of the—moving?—rock.

Kisla's boot aimed at his jaw. Becker caught her leg in one hand and jerked. She fell on her butt. Somewhat to his surprise, though her crew showed him their weapons, they did not intervene. Come to think of it, he wasn't all that surprised that they didn't. These were humans, not androids. Working for Kisla probably had a few uncomfortable side effects.

"Shoot him!" Kisla screamed.

"Calm down, princess. What did I ever do to you?" he asked. His voice was a little slurred. Apparently one or more kicks had done more damage than he thought.

"You cheated me is what! You destroyed my droids—"

"You poet, you," he said.

"And you lied about the horns! You said there was only the one! You lied! I found another horn. Where are the others?"

He sighed painfully. He really had to get rid of her and go see about the cat. "They're right here—all around. I just took a sample or two."

"He's lying," one of the crewmen said. "There's nothing here. I've been looking."

Kisla kicked herself free of him and stood up, but she stood back. "Okay, time to make him tell! Let's take him back to the ship."

"Before we go through all that, why don't I check his computer banks and see where he found the horns, and if this is the place? Meanwhile, you can keep him on ice while we make a more thorough search for the horns." This was proposed by a sane-sounding man, a high-ranking member of Kisla's new crew, judging by the decorations on his uniform.

"I give the orders here," Kisla said.

"Yes, ma'am. I'm just trying to suggest a fast way to check on what the man's told us."

Kisla liked to give orders but she wasn't stupid. The guy was making sense. She hesitated.

"With your permission then," the man said, not making it a question, and turned to go.

Becker sat up again, unhooking the remote from his belt. "Here, buddy, you'll need this. Red green blue red." He could cooperate with sane people. It wouldn't do to get Kisla excited again.

It was a good move. The other two crewmen tied Becker up—well, taped him up, having apparently brought along a roll of silver tape just for the occasion. They only let Kisla get in two more kicks before they distracted her by rooting around, looking for horns. During the time they were doing this, Becker noticed that RK was no longer lying where he had been. That was interesting. Could the little guy fake being hurt? Nah, surely not!

After a while—Becker didn't know how long as his consciousness seemed to fade in and out, along with Kisla's dainty little foot—the crewman who had gone up into the *Condor* returned. He was carrying the sack that contained the horns. Becker groaned. He'd gotten used to a sweet-smelling spaceship and had been sort of hoping Kisla wouldn't find the horns so he could heal himself.

"Well?" she demanded.

"This is the place all right. Not on any of our maps but the coordinates are the same ones he marked before. Here are the horns. This all there were, buddy?"

"I didn't think so," Becker said truthfully. "That's why I came back. But the light's not that good. Maybe we took them all the first time." He tried to shrug but his shoulder had stiffened up too badly.

"Your droid is a mess," the crewman continued his report to Kisla. He brought out the mess of wires and syn-tissue that Becker had extracted from the droid. "Here's the homing beacon. You know, your uncle—I mean you—figured Becker here would make a beeline back for where he found the horns. This very likely is the place."

"Maybe," she said. She had the sack now and was pawing through it. "Where did you find these, junk man?"

"Lying around on the ground here. Don't ask me why. I didn't get it off any living girl, if that's what you're thinking."

"That's too bad, but it can be remedied later," Kisla said.

And just then a series of explosions shook the ground, shooting blossoms of dirt and fire in a more or less straight line toward the *Midas.*

"What the hell is that?" one of the crewmen asked.

"Asteroid shower?"

"This planet has obviously undergone some kind of destabilization recently," the fellow who had boarded the *Condor* said. "I don't think we'd better hang around very long. Want to take Becker here along with us, ma'am?"

Kisla grinned through her sharp little teeth as another

explosion rocked both the *Midas* and the *Condor*. "No." She snatched the remote from the crewman's hand, threw the unit to the ground and stomped on it, grinding it under her heel. "We'll leave him. No food or water here except on his ship, which he can no longer board. He'll have to eat the cat—hey, where did the cat go?"

Another explosion erupted beside her before she could answer. She kept her mouth shut as the crewmen herded her aboard the *Midas*, which prepped for takeoff in record time. The ship rocketed back into space like a scalded cat.

Speaking of cats . . .

Becker passed out, only to awaken when something wet hit his face. Cat drool. RK, looking no worse for wear, stood on his chest, kneading sharp claws into it. He no longer lay beside the *Condor*. It was dark, and he didn't hurt anymore. Not anywhere.

If someone had offered to make Edacki Ganoosh king or emperor of the universe, he would have turned them down. He did not wish to have ultimate power or ultimate responsibility or ultimate visibility. He far preferred the joy of playing puppet master and pulling the strings that manipulated people and events for his amusement. Presently, he was both very happy and highly amused.

His network's tentacles had extended far beyond his customary haunts, into new galaxies where his allies had allies who had allies and those allies had allies who were quite accustomed to dealing with people who fit the description of the Linyaari. Also, like the Linyaari, these particular people were said to be quite advanced and peaceable and law-abiding by nature. Ganoosh, though he was not fond of abiding by rules himself, was very fond of such people. They were so much easier to control. Sometimes he wished his ward were more law-abiding but then, if she were, she probably still wouldn't be alive now. She would have been much less trouble, but also much less useful.

He was, in fact, quite anxious to hear from the dear girl. The *Midas* had not communicated for a very long time. The willful child was probably just trying to keep her dear guardian in the dark. He was greatly pleased at how quickly Ikwaskwan had taken control of the situation, his mercenaries now patriotically serving as Federation peacekeepers, traveling to the far-flung, non-Federation worlds that had been harboring the Linyaari renegades. These staunch uniformed troops let the non-Federation worlds know that continuing to aid and abet the Linyaari would sadly lead to a show of force on behalf of the Federation, which could not allow such people to just go running out of its jurisdiction after committing the interesting array of offenses Ikwaskwan and the others had dreamed up. As Ganoosh had suspected, the worlds frequented by Linyaari were as staid and peaceful and law-abiding as the unicorn girl's visitors had claimed their own world was.

Ganoosh considered it a great pity that the Khleevi Ikwaskwan's men had helped defeat had no known allies or common language or communication with any other race. He felt that such ferocity as they were known to exhibit could be of value to his enterprises.

The com unit sent forth a blast of the static that it was patented not to emit and then Kisla's voice preceded her indistinct image on the comscreen. "Oh, Uncle Edacki, we have failed! Daddy is furious with me, I'm afraid, and says I am not fit to command a starship. Please please please don't be mad at me! It was the crew's fault really. They were such sissies when I wanted to torture Becker. They didn't even want me to kick him around or kill the nasty cat."

"Calm down, sweetheart, and tell Uncle Edacki all about it now. You must remember the crew are corporate employees, not information-gathering specialists. I should have thought to send one along but I was trusting to your natural talent. I can scarcely believe you got your hands on the man and did not find the place from which the horns came or secure any more of them."

"Oh, I found it, all right. At least, I found the place he got the first ones from. But there weren't any more and there are only a dozen or so in his sack."

"I have a hunch he is holding out on you, darling girl. Do ask him again nicely."

"I *ca-a-a-n't*," she wailed miserably.

"He got away?"

"No—I sort of, you know . . ." She made an approximation of the sound of a laser burning through flesh. She did it very well, and it was a difficult and unpleasant noise to reproduce.

"Did you let your enthusiasm get away with you before you investigated thoroughly, Kisla Manjari?" Ganoosh asked her sternly.

"Nooo! Really, Uncle! We checked his computers and according to them it was the right place. But after I zapped him, these little explosions started going off everywhere and the *Midas* was about to be hit so we took off and left him. We can always go back if you want us to, and take his ship and check the computers again."

"No, no, my dear, that would most likely be unproductive. I should have known persons such as the late Mr. Becker would have no truly valuable finds to share with us, no matter how prettily you asked."

"You're not cross, are you, Uncle? Perhaps you could send me to the school, you know, where your information extraction specialists learn their trade. I know I can very helpful in this work if you'll just give me another chance."

"Oh, precious, don't fret your little head about it. Of course I'm not cross with you. You did get more horns. All the horns Mr. Becker had. And I have no doubt but what, if a school for information extraction specialists existed, you would, except for that little tendency toward impatience of yours, be at the head of the class in no time. In fact, with your natural talent, I'm sure you could be an instructor."

He saw her well enough now to discern that she was blushing with pleasure. Positive reinforcement worked well with this girl.

"I have so much faith in you, in fact, that I want you and the *Midas* to undertake a new mission."

"Oh, goody! What is it? Do I get to extract information?"

"Certainly, my darling girl, and from a wealthy and pampered pair of newlyweds, one of whom is a very close personal friend of your own close personal enemy . . ."

"Which one?" she asked eagerly and he could see her taking inventory of people she knew of who filled his description. "Oh, Uncle, you don't *mean* that wily old sheik, do you?"

"Now who is wily? You figured that out immediately. Bright girl. Good girl. Yes, I'm afraid the stupid Yasmin allowed herself to be found. To buy her own head she betrayed the tail I had on her. I expected no better, to tell you the truth. However, Harakamian's ship the *Shahrazad* has just left the Rushiman orbit. Fortunately, Yasmin apparently did not feel it necessary to tell her captors about the secondary monitoring devices she placed aboard the ship. We are still able to get a fix on the Shahrazad without difficulty."

"Can I kill Yasmin for you when we get back?" Kisla asked. "She shouldn't have tattled on our surveillance ship."

"I'll think about it. Patience, remember, darling. Yasmin has her limitations but she may still prove useful if I can retrieve her from the settlers—preferably after she's done a bit of hard penal labor to remind her who her friends are. No, I want you to follow, properly cloaked and shielded, until such time as you can board the *Shahrazad* and take the Harakamians prisoner. At that time you may use any methods you wish to determine the course Hafiz is employing to reach the unicorn girl's home world."

Kisla was beaming. "Uncle Edacki, you are the *best*. I'll find out for you at once!"

"Make it so, sweetie. And Kisla? Lovie?"

"Yes, Uncle?" Her impatience was now again evident, along with a certain defensiveness, like a dog who was afraid its treat would be snatched back.

"You're not to go there once you find out. Just relay the

information and detain the Harakamians until I give you further orders."

"Awww, *Un*cle!"

"Kisla!" he said warningly.

"Oh, all right. May I hurt them while I detain them? Even if I can get the information some other way?"

"There will be sufficient opportunity for that, dear heart, once we have the information you are after. Hafiz Harakamian has many secrets and I'm sure you will enjoy cajoling him to confide in you once I tell you what it is I wish to know. But that can wait. Now, scoot! You've a job to do, Commander Kisla!"

"Yes, *sir*," she said, blew him a kiss, and the screen went dark.

Some aspects of Ganoosh's plans were going even better than he could have hoped.

His teams had found an entire chain of planets destroyed by the Khleevi. While the planets themselves were depressingly without commercial value, one of them had a serviceable moon. With the help of biosphere-type prefab experimental stations, it was soon able to support sufficient personnel for his purposes. Ganoosh installed his teams of scientists and security forces. The former were told what to look for and the latter were told where to find subjects. Nothing could be simpler.

General Ikwaskwan reported back to him via remote relay, and the reports were enormously satisfying to both Ganoosh and the general.

One by one, the Linyaari trade partners were being identified—occasionally by the Linyaari taken into custody, and more often by the trading partners themselves. A few of the trading partners had proved awkward, but forceful persuasion generally was all it took to sway them into surrendering their Linyaari guests, and the location of any trading partners they knew about.

Two large, secure wards were currently filled with the white, single-horned humanoids. If things went well, there would soon be more. More horns and more likelihood of breaking one of the Linyaari and finding the location of their home world.

When the most recent arrivals were herded into the biosphere, General Ikwaskwan was in residence, listening to the complaints of the scientists. These unimaginative men claimed that they had all of these subjects, but unless the subjects could be observed doing whatever it was they supposedly did, the scientists would be unable to proceed. Linyaari were extremely stubborn, for a peaceful people. They seemed to be able to communicate without words, leaving the scientists continually feeling as if they were being discussed, even though the Linyaari never spoke in their presence, not even to complain, once they realized what the scientists wanted.

"Sedate them," Ikwaskwan said. "Put them in cold sleep until you need them. I don't care."

"I thought so!" a loud, nasal, feminine Linyaari voice rang through the sphere. "General Ikwaskwan! Are these your people? There has been some mistake. You know who I am. Please tell them to release me and my crew and our people at once."

Ikwaskwan didn't know the lady in question at first. For a heart-stopping moment, he thought he had actually captured Harakamian's niece, Acorna. But no, there was something — older, about this woman. "Madam, you have the advantage of me," he said, with a mocking, courtly bow.

"I'll refresh your memory then," she said, dragging her captors nearer to him. He signaled for them to let her go. "I am *Visedhaanye ferilii* Neeva of the Linyaari people of narhii-Vhiliinyar. I demand to know the meaning of this outrageous imprisonment of myself and my people. The trumped-up charges your people used to abduct us are so patently ridiculous, I'm amazed you were able to take us without a formal protest from our hosts."

"Your hosts stood to gain a great deal by the transaction,

madam, if you know what I mean," Ikwaskwan said. "Besides, we were able to convince them that while you may be well-behaved in your own sector, you were definitely a criminally disruptive influence in ours. You are to be congratulated on finding so many supremely stodgy allies."

"Neeva, save your breath," said another of the newcomers just as loudly, as if she thought they were all deaf. "There's been no mistake. Obviously he is no longer an ally."

"Very astute, dear lady. I put my superb mercenary forces at the service of the highest bidder. As you see, the highest bidder has changed since our last meeting."

(Neeva! Is it really you? Oh, beloved lifemate, how I have longed to see you, but not here and now.)

Ikwaskwan was rather amused to see the fight go out of Neeva as her attention was drawn to the others of her kind in the biosphere. He hoped what was said but so far unproven about this race was accurate. Otherwise they were a waste of good air and food, as far as he was concerned.

He shrugged and left them to the scientists. He was ready to return to his own compound for a time and reunite with Nadhari. He had some rather splendid plans that would make good use of her. He planned to put her at the service of Ganoosh, whether or not she was willing.

The titillating but distracting struggle for power between them would be over for the moment, if he did so, but it would be delicious to break her time and time again. Of course, the real point was to see how thoroughly these supposedly miracle-working Linyaari could put her back together again. She would never forgive him, of course, but that was part of the fun of it. The joy in conquering a woman was in playing the last trick and this, surely, would be the best trick anyone had ever played on Nadhari. Just to be sure he would be the one doing the taking, not the other way around, he brought along a company of the best troops he had who had *not* been trained by her.

* * *

When the remaining communications officer buzzed the comlink in her room to tell Nadhari she was being hailed, she asked, "The general, I presume?"

"As a matter of fact, ma'am, no," the officer said. "This is another party. They've been cleared to speak to you, with your permission."

"You have it," she said abruptly. She hadn't spoken to anyone outside the station since the day Ganoosh called Ikky. Ikky had pretended nothing was happening, and Nadhari, aware of her precarious position, had gone along with the pretense, while keeping her senses tuned for an opportunity to turn the tables, escape, or at least get a message through to let the Kendoros know of the alliance.

Fortunately, she hadn't needed to maintain appearances for long before Ikky and most of his troops departed.

She switched on the comlink. "Colonel Kando?" The halting question came from a young Starfarer girl she recognized from the Khleevi invasion of Rushima.

"Yes?"

"We would like to retain your services as a combat instructor, please," the girl said.

Nadhari watched a figure move into the comscreen. When the face appeared, she saw with relief that it belonged to Pal Kendoro.

She knew she was being monitored and tried to figure out what she could say to tip them off to her situation.

"Hello, Pal, long time no see. Are you running a day care facility these days?" she asked.

"You know better than that, Nadhari," Pal said. "Look, we've come to try to recruit your help, and the general's if he's available. We would like to dock and speak with you face to face, if possible."

"I don't think that's a good idea, Pal. I'm not at liberty to receive guests right now and the general isn't here."

"Be that as it may, we've come all this way to talk to you. We request permission to dock. We have reason to believe there's a threat to Acorna and her people. House Harakamian has authorized us to retain your services and the gen—"

"This isn't a good time to talk about it, Pal," Nadhari said. "The general already knows—"

Her transmission was suddenly interrupted by the smooth and friendly voice of Sergeant Erikson. "Permission to land granted, *Haven*. Just come on in and set 'er down. We have a lot of vacancies right now."

Damn! How could she warn them off now?

She was both pleased and surprised to find that her door irised open to her touch as usual, so she had not been confined to quarters. There was a trap in this situation somewhere. She knew it, and if she could keep the *Haven* from falling into it, she had to try. She sprinted for the docking bay.

The canopy was open and the *Haven* was already landing before she could pull on her pressure suit and gravity boots. She waved at them to go back as she stood in the transparent viewport between the air lock and the open landing bay, but of course they didn't understand. They thought she was greeting them. Damn. If she'd had a rock she'd have thrown it. The *Haven* set down as trustingly as a child settling onto its mother's lap.

Immediately afterward, as if by magic, Ikwaskwan's flagship suddenly appeared above the bay. It had been cloaked, she realized. Lurking. It probably picked up the *Haven*'s signal from some distance away. Ikky apparently felt he had some business with the *Haven*, because Erikson would never have welcomed them without orders to do so.

What was the general playing at now?

The docking bay boasted a huge comscreen with loudspeakers and Ikky's face appeared before them. Nadhari pulled on her helmet and stepped out into the bay. Despite the bulkiness of her suit, she felt naked without a side arm.

The big face on the comscreen looked down at her as if she were a bacteria under a microscope. "Nadhari, you didn't tell me you were expecting visitors or we'd have tried to make it home sooner. This is my lucky day! I get to see you again and also those plucky Starfarer kids."

Plucky? Oh, God, if he was being that phony the kids were done for, too. But if he was keeping up pretenses, she had one of her own to try. The mike in her helmet worked. "It was unexpected. They came on behalf of House Harakamian to retain our services. Thye've brought us, General, a substantial offer," she said, almost hopeful that it would work. Money was Ikky's native language. Maybe House Harakamian could buy him off?

But as the flagship came to rest beside the *Haven* and the dome of the docking bay closed over them, a weapon she had not been aware of was deployed by Ikky from the safety of his ship. The air in the bay turned oddly greenish and a strong noxious-smelling mist soon filled the interior of the docking facility.

She was staring at it in horrified fascination when Erikson and five other mercenaries entered the lock. She was suited up, and clumsy. They wore simple gas masks and were armed. She tore the mask off one of them and broke Erikson's leg, but they didn't fire on her. Instead, three of them subdued her while the others snatched her helmet off before raising their weapons. When the stun bolts hit her, the last thing she saw before the world faded to black was Erikson's satisfied smile.

She was not conscious when the *Haven* was boarded, after the hatch had been forced open by masked troops to allow the ship to fill with gas. One by one the Starfarers were carried out of their own ship and aboard the general's, while Nadhari herself was tenderly scooped up by Ikwaskwan and later just as tenderly chained to his berth aboard the flagship. She did not feel this either. The flagship, full of this unexpected human bounty, began the voyage back to the experimental station, leaving the *Haven,* standing alone in the docking bay, forlorn and seemingly empty.

Sixteen

oadkill!" Becker cried, and the cat jumped back as if scalded. But there was nothing wrong with the critter. Not a thing. "Hey, buddy, I got hit and from what I could see, you got hit. Why don't we hurt? If we already died and went to heaven, it's a lot darker than advertised up here."

"Riidkiii?" a voice asked. It was not the cat's voice. The cat was washing vigorously, taking inventory of all of his parts. A gray, shambling, lumpish form appeared, hovering over Becker. The face was long and the forehead had a caved-in look to it. Matted, filthy hair surrounded it. The figure was pointing to the cat.

"No, man. Roadkill. Road. Kill. It's a joke."

"Riid. Kiiyi." The figure tried hard, but his tongue couldn't seem to cut through.

"Yeah, see, the joke is from back before flitters, when we all traveled in wheeled conveyances which rolled on the ground along paved stretches on planetary surfaces called roads. Critters like RK here—okay, Riid Kiiyi, if you insist—critters like him would wander out on the road and get squashed. Like he almost did."

The figure stroked RK's back and the cat rose up to meet the clubbed-looking hand. Becker had thought something was wrong with the hand before, and now he saw that each finger lacked a knuckle, and the hand didn't have enough fingers. The guy's feet were screwed up, too. They looked more like a goat's feet—cloven hooves—than like a person's feet.

"Riid Kiiyi Khleevi?" inquired the figure—a male, Becker decided, from the overall stance and bearing of the creature.

"No, Riid—Roadkill isn't whatever you said. Roadkill is a cat. A Makahomian Temple Cat, to be precise. Makahomian Temple Cats are bred from ancient Makahomian Cat God stock to be defenders of the temples of—ah—Makahoma. They are very fierce fighters. I guess RK kinda thinks of the *Condor* as his temple now and me—I must be the pope at least! That's how come the little guy waded into Kisla's gang, even when he could have got away. *Nice* kitty," he said, and petted RK, who growled a little.

That was when Becker noticed that the funny looking guy had a little boxy device he had positioned between himself and Becker. Becker touched it. "What's this?"

The other guy pointed to Becker's mouth and made a shadow duck quacking in the flickering light cast on the wall by the fire burning in the—cave? It had to be a cave they were in. When had the fire been lit? Becker didn't remember a fire. Maybe he wasn't yet one hundred percent recovered. Must be still lapsing in and out of consciousness.

So—Becker's mouth, quacking—speaking maybe—then the man made a sweeping motion with both hands that clearly meant exchange—and pointed to his own mouth. "Linyaari."

"That your name? Linyaari? I'm Becker. Me. Becker," he said, feeling like the lead character in one of those ancient icons of classic film, Tarzan. He pointed to himself. "Becker." To the cat, who rose up again, to allow himself to be stroked, "Roadkill." Back to himself: "Becker." He pointed to the man again and asked, "Linyaari?"

The man made a sweeping motion with both hands and

arms to indicate either the whole cave or possibly the whole planet. "Linyaari." Then pointed to himself. "Aari."

"Ari? You're Ari! Hi, Ari. Jonas Becker. Much obliged for the rescue."

"Muk oblii!" Aari responded. "Hii, Biickir." The filth on his face ran with wet streaks, glistening in the firelight. "Hii, Riid. Kiiyi." The cat climbed onto Aari's folded legs and began to purr.

Over time, Becker wasn't sure how much time exactly, Aari's grasp of Standard improved. Aari encouraged Becker to talk and used different words as Becker brought them up. The little translator didn't give Becker much of a grasp of Linyaari, which was clearly the language and race that Aari belonged to, and the race that had once occupied this planet.

The coin dropped after Becker had more sleep under his belt. This planet was the one with the horns. The horns that had been mistaken for a very personal horn belonging to the Lady Acorna, the unicorn girl. That must be her race. Linyaari. The same as this guy.

Except this guy didn't have a unicorn horn. Maybe only the girls did? Nah—quite unwillingly, Becker looked more closely at the injury to Aari's forehead. Then he threw up what was left of the last handful of cat food. Oh, great, pretty soon he'd be hacking up hairballs, too.

But what he had seen, when he looked, was that there was a place where Aari probably had had a horn. Now it was a deep, partially scarred-over crater that gave the guy the appearance of having a crushed forehead.

Aari saw him looking and pulled the matted hair down over the wound as far as he could, shaking his head and weeping again.

"Aari, buddy, what happened here? What happened to you?"

"Khleevi," he said, and then made motions where his horn should have been that made Becker want to vomit again, only there was nothing there to vomit, just as there was nothing more on Aari's forehead for anyone to torture him with.

"How in the hell did you get away? How did you survive?" Becker asked.

"Vhiliinyar," was the only Linyaari word Becker heard and then, the funny thing was, he sort of understood the rest of what had happened without actually being aware of anything Aari was saying. At first he thought that the universal translator gadget *was* actually working both ways, and then something made him realize that he and Aari were reading each other's minds—and a third mind as well.

RK very carefully sunk a single claw into Becker's leg and Becker knew beyond a shadow of a doubt that RK could hear and understand the thoughts of both of them and could have transmitted thoughts, too, if he'd wanted to. The cat just preferred body language. As far as he could see, RK wanted Becker to try to learn Cat. It was beneath a cat's dignity to speak human Standard, Becker figured. Then it hit him.

"Hey, you're telepathic! And so are we, when we're with you!"

Aari shook his head and picked up one of the horns, then made a sweeping motion with his hands, and an exchanging motion between his head, Becker's and RK's. Then he pointed to his own forehead, made a negative swipe with his hand, and hung his head.

"So we understand each other telepathically because of the horns, huh?" Becker asked.

Aari sighed deeply, shook his head to indicate that wasn't the case, shrugged, and looked perplexed. RK sunk his claw into Becker's leg again and fixed him with another stare, which to Becker's somewhat rattled brain seemed to say that RK had been reading his mind all along; he just didn't much *care* what Becker thought. Becker guessed he was reading the cat because—well, he had always read the cat, really, but now he had nothing better to do so he noticed.

Aari smiled a little, and Becker could tell the Linyaari was reading him.

Aari projected a few careful images that showed him with his horn, communing wordlessly with other people that looked just like him. So, he had been telepathic when he had his own horn. Fair enough.

Becker didn't ask again what had happened to the guy's horn but Aari grimly showed them how it had been when the Khleevi were about to finish him off and, having broken his body, excised his horn in a particularly slow and painful way. He backtracked to show them how he had been captured. Aari had stayed behind during the Khleevi invasion to help his brother, who had been stuck in this cave, badly injured, too far away from the spaceport for them to get help from the ships departing with all of their people during the great evacuation. Aari had been unable to reach him in time to heal him.

The Khleevi had captured Aari when he was out gathering rope for the rescue, and had begun long, long tortures of their captive, all the time probing, probing, as if trying to feast on his grief. They had captured some of the translator boxes from previous diplomatic missions—LAANYE, Aari called them—and used them to communicate with him, to interrogate him, though they surely learned little that could be of help to them. What he knew that they might have wished to know, he never told.

Aari did not speak of his brother, or of the new planet his people had found. The foremost thoughts in his mind were grief. His brother would be dead from his wounds by now, so he grieved, and grieved more as the Khleevi destroyed him, along with his planet. He grieved for the loss of his people, for the simultaneous destruction of his own body and the body of his home world, grieved at the pain, and the memories of better times. And all the time the Khleevi stood by jeering and gloating over their methodical ravaging of the beauty and life force of a planet and one of its children, the only one within their grasp.

"Did they kill all those other people, too?" Becker wanted to know. "I found all those horns."

"No," Aari said, and Becker felt triumph in the thought as Aari carried a light to the back of the cave. It was filled with horns and bones, carefully arranged into individual skeletons whenever possible. "These are the bones of my Ancestors. When you landed the first time, you discovered our graveyard. The residual power of the horns kept that area living when the rest of the world was destroyed. The Khleevi never knew of this sacred place, and I did not tell them. They found me some distance from it.

"When the instability they caused in Vhiliinyar by their destruction caused the planet to drive them from its face, leaving me behind for dead, I dragged myself back here, and slept among the horns. Most of my wounds were healed—you cannot imagine the shape I was in before then. I did not resemble anything Linyaari. But the Khleevi had done something to me that prevented the horns from truly healing me, though nothing could block the process completely.

"And so—" His eyes rolled slightly up, to where his horn had been. "And so even the healing power of the horns did not make me truly whole again, for among the Linyaari healing rests not only in the horn but in the guiding intelligence and empathy of the healer. After the Khleevi tortured me, I was incapable of participating in my healing. The horn merely knit together that which was broken. Except for my own horn. All of the horns of our dead could not give me back my own horn.

"Still, the healing was enough that I could gather a few of the horns that lay on top of the ground and return to the cave. But the Khleevi had held me a long time and my brother had lain injured for a long time, waiting for my return to rescue and heal him. He was with the Ancestors, beyond the power of the horns to heal."

"But even without your horn, you can still read minds and everything, right? 'Cause you were telepathic before and—"

"The horns are like—um—things on the heads of insects?" Aari put his hands up to make antennae and Becker supplied the word. "They transmit our thoughts but the ability is in the

Linyaari. Without my own horn, I cannot make myself heard. I do not know how. But surrounded by so many, many horns, I have many antennae. You have antennae, too, and Riid Kiiyi."

"I get it. I think," Becker said. "So, tell me, why didn't you let me know you were here when I came the first time?" Becker said. "I would have helped you. I could have taken you to your people at their new place."

"You were robbing graves," Aari said with a little shrug. "I thought you might be Khleevi of another sort. Besides, I feel— shame—at my own appearance. I do not wish to see my people again—well, more precisely, I do not wish for them to see me as I am now. *They* will shudder to look upon me. But I could not let the bones of our Ancestors be defiled any more. So when you left, I disinterred the Ancestors, and brought them here to a new place."

"*That's* why there weren't any horns there. Well, look, Aari, it's a good thing you did that because that gal you saw kicking the shit out of me? She has some use for the horns, and I can almost guarantee you it isn't a happy one. Good thing your home world here decided to pop off a few explosions—"

Aari pointed to himself again.

"*You* did that?" Becker asked. "How?"

Aari walked to the back of the cave and picked up something that was obviously a very nasty weapon. He pointed to it, said, "Khleevi," and made a booming sound, then set it back down.

"Is there anything to eat around here, by the way?"

"Oh, of course. Excuse my rudeness." Aari bent down, there was a tearing sound, and he returned with a big handful of grass.

RK put it better than Becker could have. He looked at the grass and meowed piteously.

Aari looked crestfallen and again Becker caught an impression of overwhelming shame.

"You will starve because I cannot feed you that which you need to sustain life. Riid Kiiyi will starve also," Aari said.

"Not if we can help it. We just have to find a way to get back into the *Condor*. Kisla-baby tap-danced on my remote."

The three of them returned to the former graveyard. The grass was dying already, turning brown and brittle without the power of the horns. Becker found the pieces of his remote where Kisla had left it. It was smashed so badly even he couldn't fix it.

They tried a couple of horns but the horns didn't seem to work on electronics. However, Becker did have some emergency backups. Not easy ones, not convenient ones, but he had them.

By standing on Aari's shoulders, he was able to grasp a tail fin and haul himself to within reaching distance of a particular area near the hatch. Touching that, he whistled the bar of "Dixie" that was the opening code. An encoder implanted inside the hull translated his whistle into electronic code. Then all he had to do was slide back down the tail fin and drop to the ground before the robolift descended on his head.

He and RK climbed aboard and chowed down. He grabbed the spare remote he had stashed in the ventilation duct, and then he and RK returned to the surface with a bag of freeze-dried veggies for Aari.

The Linyaari was busy hauling loads of bones to the *Condor*.

"I must set aside my shame now and ask you to take me to narhii-Vhiliinyar, the new home of my people. I must take the remains of our forebears with me. This world has become unsafe even for the dead."

For Markel, the *Haven*'s ventilation system was home sweet home. He had hidden in it and made his way around the ship after the Palomellese bandits had killed his father.

Trained in warfare or not, the Starfarers did have one advantage over the Red Bracelets, and that was that they knew their ship. When it became clear they were caught in a trap, Markel had naturally suggested the ventilation system as a hiding place for the younger ones and the ship's "guests." He,

Johnny Greene, and Khetala, along with the Reamer family and Starfarers under the age of five, would hide in the ducts from Decks A to D, which could be blocked off from the rest of the ship and supplied with their own oxygen.

Of them all, only Markel realized that this section was also where many of the bandits had been gassed to death while trying to pursue him, Acorna, Calum Baird, and Dr. Hoa after Markel had rescued Acorna. As he lay flat in the duct, not speaking, hardly breathing, with perhaps a hundred other bodies lying in the same fashion down the length of the ducts, he thought he could still smell the lingering pong of the poison gas they had used. But, of course, that was ridiculous. It had been many months since the Palomellese had been overwhelmed, gassed, or spaced.

He waited for the cries of his shipmates below—for 'Ziana and Pal to shout orders, a surrender, anything. Their faces had appeared on the comscreen and so his friends could not be hidden from any possible attackers, lest their enemies realize they were not dealing with *all* of the Starfarers. But he heard very little from below—no screams, no shouts, just sighs and slight shuffling sounds, before the boots of the enemy tramped across the *Haven*'s decks and retreated again, even more heavily.

The bay vibrated with the noise of other ships taking off. And still no noise from below.

Markel had positioned himself strategically above the supply lockers, a bit separated from the others so that if he was discovered, it might be presumed he was alone. Or if the others were discovered, he might not be, and would be able to help them escape.

Johnny Greene was above his duty station, the computation and navigation room. Khetala, Reamer, and some of the more mature children were placed among the younger children, to keep them quiet. Not that there were many among the very young who couldn't fight and think extremely well under pressure. But the little kids were also the smallest and the most easily captured.

Markel took a deep breath and lifted the seal that was also the entrance to the room below. The acrid stench of some kind of gas caused his eyes to water and made him feel sleepy. He managed to wrestle the seal closed, and let his drowsiness pass while he thought about what to do next.

He didn't know what kind of gas it was, though judging from his own reaction, it was supposed to knock people out, if not kill them. There were gas masks in the lockers. If he could hold his breath until he could access one of the masks and put it on, then he could get masks for the others. He could also check out the status of their shipmates and see what damage was done to the ship.

He would have liked to have communicated this plan to Johnny but the distance was great and time was short. Before they'd hidden, they had all agreed they would wait until they heard from him, or at least send someone to check on his position before anyone else acted. He was the acknowledged expert vent rat of the crew. Admiral of the vent rats, even.

The vent rat admiral held his breath and opened the seal again. Quickly, he dropped down, letting the seal close behind him as he slipped out so it would not allow much of the gas into the system where his shipmates hid.

The maneuver was tricky and cost him precious seconds. The greenish gas draped the room heavily but Markel held his breath and lay on his stomach, crawling for one of the lower lockers. The air was always better close to the floor, in case he had to breathe before he got to the lockers. He figured he was going to have to. He couldn't see the lockers from here. The vent opened into the middle of the room and the lockers were along the sides.

Then his hand, outstretched to help him swim-crawl through the miasma, touched something soft and fleshy-warm. He heaved himself up so his eyes were level with his hand. Annella! Annella Carter lay there, knocked out by the gas but still breathing, though very shallowly. And as he drew closer, wondering how on earth he would manage to hold his breath one more second, he saw that she held a gas mask in her out-stretched hand. Her other hand, holding two more masks, lay near an open locker door. He knew at once that she had grabbed the masks to get them to him and the others in the ventilation system, but had already breathed too much gas. It had knocked her out before she could get her own mask on.

He fitted a mask over his face, then put one on her. After he got masks to Johnny and some of the others, they could clear the ship of this gas and work to wake her up, if the mask didn't do the trick. But right now he had to try to save the others. Carrying as many masks as he could hold, he ducked out into the passage and down the next one which led to the computation/navigation center.

He saw no more bodies, living or dead. The door to the locker area was concealed behind some pipes, so the enemy had missed it—and Annella—when they boarded. He wished he knew what had gone on while they were in hiding. Really, he'd have to talk to Johnny about rigging the vents with visual surveillance equipment in the future. Maybe bunks and hot and cold running water and battery-powered lights, too. He grinned at his own wild ideas.

Tapping on the vent, he waited until it was pulled open and shoved a mask up at Johnny, who took it, then reached back for the other masks. The vent closed again—Markel assumed everybody was masking up. Johnny and other masked ship-mates finally began dropping through the ceiling. Markel directed them to the lockers, to gather more masks for their remaining shipmates in the vents.

All of this was done in eerie green silence. The only sounds on the ship were clanking chain sounds of opening and closing locks, seals, and hatches, and the soft sound of Markel's ship-mates' phantomlike movements—or maybe elflike movements, in the case of some of the smaller kids.

Markel himself made for the main hatch, warily, laser can-non in hand, alert for any intruders who had remained behind. But none had. Nor had they left behind any of his other friends.

The gas was even thicker outside the ship than it was inside. He closed the hatch behind him and went to search for the ventilation control of the docking bay. He didn't locate it, but he did find the pressurized transparent control shed. This was not full of the gas. Once inside, he was able to remove his mask as he studied the controls, finding by trial and error the panel that opened the overhead portal that allowed ships to take off and to dock.

This he opened. The green gas was sucked into the vaccuum of space. When all tinge of green was gone, he closed the portal once more and adjusted the oxygen, pressurization, and ventilation fans. The air in the bay was soon breathable. He returned to the ship, opened the hatch, and allowed the bay's vented fans to pull the gas from the interior of the *Haven*. Johnny Greene called softly from the open hatch. "Rocky used the healing horn to help Annella. She'll be grand now."

"Fine. Nobody's tried to kill me for at least ten minutes. I don't think much of anybody's left here."

"Good. Then maybe we should take advantage of that hospitality the general offered."

With Johnny's help, Markel raided the airlock adjoining the bay, and two of the adjacent, unattended rooms. With the general and his troops gone, the place was virtually deserted. Johnny found station security headquarters, and took out the guard. There was only one. He had been watching reruns of the *Haven*'s capture. For a few mesmerizing moments, Johnny and Markel stood over the body of their unconscious captive and watched first Nadhari Kando, then their shipmates, being gassed and dragged or carried aboard the general's flagship, now painted to look like a Federation Forces vessel. So that's what those footsteps had meant. Thoroughly angry now, Markel and company had disabled the monitors and raided the unattended areas of the base. They took all the weapons and food they could find, and—as an afterthought on Johnny's part—any uniforms they found lying around. They also removed all of the pressure suits from the lock. Johnny downloaded a copy of the flagship's course from the computer in the security room. The security room guard was still unconscious, so they tied him up and took him along.

It had taken them three trips back and forth to the *Haven* and about forty-five minutes to accomplish all this, before Markel, loaded with the last of the booty, returned to the *Haven*. Johnny, wearing one of the purloined pressure suits, opened the canopy and boarded the *Haven* through the air lock. Once they were well away from the general's compound, Johnny adjusted their course to follow that of the general's flagship.

Seventeen

Becker had never felt awe for anyone except his dad in his whole life until he met Aari, but his respect for the maimed Linyaari grew on the journey from the old Linyaari home to the new one. Aari knew exactly how to get there. In spite of having endured tortures that would drive anyone else insane, he had kept the memory of the Linyaari escape route, drummed into him since boyhood, not only intact, but also secret from the Khleevi. He tidied up the *Condor*, which was, thanks to Kisla Manjari, almost vacant. Becker still had the money she'd paid him back on Kezdet, money that had nearly emptied his ship. Come to think of it, Becker was almost willing to bet Kisla's credits were somehow fraudulent. He didn't trust anything about that venomous little psycho.

After cleaning the holds, Aari had reverently placed each Linyaari skeleton, from the most recent one of his brother, to the most ancient fragments, side by side throughout the ship. Becker helped him until Aari saw the android. Both men realized just how useful that android could be in the current situation. The horn would not work on its electronics, which Becker had already mostly repaired, but did a great job on shredded plastiskin. Soon the reprogrammed, aesthetically pleasing, and now very helpful KEN640 was back in business as official assistant keeper of the *Condor*'s charnel holds. With KEN640's help, every skeleton was loaded aboard the *Condor*'s holds. Aari slept there every night among the bones of his ancestors.

Away from those holds, Aari had a tougher time talking to Becker. He was trying hard to pick up Standard and Becker was trying hard to pick up Linyaari, and Roadkill wasn't interested in speaking anything except Cat. Which meant that Aari and Becker indulged in a lot of communication through body language and charades. But that was more of an exchange than Becker usually had with the cat. Becker was enjoying the trip and the company.

RK apparently felt the same way. He showed Aari the sort of kitty cat affection he had not thus far deemed appropriate to bestow upon Becker. He sat on Aari's lap and took to sleeping beside him in the Linyaari graveyard. The KEN unit came in handy for changing the litter box. He was not the brainiest droid in the universe, but he was rehabilitated, thanks to Becker's new programs, and no longer said things like, "Do you wish me to tear his arm from his socket now, or would you prefer I punch out one eye in a painful and maiming, yet not life-threatening, manner, Lady Kisla?" It had taken Aari and Becker both a lot more work to get KEN640 over some of these socially unacceptable utterances. These guys might be computers on feet and have opposable thumbs, but the computer was only there to operate the feet and thumbs in a useful way. KEN's processor was an idiot compared to, say, the ship's computer.

KEN was also somebody who could play gin rummy with Becker when Aari was feeling antisocial, which happened fairly often. It didn't take a rocket scientist to figure out why a guy who'd been left behind by his people, who felt he'd failed to take care of his brother who died while the guy himself was being slowly tortured to death by alien invaders who were also destroying his home world—why a guy like that might need a little down time once in a while. And Becker *was* a rocket scientist, albeit an idiosyncratically privately tutored and self-taught one.

Aari didn't spend all of his unsocial time in pity-party mode, however. His Standard improved by leaps and bounds as he watched the store of ancient films and clips stored in the ship's computer, as well as read the hard copy books.

"Did you see this one, Joh?" he asked, pronouncing Becker's first name with a sort of a whuff through his nostrils. Aari was brandishing the *How to Care for Your Kittycat* book. Becker noticed that RK for once was not clinging to the Linyaari like a fuzzy leech.

"Yeah. Skip the part on interfering in a feline's sex life. I tried it and RK was not amused. That cat on a bad fur day could give those Khleevi bugs a run for their money."

Aari looked puzzled and retreated to the now-cleared-of-debris berth in the newly organized crew's quarters to pursue the cat care trends of several hundred years ago.

Becker hardly recognized the *Condor*. The KEN unit had tidied up the ship so that things were stored and catalogued and there was actually room to move around. Becker wasn't at all sure he liked it. The other way had been sort of cozy.

After a while he found that having two other—well, one and a half other—people on board was distracting, so he had the KEN unit turn itself off between bouts of housekeeping. And Aari was busy studying or brooding (or both) a lot of the time, so that wasn't too much of a problem. Becker's real adjustment was that RK was spending most of his time with Aari and Becker missed the onery feline.

He was thinking that he had been a real sucker to think that because the cat tried to rescue him from Kisla and her men that it meant the animal harbored any affection for him. Why, he showed his fuzzy purry side more to Khetala on first acquaintance, or to this Aari guy, than he ever did to Becker. As Becker was thinking this, he felt a familiar pain in his thigh and looked down to see RK sitting there, switching his tail back and forth, and looking expectantly up at Becker.

As soon as Becker paid attention, the cat sprang up to his shoulder, lay against his neck and purred with a noise that rivaled that of the rustiest rattletrap engine of an outmoded junker ship. "Aw, RK. I didn't know you cared."

RK backed down and proceeded to rub his face all over Becker's, marking him in one of the less objectionable ways the cat had of performing that task. And it occurred to Becker that he really hadn't previously actually solicited the cat's actual affection—theirs had been a more rough and ready relationship. Man-to-man or cat-to-cat as it were, depending on the viewpoint. Of course Roadkill *liked* him. Otherwise the cat would have found himself new quarters the first time the *Condor* docked.

Becker suddenly realized he was also thinking a lot like a cat and he looked at RK suspiciously. The cat, whose fur was lightly coated with white dust from the Linyaari boneyard, blinked back at him three times and intensified the purr.

Thereafter on the journey, the cat spent a little more time on the bridge and after a while so did Aari, asking Becker questions about the things he was learning and trying out words on him, getting his accent corrected. Becker, in return, tried to learn Linyaari words and phrases. The little box, a LAANYE in Linyaari, took only a bit of tampering with on Becker's part, with the technical assistance of Aari, to translate in both directions.

Meanwhile, they came within shouting distance of narhii-Vhiliinyar. "Shall I hail them or will they be less freaked out if you do it?" Becker asked Aari. "My accent isn't as good as it should be yet."

"I will speak if only you will not turn on the visual projector," Aari said. He had stayed with the bones for days on end the first time he got a look at himself in Becker's shaving mirror. "I—I do not wish to frighten my people."

He did anyway.

Becker got his first visual of a Linyaari female when the communications officer, a white-skinned, white-haired girl with a pretty shiny spiraled horn growing out of her forehead, said, "Please adjust your visual transmission, *Condor*. We are not receiving you."

"This is Aari of Clan Nyaarya, narhii-Vhiliinyar port," Aari repeated. "Our visual projector is temporarily out of service. Request permission to land."

There was silence, while the communications officer presumably conferred with someone else, and then her skeptical voice said, "Aari of Clan Nyaarya was lost to us during the evacuation of Vhiliinyar prior to the Khleevi attack. Please adjust your transmission and properly identify yourself."

Aari's voice was tight as he said, "I have been imprisoned on Vhiliinyar by the Khleevi but escaped them, and have been rescued by the captain and crew of the *Condor*. I have recovered the bones of our forebears from the sacred cemetery, to save them from plundering and bring them back to their children for reinterment. Now please give us permission to land so that I may rejoin my family."

"Really?" The communications officer forgot to use the official language and lapsed into vernacular Linyaari. "You actually escaped the Khleevi after they captured you? I'll have to apply for official permission but—oh, welcome home, Aari! Everyone will be so happy to see you!"

By the time she came back on screen, the *Condor*'s fuel supply was running dangerously low.

The communications officer's face was closed again as she said, "Aari, the ship may land long enough for you to meet a greeting committee who validate your identity, but all non-Linyaari personnel aboard the vessel must remain aboard and the vessel itself must depart immediately after you have been identified."

"Tell her we're out of fuel," Becker said.

"The *Condor* will need to refuel," Aari said.

"Permission denied," the communications officer said.

"Gimme that thing," Becker said, and took the portable transmitter from Aari. "Look, lady, I know your people have been through a lot," he said in the best Linyaari he could muster. "Aari explained all that to me. But he's been through whatever you people use for hell himself, and my crew and I went through a lot to get him here. The least you could do is have the common courtesy not to make us take off again without enough fuel to get to the next stop."

Another long silence before she returned to say, "Permission to land granted. Prepare to be boarded upon docking."

The *Condor* was forced to land in a field outside the regular port, as all of the docking bays were hollowed into deep ovals, the wrong shape for the ship's alien tail. Becker sent down the robolift. He was busy talking to Aari and didn't notice RK scooting out down the emergency cat flap chute. The cat depressed the exit mechanism himself and landed neatly on the deck of the lift, thereby forming his own greeting committee.

Aboard the *Condor*, Aari was letting Becker know that he was just as glad the inspection committee was going to come aboard instead of the other way around. He was seemingly as afraid to meet his people again as he had ever been of the Khleevi.

Becker turned on the outside visual and saw Roadkill being lowered with the robolift. Four of the white unicorn people, three females and one male, and two brown male ones plus one small female spotty one, stood below watching as the cat joined them. The little spotted one clapped her hands but was held by one of the white females, while another gently reached onto the lift to receive RK, who jumped up to meet her. While the women were occupied, the white male and the two brown ones climbed onto the lift. They did not look happy about it.

In the middle of the night, Thariinye appeared in the flap of Grandam's pavilion, insisting that Grandam, Acorna, and Maati all rise, dress for a long walk, and hurry with him to *viizaar*'s pavilion immediately.

When they got there, *Viizaar* Liriili's eyes showed white all around the pupils, and Acorna could smell her fear, strong and goatishly acrid.

Grandam asked, "What in the name of the Ancestors is wrong?" None of them asked why the problem couldn't wait until morning.

"An alien ship is entering our atmosphere," Liriili told them. "It refuses to transmit visuals, but the person who initially contacted us claims to be Maati's brother Aari, who was missing at the time of the evacuation along with Maati's other brother, Laarye. You know as well as I do, Grandam, that it's absolutely inconceivable that anyone escaped the Khleevi or the destruction of the planet."

Acorna cleared her throat. "I escaped."

"What?" Liriili asked and Acorna read her clearly to mean, "How dare you interrupt?"

"Everyone presumed all were lost when my parents' ship exploded, but I escaped. Perhaps Maati's brother did, too."

Maati, who had never known her brother, glanced agitatedly from one of the adults to the other, her sleepiness completely overcome by the excitement.

"I believe it is a trick," Liriili said.

"How can that be?" Grandam asked. "No one knows of Aari and Laarye except a few of us."

Liriili shook her head violently. "Everyone we have sent into space has disappeared without so much as a hailing," she said. "I can't help but believe they have come to harm. If they haven't actually fallen into the hands of the Khleevi, then they've run afoul of some other race, one that seeks to know us. Our people may have been interrogated for anything that would get the captors past our defenses."

"Yes," said Grandam. "That may be true. But it may also be true that somehow Aari has found his way home. Though I can't think how."

"In an alien vessel with a very bad-tempered alien with an atrocious Linyaari accent, according to Saari, the duty officer at the space port. Here is a tape of the transmission."

She played it for them.

"That's a human!" Acorna said.

Liriili glowered at her. "I thought that might be so. One of *your* people. Who is it?"

"How should I know?" Acorna asked. "It doesn't sound like any of my friends."

"It doesn't?" Liriili was surprised. Acorna was a little amused in spite of herself. The *viizaar* sounded like the old joke that went, "Hi, I'm Mirajik. I'm from Mars." "Hi, I'm Sarah from Earth Prime." "Earth Prime? Oh, say, I have a friend from there. Do you know John Smith?" The *viizaar* seemed incredulous that since Acorna knew some humans they would not be the same ones currently on the "doorstep" of narhii-Vhiliinyar.

"No," Acorna said, trying to keep both the amusement and her own excitement out of her voice. It would be *good* to hear Standard spoken again. "But if you need an interpreter, I'll be glad to help in any way I can."

"Very good of you, Khornya," Grandam said. "I'm sure that's why the *viizaar* included you in this group. And I am here as the elder and Maati because if this is indeed Aari in our midst, she should be there to greet her brother. And Thariinye?" The last was a question aimed at Liriili.

"Thariinye also speaks the tongue of Khornya's adopted people and can serve as a second interpreter."

Acorna made a noise of protest. What Liriili meant was that Thariinye was supposed to report if she was translating truthfully or not.

"I am keeping this party small," the *viizaar* continued. "A couple of the other young men will accompany us but there is no need for everyone to know about this until we have determined the nature of the intrusion. I have asked my vice-*viizaar* to be prepared to evacuate the city in the event that we are being invaded again, however. I can only hope we can prepare for our escape in time."

"How about the ships Khornya and I saw the other day, Liriili?" Thariinye asked. "I am a qualified pilot. I could certainly fly any of them. And I can organize a crew among the elders who have retired from active duty."

"I hope you will not be called upon to try, but it is a noble thought," Liriili said.

"Before we go running off in all directions, I think we'd better see what's coming our way," Grandam said sensibly. "There's no need to alarm the Ancestors yet. Besides, even in an emergency, the Ancestors move at a stately pace."

"Yes," Thariinye agreed. "So stately a pace that a full invasion could wipe everyone out before we arrived at the spaceport."

Liriili, with a slight nod to acknowledge the jest—and that only because it came from Thariinye, Acorna thought—inclined her head in agreement and they set out, the *viizaar*, Grandam, Thariinye, Maati, and two young males, presumably as a security presence.

Watching the ship land, Acorna relaxed. The tail looked Federation, but that was a Mytherian toxic waste chute if she ever saw one sticking out the bottom, and the hull itself was composed of a strange patchwork of metals, not to mention the somewhat eccentric structural design of the nose. Where the hatch should have been was what looked like a pocket of some sort. As the ship landed, it caused the ground to quake. The engine sounded as if it was about to fall to pieces. (That is no battleship, Liriili,) she said with a smile, in thought-talk. She was getting much better at it, fortunately, since verbalizations would have been drowned out in the roar of the landing. (It is not any one sort of ship at all. It looks like a junker to me.)

(The alien aboard claims that it is out of fuel,) Liriili replied. (He demands that we refuel it.)

(I'd believe him,) Acorna said. (That vessel looks like it needs all the help it can get.)

(It could be a trick,) Thariinye said. (To lull us into complacency.)

(It's working for me,) Grandam said. (And—does no one else feel it? I have a definite impression of a Linyaari aboard.)

(I felt that, too,) Liriili said. (But there is something wrong about it. Something terribly wrong.)

The noise stopped and another series of sounds began, with first a thunk, then a whoosh, and then, slowly, the hydraulic hum of a platform being lowered out of the Mytherian toxic waste chute.

Suddenly, Maati clapped her hands and pointed. "Oh, look!" she cried aloud. "Look at the furry little alien! He must have come so far in that big old ship! I'll bet he's hungry, as well as needing fuel." She ran over to a patch of fairly healthy looking grass and pulled it up, along with some purple flowers Acorna had learned were very tasty.

Tears formed in Grandam's eyes and her voice choked a little as she said, "The little alien reminds me of a *pahaantiyir*." Acorna caught a thought-picture of a furry cat-like being.

"It does, doesn't it?" Liriili asked, sounding teary herself. "I had the dearest little *pahaantiyir* when I was at home, but it ran away just before the evacuation and I couldn't find it in time."

Maati was reaching forward, coaxing the "alien" with her bundle of succulent grasses and flowers. "You'll find these delicious, alien entity," she said politely.

"I doubt it," Acorna said. "That looks to me very much like a Makahomian Temple Cat. They are carnivores, I believe."

The cat gave her an indignant look and daintily stepped forward to sniff the flowers, then began to eat one. Just one. All of the Linyaari watched it with awe. It sat back on its haunches, surveyed its audience complacently, and began to wash.

Acorna reached over and lifted the cat into her arms, then handed him over to Maati. The youngling squealed with delight as the creature snuggled against her neck and then settled into purring.

"The alien likes me!" Maati said

"I wouldn't be too impressed," Acorna replied with a smile. "This fellow is probably not the captain. Nor does it appear to be Linyaari, so it can hardly be your brother."

Thariinye and the other young males stroked the animal, too, as did Liriili.

"It's *so* soft," Maati said blissfully.

"Since they sent the lift down, perhaps they mean for us to board," Acorna said.

"It could be a trap," Thariinye said.

"I've only heard of cats practicing mind control when they are looking for homes or a meal," Acorna said. "I very much doubt this one is a spy. I would like to see who inside the ship. Perhaps they have news of my friends."

"You're not going up there without me," Thariinye said. "Unless—uh—unless you think it best."

"*I* think it best," Liriili said, firmly putting her hands behind her to stop petting the cat. "It is why you were sent for. And you two—go with them."

"Yes, *Viizaar*," the two young males said in tandem.

"I want to go see if there are more of these—kaaats?" Maati said.

"Mrow?" the creature said.

"You must stay here until we know if it is safe," Liriili said.

"But you said my brother . . ."

"Someone who claims to be, yes. It is best that Khornya and Thariinye handle first contact."

Eighteen

*A*corna stepped onto the platform and was followed by the males. The cat leaped from Maati's arms and sat on the platform with them.

The platform rose through the tube until it was level with one of the decks. A stocky, barrel-chested, curly-haired man with a bristling mustache watched their arrival, then reached forward to help Acorna off the platform. "Hi, there, ma'am, boys," he greeted them in a deep and slightly gravelly voice. "I don't know which line to use — 'We've come in peace' or 'Take me to your leader.' Aari tells me you folks aren't used to visitors."

The cat jumped from the platform and onto the man's shoulder, to curl around his neck. "I see you've already met our leader, or the self-appointed glad-handing committee anyway."

The funny thing was that he was using all of these Standard idiomatic expressions, but in the Linyaari tongue. Acorna understood him but she could also understand the puzzled expressions on the faces of the other three Linyaari.

"My name's Jonas Becker," the man continued, as the males joined them on deck. "I am captain of the *Condor* here, and Chief Executive Officer, Chairman of the Board, and — until recently —

Chief Cook and Bottle Washer of Becker Interplanetary Salvage and Recycling Enterprises, Limited. It was going to be Becker and Sons but my dad didn't get around to changing the sign before he died so there's still only one Becker. And you folks are?"

Acorna was grinning again, enjoying the fact that Becker, whom she liked at once and from whom she was sensing very positive energy, would know that she was being friendly while the other three Linyaari would probably be under the impression she was fearlessly baring her teeth at the "alien." This man reminded her a great deal of her beloved uncles. The same brand of individualistic and independent intelligence, curiosity, and kindness radiated from him. "I was named Acorna by my foster parents," she told him. "In Linyaari—our language—I am known as Khornya."

"Bingo!" he said. "I mean, no kidding? I've been hearing about you all over the place, Lady Acorna, nothing but good things, and here you're the first person I meet when I get here. Pleased to meet you, ma'am, and I mean that sincerely. I used to be a farm slave on Kezdet when I was a kid and what you did for those children was wonderful, from what I hear. I know your daddies, too. Good men."

Thariinye cleared his throat in a gruff, manly sort of way. "We are told you were permitted to land because you claim to have a Linyaari aboard?"

Becker's demeanor altered subtly to be as gruff as Thaarinye's and twice as threatening. "I didn't claim it, no, sir. Aari himself did."

Acorna touched Becker's arm lightly. "My people are unused to visitors. They have had some bad experiences, especially recently. Please do not take offense. May I present Ambassador Thariinye, who was among the party that came to Manganos to bring me back to narhii-Vhiliinyar, and these fellows are"—she caught their thoughts—"Iiryn and Yiirl."

Becker nodded, a short and wary and not nearly so friendly gesture. "Boys," he said in acknowledgement. "Well, Aari got a little shy all of a sudden when he saw you coming and he's back in the holds sorting out the graveyard. I guess if we each take a few loads of bones down we'll have it dirtside soon enough."

Thariinye and the other two males looked, if anything, whiter at the mention of bones. Becker examined their faces for a moment, and then seemed to be looking them over in general, and Acorna as well, then he said, "Make yourselves at home. I'm going to go check on KEN and see what's keeping Aari. He's probably working so hard back there he didn't hear you board."

(That is very strange behavior for one gone so long from us,) Iiryn said.

(Well, he is very old, from back before the evacuation,) Yiirl replied. (Perhaps he grows forgetful.)

(You were certainly friendly to that Becker person,) Thariinye said.

(He's a good man,) Acorna replied. (Could you not feel it?)

(Hmph. No. He didn't have the same energy with me that he did with you. He is very hostile and suspicious and, I would say, can be violent.)

(We shouldn't judge him without knowing him,) Acorna said.

(Not much chance of that, fortunately,) Thariinye said. (You realize, of course, he and this ship must leave immediately after refueling. Their presence contaminates and endangers all of us.)

(I hardly see how,) Acorna was thinking when Becker, looking extremely troubled, reappeared and crooked his finger at her. Thariinye started forward and Becker said, "Hold it, sport. Just the Lady Acorna for now, please." He started up the ladder connecting the decks.

"Very well," Thariinye said. "But do not try any unacceptable behaviors with her or I will cause you to be remorseful that you did."

(Why, Thariinye,) Acorna shot at him in passing, (that sounded hostile and aggressive and maybe even violent.)

She climbed to the upper deck where Becker waited for her.

"Aari's in a bad way, to tell you the truth, Lady Acorna," Becker said. "I met him when I was hurt worse than he is, and I hadn't met any regular people like you then—but looking at you—well, let me prepare you. Those Khleevis messed him up pretty bad. He's missing his horn, that's the most obvious thing, but from the looks of you people, there's other stuff that hasn't healed right either. The way he explained it to me was that he was all busted up when he collapsed in the cemetery and the power in all those old horns healed him, except the Khleevi had done to him something that kept the healing from proceeding normally. Without someone who knew what they were doing to guide the healing, his bones just knit together wherever one end touched the other. I guess now that he's almost safe back home again and doesn't have to be on alert all the time, the impact of everything he's been through is starting to hit him. I found him curled up in a corner sobbing his eyes out. I thought maybe if you came back alone with me and talked to him, told him it would be okay, that his folks are looking forward to having him back, it would be better."

"I'll do what I can," Acorna said, grateful to the man for his thoughtfulness on behalf of the former captive.

They clanked across open metal grating on their way back to some of what would have been cargo holds and crew's quarters on a standard vessel. Following Becker into one of the holds, Acorna heard the clatter of bone on bone. Then a monster arose before them.

Even as hunched up and crooked as he was, Aari towered over Becker and was taller than Acorna. But his joints did not articulate properly and there was a huge hump on his back. His legs bent incorrectly and his head was at an odd angle—and then there was the stomach-churning sight of that sunken-in forehead.

She tried to take this all in only on a physical, visual level and not think about it, not react to it at all. The expression in his deeply haunted eyes showed that he could read her before she sent or he received a thought.

She extended her hand to him—horn touching would be inappropriate in this instance with no other horn to meet it. "I am called Khornya. I was born in space after the evacuation and have only just arrived here myself. But welcome home."

He dipped his head, and though he was trying to sound composed, his voice trembled as he replied, "I was Aari. I thank you."

And then, from behind her, she heard the clatter of hard soled feet on metal grating. The three males entered the hold behind them, and made gasping noises.

(What *is* it?)

(I think I'm going to be sick!)

(They really made a mess out of you, didn't they?) from Thariinye.

Acorna closed the distance between them before Aari could retreat farther back into the hold. She took his hand with hers and this time did lean her horn against his cheek, for healing, for calming. (They are young and stupid and know nothing of anything outside this world,) she told him. (I'm sure the physicians here can put you right in no time.)

Thariinye, who was thoughtless but not intentionally unkind, realized his error at once and crossed to them as well, also, with only slight reluctance, laying his horn against the newcomer. (Khornya is right. I was rude and cruel. The physicians will be sent for at once.)

"Maybe before we unload the Ancestors' bones, you people would want to take Aari to some kind of hospital or clinic with you?" Becker asked, and Acorna realized that he, too, had a definite, if somewhat limited, ability to read thoughts.

"I will go below and discuss the matter with the *viizaar*. But, my brother," Thariinye said to Aari, "would you not be happier if we brought physicians to you before you meet your little sister and old friends again?"

Aari gave him a glance full of bitterness. "You mean so that I don't frighten them? You are very thoughtful, my brother."

"Okay, that's it," Becker said. "I think we'll just stow the moving of the bones until your docs see what they can do for Aari, here or there, I don't care. Just get off my ship for now, all you guys. Lady Acorna is welcome any time she wants to come, but the rest of you do me a favor and wait for an engraved invitation, huh? Tell your leader lady that I still need fuel and I hope they got a long hose on the gas pump at the spaceport to bring the fuel to me since I can't get to it."

(*Very* hostile and aggressive,) Thariinye told Acorna in passing.

"I heard that!" Becker said.

"I think I should go, too," Acorna said. "You will need someone to speak for you. Not that my opinion is much valued by the *viizaar*, but if Grandam Naadiina, the elder, backs me, they will have to listen."

Aari almost smiled at her. "Is Grandam still with us, then?"

"Very much so," Acorna said.

"I would like to see her. She will not be frightened of me, though she may be sad. Grandam was always kind to Laarye and me when we were small."

"She has taken care of your little sister since your parents—"

Pain spasmed over his face and she realized that if his parents had been lost before they reached Vhiliinyar, he would not have known he wouldn't be reunited with them here. "Oh, I'm sorry. You shouldn't have found out that way," she said.

His broken hand rested on her shoulder, comfortingly. "I knew they could no longer be alive or they would have been here to meet me. It was my choice to remain behind, not theirs to abandon me. You only confirmed what I knew already."

Acorna hurried to catch up with the others and Becker lowered the robolift once more. This time the cat stayed firmly onboard, sitting protectively between Aari's feet.

"I'm happy to report, Count Edacki, that the experimental station is now fully operational and the testing has begun." General

Ikwaskwan gave the news to his employer on his private and secure channel. "Our technicians are going over the computers of the captured Linyaari ships, trying to find a way to open the navigation programs and decode the course to the home world. It seems there is an autodestruct device on such programs, but we are unsure as to how it can be reconstructed when the—creatures—wish to return to their home world."

"Perhaps you can cajole our guests into providing you with the information verbally," Ganoosh suggested.

"Well, there's a little problem with that, sir. Except for three of the captives, the ones who came for the Acorna girl a few months ago, none of these—creatures—speak anything resembling Standard. We tried forcing the ones who do understand to translate, but they refuse and there is no budging them. Torture doesn't work. They don't say anything, even though they feel it. They pretty well heal immediately. Or die. We've almost lost the ambassador—whatsername—the one who is Acorna's aunt. At least that's who she said she was. It's hard to tell. They all look alike. It's hard to tell the men from the women even."

"Hmmm—are they being recalcitrant about using their other powers?"

"Oh, no siree. We've got that under control. Put one or two of them in a gas chamber and the air is sweet as springtime when you let them out. Poison one of them with drain cleaner and it's crystal clear water before you know it. That's well documented. You can feel free to dump toxic waste, pollute anything you want, and what we have here is a cure-all. Of course, I'm not sure how well they'll perform outside a controlled environment."

"It's not like you to mince words, General." Ganoosh smiled. "You mean outside of captivity. Well, there are some other little tests I want you to run. I have had my ward divert her course, but soon she will be arriving with a very important guest, I hope, and possibly some information regarding the location of the central nesting place of our fine horned friends.

She will also have with her some horns which have been removed from their original owners. I would like you to do some testing to determine the qualitative difference in the performance of the horn on a live animal, as opposed to one that's detached. If it is not great, well, then—"

"I understand perfectly, Count Edacki. I wish also to report, by the way, that I have myself devised an interesting and entertaining way of testing the horns' healing powers."

"How is that?" Ganoosh asked.

"By reviving the idea of the Roman amphitheater and gladiator contests. You'll recall my associate, Nadhari Kando?" the general asked.

"You haven't made her privy to our little secret, have you? The woman was in league with that bleeding-heart Delszaki Li," the count said with some disgust.

"We seem to have solved the problem of Nadhari's tender heart with liberal infusions of drugs that produce hostility and aggression. They seem to overcome her natural inhibitions to violence, which were never all that strong anyway." Ikwaskwan's smile was feral.

"I recall that from another conversation we had," Ganoosh said.

"We lucked upon a ship full of children, enemies of your late associate, the Piper, I might add. They had hoped, I understand, to enlist Nadhari to teach them the art of war. So I am accommodating them. Have a peek," he said.

The general switched the view on the comscreen so that Ganoosh saw an amphitheater constructed by building bleachers up the sides of a biosphere bubble. The soldiers in the bleachers were protected from the combatants by walls of reinforced plascrete. In the center of the ring, tethered by the neck and foot to a pillar, was Nadhari Kando, the lithe and dangerous-looking female Ganoosh had seen previously in Ikwaskwan's company. She was armed with daggers and whips. And a tall, rather lovely teenaged girl, dressed in what was apparently Ikwaskwan's scanty idealized version of a Roman toga, was forced into her path by soldiers carrying laser prods. The girl had only a dagger and a net.

An anguished cry rose from somewhere in the background. "'Ziana! No!"

"Is that her name?" Ganoosh asked.

"Yes, sir. She is Adreziana Starborne, the captain of the Starfarer children I spoke of. How touching. She is trying to talk to Nadhari through the drugs, you see? But Nadhari is no more likely to listen to her than the lions once did the Christians."

"And the male voice I heard just now crying her name in such a tender fashion?"

"That would be Pal Kendoro, Count Edacki. Like Nadhari herself, a former lackey of Delszaki Li. A friend of Nadhari's, actually. The old Nadhari, that is, not this new, improved model."

"It is unfair and unchivalrous of you to send that sweet child out there to face the madwoman on her own, General. May I suggest a refinement?"

"Yes, sir, of course."

"Bind the lovers together. Two love birds with one stoned warrior woman." He began to giggle. "Oh, that tickles my fancy! Yes it does! I shall have to come out there immediately to view it in person. Save that spectacle for me, will you?"

"No need, Count. No matter how badly Nadhari hurts them or, if they are lucky, one of them hurts her, the Linyaari will certainly cooperate to heal such innocent hides. We can recycle both Nadhari and the children indefinitely, if the healing powers work as well as we've been led to believe."

"Splendid, General, splendid! How I have missed these little entertainments—the sort the Didis used to dream up to interest me back in the old days before the unicorn girl showed up. How very fitting that her own species should make such pleasures feasible and cost effective again."

Nineteen

aati wanted to know where her brother was and why he had not come out with the others. "He was hurt, Maati," Liriili told her when the child refused to leave. "The aliens we fled when your parents came here hurt him very badly. He does not want you to see him until we can heal him."

All of the adults were now trying to project calm and patience like crazy but Maati had learned a thing or two as a government page.

"You didn't want him to come!" she said. "You were scared of him. But he wouldn't hurt me. He's the only family I have and I'm the only family he has. I want to see him."

Acorna said, "You will, Maati. You will. But he *is* hurt by the way people look at him and he doesn't want to be pitied. He wants you to look up to him, not feel sorry for him. So we have to go get the physicians now and bring them right back here to heal him."

"I want to be there," Maati said firmly. "We are family and I want to help him. If I was hurt and he knew it, I bet he would be there. My parents would have been, wouldn't they, Grandam?"

"Yes, Maati. And I see no reason why you shouldn't come, too."

Thariinye sent the adults in the group a somewhat distorted mental picture, in Acorna's opinion, of Aari and Becker. Grandam gasped and Acorna, who had been trying hard not to project, snapped at him.

(Well, Grandam said she didn't see why,) Thariinye declared in his own defense.

The other two males had scurried off immediately, looking distinctly unwell.

"Thariinye," Liriili said. "Please ask the communications duty officer to contact the physicians' college and have Baaksi Bidiila and Baaksi M'kaarin come here at once with their staff and any necessary equipment."

"Yes, *Viizaar* Liriili," Thariinye said, relieved to be away from there for even a moment. "At once."

When he had gone, Liriili confronted Acorna and Grandam. "It is not helpful that you two judge him or me or the others for reacting in this way to one who has been so badly maimed," she said. "The Khleevi sent the vids of our people under torture to us in order to deliberately terrorize us. As you can see, it works. Our people are not cowards, but we *are* peaceful. We're healers. We would never do anything so dreadful to other living creatures. It is horrifying to us in the extreme. To see what can be done to us while we still live and breathe and walk—well, that would be far too upsetting for most of our people to be able to continue functioning. Such a sight would upset the balance and harmony we have achieved since coming here. Besides, it is in the best interests of Aari himself that he be healed before he rejoins us."

"How bad is it?" Maati wanted to know. "*I'm* his sister. You shouldn't all try to keep this from me."

Before Liriili could tell her what she'd seen in Thariinye's image, Acorna described Aari's wounds herself, focusing on the pain in his eyes. Maati started to cry, big grieving tears rolling down her cheeks. "*Nooo!* Why did they do such a thing? Poor Aari! I want to help him."

Grandam patted her shoulder. "You shall, child, you shall. Liriili, I feel it would be a good idea if Acorna, Maati, and I went to the communications shed and asked to be allowed to speak with Aari."

"I really discourage any further communication with those aliens until we can bring Aari back among us," Liriili said.

"Child, I do understand your objections and your responsibility to the rest of our people, but in this case, our responsibility to Maati must come first—if she feels she can handle this, then we must not stand in her way. Aari is her family, almost all the family she has left. Hasn't she lost enough? Hasn't her brother? We left him behind once for the sake of us all; isn't it his turn to come first, now that he's back among us?"

"I will bow to your wisdom, Grandam. But I still feel that the sight of Aari would be unnecessarily frightening to the public. The images projected by Iiryn and Yiirl alone will be giving many of our people nightmares."

"In that case, *Viizaar*," Grandam said, "perhaps if you feel so strongly about that, it must be your immediate priority to return to the city and give our people the correct and actually—and we seem to have overlooked this—quite *joyous* news that one we all believed was lost has not only returned, but is the first person to have survived capture and torture by the Khleevi; that he is in the process of having his wounds healed, and should soon be among his friends and loved ones once more. Meanwhile, since according to Thariinye, Acorna is the only one of us capable of reasoning with the belligerent Captain Becker, she, Maati as next of kin, and I as a friend and elder from the boy's youth, should remain to help the physicians with their work and provide moral support." Grandam's words were clearly an order to the flustered *viizaar*.

"As you wish, Grandam." Liriili withdrew and headed back to the city. The rest of them walked to the communications shed.

The communications officer gladly ceded his seat to them and watched as Acorna hailed the *Condor.*

"Well, Lady Acorna, fancy seeing you there. What's on your mind, hon?" The honest face of Jonas Becker reflected pleasure at the sight of her in his viewscreen.

"Captain Becker, Grandam Naadiina, whom you heard Aari say he knew and was fond of, is here, and she would like to speak to him. Aari's younger sister, Maati, who is Grandam's ward, is here as well. Maati has been informed of the nature of Aari's wounds but she wants very much to speak to him and—well, I think it would be best if she could speak for herself."

"Right. If you think it's best, then I'll try to get him in here. But those jerks who were here with you are not welcome aboard this vessel again. I hope everybody understands that."

Acorna smiled. "I believe you made yourself abundantly clear on that issue, Captain." She looked around. "Thariinye doesn't seem to be here now, but Liriili asked him to send for the physicians. They should be arriving soon. We three would like to return to your ship with them, with your permission."

"Granted, with pleasure," he said. "Wait a minute and I'll see if Aari will come out to talk to his sister."

"I'm not entirely sure this contact is authorized," the communications officer said.

"No?" Grandam said. "Well, it is. Liriili appointed Khornya and me as her liaisons in this affair. Khornya is already showing great talent as an alien ambassador, don't you think?"

"Yes, Grandam," the officer said meekly.

"That's a good lad," Grandam said with an indulgent smile.

A moment later Becker appeared back on screen. Behind him loomed a tall figure with a cat wound around his neck. Maati had her jaw thrust forward and set. As Aari's ruined face appeared on the screen, she blinked twice but that was all. Aari also blinked, so perhaps he didn't see her first instinctive reaction. Acorna thought he was trying not to weep again.

"Welcome home, elder brother," the little girl said, sounding less like a little girl than Acorna had ever heard her. "I am Maati, born here on narhii-Vhiliinyar to our parents before they returned to search for you and our brother. They—they never found you?" She had tried, Acorna knew, not to make it a question but could not quite keep the note of hope from her voice.

"To my sorrow, no. It is also my great sorrow to tell you that our brother has passed this life, but it gives me more joy than I have known in all of these *ghaanye* to see you and to hear your voice, younger sister. I am Aari, born many *ghaanye* and a world before you, but I am your kinsman and I love you already."

"And I you," Maati said. "Aari, when the doctors come, tell your friend I will come, too. I'll lay my horn upon you and keep you from any pain and speed your healing."

Tears did fall from Aari's eyes as she spoke. "My gratitude, Maati," he said, but his response was almost drowned out as both Acorna and Grandam said, "And I will do the same," in response to Maati's declaration.

"My gratitude, Grandam Naadiina, and to Khornya, who has already—my gratitude."

"Okay," Becker said. "But if you ladies are coming you'd better step on it. I see a bunch of people coming up the road right now. I'll send down the robolift for you so you'll be on board when they arrive."

"Thanks, Captain Becker," Acorna said.

"Thank *you*, lady. You, too, ladies."

The physicians were those most skilled in the healing arts, much more than the average Linyaari. Many of them, Grandam told Acorna, had studied off-planet, where there were more ills to be healed. Most Linyaari were never ill or hurt for more than a few moments, or at least not until they found the next Linyaari. In fact, being a physician on narhii-Vhiliinyar was largely an intellectual rather than a practical profession. The physicians didn't gasp when they saw Aari, but they shook their heads, regarded him with clinical interest, tried a few applications of their own horns with little effect, and then turned to look with interest at the piles of bones in the holds beyond their patient.

"So you say, Aari, that after you were injured you dragged yourself to the burial place and the power of the horns of our departed forebears healed you of your injuries—at least to a degree? As much as the lasting damage done to you by the Khleevi would allow?"

"Yes."

The physicians looked uncomfortably at each other. "Unfortunately, given the special nature of the tortures inflicted by the Khleevi, the horns' healing power only knit that which was broken—it did not straighten anything into proper position first. Khleevi take special pains when working with Linyaari to try and short-circuit the healing processes."

"I had suspected as much," Aari said dryly, regarding his own misshapen arm.

"But now that your arm is healed this way, there is little *we* can do. The tissue is not injured, as far as our abilities are concerned. As for your horn—well, a transplant might be possible when Maati is older, if she could spare a piece of her horn. But she and it are too immature to risk that at this time. And such a procedure has never been tried, you know. No one has—ever survived such an injury in the past."

"Oh, do try!" Maati cried. "I don't care if it hurts. It can't hurt anything like Aari has hurt. Please, can't you do something for him?"

One of the doctors, a female, Bidiila, knelt beside Maati and took her hand. "We wish we could, youngling," she said, and Acorna could see she was close to tears herself. "But he has suffered great harm at the hands of our enemies. Some will see his wounds and blame him for receiving them, as irrational as that may be, but some will be as wise as you and know that he is living proof of Linyaari courage and fortitude. You must be very proud of him."

"I *am*," Maati said, taking the doctor's hand and trying to put it in Aari's, "but he hurts so terribly—am I the only one who feels it? Can nobody help him?"

Aari gathered her up and stroked her hair with his broken hand, shushing her. "I am used to it now, little sister. Please don't weep for me. Did you not hear what they said? Later, perhaps, when they know more, they can do more."

"But there must be something they can do *now*," the child insisted.

"Well, actually, there is," Becker said. "We could break the old injuries, one at a time, and you could reheal them. That should work." He looked at the doctors and cocked an eyebrow. Acorna translated.

"We do not do such things, Captain. Even in a therapeutic way, and to heal. Injuring any living creature is an act of violence and not our way."

When Acorna gave Becker the doctor's reply, he shrugged and asked, "They don't mind finishing the job if I do the dirty work though, do they?"

Acorna translated. "They have no objection."

Acorna asked Becker, "What do you have in mind?"

"Well, first, I just want to make certain of something. The way Aari healed me and RK when we were hurt, you can do that for him? I mean, make it so he gets patched up completely almost at the same time he's hurt so he doesn't feel anything for more than say, a split second?"

The others looked dubious, but Acorna, who had had considerable experience with the healing properties of her own horn, nodded. "Yes. Probably even more effectively than Aari healed you since he had to use the dead horns to accomplish the healing."

"Well then, all we have to do is rebreak the places that have set wrong and heal them again. I hate to put Aari through it, but it's the only solution," Becker said. "Your docs may have principles against it, but I don't."

Bidiila said, "I personally have never encountered old fractures such as these. Few of us have. When one can heal almost any wound immediately, one seldom sees old wounds, and even then, usually they have received some sort of attention prior to ours that keeps them from being in such sad shape as Aari's."

"I understand, doc. You people don't want to do it because the way you see it, hurting people is the opposite of healing. Me, I don't have any problem with breaking a few bones, especially in a good cause." He touched Aari's shoulder. "How about it, buddy?" he asked Aari. "You willing to let me bust you up a little so your medics can heal you right this time? I can't do much about the horn, but I got me a crowbar that will do a good job with a few surgical strikes. They promise it'll only hurt for a little while."

Aari only glanced at the doctors, who, except for Bidiila, had backed off slightly. "I can bear pain at the hand of a friend," he said. "Part of the pain of the torture was knowing that my captors intended their cruelty and delighted in my pain. They even amplified it. I know that you will be sharing it and helping me bear it."

"Maybe Maati and you other ladies should leave now," Becker told Acorna.

Acorna didn't need to translate. Maati was shaking her head, and clinging to Aari. Grandam said simply, in clear thought-speak, without hesitation or question so that even Becker could understand her, (Your concern for our sensitivities does you credit, Captain, but Aari will need our support more than ever. We will stay in contact with him as you perform your task. In that way, he may feel far less pain.)

Becker nodded. The other doctors were all protesting but Bidiila spoke to them sharply and, although they looked away as Becker fetched his crowbar, they remained close. Aari reclined on a table and Grandam, Acorna, and Maati stayed close by his head, their horns touching his face and neck, and their hands on his arms and shoulders. Becker, without fear or squeamishness, and with the efficiency he might give to hammering some bent object into shape, brought the heavy tool down sharply on the misshapen part of Aari's leg. Aari let his breath out in a huff and a high-pitched whistle, and by then the doctors were closing in, applying their horns to the fresh wound as they manipulated the leg so that it would set correctly.

"You okay, buddy?" Becker asked Aari gently.

With great effort, Aari said, "Yes." And in a moment, after

several deep breaths, added, "My left foot now, please, Joh."

Maati had buried her face against his mane and Acorna felt that he was more concerned about her reaction than about the pain, which was dulled by their contact and quite brief compared to what he had endured walking around with misaligned bones, twisted tendons, and atrophied, overly strained muscles. Each break and healing found him breathing easier, though all of them, especially Aari and Becker, had sweat running from every pore. Worse yet was that the sound of Aari's crunching bones was drowned out only by the high, eerie keening of the Makahomian Temple Cat, who cowered beneath the table.

The process took hours and Acorna was very weary, as was Grandam. Acorna could see that Grandam's horn and those of the doctors were all becoming translucent, as hers had when she had cured the wounded following the battle between Rushima and the Khleevi.

Aari opened his eyes only after he had healed from the last break. Becker, jaw set, functioned like a machine but his voice was always controlled, and always gentle and concerned when speaking to Aari or any of them. He knew that he was hurting to help the healing and had to keep a firm grip on himself so that each blow did not cause him almost as much pain as it did Aari.

When at last they were done and Aari sat up, straight and five inches taller, Acorna went to Becker and laid her horn against his forehead.

"Thank you, Khornya," Aari said. "I wish I was able to do that, too. You are spent."

"We are all spent," Grandam said.

The cat shot from beneath the table. Maati caught and held him, soothing him with a touch of her horn that soon had the beast purring.

Bidiila said, "We have been thinking about your horn, Aari. It is a new problem, as I said, but did you not say your brother perished on Vhiliinyar and that you have brought his bones back for reburial? Do you feel that his spirit would be offended if we took a small piece from his horn, which would have similar DNA to yours and therefore be less likely to be rejected, and tried to coax it to grow on the root of your own horn?"

This was done, with Aari's and Maati's agreement.

"Now you can come back with us," Maati told her brother.

He put his hand up to the bandaged place where the horn implant had been. "I don't think so. I'll still be an outcast."

Acorna said, "Maybe you could wear a prosthetic hidden by a horn-hat."

"A what?" Becker and Aari asked together.

Acorna explained and Becker said, "Yeah, we could give you a fake horn inside to stiffen it. Nobody would know if you didn't want them to."

"Aside from the people all over the planet who already do, thanks to those who were here earlier," Aari said.

"Never mind them. You want to see your old friends, and what this new world is like, or not?"

Acorna thought it was a good thing Becker didn't really wait for an answer.

The com unit came on again and the officer on the other end said, "Captain Becker, the people have gathered to rebury the bones of our dead."

"Okay. We'll get them onto the robolift and send them down load by load."

"I will need to supervise," Aari said. "I am the only one who still knows who was buried where and remembers the clan designations of each body. Where would I find a—horn-hat?"

Bidiila reached into her lab coat pocket. "Take mine," she said. "I have several others. They come in handy when you spend the day listening to minor complaints from patients who should have had the sense not to overgraze."

Becker had gone to work with a torch and hammer on a piece of lightweight alloy and in no time fashioned it into the semblance of a horn. A slot on either side held a band that slid beneath Aari's mane to hold it in place. With Bidiila's horn-hat, it was difficult to tell him from another Linyaari.

The three women stayed aboard the ship and helped Aari and Becker load the robolift time after time. Then Becker remembered something and came back with what looked like another man, albeit one somewhat scarred and with a peculiar skin tint. This, Acorna learned, was a KEN unit, an android, and he was able to work five times faster, if not more accurately, than any of them. Aari had to indicate to Becker whose bones were whose before riding down with each load and supervising its disposition. The road to the spaceport was lined with Linyaari of all clans, all come to claim the bones of their dead.

"How did they find out so fast?" Becker asked.

"Thought transference is a very swift form of communication when used correctly," Grandam said. "I suspect Liriili set up a relay of some sort to inform the clans."

"Will you look at that guy?" Becker asked, nodding toward Aari. "I was the pounder and he was the poundee and he is working rings around me. You'd think he'd been sitting around watching the stars go by all morning instead of getting every bone in his body rebroken and mended."

"He is a very determined young man," Grandam said. "He had to be or he would not have survived all that he has."

When Aari returned for the last time, he carried a single skeleton, this one carefully wrapped in the thermal blanket Becker had given Aari to sleep with.

"Grandam, I was very careful with Grandsire Niciirye but I brought him back to you. I do not wish you to be concerned, but Grandsire's horn is missing from his remains."

"His horn?" Grandam asked, and Acorna saw that she was trying to picture her lifemate as Aari was now. "Not the Khleevi?"

"Captain Becker will explain," Aari said. "I must go below now."

"Thanks a lot, buddy," Becker said.

Aari allowed himself a small grim smile. "You have nothing to worry about, Joh, even if I had not already hidden your surgical instrument. We are a nonviolent people. Grandam will not cause you much physical damage for desecrating the remains of her lifemate. I do not know if that will be true for the others whose kin are missing their horns. Those bones I have left in the hold for now, but Grandsire's at least I can return."

His voice contained elements of black humor, but his emotions were hollow and cold with grief, as they came to Acorna. His thoughts had been harder and harder to detect as the bones and horns left the ship and it came to Acorna that he might be lonely without them.

She turned back to Becker and to Grandam, who was watching the salvage man with a curious mixture of pain and reproach. "You are a grave robber, Captain?" she asked.

"I take full responsibility, ma'am," Becker said, and pointed at RK, washing on top of the control console. "It was the cat's fault. Your old planet is a mess. We landed there looking for salvage. Some of your people's horns were laying around on the ground. It was night, the light was poor, and I thought since the cat liked them I'd pick up a few and see what they were. Well, *honest*, they really were just laying around."

"So you took them?" she asked, the reproach still there.

"I'm a *salvage* expert, for pity's sake!" he said. "I pick up stuff nobody claims—and it sure didn't look like there was a living soul there at the time. I didn't even know what they were till we got back to Kezdet and a couple of people thought they belonged to the Lady Acorna or her shipmates."

Acorna was a little startled at the idea at first but it made sense. She and then her aunt and the others were the only Linyaari the people of Kezdet and Manganos had met.

"One fellow was ready to turn me over to the cops for murder, and one nasty little—female individual, an old enemy of Acorna's—tried to kill me more than once to take the horns. Then she followed us to your old planet and took the horns I had with me. If she hadn't I swear I would have returned them, I don't care how much they were worth."

"Were—*worth*, Captain?" Maati asked, touching hers.

Grandam looked horrified, and Maati said, "Oh, no! You mean like in the story of the Ancestors? How the people didn't want them, they only wanted the horns? But dead horn? Healing using dead horn doesn't work nearly as well as healing done by a living person!"

"It works better than no horn at all, I'm afraid, honey," Becker said. "And there are a lot of us out there in the galaxy without healing horns."

"You say this woman knew me?" Acorna asked. "Who is she?"

"Kisla Manjari." Becker filled her in on Kisla's attempts to murder him and RK.

Acorna sighed. She had hoped that perhaps when Kisla learned of her own humble birth from her adopted mother, the girl might have been cured of some of her arrogance, but apparently she was even worse. Becker's thoughts were not as easily discernible now, nor were the cat's thought patterns as clear as they had been with the bones aboard, but from what she could tell, Kisla was more badly disturbed than ever.

"Could she have followed you here?" Acorna asked Becker.

Becker shook his head. "We lost her this time. Aari scared her away with a Khleevi weapon."

Grandam looked vaguely shocked but Becker said, "It simulated explosions in the earth—maybe it was a mining tool instead of a weapon to use against people—he said they used things like that to destabilize the whole planet. Anyway, it worked, and she took off. She only found us that time because of a homing device on the droid, but we got rid of that finally."

Acorna sighed. "That's good, then."

"I also have an—idiosyncratic way of navigating that's unpredictable to me as well as other ships. Besides which, I had no idea where we were going. We steered by Aari's memory of what he had been told was the evacuation route before the invasion."

Grandam sighed. "I think that whatever the others do, I shall bury Niciirye in the field beyond my back door. And Captain—if you—if you should recover the horns, by any chance, I wonder if there is any way you could somehow return them to us? It is a very important link between us and our dead. I don't know why; maybe scientists would say that an extraordinary amount of DNA material is encoded in the horn and survives death. But however it is that it works, it is a connection and now—"

She looked away but Acorna felt Grandam's pain as if it were her own, a sudden cold void, an open pit of grief she had never before sensed in Grandam.

Twenty

It took nearly a week—a *ghiiri-ghaanye*—from the time the bones were unloaded from the *Condor* and handed over to their descendants for the Council to decide where the burials were to take place. During this time, the bones stayed in the homes of their respective clan members.

The presence of the dead from the past cast a pall over the living that was at least partially connected to their fears for those who were currently voyaging through space and had been out of communication for days now, completely silent.

Grandam had accompanied Aari to a Council session where he told the story of the cemetery's unwitting desecration and how he had preserved the bones against further pilfering. He described the thought-images he had received from Becker regarding the unwholesome interest in the horns by some of Becker's fellow humans. The Council, Grandam said, had become rather agitated after hearing that, both concerned about the possible invasion of other horn-seeking aliens and troubled that there could be some connection between the alien interest in the horns of the Linyaari dead and the lack of contact with the space-faring Linyaari.

Liriili had dismissed that concern (rather shrilly, Grandam

noted). "These particular aliens are galaxies away. This one found us only because of Aari's memory. And these humans had never seen one of us before Khornya." The *viizaar* did not say that she wished the aliens had never seen Khornya, that she could almost wish the girl had perished with her parents rather than be the instrument of bringing such danger upon them. But Grandam heard the thought, even concealed. And worse, she knew that others on the Council shared it. The possible threat from aliens preoccupied the Council during that session to the extent that discussion of burial sites was temporarily tabled.

Later, Aari told Grandam, "I hope they will put the burial ground somewhere protected, where the graves will not be disturbed again. A cave would be good. Like the one I hid them in on Vhiliinyar. The bones were easy to guard there, and the cave could always be collapsed upon them if outsiders came to disturb them again."

Grandam told Acorna about it later, when Aari had returned to the *Condor* with food for Becker. "I got the strongest impression that what he intends to do the rest of his life is guard the burial ground."

Acorna could not suppress a shudder. "I suppose that's what the Khleevi did to him that none of our horns can touch."

"Yes, well, perhaps. But it's nonsense. That is a brilliant young man. He excelled at every aspect of our culture and had already traveled to other worlds as an ambassador and educator. He is like a shell, from which the little creature within has been stolen. No—I exaggerate. Perhaps his essence is only hidden, but hidden from himself as well as from others."

Later, when the Council decided that each clan would be responsible for burying its own dead in separate burial places, Aari insisted on attending all reinterments. The clans whose dead were not returned to them with the rest of the bones did not mention the missing remains, which Acorna found odd. However, the entire city of Kubiilikhan was actively, prematurely, mourning the ones now believed to be lost in the cosmos and so a few absent dead from the past mattered less than the burial of the many bones reclaimed.

Acorna accompanied Aari as he attended the first reinterment.

The sky looked like an open wound that day, yellow, with huge red and burgundy clouds boiling in the west, split now and then by the green lightning she remembered from before. The pavilions creaked, extruding and retracting their ramps like snakes' tongues, raising and lowering their floors as the breezes and dampness shifted.

Aari was very quiet and Acorna felt from him confusion and grief, and sensed this might be coming from the Council's decision to have no central burial place, so that even the tenuous position he had found for himself as guardian of the dead was now lost to him.

This was confirmed when she noticed that when a few people addressed him, he ignored them.

"Aari," she said softly, "Techno-artisan Maarye just greeted you."

Aari looked genuinely startled. "Oh. I'm sorry. That was real then?" He passed his hand over his face. Healed and wearing the prosthetic horn Becker had devised for him, he seemed a handsome, stalwart example of Linyaari manhood.

"Of course it was real," she said. "You looked right through him."

"I'm sorry. I should apologize. I've kept company with phantoms for a long time, Khornya. They don't generally expect manners, or even answers."

Thunder cracked just then and the rain drenched everyone within a single moment. No one ran for cover, however. This was a solemn moment. All of Kubiilikhan and most of the rest of narhii-Vhiliinyar was here. All of the clans had at least sent representatives, gathered up in the shuttle belonging to the new ship being assembled by the techno-artisans. Only one communications officer remained on duty at the spaceport, and even that officer was frequently relieved so that everyone could attend the appropriate burials.

The rain was welcome, even fitting. It made the new ground softer for burial of the old bones. The Ancestors were in attendance, and that alone kept the procession from speeding its slow, mournful pace.

This was the burial ceremony of Clan Neeyeereeya, the clan with the most members to be interred, and the most above ground, though many of the latter were far too young to remember those buried on the world they had never known.

And yet, the atmosphere was as heavy with sorrow as the sky was with clouds. Clansmen with heads bowed against the torrential rain carried the burial baskets containing the remains of their kinfolk to dark holes in the long blue grass. Acorna had sorely missed her dear, departed Mr. Li, but though her loss had been new while these losses were old ones, she had not previously experienced the raw expression of grief she felt from the other Linyaari. Unlike the grief of men, this feeling carried no morbidity about it, no consciousness of the flesh rotting or ghoulish fascination with death. There was no threat or anger here, only a kind of wounded wonder at the mystery of how a loved one who had walked, slept, and eaten beside you could be rendered to a few calcified fragments.

She picked up the clearest image of bones, not these bones wrapped for this burial, but of the bones of the Linyaari missing in space, as their relatives and loved ones imagined burying them. The grief for the long-dead kin was only part of the loss being mourned here. The planetbound Linyaari cried for future as well as past deaths, grief joined with fear for the safety of the missing husbands and wives, fathers and mothers, sons and daughters, brothers and sisters. Acorna suddenly felt tremendously protective of her own people, and wished she could do something, anything, to help.

Aari stood perfectly still as horns touched in silent remembrance, and then, startlingly, clearly even to him, a keening began inside him, low at first, then rising and falling, until it turned into a melody and Acorna realized he was singing. As the first chorus began, other voices rose to join his, those of the older Linyaari, and then, more tentatively, a few of the younger ones, singing their lament for those missing as well as the dead.

Where do you graze now that you've gone away?
I no longer see you, we no longer play
Together at sunrise, together at night,
Gone is your laughter and gone your eye's light.

Your horn now is dull, it cannot ease my heart,
It cannot ease my pain now that we are apart.
I seek you in silence, I seek you in crowds,
I look for your face in the shape of the clouds.

Is that your laughter in the voice of the stream
Where we drank together when our world was green?
My colors are dark now that you've gone away
And I cannot hear words that you used to say.

They tell me you live in my thoughts and my dreams,
Someday you'll return in a newborn youngling.
But my tears keep on falling till someday you do,
And they'll make a new river I'll name after you.

The song continued throughout the burial and on to the next and the next until the dead of all of the clans were buried. The procession ended at last at Grandam's pavilion, where she and Maati stood beside the burial baskets of Grandsire Niciirye and Aari's and Maati's brother, Laarye. Grandam joined in the song, and Maati, too, their tears indistinguishable from the rain washing down their faces as the baskets were gently put in the ground.

Acorna had sung with her people as the verses were repeated over and over again, to no music but the beat of the hard Linyaari feet pawing the soaked ground and throwing mud back over the baskets.

She was crying, too, for the parents she had known so short a time, for Delszaki Li, for all of the children she had not been able to save, but most of all she was finally feeling what had made this place so cold and strange and distant, how the heart had been cut out of her people when they left behind the continuity of their own lines, when they left behind their home. Acorna cried for little Maati, who was left alone except for Grandam and her strange, sad brother. But it was for Aari himself that she cried hardest, Aari who had suffered as no other Linyaari had ever suffered, and lived, who had been abandoned and who had lost everything he had ever held dear, including a vital part of himself. And yet, when he had the chance to save himself, he had thought mostly of saving from pillage the bones of his people. Acorna had the distinct impression that he might never have returned except for that mission.

As the last strains of the song drained into the ground with the rain, Acorna noticed that people were standing closer together, males and females touching horns, arms around each other's backs and waists, walking away side by side, gazing into each others' eyes. No one was wearing horn-hats today except Aari, and increasingly the thoughts being projected were unmistakably amorous.

Acorna felt a rather embarrassing warmth flooding through herself as well, and Grandam, wiping her eyes and nose on the sleeve of her garment, smiled at her. "It's a natural reaction, child. During these hard years our population has fallen off and as the song says, our loved ones will only return with future generations—so our bodies tell us it is time to start making babies."

Before Acorna could reply, she saw Thariinye coming toward her and warm feeling or no, she stepped behind Aari, back into the shelter of Grandam's pavilion. This did not seem to be the smart thing to do either as other people, couples, were disappearing into the nearest pavilions with an urgency that left no doubt that they were taking care of needs far more interesting than a wish to escape the rain.

Acorna turned away from the dispersing crowd.

Suddenly, the front flap of Grandam's pavilion burst open and Captain Becker ran into the middle of the room, panting, the uniformed communications officer close on his heels.

He was shouting. "Okay, okay, I know I'm not allowed but this is an emergency! I need to find Aari and Lady Acor — Khornya. *Now!* Where are they?" he demanded of Acorna, evidently not able to see her in the dim interior of the pavilion, darkened both by rain and out of respect for the ceremony.

"I'm here, Captain Becker. It's me, Acorna. What's the matter?"

Aari ducked inside behind her. "Joh?"

"I just got a Mayday on my remotest remote scanner. It's from a ship called *Shahrazad*, Lady Acorna, registered on a planet called Laboue to the House of Harakamian."

"Uncle Hafiz!"

"Yeah, that's right, Hafiz Harakamian. They're under attack."

"This is nonsense!" the communications officer sputtered as Becker's arrival began drawing a crowd, including Liriili. "We picked up no such communication!"

"No, well, maybe that's because you people don't want anybody to know you're here so you don't look very hard," Becker said. "But I have equipment that lets me pick up signals two galaxies away. Can you get somebody to sell me the damn fuel so I can go help them?"

"I will come, too, Joh," Aari said. "My work here is done and Grandam is taking good care of my sister."

"Me too," Acorna said. She thought someone would protest but Liriili actually looked relieved.

"I will also come," Thariinye said.

"No way," Becker told him. "You make a crowd all by yourself, buddy. Unless you Linyaari happen to maintain a cavalry, which, since you're pacifists, I'm inclined to doubt, all I want from the rest of you is refueling and we're outta here."

"Make it so," Liriili said with great relief to the communications officer and to the spaceport personnel among the crowd. She didn't bother to hide her thoughts, and Acorna and everyone else could read her clearly. Liriili was more than a little pleased to see the backs of the contentious Becker, and the troublesome Khornya. And Aari's presence was, as she had predicted, upsetting to many of the inhabitants. He didn't truly belong among normal Linyaari any more. Yes, off-planet was a very good place for them all, as far as Liriili was concerned, as far out into outer space as they could possibly go.

Acorna turned as she heard feet galloping up beside her. Maati called out to her to wait. She did so—there was no immediate need for haste. The *Condor* was being refueled with one of the several mixtures that would power it.

"I like diversity, in case you didn't notice," Becker said to the world at large since Aari was already back in the ship and Acorna had turned to meet Maati. The Linyaari fueling the ship did so quickly and efficiently but paid the human no undue attention. "The hatch is the Mytherian toxic waste chute, got the robolift off a Pachean tanker, and the nose cone is from a Nupiak asteroid breaker. It can take any one of a dozen different fuels and runs good on all of them or a mix."

Maati's demands drowned out Becker's voice to Acorna. "I want to go *with* you!" she cried. "How can he leave again when I just got him?"

Grandam, panting a little, caught up with them.

"Maati, we're answering a distress call. It will be dangerous. Your brother is going to help Captain Becker and I'm going in case someone needs healing," Acorna said.

"I can heal, too!" Maati said. "I helped Aari. I did! He said I was the most help of everybody. I want to go into space, too, and be star-clad like he is and you are, Khornya. Make them take me along."

Grandam put her hand on Maati's shoulder. "Maybe next

time, child. This time I need you here. We have lost too many already."

"Well, then, he should stay, too," Maati said stubbornly. "He only just got here. Captain Becker hasn't had him always. He can do things by himself or with the cat or — Khornya can help him."

"Being traded in, am I?" Acorna asked, chiding just a little. She squatted on her heels and said, "Maati, I don't think Aari can stay right now."

"Why not? We healed him. All but his horn."

"The thing is, we didn't. Not entirely. He is not used to being with people any more."

"I will tell you a state secret, child," Grandam said. "Do you know why the Council decided that the graves should be spread out according to clan?"

"I don't care about that!" Maati said.

"No, but Aari does. Do you know that if we had buried them all together, all he wanted to do here was what he has done these last few *ghaanyi* and made himself guardian of the graves?"

"You felt that, too?" Acorna asked.

"He broadcasts quite well, even without a horn," Grandam said. "I — rather think he believes he belongs with the dead, no matter how much the living may care for him."

"That's Khleevi!" Maati declared. "Why would he think that?"

"That's just it, Maati," Acorna said. "He spent a long time with the Khleevi. You saw some of what they did to his body — could you feel what they did to him inside?"

"Yes," Maati said. "Yes, but he'll get better."

"Yes, he will," Acorna said. "But he needs time to get used to being alive. If he stays among our people now, they will never forget how he is now, and it will be much harder for him to grow into his life and become again the man he once was or could have been. Captain Becker may be a little Khleevi around the edges, but he is a good man and he does not let Aari go into himself too much. I will go and make as sure as I can that he comes to no harm and comes back to you. Then, when you're a little older, you can come into space with us if you like."

"Into space—with you? Aren't you coming back, Khornya?"

"I'm not sure," she said. "But my adopted uncle is out there in trouble."

"So is your aunt, don't forget, child," Grandam said, taking Maati by the shoulders. The girl was only partially mollified and later, as Acorna, Aari, and Becker watched the ground from the comscreen, they saw her looking after them as the ship lifted off.

Twenty-One

The *Shahrazad* was still transmitting her distress signal when she was boarded. Hafiz had taken the helm after the captain was hit by falling debris from the first volley fired against the ship. It had come from nowhere, before the *Shahrazad* was able to deploy her shields. Their attacker was cloaked.

Fortunately, the *Shahrazad* was as spacious vertically as the villa on Laboue was horizontally. And there was only one entrance, on the lower levels, and in between, the ship had a labyrinth of defenses.

Karina watched, with a sort of horrified fascination, as pressure-suited individuals entered the main air lock, brandishing large, gleaming, fearsome-looking weapons. The leader, a small person, shucked off her garment to reveal a form-fitting silver garment much like the ones worn by ancient film starlets in vintage Asian space operas. The invader fluffed her hair and demanded of the ship at large, "Hafiz Harakamian, your guests have arrived. Surrender now and save yourself a great deal of pain later."

Hafiz smiled and said softly to the computer, "The baths." Dr. Hoa, standing nearby, nodded, and pressed the control buttons for the little bubble of weather he was not averse to using as a weapon under these circumstances.

Kisla and her phalanx of soldiers blasted open the air lock from the inside, as Hafiz had known they surely would do, disrespectful as they were of his investment in the finest, smoothest, and most aesthetic possible technology. The blast caused the onion-domed portal to the air lock to disassemble into a waterfall of beads which then tinkled away to a mere shimmer of energy as they were penetrated.

Once outside the lock, the invaders were quickly lost in a miasma of swirling steam. The last Karina saw of Kisla or her soldiers for quite some time was the sight of Kisla pulling frantically at the neck of her silvery garment. The invaders mopped sweat out of their eyes and tore off whatever bits of clothing they could spare. They were desperate to keep themselves from broiling in the 135 degree steam heat of the artificial Turkish bath generated by a combination of Hoa's weather wizardry and Hafiz's design for another homey little luxury he had planned to add to the *Shahrazad*.

After a bit, though, the invaders flashed their weapons again, and another of Hafiz's elegant portals was blown open. "The camels, please," Hafiz told the computer.

"What will those do, Hafiz?" Karina asked. "Where have you been hiding camels?"

"They are holograms, my beloved," Hafiz said. "Only holograms, but we have arranged for them to appear to spit great boluses of the most noisome and slimy mixture ever to spoil the high tone of a caravan. Sadly, we did not mix the stuff with acid or poison or something a bit more lethal for fear of harming my own people. These are delaying tactics only, you understand, but perhaps this spawn of scum-born scorpions will find it sufficiently distracting that we will buy time until assistance may arrive. Meanwhile, the navigation officer is deleting our course from the ship's computer."

"Won't Yasmin have warned them about these things?"

Karina asked. "You did say she knew all of your security precautions."

Hafiz smiled sweetly. "Not these. The good doctor Hoa and I have been amusing ourselves with these little diversions only since we left Rushima—while you were involved in your spiritual activities, o pot of passion."

The camel charge was a sight to behold and it certainly did have the element of surprise. If only Hafiz and Dr. Hoa could have made the camels spit something as deadly as it was disgusting, Karina thought, so that these miscreants could be sent back to their creator to have their spirits adjusted and be refitted for their next lives as lizards, snakes, and insects of various species.

The girl pirate's head was encased almost immediately in a blob of green goo. Soon enough, all the invaders were wiping their eyes, coughing from the fumes, and otherwise displaying their displeasure at the welcome they were receiving from the *Shahrazad*. They realized quickly enough that the camels were holograms, of course, but that did not stop them from slipping and falling on the pseudospit, causing their weapons to discharge accidentally. Two of the invaders were wounded in the struggle.

The ship's computer tracked their progress on the diagram of the hull's interior and showed that the next portal they blasted open led them through a maze of halls that caused them to actually go back the way they had come, though not through the Turkish bath.

Instead, the hologram this time was of a vast and endless desert and the walkway designed to help load the ship before takeoff was looped to operate treadmill fashion. The invaders walked, then ran, then walked, but never escaped the desert hologram, nor its arid climate, also courtesy of Dr. Hoa and the ship's computer. By the time someone had the presence of mind to shoot into the simulated rolling sand dunes beneath their feet, the tongues of all of the invaders, at least the human ones, were hanging out, and they were looking parched dry and burned from the sunlamps, fixtures from the ship's spa, that augmented the artificial climate.

The desert disappeared, the portal opened, and the very hot and weary invaders stumbled through to the desert oasis.

"Dancing girls," Hafiz said. The diagram showed that the invaders had climbed through the desert up to the next level. The oasis looked as inviting as it was supposed to, and featured a hologram of Hafiz's favorite garden with a fifteen-layer cascading fountain looking like a waterfall. At this point, Karina noticed that all of the crew except for themselves, Dr. Hoa, and the fallen captain had disappeared. "Where?" she began.

"Watch," Hafiz said. "In deference to the pacifistic nature of our dear Acorna's people, we brought no deadly weapons—but this does not mean my crew has suffered a lapse of their very fine training that makes them the most skilled of warriors in all manner of martial arts and hand-to-hand combat. See you, my blossom, this is what the intruders will behold." And a squad of improbably endowed and incredibly agile and flexible dancing girls—well, persons, as Hafiz had added a pair of dancing boys to the troop, all muscles and flashing dark eyes, with skills to match those of the women. Clad, but not very, in peekaboo veils of glowing, translucent silk in emerald, sapphire, garnet, raspberry, saffron, all were likewise adorned with jingling coins of purest gold fluttering from between lush breasts, cascading over rippling abdominal muscles, twinkling with the twitching of hips, sliding over sinuous arms and necks, and flirting from between brows and just under the lower eyelashes where coy veilings began. Two dancers for each invader, Karina saw, and the invaders, who surely knew this must be a hologram also, could not quite bring themselves to shoot. In fact, as the dancers kicked up little sprays of water from the quite-real fountain, quite-real water touched the parched, would-be conquerors, who disregarded their weapons long enough to drink, to wash their hot faces, to reach for proffered flesh.

Meanwhile, the crew members, clad in blue from head to toe, including transparent facemasks, were concealed by the dancing holograms. They snatched up weapons and disabled the invading troops before any of them knew what was happening.

Kisla Manjari squealed as the dancing boys disappeared and she found herself hoisted aloft by two blue clad crewmen.

"Oh, Hafiz, you are wonderful!" Karina cried. "You've saved us! Was it your ancient Hadathian spirit guides who told you how to do all of this?"

"Very close, o luscious lemon drop, it was the strategy of an ancestor portrayed in one of my collections of rare and venerable vids. The occasion was an athletic contest but the principles were much the same—except we had to employ holograms and our own humble resources instead of the living creatures at the disposal of my ancestor."

"The invaders have been taken prisoner and the ship secured, my Lord," one of the blue-clad crewmen said across the ship's computer's com system. "What shall we do with them now?"

"I haven't decided," Hafiz said. "The crocodile pit or being staked out in the desert. What do you think, my darling?"

"Oh, Hafiz, that's so very unevolved. Besides, the crocodiles would probably give Ms. Manjari professional courtesy, or perhaps die of indigestion. Why not just confine them to the ship's dungeons until such time as they may attain enlightenment?"

"Yes, my angel, but I am very cross with them. Because of them we may not continue our journey. Perhaps we should teach them the joys of spacial liberation?"

"It's a thought," Karina conceded. But they had delayed a bit too long.

Kisla Manjari broke loose from her dancing boys and pushed a button on her inconsequential left breast. "*Midas*, send over the second, third, and fourth phalanxes! And watch out for the biohazards and the dancing girls!"

Her former captors recaptured her, menacing her with her own weapon. She simpered at them, "You wouldn't blast a girl for making a little call, would you?"

Karina looked at her husband hopefully but he shook his head. "Alas, we have no second line of defense."

"*Shahrazad*, this is the *Condor*. You still in one piece?"

"*Condor*?" Hafiz said. "We are just barely. We are about to be boarded a second time."

"They're probably coming through that piece of oversized tubing linking their ship to yours, right?" the voice asked.

"That seems a safe assumption," Hafiz said.

"None of your people coming through, right?"

"No one but pirates."

"Okay, we're on the case, but *Shahrazad*?"

"Yes, *Condor*?"

"Dibs on what's left of the tubing afterward. We're a salvage ship."

"With my compliments, *Condor*."

"Okay, then. Brace yourselves. You may get a little shook up."

Acorna had not realized quite the extent of the adventure she was in for merely by becoming part of the *Condor*'s growing crew.

"How close are they, Captain Becker?" she had asked.

"Only a wormhole away," he replied. "Looks stable, and it should let us out within striking range of the target. Hold onto your horn-hats, boys and girls, here we go." He had taken what he said was the unprecedented move of strapping the cat in, too, a procedure which caused RK's ears to flatten against his head. RK's tail would have lashed as well but it had no place to go. "Sorry about this, shipmate, but we gotta make up some time here."

He called back to the rest of them as he plunged the *Condor* into the first hole, "Salvage and recycling's usually a more leisurely kind of business, you understand."

Acorna smiled. He reminded her so much of her uncles. And Aari, for the first time since she had seen him, seemed to be actively enjoying himself. Or maybe not. He was baring his teeth. Was that hostile or had he just been around Becker too long? No, she thought he was happy. He *felt* happy to her.

The ship jolted as it surged out of the wormhole and through the first of the two "pleats" as Becker called them. "Little speed bump there, ladies and gentlemen. Black water, as my daddy used to call it. Space rapids. Yahoo!"

One more of those and suddenly they were no longer in empty space. They were making visual contact with two similar ships, both posh spaceliners, connected by a long white umbilical cord.

Becker hailed the *Shahrazad*. Acorna nearly wept with relief to hear her uncle Hafiz's voice apprising them of the situation.

She was about to ask to speak to him when Becker declared he had dibs on the tubing and accelerated, aiming the *Condor*'s nose between the two liners.

The tubing was no impediment at all for the Nupiak asteroid breaker nose cone. Space-suited bodies tumbled like corpuscles on a microscope slide of a broken capillary. Gravity boots were locking onto hulls and gloves grasping the gloves of spinning crewmates. Acorna was glad to see that most of them were managing to save themselves but even gladder to see that in order to do so, they had to let their weapons twirl out into the blackness of space.

Acorna and Aari watched for a moment, and Acorna thought again how terribly lonely it would be to go drifting in space till you died. She glanced at Becker, and at the pressure suits on the wall. Becker looked completely serious for one moment, then got up, threw pressure suits and jet packs at them and said, "Okay, boys and girls, salvage time. You too, KEN-bo, but you won't need a suit, right? When that little—female individual was kicking the stuffing out of me, some of her boys stopped her from making it worse so I guess I owe them. Besides, I want that tubing! And then we'll make a house call on your uncle, Lady."

Acorna was well used to maneuvering in jets and pressure suits from her childhood mining asteroids with her uncles, and Aari also had used them before his captivity on Vhiliinyar. Fortunately, Acorna's horn was not so long that it required a special helmet. Maneuvering in space was a lot like swimming, using the jets as fins, grabbing the drifting crewmen and bringing them back to the *Shahrazad* and shoving them through an airlock before going after the next one.

They managed to pluck two off the hull of their own ship where they clung like barnacles before that ship took off. As soon as they shoved the last one aboard Becker said, "Lady, you may want to visit the *Shahrazad* and make sure your uncle is okay. Aari and KEN, unless you like family reunions, come on back to the *Condor* and we'll eat our humble din-din of plant seeds and cat food and hope Acorna brings us back some high-class chow from her rich relative."

Acorna waved and climbed through the airlock. The previous hitchhikers had been taken into custody by the *Shahrazad*'s crew but once she drew off her helmet, Hafiz himself was there to embrace her and welcome her aboard. As they repaired to the ship's lounge, she felt it suddenly lurch, and saw a bolt of light zipping across the view screen from the *Shahrazad* to the departing *Midas*. The *Midas* exploded in a ball of flame.

From the com set, she heard Becker yelling, "Yahoo! Instant karma for coming to the rescue, Aari, my man! Lookit the salvage! See ya later, Lady!" and the *Condor* with a wee waggle of its chassis zoomed off to retrieve its prizes.

"No!" cried Kisla Manjari, bound hand and foot to a chair in the corner of the lounge. "It's not fair! That junk man can't have the nice new ship my uncle gave me. Daddy, do something really nasty to him and his horrible cat."

Acorna saw that Kisla's eyes were turned up in her head so only white showed through her lids.

"As you see, dear Acorna, we are playing host, somewhat unwillingly, to an old schoolmate of yours."

Acorna rose and crossed the room, kneeling beside Kisla

and looking into her face. She started to touch the girl's head with her horn but Kisla jerked away, batting at her with manacled hands.

"She's had some sort of psychotic break," Acorna said, recoiling slightly from the ugly chaos of the girl's mind. "She followed Captain Becker and took away the horns of the Ancestors he had gathered. She tried to kill him to make him tell where the Linyaari home world is."

"And no doubt it was for the same reason that she pursued us," Hafiz said with a heavy sigh.

"I wonder if she knows anything about the disappearance of my people," Acorna mused.

Before she or anyone else could pursue that line of inquiry, a familiar voice penetrated the room. "*Shahrazad*, this is the *Haven*. We received your Mayday. *Shahrazad*, come in. For the love of all the moons of Mithra, *Shahrazad*, don't tell us we're too late and that explosion was you! Please come in, Hafiz, you old camel molester, you."

"Mr. Greene," Hafiz said to the room at large. "There are ladies present, if you please. And no, quite happily, the explosion was that of a ship called the *Midas* registered to Count Edacki Ganoosh. The *Midas* attacked us and launched a boarding party. We managed to capture most of the party, and then we blew up the ship, once it uncloaked, in order to forestall future difficulty."

The sound of youthful cheering and squealing and one shrill celebratory whistle overcame Greene's transmission for a moment.

"Johnny, it's Acorna," she said. "What are you and the *Haven* doing out here?"

"We originally came thinking to give safe escort to the *Shahrazad*, Acorna, but things have gotten a little complicated. What are *you* doing *there*?"

"That also is complicated, Johnny," Acorna said.

"Ladies and gentlemen and children of all ages," Becker's voice crackled in on top of the others, "I think it's time we all had a little real-time interfacing here. What say we pop over to the nearest dirt, set our respective vessels on their tails, and climb aboard *Shahrazad* so Mr. Harakamian can entertain us in the style to which it would be nice to become accustomed while we tell our respective war stories, hmm?"

"A very sound suggestion, Captain Becker," Hafiz said. "Please, bring your excellent crew."

"Bring the kitty, too, Captain," a young voice piped up.

"That request was brought to you by Ms. Turi Reamer, jeweler at large, Becker," Johnny Greene said.

"'Course it was," Becker replied. "I'da known Turi's voice anywhere, Greene. You best not be coming between me and my lady friends now, John, you hear?"

"Lordee, I can tell you are on a salvage high, Joe. Get much from the wreck?"

"I did not. It's in a bazillion teeny pieces all moving rapidly away at warp speed. Not really worth my while."

"Gentlemen, when you have finished your bonding ritual, perhaps we might agree upon a place to meet?"

"There's a puny little planetoid not far from here that doesn't seem to have any life or want any," Becker said. "Let's set down there."

This they did. As Becker, Aari, RK, and the KEN unit boarded, Acorna and the Harakamians greeted them.

"What a splendid specimen of a Makahomian Temple Cat you have on your shoulder, Mr. Becker!" Karina said, clapping her hands. "I understand they are among the most enlightened of all creatures. It is said that when the Makahomian elders and priests begin to consider their next incarnations, the most favored of all possible fates is to be born again as a Temple Cat."

RK licked his paw, swiped it across his whiskers, narrowed his eyes, and purred appreciatively.

Becker was more single-minded. "I'd like to have a look at the human space salvage you and Aari retrieved, Acorna, if your uncle doesn't mind," he said. "Like I said, a couple of those guys who were with Manjari were not half bad. I'm sort of hoping they were among the survivors."

Acorna was pleased that he had dropped the "Lady" part now. It meant that he was starting to consider her a friend, instead of some legendary character he had heard about on Earth, which had been how he had regarded her before.

Uncle Hafiz waved his hand graciously. "Please consider my dungeon as your dungeon," he said.

Becker strolled up to the force field where Hafiz had confined the miscreants. The hologram behind them showed a Crusades-style dungeon, complete with sound effects of someone being dismembered in the background. Acorna was very glad it was just a hologram.

Becker said, "I like the ambience, sir. Amnesty Interplanetary would be less enthused, I'm sure, but if they ever come aboard because someone who deserves this has the brass to complain, there will be nothing anyone can put a finger on in the way of cruel or unusual punishment." Kisla Manjari was by now confined in a separate cell. Karina Harakamian kept sending troubled glances in the deranged girl's direction.

"Can you wall off her cell from visual or auditory contact for a little while, please, Mr. Harakamian?"

"My dear Becker, we are fellow entrepreneurs, businessmen, and adventurers. Do call me Hafiz, my friend, and I shall call you . . ."

"Becker's okay, but Aari here calls me Joe."

"Joh," Aari said, and looked challengingly at Uncle Hafiz. Acorna was pleased to note that either Aari's appearance was so much improved by his surgery, prosthesis, and horn-hat that the Harakamians noticed nothing unusual, or else Aari's wounds had only been particularly repugnant to Linyaari. Hafiz smiled and said, "And you too, my dear fellow, must call me Hafiz. Our beloved Acorna calls me uncle. I practically raised her, you know. Why, I am all but a kinsman to your people!"

Acorna stifled a giggle and Aari gave Hafiz a slow baring of his teeth, rather like Becker's more wolfish grins. "I am Aari, Uncle Hafiz. I have lost much of my own family and will happily adopt you, since you wish it."

Oops. She wished she and Aari could thought-speak as easily as they had been able to among the horns of the dead. She could have warned him. Uncle Hafiz was a very nice man in many respects but he was not exactly to be trusted—not even by members of his blood kin.

"Splendid, splendid." Hafiz erected a hologramatic wall in front of Kisla's cell, adding some decorative manacles with a skeleton dangling from them on the outside, a burning brazier with implements of torture heating in it, and, as a finishing touch, a dish of greenish gruel crawling with virtual maggots. It matched the decor of the interior of her cell nicely, though that now was wholly blocked by a slimy looking stone wall. Had Acorna not witnessed some of the conditions in the child labor camps of Kisla Manjari's adoptive father, the Piper, she would never have believed human beings could incarcerate each other in such dreadful nonhologramatic conditions.

RK sat with lashing tail and narrowed eyes watching as Becker paced with his hands clasped behind him, studying the faces of the men Acorna and Aari had rescued. They were all men, which did not surprise Acorna. Kisla Manjari would have no other women in her entourage. Her ego was such that she would see any other woman as competition.

"I think I recognize a couple of you fellows," Becker said. "Pardon me if I don't quite remember your faces. I was dying at the time. But you failed to kick me when I was down and I like that in an enemy, fortunately for you. Now then, I'm wondering if any of you, being the lickspittles of Kisla Manjari and her uncle as you must be to find yourselves in this charming accommodation, would care to redeem yourselves a little further and fill us in about your employers' plans. You understand we're wondering why we have been singled out for the honor and distinction of being Kisla and Ganoosh's enemies."

Acorna saw them hesitate, and quite without shame she

used some of the new skills she had acquired on narhii-Vhiliinyar to give her wily old uncle a small psychic push in the right direction.

"I can assure you," Uncle Hafiz said suddenly, an inner smile lighting his eyes as if the brilliant idea he had just had was his very own, which, for all Acorna knew, it may have been. Perhaps her push was merely giving him the sort of cue an actor needed to speak his lines at the proper time. "That the man who proves to be of the most assistance to us will no longer need be in anyone's employ.

"So grateful for his services shall the House of Harakamian be that it shall reward him so that he will believe he has found the universe's most generous djinn in the most secluded and luxuriously appointed bottle in the universe. Should he be kissing his own mother on the lips, his identity would yet be a mystery to her when our physicians have concluded his transformation and yet, so handsome a—what is that idiomatic expression you so charmingly employ, o incomparable jewel among jewels, when referring to my personal physique and sexual prowess?"

"Studmuffin, Lord and Master," Karina replied with a demure lowering of her lashes and a coy curtsey.

"So handsome a studmuffin shall he be that all women will desire him and all men admire him. A far more attractive retirement program than being left adrift in space, would you not say, gentlemen?"

There was only a moment of silence before one of the men Acorna had rescued, one whose face wore a careworn expression that was perhaps the result of a troubled conscience, spoke up. "I'd do it for a new job and protection for my family, Mr. Harakamian. I understood that I was being employed to pilot an executive liner to take VIPs to business appointments. This kidnapping and torture stuff and posing as Federation Forces was not in my contract."

Acorna did not stay for the bidding war that ensued, each prisoner vying to give the most accurate details to which he was privy concerning Ganoosh's operation and plans. For at that moment, Johnny Greene and what remained for the crew of the *Haven* were boarding the *Shahrazad*. Acorna ran to greet them. It was so good to see her old friends again! She could hardly wait to see Pal Kendoro and 'Ziana. She wondered if 'Ziana realized yet how much Pal cared for her. And if Markel and Johnny Greene would be there.

Markel and Johnny were there, it was true, and Khetala, who stepped forward and hugged Acorna in an embrace that quickly degenerated into sobs. Acorna wondered what could be upsetting her so until she realized that here were Johnny, Markel, Khetala, red-haired Annella, a tall red-haired man with two children of the same coloring, and a passel of very young children. And that was all.

"Kheti, where are the others?" Acorna asked. "Johnny? They're not on the *Haven*, are they? What happened?"

Johnny took a deep breath. Becker and Hafiz had by that time noted that something else was amiss and joined Acorna and Karina.

"Well, honey, there's good news and bad news," Johnny said. "The bad news is, General Ikwaskwan is working for the bad guys. He and a bunch of his fake Federation Forces troops came home to roost about the time the Starfarers arrived to pick up Nadhari Kando for combat lessons. Ikwaskwan gassed Nadhari and our ship and took most of the Starfarers prisoner. If it hadn't been for Markel knowing how to use the vents and suggesting them as a safe space, we, too, would be guests of the general."

"Was that last part the good news?" Acorna asked.

Johnny shook his head. "No, the good news—though it's also kind of mixed—is that we know the course the general's ships took when they returned to their lair. We followed, and we know exactly where it is, but we couldn't take them on with only kiddy power to draw on. While we were trying to decide what our next move was, we picked up the Mayday from the *Shahrazad*."

When that and all of the other information had been shared and a plan requiring Acorna and Aari to be in two places at once had been formed, Hafiz Harakamian demonstrated the skill upon which his first fortune had been founded.

"My enemies have told many lies about me," Hafiz said. "Among them is the tale that my earliest enterprises involved the sale of addictive substances, with hints that these were illegal drugs. As any of my people can tell you, I am a devout man and am guided by the Three Books and the Three Prophets. I would never consider such a thing. However, in one way, my enemies are correct. My fortune was founded on items that many find addictive. You will have noticed some of my specialty work here aboard the *Shahrazad*. Mr. Greene, I believe, will recall when I fulfilled my family obligation to make a profitable business of my own before I was named heir by running my business from a storefront on Todo Street."

Johnny snapped his fingers. "Harakamian Hologramatics! Fondest Fantasies Fulfilled! I remember it! I loved the holo of the music session in the Dublin pub."

"I think Dad mentioned your company a time or two, too, now that I think about it," Becker said.

"Why, Uncle Hafiz!" Acorna said. "I knew you had wonderful taste, but I had no idea you were an artist as well."

"Oh, yes, my dearest, and now, with your help and Aari's, I will create the vision of a lifetime. Meanwhile, the rest of you — get to work."

"We're on it, Hafiz," Becker said. "C'mon, folks," he said, and the KEN unit as well as the crew of the *Haven* followed him to first the *Condor* and then, laden with various tools and spare parts, back to the *Haven*.

Twenty-two

D ay after day and hour after hour the tortured bodies of the children were dragged into the bubble—badly bruised, broken, and cut; some with ruptured organs and splintered bone. The Linyaari on the healing rotation did their best for them, working until the healers were past the point of total exhaustion.

And all night long another team worked on Nadhari Kando, healing her flesh and bone, cleansing her spirit of the drugs which caused the disciplined woman warrior to behave in a way her sense of honor otherwise would not have allowed. The Linyaari were reaching their limits and feared they would soon become too exhausted to help.

It would have been different if the Linyaari had been given time to rest between rotations but they were not. Ikwaskwan's pet scientists were deliberately pushing the unicorn people to the limits.

Melireenya had often been taken to her ship and interrogated again about the computer system. Every Linyaari underwent this, usually in the middle of the night or before a long-delayed meal time. Not that the meals were in any way adequate. Bales of old hay were all that Ikwaskwan provided for food for the Linyaari.

After the interrogation, Melireenya had been shoved into the gas chamber. She had needed healing herself afterwards. So depleted had her horn become from the interrogation, it took much longer to purify the air than usual, and she absorbed some of the toxins before her system could purify them. Then it was on to the dismal swamp known among the inmates as "the pool." It took her hours of lying on her belly with her face almost submerged in scummy, stinking sewage to clear this water.

There were several different gas chambers and several different pools, actually, so that many Linyaari could undergo the same ordeals at once.

Melireenya's joy at seeing Hrronye, her lifemate, again was quickly dampened when others told her in whispers of thought-speak that they had been separated from their own families and told they would not see them again until they gave the soldiers the information they demanded. Nobody did, of course. The location of the Linyaari home world and the secrets of the horn were as locked into Linyaari psyches as their own DNA codes. Those who traveled from the planet learned from their superiors how to navigate from memory, and it became a part of them along with their newly white skins and silvery manes.

But she seldom saw Hrronye now, and wished she had dared embrace him, as they were kept apart anyway on the tedious deadly treadmill of torture called the "duty roster."

By far the worst part of it all was the healing. At first, it was not so bad. The average Linyaari in good physical condition could heal a deep wound within moments. And there were many Linyaari in the compound. Only four were assigned to heal at the same time, and this was after their resources had been depleted by the other "duties," lack of sleep, and increasingly, by malnutrition.

Neeva had tried to reason with Ikwaskwan. "This is hardly a fair representation of our skills that you are seeing, General," she said in her best diplomat's manner. "We could show you so much more were we properly fed and rested."

He had actually reached out and run his hand down her horn, a violation of privacy that ran very deep among their people. Neeva had tried to pretend it did not distress her but of course it did. "And we could feed you so much better, dear ambassador, if you would tell us the location of the place where we might find your native grasses and other foods. If you continue to refuse to satisfy our very reasonable curiosity, why then . . ." He stroked her horn with his fingers again and when she winced away from him, she was forced to stand still by two of the soldiers, and he repeated his repugnant gesture several more times. "The horns will survive all of you, I'm told. Perhaps they alter to their translucent and less useful state because, while on a living member of your species, they are less stable—having to self-heal as it were. It may be that detached horns, having fewer frivolous demands made on their powers, will be of more use to us. I understand these things have aphrodisiac properties. Is that true?"

"How would I know?" Neeva asked, undiplomatically.

He retaliated by grabbing her horn with his fist and yanking on it so that she sobbed with pain and humiliation. "One way or another, dear ambassador, I will have yours for myself."

This had been too much for her lifemate, who, like other Linyaari present at the pond where she approached the general, was listening.

"Leave her alone!" Virii demanded, stepping forward, only to be grabbed by two more of the soldiers. He had spoken in Linyaari, of course, but his meaning was taken by Ikwaskwan, who wagged a scolding finger at him. "I'll have yours, too, stud. I wonder—are they a pair? How interesting." He had nodded at the pond. "Let's see how long it takes these two to purify that. Make sure it's good and foul."

The soldiers had eliminated in the pond and then forced the heads of both Neeva and Virii into the filth, not bothering to make sure their noses and mouths were clear of the water. No one else had been allowed to help. It was horrible. In the shape they were in it took both of them almost ten minutes to purify the water and by the end of it both had nearly drowned. Thereafter they underwent a joint interrogation session. Melireenya and the others had not so much as dared to whisper while the interrogation was broadcast throughout the compound.

Today it was rumored something even worse would happen. The architect of this horror, the one who had retained the services of Ikwaskwan and his mercenaries, had arrived during the night. Ikwaskwan told everyone he had special entertainments planned for their distinguished guest.

(They almost make you miss the Khleevi, don't they?) Khaari asked sadly. (At least with the Khleevi, we were never sure if they understood what they were doing to us or not. The calculation of this is repulsive.)

The tournament was about to begin and during it, Melireenya had been specifically chosen for healing duty. Her horn was translucent, difficult to see now in some light, and it had even begun to droop. It was awful enough to think of its powers failing while she was up to her ears in fouled water or breathing poisoned air or enduring the mistreatment of the interrogators—but worst of all for her was the thought that it, and she, would fail in the middle of trying to heal a massively wounded child.

So far this had not happened but it now took all the Linyaari on duty many many long moments to heal each and every wound. All the time the victims were in terrible pain.

Now the soldiers and their masters had assembled in the stadium, and this time all of the Linyaari and all of the children of the *Haven* were being forced to watch as well. The lovely young captain 'Ziana of the *Haven* was bound at the wrist and ankle to that young man who would someday, if they lived through this, surely be her lifemate.

Poor Nadhari was healed once more of all but the massive amounts of drugs Ikwaskwan had injected into her system. The last three nights she had seen patients still undergoing healing. Once the drugs were leeched from her system, she had begged them to kill her, or to at least let her die so she could no longer be used in this fashion. But of course, no Linyaari could do such a thing.

The soldiers were using their prods to push the young couple out to Nadhari when a soldier came running through the crowd and bounded up to the box where Ikwaskwan and Ganoosh sat waiting for the maiming to begin. The soldier saluted and said something to Ikwaskwan, who looked very pleased, which was not at all good, and nodded to him, then held his hand up to the soldiers below to desist for a moment. The first soldier bounded down the steps and out of the stadium bubble. He was headed in the direction of the bubble where the captured Linyaari ships were stored and the interrogations took place.

A moment or two passed, and Melireenya was wondering, along with the other Linyaari linked in thought-speak, what fresh horror was about to be visited upon them. Then the light shifted and the top of the bubble was filled with oversize faces and forms of richly dressed Linyaari people standing in front of colorful pavilions with a stately hill in the background cradling more egg ships than could possibly be left on narhii-Vhiliinyar.

"Dearest ambassadors, tradesmen, students, and scientists, this is your *viizaar* speaking," said the woman, who was *not* the *viizaar* at all, not unless Khornya had rapidly risen to power. She was speaking in her rather broken version of Linyaari, so Melireenya was inclined to doubt she had become the planet's administrator already. Beside her was a fellow who was vaguely familiar, and yet, different somehow. Melireenya was far too weary to try to place him. "Dr. Vaanye" — Khornya indicated the man beside her who was hardly old enough to be the Dr. Vaanye who was her late father — "has finally succeeded in widening the band of our broadcast so it can reach to the various planets upon which you should now be posted. We have had no word of you in a long while. Have you lost your way home? Have you forgotten how to contact your loved ones? In case such a disaster is happening, we will rebroadcast our coordinates on this band only."

Ikwaskwan was impatiently gesturing to a soldier who dragged Neeva and Virii, bound at wrist and ankle like the young Starfarer couple, out into the arena.

"Well, Ambassador? What's the message?"

Neeva raised her filthy face, her mane matted and chunks of it torn loose in parts, her horn barely visible.

She spat.

Ikwaskwan roared. "Let Nadhari have them both and bring me their horns when she's done with them!"

Melireenya and Khaari passed a signal between them and Melireenya sprang up and cried, "No! General, please don't hurt them any more! I'll tell you what it says! I know it will harm the rest of my people but I simply can't take it any more! Please let Neeva and Virii go and I'll tell you anything you want to."

Khaari ran into the arena after her and tried to pull her back. "Melireenya, you don't know what you're saying. You mustn't betray all of us for one person, not even Neeva."

Perhaps the general would not notice in the heat of the moment that they were both speaking Standard, for his benefit.

The message overhead was in a loop, repeating over and over again. Melireenya, babbling, stumbling over her words, forgetting the Standard that she had learned from Khornya's people what seemed like *ghaanyi* and *ghaanyi* ago, told Ikwaskwan what the transmission said. She hesitated over the coordinates until he threatened Neeva and Virii again, and then she allowed herself to cave in under the weight of his cruelty, as she had wanted to do for days. She lay in the dirt of this strange moon beside her poor tortured friends and wept and wept and wept until she thought her weeping would never cease. When at long last someone, Khaari, thought-touched her and she looked up, everything around her had changed. The most drastic change was that the bleachers were empty, with most of the soldiers, Ikwaskwan and Ganoosh, gone. Although the broadcast was still playing and replaying overhead, it was infused with far more light, and Melireenya realized that this was because there were no longer the shadows being cast by the towering fence of bullet-shaped troop ships that had sur- rounded the biosphere bubbles. All of these ships were also gone, and the atmosphere outside the bubbles was clouded only by settling dust and debris. The bubbles still resounded with the roaring of the troop ship drives as they lifted off.

That roaring seemed to continue for an awfully long time, Melireenya thought. With the games over, Nadhari was netted, sedated, and Melireenya and the other three on her shift went to work healing her. This day there were no wounds except the psychic ones from the drugs and the shame she suffered to be so badly misused. So far this day she had maimed no one.

The lone sentry left to guard the Linyaari ship bubble was sur- prised to see two troop ships land so soon after the others had left. He thought he understood when he saw the cadre of uni- formed Federation Forces men and women pushing one of the corns in front of them. This one was lipping off to them in her own horsey-sounding babble.

"Got another live one for the general," the short, barrel- chested master sergeant said. "He's gonna want to interrogate this one personally."

"Well, he'll have to do it when he gets back from the Linyaari home world then," the sentry smirked.

"What?"

"Didn't you get the message? The stupid corns broadcast to all of their ships, which we intercepted, of course, the coordi- nates to their planet. The general and the boss have taken off with most of the personnel to check it out."

"No kiddin'? Well, we'll just park her with the others then. What'd they have in the mess hall tonight?"

The sentry told him while the rest of the cadre marched the corn past him, and past the ships, into the biosphere where most of her kind were kept.

"Where'd you find her?"

"Pleasure house on Rahab Three."

"No kidding? You mean somebody wanted to do it with one of . . ." The sentry didn't finish his sentence. Something banged against the backs of his knees, knocking him into the sergeant. The last thing he saw was the sergeant's belt buckle as the newcomer raised both fists and brought them down hard on the back of the sentry's skull.

Acorna heard the thump when the sentry hit the ground and saw only a brief flash of movement as Aari penetrated the biosphere. He had an uncanny talent for taking on the coloring of his surroundings, she saw. It was augmented by smearing himself with soil, but it was more in the way he *became* whatever was around him, though she would have said if asked previously that it was impossible for anyone to blend with a plastic bubble.

Khetala was giving the next trooper they encountered the same story Becker had about Acorna being a special prisoner they'd found in a pleasure house. Meanwhile Reamer guided her to the bubble where many other Linyaari were crammed into a place far too small for them. They were very subdued. At first she thought they all wore horn-hats to mute their thoughts, but then she saw that their horns were in very bad condition — that they were emaciated and filthy, their bones protruding and their postures drooping.

She began to pick out the ones who looked the strongest and ablest and used her horn judiciously on them, meanwhile broadcasting in thought-speak, (We have come to take you home. Please be ready. Do as you are directed and with any luck, we will all leave here safely.)

(Khornya?) Her name spoken in her aunt's thought-speak sounded as if Neeva was seeing her as a ghost. Acorna waded through her people until she found an adjoining bubble where four Linyaari were laying horns on Neeva and a male Linyaari, and also on someone who vaguely resembled the Red Bracelet who had once been Delszaki Li's chief of security, Nadhari Kando.

(Neeva!)

(We are doing what we can for her, Khornya, but she and Virii have been badly abused.)

(Melireenya! Khaari, I am so glad to have found you. Stand aside a moment—no, wait.) She laid her horn on all of them and in a few moments, except for looking very thin, they had recovered to the point that they once more resembled her old shipmates and her aunt.

(Oh, Khornya! You see how low we have fallen. Thanks be that your horn is still fresh. Can you help Nadhari? They have almost killed her with their wicked drugs that make her do terrible things to us all.)

Nadhari was feverish, and her eyes were staring, the blood vessels in her neck and upper chest standing out like those of her arms, seemingly in spasm. Acorna laid her horn against them and Nadhari relaxed.

Becker poked his head in. "Khetala, Reamer, Markel, and Hafiz's people have taken care of the guards. You got enough pilots for the Linyaari vessels?"

"Yes. But none of them are very strong."

"That's okay. They don't have to fly far. I swept all the ships for homing devices. Learned that lesson once already. Let's go, then."

"It is a fortunate thing that all of my gardens are not of the illusory variety," Hafiz said as he, Acorna, and Aari watched the Linyaari former prisoners stripping his hydroponics gardens like locusts in a field. The gardens in the Linyaari ships, which could have fed the prisoners, had been deliberately killed by Ikwaskwan's men or allowed to die.

"Very good," Acorna agreed. "Our people are looking much improved. But we need to get them home where they can graze and rest and have the wounds to their spirits salved."

"I hope," Aari said in a voice so tight that it came out rather high, "that their families will not fear them, too."

Acorna laid her horn against his shoulder. "Your family did not fear you. Maati was very put out we didn't bring her along, in fact."

In the lounge and on the mess deck, the Starfarers were putting all of the gourmet selections in the *Shahrazad*'s replicators to the test, while Karina and the staff busied themselves at other replicators on other parts of the ship, fixing food for the youngsters to take on their journey home.

Becker stuck his head through the onion-domed port, nodded to Aari and Acorna, and said, "Saddle up, crew. Time to go back in the sky now."

So they left Hafiz and the *Haven* in charge of the former prisoners, both human and Linyaari, and boarded the *Condor* once more, setting off for the coordinates that the hologram had given as those of narhii-Vhiliinyar.

Acorna was a little surprised to see Nadhari Kando, Neeva and Virii, and 'Ziana and Pal already aboard. "I'm amazed Johnny Greene isn't here, too," she said.

"He's still back on the *Shahrazad* generating those messages with the coordinates, sending out fresh holovids every little once in a while just to keep Ganoosh and Ikwaskwan interested," Becker told her. "I figure they've been traveling maybe forty-eight hours by now, but using my special navigational methods, we'll be there several hours before them."

He was correct as, Acorna was learning, was usual. The *Condor* arrived at the Federation outpost well before the mercenary fleet. When the post commander heard the stories of the Linyaari ambassador, the legendary Nadhari Kando, and the young Starfarers, he was at first hesitant until Acorna said, "I can only bring you the words of my uncle, whom the Linyaari people regard as a sort of honorary kinsman and who considers

all of my people to be under his protection while they are outside their own territory."

"Yes, ma'am," the Federation commander said. "And your
uncle, can you give me a name?"

"Hafiz Harakamian," she said. "You may have heard of him.
Patron Emeritus of the House of Harakamian? My other uncle
Rafik Nadezda is the current patron and he naturally shares
Uncle Hafiz's concern. In fact, Mr. Kendoro and Ms. Kando are
close personal friends of Uncle Rafik's as well as mine."

The commander's demeanor changed. "You're Lady
Acorna Harakamian-Li! At the behest of Mr. Rafik Nadezda,
the Federation has been investigating certain crimes against it
and unaffiliated races."

Acorna nodded.

"And—uh—two other uncles—your parents seem to have
had a lot of brothers, ma'am." Acorna nodded. "Two other
uncles were so insistent that we send Federation troops that
there is a detachment on the way already. I'm afraid your
uncles were so upset that they had to be forcibly detained to
keep them from coming along. No civilians on troop ships,
ma'am. I'm sure you understand."

"If you could just send them word that you've spoken with
me and I am"—she started to say fine but then amended it to, "I
have survived, Mr. Harakamian is safe, and we are among
friends, I would appreciate it."

"Roger that, ma'am." Within a few hours real Federation
ships began arriving from outposts all over nearby quadrants,
creating a formidable welcoming committee for Ikwaskwan's
fake ships.

When Ikwaskwan's troops arrived, bristling with weapons
but speaking words of peace to what they fondly supposed to
be the Linyaari home world, they were flanked by the real
Federation ships, locked into tractor beams, and escorted to the
outpost, after a brief skirmish ending in the Federation's favor
and providing so much salvage for Becker that he had to put it
on the tractor beam to tow behind the *Condor*.

"Now then, Aari, here's something my daddy taught me about towing salvage. You always tow it at a thirty degree angle from your flight pattern. You know why that is?"

"Perhaps so it does not hit your ship if you must suddenly cease acceleration or reverse course?" Aari asked.

Becker looked disappointed, Acorna thought. He loved to lecture. "Very good. But that's not all. You know what else?"

"No, Joh," Aari said.

"Well, it's the ions we leave behind in our wake, see. They discolor some of the metals, pock others, can completely ruin a good load of salvage so it's not worth jack. This way, you tow it at an angle, you don't get hit in the butt or ruin your cargo. Only problem is, we can't tow through the worms and pleats so we gotta go the long way."

"Joh," Aari said. "The scanners."

The scanners had picked up the cloaked vessel ahead of them, now uncloaking to turn on them. The comscreen never brightened. It didn't have to.

"Ahh," Nadhari said in a hoarse and cracked voice. She had spent hours giving her deposition. "Ikky's flagship."

Becker bared his teeth at her in the grin Aari had learned to mimic. "So, Nadhari, I heard about what this old boyfriend of yours did to you. How about we send him a little love letter?"

Nadhari returned the grin with the first one of hers Acorna had seen since they left the biospheres. "Oh, Becker, sweetie, *can* we?"

"For you, no sacrifice is too much," Becker said. "It's a good place to die—for them. We got black water behind us—everybody strap down."

Acorna reached for RK to secure the cat, as well, but he had made other plans. He lay inside the same harness that held the unhealthily thin form of Nadhari Kando.

Becker said, "Nadhari? Pretty name. Makahomian, isn't it?"

A bolt of light snapped toward them.

She nodded just before he said, "Okay, here it comes, three–two–one, *reverse thrusters!*"

Acorna didn't quite take it all in. One moment the ship loomed large on their screens and the *Condor* seemed to be standing still. The next moment, Nadhari's smile turned down, everyone unstrapped themselves and Aari unpointed at the comscreen. And in the midst of it all, several tons of wreckage were slingshot from the tractor beam on their starboard side.

After a moment or two the *Condor* slowed, and all movement reversed once more for a forward thrust. They reemerged from the "black water" just as the first red ball of light was dimming and the pieces of Ikwaskwan's flagship were making that part of space a dangerous place to be.

Nadhari Kando laughed and Becker winked at her. "Sending them a frag-load of salvage ricocheted their shot right back at them." He shook his head regretfully. "Just like the sick sucker to explode in too many pieces to make it worthwhile to collect."

"I appreciate your sacrifice, Becker," Nadhari said.

"Then it was worth it," he said, with grim satisfaction.

Karina was the one who thought of the brilliant idea of taking some of each of the grasses favored by the Linyaari and putting them in the replicator. And belatedly, Becker and Aari remembered the sacks of seed that had been blocking the crew quarters before the KEN unit cleared them out to make room for the bones.

With these resources, the Linyaari were soon restored to relative health.

Karina again offered her services and Hafiz's to Acorna for her spiritual training. Neeva, who overheard the offer, thought-spoke to Acorna, (Ask her to tell you how she manages to shield her thoughts so well, Khornya. When we first met her, just about the time we thought we had made contact, her mind became a complete blank.)

"Karina, you were the first contact for my people when they came to fetch me," Acorna said. "You learned thought-speech before I did, I'm told."

"Oh, yes," Karina said, "And thanks to my heightened level

of enlightenment, I was able instantly to communicate with your species."

"Didn't you find it difficult at all? I certainly did—I have had so much trouble sorting out the thoughts of those around me from each other and not broadcasting every little notion."

"I had just the opposite problem, to tell you the truth," Karina said confidentially. "I would start receiving them and, knowing they were trying to reach me, I naturally made my mind completely open and blank to receive their thoughts—and then I could hear nothing at all."

"Hmmm," Acorna said. "I'll have to try that."

"What?"

"I said, 'imagine that,'" Acorna replied. "When you were expecting just the opposite, I mean."

While everyone worked to regain the strength they needed to make the journey home, Acorna and her aunt talked.

Acorna was almost startled to find that of everything that had happened to her, what she wanted to talk about most was Aari and what had been done to him. After her aunt's ordeal, Acorna felt that she would understand what Aari had undergone. "Maybe you can make our people understand, help him fit in again," Acorna said.

"Do you think that's still necessary?" Neeva asked. "Look. Does he seem to be having a hard time fitting in now?"

Indeed, he did not, but was grazing with the others, listening to them talk and nodding, occasionally adding something of his own.

"He seems fine now but when we get home, when everyone's normal, will they be so upset by memories of their own ordeal that just *seeing* him—or me—might bring back, that they will be afraid to look at—well, especially him again?"

"Khornya, we're not all like that. You must realize that this particular crisis affected you and the people at home as well as us. We spaceborn and spacechosen are *your* kind, but because of circumstances, none of us stayed dirtside while you were there. You met only the most conservative element of our society. And the most fearful, because they look to the past for their strength. They have a strong aversion to change of any kind. And they don't like anyone who is the least bit different. Don't get me wrong. It is necessary that there be both traditional or agrarian, and progressive or technological and scientific Linyaari. The traditionalists give us our stability and sense of self and we—we give them the ability to continue to live. I don't suppose they mentioned that it was necessary to partially reform narhii-Vhiliinyar to make it habitable for our people?"

"Not in any detail," Acorna said.

"Well, it was. Thanks be to the Ancestors that Grandam was there to help you."

"And Maati."

"And Maati," Neeva agreed. "My point is, you are one of us. Aari is one of us. Nothing can change that, ever, not distance or time or even the sort of thing that has happened to Aari—and almost to all of us. Wherever you are, wherever *we* are, you are still ours and we are still your people."

Except for the inclusion of the *Condor*, Acorna's second home-coming was almost a reversal of her first. This time the bright Fabergé egg ships bounced *toward* narhii-Vhiliinyar rather than from it, and only one lone ship, the new one she'd seen the techo-artisans working on with the clan colors of Acorna's illustrious clan ancestress, bounced up from the planet's surface. Thariinye beamed at them from the comscreen until Becker switched it off.

"I don't like that guy," he grumbled.

The Linyaari band was there to greet more than one person this time, Acorna could see from the viewport of the *Condor*. Grandam and Maati alone separated from the crowd and walked across the field to wait for the robolift to lower, and Acorna and Aari to join them on the surface. The *viizaar* herself had extended the invitation to the welcome home fete to Becker as well, but if she had reversed her opinion of Becker, the same was not true of his opinion of her.

"Bureaucrats," he said. "They're all alike."

Maati gave Acorna a brief horn touch and then held onto her brother's waist with both arms until he picked her up in his and hugged her. Acorna touched horns with Grandam. "Perhaps we'd better leave them to catch up with us," Grandam said.

They walked slowly and silently toward the crowd. The returnees were being given wreaths of flowers by those greeting them, and there were many tears and much laughter. Neeva was explaining to Liriili that without the good or "Linyaari barbarians" their people would never have survived the bad or "Khleevi barbarians."

"In fact," Neeva said loudly enough for all to hear, "we Linyaari now have a kinsman among the barbarians. Khornya's uncle Hafiz, who fed us and helped us regain our health after our imprisonment, said that since he was Khornya's kinsman, he felt that all of the rest of us were also members of his clan, a very wealthy and aristocratic lineage of merchant traders."

"Hmmm," Liriili said, "It is wise to keep one's assets in the family. Perhaps we should send emissaries back to this new uncle of our people to discuss a favored trade agreement."

"I believe that would please him a great deal," Neeva said. "Some of us who spend much time off-world learning and bringing back technologies and trade items need to spend more time at home for a while, as we recover. This Harakamian is a genius at making holograms. Perhaps he could be persuaded to produce some hologramatic learning programs for the various guilds?"

Liriili gave Acorna a guilty, but still slightly frosty smile. "Perhaps. Perhaps Khornya would care to discuss it with him on our behalf? Now that she has spent time among us, in my estimation she is ready to assume her own mantle as *visedhaanye*."

"Perhaps," Neeva said.

"But surely she will want to stay home and rest for a time, too," Grandam said.

At that moment, Acorna looked across the field and saw Maati walking slowly toward them, alone. Acorna fought her way through the crowd to the comscreen and hailed the *Condor*.

"There you are, Acorna. *If* you can tear yourself away from that mob down there, you might want to join me and Aari and the cat again. The board here is lit up like a pinball machine all of a sudden. We have us some serious salvage opportunities and they won't wait forever. Stay there or come along. What's your pleasure?"

Acorna, Grandam, and Neeva exchanged looks and thoughts. They were her people, it was true, but so were Uncle Hafiz, Rafik, Gil, Calum, the Kendoros, and so many others.

On the comscreen, over Becker's shoulder, she saw Aari's face, regrets and sorrow mixing with anticipation of rejection and—just a little—hope.

Grandam's eyes twinkled.

Acorna turned back to the *Condor* and then swung back to face Liriili again. "I'm honored by the ambassadorship, of course, but for right now, there is still something I must try to"—she glanced once more at the comscreen, the cat's impatiently flicking tail, Becker's welcoming expression and most of all, Aari, and said aloud, in answer to Becker—"salvage."

Glossary of Terms Used in the Acorna Universe

aagroni—Linyaari name for a vocation that is a combination of ecologist, agriculturalist, botanist, and biologist. Aagroni are responsible for terra-forming new planets for settlement as well as maintaining the well-being of populated planets.

Aari—a Linyaari of the Nyaarya clan, captured by the Khleevi during the invasion of Vhiliinyar, tortured, and left for dead on the abandoned planet. He's Maati's brother. Aari survived and was rescued and restored to his people by Jonas Becker and Roadkill. But Aari's differences, the physical and psychological scars left behind by his adventures, make it difficult for him to fit in among the Linyaari.

Acadecki—the ship Calum and Acorna journey in to find Acorna's people.

Acorna—a unicorn-like humanoid alien discovered as an infant by three miners—Calum, Gill, and Rafik. She has the power to heal and purify with her horn. Her uniqueness has already shaken up the galaxy, especially the planet Kezdet. She's now fully grown and searching for her people.

Aiora—Markel's mother, now dead.

Almah—Rocky Reamer's wife, now deceased.

Amalgamated Mining—a vicious intergalactic mining corporation, famous for bad business dealings and for using bribes, extortion, and muscle to accomplish their corporate goals or cut their costs.

Ancestors—unicorn-like sentient species, precursor race to the Linyaari. Also known as *ki-lin*.

Ancestral Hosts—ancient space-faring race that rescued the Ancestors, located them on the Linyaari home planet, and created the Linyaari race from the Ancestors and their own populations through selective breeding and gene splicing.

Andreziana—second-generation Starfarer, daughter of Andrezhuria and Ezkerra.

Andrezhuria—first-generation Starfarer, and Third Speaker to the Council.

Balaküre—the Linyaari ship commanded by Acorna's aunt Neeva in which the envoys from Acorna's people reached human-populated space.

Balaave—Linyaari clan name.

barsipan—jellyfish-like animal on Linyaari home planet.

Becker—*see* Jonas Becker.

Blidkoff—Second Undersecretary of RUI Affairs, Shenjemi Federation.

Brazie—second-generation Starfarer.

Caabye—planet in the original Linyaari home world system, third from the sun.

Calum Baird—one of three miners who discovered Acorna and raised her.

Ce'skwa—a captain and unit leader in the Red Bracelets.

Child Liberation League—an organization dedicated to ending child exploitation on Kezdet.

Clackamass 2—an abandoned planet near the Kezdet system, used as a landfill site.

Coma Berenices—the quadrant of space most likely to hold Acorna's ancestors.

Condor—Jonas Becker's salvage ship, heavily modified to incorporate various "found" items Becker has come across in his space voyages.

Dajar—second-generation Starfarer.

Declan "Gill" Giloglie—one of three miners who discovered Acorna and raised her.

Deeter Reamer—five-year-old son of Rocky Reamer.

Delszaki Li—the richest man on Kezdet, opposed to child exploitation, made many political enemies. Paralyzed, he used an antigravity chair. He was clever, devious, and he both hijacked and rescued Acorna and gave her a cause—saving the children of Kezdet. His recent death is a continuing source of sorrow to Acorna.

Des Smirnoff—an unsavory sort, a former Kezdet Guardian kicked out for failure to share the proceeds of his embezzlement with appropriate superiors, now an officer with the Kilumbembese Red Bracelets.

dharmakoi—small burrowing sapient marsupials known to the Linyaari, now extinct as a result of Khleevi war.

didi—Kezdet slang for the madam of a brothel, or for one who procures children for such a madam.

Didi Badini—a madam on Kezdet who tried to kill Acorna.

Dom—a Palomellese criminal posing as a refugee aboard the *Haven*; a key member of Nueva Fallona's gang.

Edacki Ganoosh—corrupt Kezdet count, uncle of Kisla Manjari.

Ed Minkus—a companion of Des Smirnoff's who has followed him from the Kezdet Guardians of the Peace to their present employment with the Red Bracelets.

E'kosi Tahka'yaw—former ally of General Ikwaskwan's, betrayed by him in some manner which he would prefer not to discuss.

enye-ghanyii—Linyaari time unit, a small portion of a *ghaanye*.

Epona—a protective goddess identified with horses, and by some children of Kezdet, with Acorna.

Esperantza—a planet taken away from its colonists by quasi-legal manipulations on the part of Amalgamated Mining.

Esposito—a Palomellese criminal posing as a refugee aboard the *Haven*; a key member of Nueva Fallona's gang.

Eva—Kezdet orphan, training on Maganos.

Ezkerra—first-generation Starfarer, married to Andrezhuria.

Feriila—Acorna's mother.

Foli—second-generation Starfarer.

Geeyiinah—one of the Linyaari clans.

Gerezan—first-generation Starfarer, Second Speaker to the Council.

ghaanye (pl. *ghaanyi*)—a Linyaari year.

gheraalye malivii—Navigation Officer.

gheraalye ve-khanyii—Senior Communications Officer.

giirange—office of toastmaster in a Linyaari social organization.

Giryeeni—Linyaari clan name.

GSS—Gravitation Stabilization System.

Haarha Liirni—Linyaari term for advanced education, usually pursued during adulthood while on sabbatical from a previous calling.

Hafiz Harakamian—Rafik's uncle, head of the interstellar financial empire of House Harakamian, a passionate collector of rarities from throughout the galaxy and a devotee of the old-fashioned sport of horse-racing. Although basically crooked enough to hide behind a spiral staircase, he is fond of Rafik and Acorna.

Hajnal—a child rescued from thieving on Kezdet, now in training on Maganos.

Haarilnyah—the oldest clan amongst the Linyaari.

Haven—a multigeneration space colonization vehicle occupied by people pushed off the planet Esperantza by Amalgamated Mining.

Hrronye—Melireenya's lifemate.

Iirtye—chief aagroni for narhii-Vhillinyar.

Ikwaskwan—self-styled 'admiral' of the Kilumbembese Red Bracelets.

Illart—first-generation Starfarer, First Speaker to the Council, and Markel's father.

Johnny Greene—an old friend of Calum, Rafik, and Gill; joined the Starfarers when he was fired after Amalgamated Mining's takeover of MME.

Jonas Becker—interplanetary salvage artist; alias space junkman. Captain of the *Condor*. CEO of Becker Interplanetary Recycling and Salvage Enterprises, Ltd.—a one-man, one-cat salvage firm Jonas inherited from his adopted father. Jonas spent his early youth on a labor farm on the planet Kezdet before he was adopted.

Joshua Flouse—mayor of Rushima.

Judit Kendoro—assistant to psychiatrist Alton Forelle at Amalgamated Mining, saved Acorna from certain death. Later fell in love with Gill and joined with him to help care for the children employed in Delszaki Li's Maganos mining operation.

Karina—a plumply beautiful wannabe psychic with a small shred of actual talent and a large fondness for profit. Married to Hafiz Harakamian. This is her first marriage, his second.

Kass—Rushimese settler.

kava—a coffee-like hot drink produced from roasted ground beans.

Kerratz—second-generation Starfarer, son of Andrezhuria and Ezkerra.

KEN—a line of general purpose male androids, some with customized specializations, differentiated among their owners by number, for example—KEN637.

Kezdet—a backwoods planet with a labor system based on child exploitation. Currently in economic turmoil because that system has been broken by Delszaki Li and Acorna.

Khang Kieaan—a planet torn between three warring factions.

Khaari—senior Linyaari navigator on the Balakiire.

Khetala—captured as a small child for the mines of Kezdet, later sold into the planet's brothels. Rescued by Acorna, and now a beautiful young woman.

Khleevi—name given by Acorna's people to the spaceborn enemies who have attacked them without mercy.

kii—a Linyaari time measurement roughly equivalent to an hour of Standard Time.

Kilumbemba Empire—an entire society which raises and exports mercenaries for hire—the Red Bracelets.

ki-lin—oriental name for unicorn, also a name sometimes associated with Acorna.

Kirilatova—an opera singer.

Kisla Manjari—anorexic and snobbish young woman, raised as daughter of Baron Manjari; shattered when through Acorna's efforts to help the children of Kezdet her father is ruined and the truth of her lowly birth is revealed.

Kubiilikhan—capitol city of narhii-Vhiliinyar.

LAANYE—sleep learning device invented by the Linyaari which can, from a small sample of any foreign language, teach the wearer the new language overnight.

Laarye—Maati and Aari's brother. He died on Vhiliinyar during the Khleevi invasion. He was trapped in an accident in a cave far distant from the spaceport during the evacuation, and was badly injured. Aari stayed behind to rescue and heal him, but was captured by the Khleevi and tortured before he could accomplish his mission. Laarye died before Aari could escape and return.

Laboue—the planet where Hafiz Harakamian makes his headquarters.

Labrish—Rushimese settler.

Liriili—*viizaar* of narhii-Vhiliinyar.

Linyaari—Acorna's people.

Lukia of the Lights—a protective saint, identified by some children of Kezdet with Acorna.

Maati—a young Linyaari girl of the Nyaarya clan who lost most of her family during the Khleevi invasion. Aari's sister.

Ma'aowri 3—a planet populated by cat-like beings.

Makahomian Temple Cat—cats on the planet Makahoma, bred from ancient Cat God stock to protect and defend the Cat God's temples. They are—for cats—large, fiercely loyal, remarkably intelligent, and dangerous when crossed.

madigadi—a berry-like fruit whose juice is a popular beverage.

Maganos—one of the three moons of Kezdet, base for Delszaki Li's mining operation and child rehabilitation project.

Mali Bazaar—a luxurious bazaar on Laboue, famous for the intricate mosaic designs which decorate its roof.

Manjari—a baron in the Kezdet aristocracy, and a key person in the organization and protection of Kezdet's child-labor racket, in which he was known by the code name 'Piper.' He murdered his wife and then committed suicide when his identity was revealed and his organization destroyed.

Markel—first-generation Starfarer, son of First Speaker Illart.

Martin Dehoney—famous astro-architect who designed Maganos Moon Base; the coveted Dehoney Prize was named after him.

Melireenya—Linyaari communications specialist on the Balakiire, bonded to Hrronye.

Mercy Kendoro—younger sister of Pal and Judit Kendoro, saved from a life of bonded labor by Judit's efforts, she worked as a spy for the Child Liberation League in offices of Kezdet Guardians of the Peace until the child labor system was destroyed.

Midas — Count Edacki Ganoosh's private space yacht, entrusted to Kisla Manjari, used to follow Becker as he searches for the Linyaari home world.

Misra Affrendi — Hafiz's elderly trusted retainer.

mitanyaakhi — generic Linyaari term meaning a very large number.

MME — Gill, Calum, and Rafik's original mining company. Swallowed by the ruthless, consciousless, and bureaucratic Amalgamated Mining.

M'on Na'ntaw — high-ranking Red Bracelet officer, cheated by General Ikwaskwan in a way that threw the blame on someone else.

Moulay Suheil — fanatical leader of the Neo-Hadithians.

Naadiina — also known as Grandam, one of the oldest surviving Linyaari, is host to both Maati and Acorna on narhii-Vhiliinyar.

Naarye — Linyaari techno-artisan in charge of final fit-out of spaceships.

[Auntie] Nagah — Rushimese settler.

narhii-Vhiliinyar — second home of Linyaari.

Nadhari Kando — Delszaki Li's personal bodyguard, rumored to have been an officer in the Red Bracelets earlier in her career.

Neeyeereeya — the most populous of the Linyaari clans.

Neeva — Acorna's aunt and Linyaari envoy on the Balakiire, bonded to Virii.

Neggara — second-generation Starfarer.

Neo-Hadithian — an ultra-conservative, fanatical religious sect.

Ngaen Xong Hoa — a Kieaanese scientist who invented a planetary weather control system. He sought asylum on the *Haven* because he feared the warring governments on his planet would misuse his research. A mutineer faction on the *Haven* used the system to reduce the planet Rushima to ruins. The mutineers were tossed into space, and Dr. Hoa has since restored Rushima.

Niciirye — Grandam Naadiina's husband, dead and buried on Vhiliinyar.

Niikaavri — Acorna's grandmother, a member of the clan Geeyiinah, and a spaceship designer by trade.

Nirii—a planetary trading partner of the Linyaari, populated by two-horned sentients, technologically advanced, able to communicate telepathically, and phlegmatic in temperament.

Nueva Fallona—Palomellese criminal who posed as a refugee to the Starfarers until she could carry out a coup putting her and her gang in control of the *Haven*. She was defeated by the children of the Starfarers.

Nyaarya—one of the clans of the Linyaari.

One-One Otimie—a Rushimese trapper and prospector.

Order of the Iriinje—aristocratic Linyaari social organization similar to a fraternity, named after a blue-feathered bird native to Vhiliinyar.

Pal Kendoro—Delszaki Li's assistant on the planet Kezdet. Brother to Mercy and Judit. Acorna's dear friend, and once her possible love interest—though they didn't, in the end, try to do anything about it. Given that the pair came from different species, it could have been problematic. Currently in love with 'Ziana, the captain of the Starfarers.

Palomella—home planet of Nueva Fallona.

Pandora—Count Edacki Ganoosh's personal spaceship, used to track and pursue Hafiz's ship *Shahrazad* as it speeds after Acorna on her journey to narhii-Vhiliinyar.

pahaantiyir—a cougar-like animal native to Vhiliinyar.

Provola Quero—woman in charge of the Saganos operation.

Pyaka—a Rushimese settler.

Quashie—a Rushimese settler.

Qulabriel—Hafiz's assistant.

Rafik Nadezda—one of three miners who discovered Acorna and raised her.

Ramon Trinidad—one of the miners hired to direct a training program on Maganos for the freed children.

Red Bracelets—Kilumbembese mercenaries; arguably the toughest and nastiest fighting force in known space.

Renyilaaghe—Linyaari clan name.

Rezar—second-generation Starfarer.

Roadkill—otherwise known as RK. A Makahomian Temple Cat,

the only survivor of a space wreck, rescued and adopted by Jonas Becker.

Rocky Reamer—intergalactic vendor of precious stones.

Rosewater's Revelation—Uncle Hafiz's best racehorse.

Rushima—agricultural world colonized by the Shenjemi Federation.

Saganos—second of Kezdet's moons.

Sengrat—a pushy, bossy, whiney, bullying know-it-all with a political agenda on the ship *Haven*.

Shahrazad—Hafiz's personal spaceship, a luxury cruiser.

Shenjemi Federation—long-distance government of Rushima.

Sita Ram—a protective goddess, identified with Acorna by the mining children on Kezdet.

Skarness—planetary source of the famous (and rare) Singing Stones, stones that are sentient, each of which emits a single, perfectly pitched note whenever stepped upon. Collectors usually assemble one or several octave scales of the stones, including the requisite sharps and flats.

Skomitin—somebody in Admiral Ikwaskwan's past of whom he does not care to be reminded.

Starfarers—name adopted by the Experantzan settlers who were displaced by Amalgamated's manipulations. They refused unsatisfactory resettlement offers and turned their main ship, the *Haven*, into a mobile colony from which they carried on a campaign of nonviolent political protest against Amalgamated.

Ta'anisi—the Red Bracelets' flagship.

Taankaril—*visedhaanye ferilii* of the Gamma sector of Linyaari space.

Tanqque III—rainforest planet; export of its coveted purpleheart trees is illegal.

Tapha—Hafiz's ineffectual son, who made several attempts on Rafik's life before he was killed during yet another murder attempt on Rafik.

Thariinye—a handsome and conceited young spacefaring Linyaari with a crush on Acorna.

Theloi—one of the planets the miners had to leave hastily to avoid their many enemies (*see* Acorna).

Theophilus Becker — Jonas Becker's father, a salvage man and astrophysicist with a fondness for exploring uncharted wormholes.

thiilir (pl. *thilirii*) — small arboreal mammals of Linyaari home world.

Tianos — Kezdet's third moon.

Turi Reamer — seven-year-old daughter of Rocky Reamer, very business-like.

Twi Osiam — planetary site of a major financial and trade center.

twilit — small, pestiferous insect on Linyaari home planet.

Uhuru — one of the various names of the ship owned jointly by Gill, Calum, and Rafik.

Vaanye — Acorna's father.

Vhiliinyar — home planet of the Linyaari, now occupied by Khleevi.

viizaar — a high political office in the Linyaari system, roughly equivalent to president or prime minister.

Virii — Neeva's spouse.

visedhaanye ferilii — Linyaari term corresponding roughly to 'Envoy Extraordinary.'

Vlad — cousin of Des Smirnoff's, a fence, probably descended from Vlad the Impaler.

Wahanamoian Blossom of Sleep — poppy-like flowers whose pollens, when ground, are a very powerful sedative.

Winjy — a Rushimese settler.

Ximena Sengrat — Sengrat's beautiful young daughter.

Yukata Batsu — Uncle Hafiz's chief competitor on Laboue.

Yasmin — Hafiz Harakamian's first wife, mother of Tapha, faked her own death and ran away to return to her former lucrative career in the pleasure industry. After her accumulated years made that career much less lucrative, she returned to squeeze money out of Hafiz in the form of blackmail.

Zanegar — second-generation Starfarer.

Zaspala Imperium — backward planetary confederation, original home of Des Smirnoff.

Dr. Zip — an eccentric astrophysicist.

A Brief Note on the Linyaari Language

By Margaret Ball

As Anne McCaffrey's collaborator in transcribing the first two tales of Acorna, I was delighted to find that the second of these books provided an opportunity to sharpen my long-unused skills in linguistic fieldwork. This task required a sharp ear and some facility for linguistic analysis to make sense of the subtle sound-changes with which their language signaled syntactic changes; I quite enjoyed the challenge.

The notes appended here represent my first and necessarily tentative analysis of certain patterns in Linyaari phonemics and morphophonemics. If there is any inconsistency between this analysis and the Linyaari speech patterns recorded in the later adventures of Acorna, please remember that I was working from a very limited database and, what is perhaps worse, attempting to analyze a decidedly non-human language with the aid of the only paradigms I had, twentieth-century linguistic models developed exclusively from human language. The result is very likely as inaccurate as were the first attempts to describe English syntax by forcing it into the mold of Latin, if not worse. My colleague Elizabeth Ann Scarborough has by now added her own notes to the small corpus of Linyaari names and utterances, and it may well be that in the next decade there will be enough data available to publish a truly definitive dictionary and grammar of Linyaari; an undertaking which will surely be of inestimable value, not only to those members of our race who are involved in diplomatic and trade relations with this people, but also to everyone interested in the study of language.

Notes on the Linyaari Language

1. A doubled vowel indicates stress: **aavi, abaanye, khle*vii*.**

2. Stress is used as an indicator of syntactic function: in nouns stress is on the penultimate syllable, in adjectives on the last syllable, in verbs on the first.

3. Intervocalic n is always palatalized.

4. Noun plurals are formed by adding a final vowel, usually **-i**: one **Liinyar**, two **Linyaari**. Note that this causes a change in the stressed syllable (from **LI-nyar** to **Li-NYA-ri**) and hence a change in the pattern of doubled vowels.
    For nouns whose singular form ends in a vowel, the plural is formed by dropping the original vowel and adding **-i**: **ghaanye, ghaanyi.** Here the number of syllables remains the same, therefore no stress/spelling change is required.

5. Adjectives can be formed from nouns by adding a final **-ii** (again, dropping the original final vowel if one exists): **maalive, malivii; Liinyar, Linyarii.** Again, the change in stress means that the doubled vowels in the penultimate syllable of the noun disappear.

6. For nouns denoting a class or species, such as **Liinyar**, the plural form of the noun can be used as an adjective when the meaning is "of the class," as in "the Linyaari language" (the language of the Linyaari rather than the usual adjectival meaning of "having the qualities of this class") — thus, of the characters in *Acorna*, only Acorna herself could be described

as "a **Linyaari** girl" (a girl of the People), but Judit, although human, would certainly be described as "a **linyarii** girl" ("a just-as-civilized-as-a-real-member-of-the-People" girl).

7. Verbs can be formed from nouns by adding a prefix constructed by [first consonant of noun] + **ii** + **nye**: **faalar** — grief; **fiinyefalar** — to grieve.

8. The participle is formed from the verb by adding a suffix **-an** or **-en**: **thiinyethilel** — to destroy, **thiinyethilelen** — destroyed. No stress change is involved because the participle is perceived as a verb form, and therefore stress remains on the first syllable:

enye-ghanyii — time unit, small portion of a year (**ghaanye**)
fiinyefalaran — mourning, mourned
ghaanye — a Linyaari year, equivalent to about one and one-third earth years
gheraalye malivii — Navigation Officer
gheraalye ve-khanyii — Senior Communications Specialist
Khleev — originally, a small vicious carrion-feeding animal with a poisonous bite; now used by the Linyaari to denote the invaders who destroyed their home world.
khlevii — barbarous, uncivilized, vicious without reason
Liinyar — member of the People
linyarii — civilized; like a Liinyar
mitanyaakhi — large number (slang — like our "zillions")
narhii — new
thiilir, thiliiri — small arboreal mammals of the Linyaari home world
thiilel — destruction
visedhaanye ferilii — Envoy Extraordinary

9. Like all languages, Linyaari has a number of irregular constructions, each of which must be explained on a case by case basis.

About the Authors

Anne McCaffrey is considered one of the world's leading science fiction writers. She has won the Hugo and Nebula awards, as well as six Science Fiction Book Club awards for her novels. Brought up in the United States, she now lives in Ireland with her Maine Coon cats, her piebald mare, and a silver Weimaraner, and declines to travel anymore. She is best known for her unique Dragonriders of Pern series.

Elizabeth Ann Scarborough is the author of twenty-three science fiction and fantasy novels, including the 1989 Nebula Award winning *Healer's War* and the Powers series co-written with Anne McCaffrey, as well as the popular Godmother series and the Gothic fantasy mystery, *The Lady in the Loch*. She lives in a Victorian seaport town in western Washington with a lot of cats, beads, and computer stuff.